Jeffrey Speight has done it again with *Mystic Reborn*. He's delivered one of the most entertaining and enjoyable fantasy books and continues to expand on his utterly brilliant world of Evelium.

– Out of This World SFF

If books were table games, *Paladin Unbound* would be Dungeons and Dragons when everything else is simply Chutes and Ladders! This bright action-fantasy book is superbly imagined and skillfully executed, particularly with its evocative and immersive imagery.

– Indies Today

Mystic Reborn continues a series that is a masterpiece of epic fantasy.

– Witty and Sarcastic Bookclub

Paladin Unbound was a fun read, combining the feeling of real stakes, with the nostalgia of classical quest fantasy and the chaos of a D&D game.

– Beneath a Thousand Skies

Paladin Unbound is a richly imagined fantasy novel packed with adventure, creatures, gods, friendship, and goodness.

– A Pocket Full of Tomes

You'll devour this book and end up wanting for more.

– The Medjay of Fayium

Paladin Unbound really made an impression on me. I devoured it in the way I haven't devoured a book in a long time. I could feel the author's passion on each page. More, it reminded me of my early fantasy days when I would devour book after book, reading late into the night just so I could enjoy one more chapter.

– Bookworm Blues

All in all, this is easily one of the best books I have read in the past decade, and tying for my favorite fantasy book of the year with Dragon Mage is no small feat.

– Bookwyrm Speaks

If you are looking for a fantastic D&D inspired series with a great story, interesting world, and loveable characters, look no further.

– Roasted Book Reviews

To Rowena,
I can't thank you
enough for the support
you've shown me.
Enjoy your return
to Evelium!
Best,

GOD ASCENDED

AN ARCHIVES OF EVELIUM TALE

Jeffrey Speight

Literary Wanderlust | Denver, Colorado

Published in the United States by Literary Wanderlust LLC, Denver, Colorado. www.LiteraryWanderlust.com

ISBN print: 978-1-956615-44-9
ISBN digital: 978-1-956615-45-6

Library of Congress Control Number: 2024946709

Cover illustration: Ömer Burak Önal
Map illustration: Thomas Rey

Printed in the United States of America

GOD ASCENDED
AN ARCHIVES OF EVELIUM TALE

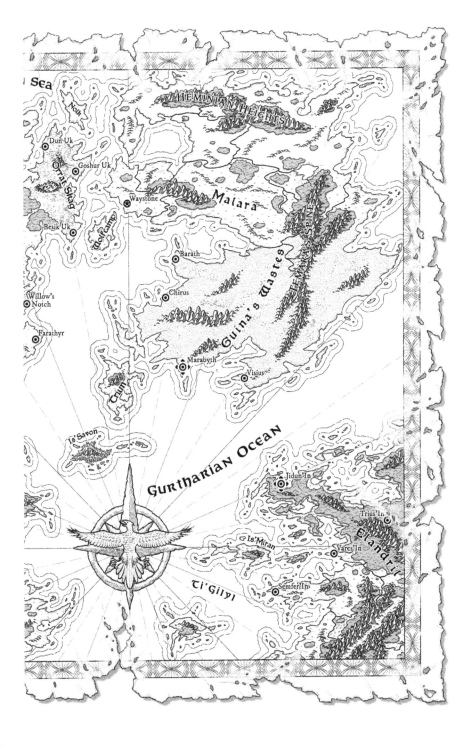

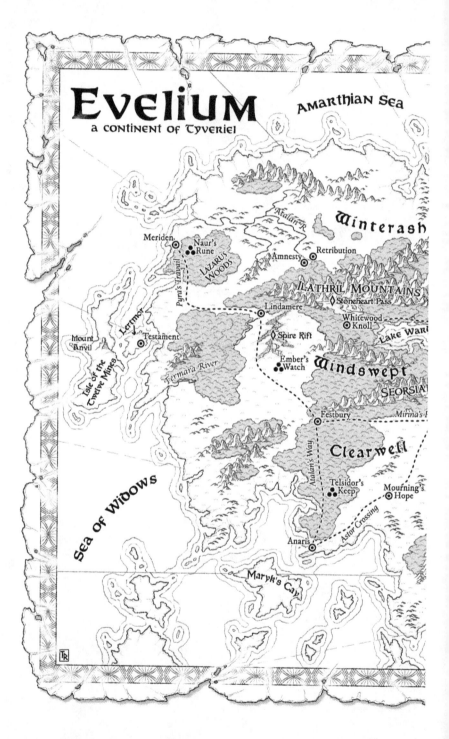

DEDICATION

To my parents

For always believing in me, even when I did not.

PROLOGUE

The gods granted the invaders safe quarter in Mount Anvil with the understanding that they would meet an approach of Evelium with an ire unmatched.

- The Gatekeeper's Abridged History of Tyveriel
Vol. 1, Chapter 5—Unearthed from the Ruins of Meriden, the month of Anar, 1217 AT

— ▲ —

Rock showered down upon Mesorith and jarred him from his sleep. He yawned, crawled to his feet, and shook the debris from his back. How he abhorred having his slumber interrupted in such a manner. Especially when he lazed beside a favored fetid pool deep within Mount Anvil.

Alas, the damage was done. His stomach growled, and he turned to his lair's exit. No doubt, Zalinrithe would awaken too. It would serve him well to find nourishment before long.

The ancient black dragon crawled from the vacuous cavern and welcomed the warm evening sun on his face. He stretched his front legs, arched his back like a cat after a long nap beside the hearth, and shook his wings to chase away the chill of his lair—a chill that always seemed to stay with him too long.

Mesorith looked himself over. Every black scale gleamed like polished obsidian. Each talon was honed to a knife's edge. He smoothed his tail through his fore claws, snagging on the lethal barb at its tip. He truly was the incarnation of beauty—the embodiment of perfection.

The second quake jolted him to his senses. Deep within his core, there His vision cleared and Zalinrithe landed in the grass with her wings splayed like a kestrel upon a starling. was a void where fear once lived. A comfort where unrest once ruled. This was it—the moment he had been waiting for. The very reason he came to Tyveriel.

Since he and Zalinrithe arrived from the Fae, he felt the Creator Gods' presence. They had long ago left his realm and, until this very afternoon, squabbled over the favor of the feeble species that somehow dominated Tyveriel. The *exalted races*, as they were called. It was laughable. They were little more than rats.

Now that the quakes subsided and his mind tore away the cobwebs of sleep, he no longer sensed Vaila and her brothers. He did not know where they went or why. Only that they were gone. And that changed everything.

Without their gods to protect them, the Mystics would now flee like rabbits in the hawk's shadow as soon as they could secure safe passage from this mortal realm. The time to exact his revenge was fleeting. And revenge he desired more than claiming Tyveriel for himself. It bore a hole in his gut like a worm through the soil. It gnawed at him that these lesser beings lived with impunity while he, Mesorith, Liege of Chaos, wallowed in squalor.

Heavy footfalls snapped him from his bellicose thoughts as Zalinrithe joined him outside the entrance of the former Zeristar stronghold they claimed as their own. Her blue eyes drew him in as though they were windows to a better life. Her ivory scales were nearly as magnificent as his own. She whipped her tail around her and sat.

"Have you felt it?" Mesorith asked. "Have you felt their departure?"

"Of course. The quakes roused me from a deep and dreamful sleep."

It pained Mesorith to think of his precious bride being disturbed in such a manner. The gods, once more, showed their selfish predilections. "I am sorry, my dear. But I promise you many nights of comfort to come."

Zalinrithe ran her tongue across her teeth. "Are we to taste the flesh of Mystics?"

"Yes, my terror. We shall travel to each of their keeps to devour them if we must. I plan to take my time with the one called Mirina."

"Lover of the metallics," Zalinrithe spat.

"Come. We begin with Ember's Watch."

Mesorith dove from the rock face and soared over the Bay of Tailings. He craned his neck to see Zalinrithe gliding in his wake.

They flew over Lertmor and the sandy shores of mainland Evelium appeared on the horizon. Mesorith's mouth watered. He never would have considered such a brazen approach when Vaila and her brothers walked these lands. Even when their petty war distracted them. But now, little stood between him and his destiny. He could taste it.

The sun hung low in the west, and the shoreline gave way to verdant forest, but they would not rest yet. Not until the Mystics were no more.

With every beat of his wings, Ember's Watch drew nearer and Mesorith's rage swelled. What began as an ulcer in the pit of his stomach grew and grew until his entire body was aflame with the desire to kill.

A dark tower pierced the horizon and Mesorith's lips quivered with anticipation. He dove toward the walled compound and landed in the courtyard. Other than the whoosh of Zalinrithe's wings as she landed beside him, all was quiet.

There was no warm glow emanating from within the keep as the weak eyes of man required.

Mesorith stooped over and peered through a window. Empty.

His lips curled into a snarl. "There's nothing here."

Zalinrithe released a blast of ice across the courtyard.

Mesorith spun to face her and saw a bulky form encased in ice between them. "What is it?" he asked.

"A construct," Zalinrithe said. "Left as a ward, no doubt."

"Pay it no mind. We move to the next keep. They must be hiding somewhere."

Zalinrithe leaped into the air. Mesorith followed.

Throughout the night and into the next morning, they visited each of the Mystic's compounds and each one they found vacant. With each disappointment, Mesorith grew more incensed. With his blood boiling, he led his bride in razing the watches to the ground. They left nothing but rubble in their path.

As the tower of Pyra's Watch crumbled to dust behind him, Mesorith stepped from the debris. "They have fled."

Zalinrithe growled. "They make for their Waystones. They plan to ascend to Kalmindon."

"Then we will not have the fortune to catch them all. But there may be time for one if we hurry to the Stoneheart Pass."

The dragons took flight on weary wings.

Fueled by his anger, Mesorith pushed through exhaustion. If he was not destined to destroy all the Mystics, he would at least devour the flesh of one.

The Ilathril Mountains pierced the dawn like serrated teeth. Below, amidst the dewy grass, sat a flat stone that cast a cerulean glow. A shadowed form stood at its center, the light of the stone growing with every passing second.

Mesorith dove from the sky, the figure his sole focus.

He crashed into his target, the aura of the Waystone temporarily blinding him. He heard his enemy tumble through the grass, the grunts and groans that followed every thud was acknowledgment that he had interrupted Torrent's ascension.

His vision cleared and Zalinrithe landed in the grass with her wings splayed like a kestrel upon a starling.

A burst of energy threw her backward just enough for the Mystic to crawl out from beneath her.

Torrent climbed to his feet, and the earth shook. Blood trickled from his white beard. He removed a rod of solid rhodium from his belt and held it out before him. It flowed like liquid metal into a javelin with a point at each end.

Rocks cascaded from the cliff face that marked the entrance to the Stoneheart Pass. The ground once more trembled between them.

Torrent jabbed his javelin at Zalinrithe. "You're too late, wyrms."

"I stand between you and your precious Waystone," Mesorith said. "It would seem we are just in time."

The earth shook again, stronger than before. The ground beside Zalinrithe caved in and an enormous myriapede burst to the surface.

Zalinrithe reeled to defend herself against the unexpected attack.

"Ballan might say otherwise," Torrent said.

The myriapede's pincers clamped down around Zalinrithe's neck. Its countless spiked legs probed her scales, searching for a gap through which to impale her.

Zalinrithe's tail lashed wildly. Her talons scraped against Ballan's carapace.

Mesorith eyed Torrent—who wore a smug smile across his bloodied chin—and then his struggling bride. He unleashed a flood of acid in an attempt to stall the Mystic from reaching his Waystone and then lunged for the myriapede.

He bit into the back of Ballan's head, the brittle carapace crunching as he bore down.

Ballan stabbed Mesorith's underbelly with the stinger at the base of his tail. A pulse of pain flooded Mesorith's body.

Torrent leaped over Mesorith's acid pool and landed upon the Waystone.

Mesorith released Ballan's neck and bound after the Mystic.

Ballan spun from Zalinrithe and swiped Mesorith's legs out from under him.

The great dragon toppled forward, his chin hitting the earth and jarring his teeth together. The smell of damp soil flooded his nostrils. He regained his footing and made for the Waystone.

In a burst of light, Torrent vanished.

The Waystone's aura diminished to a dull, erratic flicker. It was over. He had failed to destroy even one Mystic. He had broken his promise to deliver Zalinrithe the taste of their flesh.

Ballan dove beneath the surface, a gaping hole left in the ground between Mesorith and Zalinrithe.

Enraged, Mesorith said nothing. If he could not have the satisfaction of smiting his enemy, he would gladly take it out on what his enemy treasured most. He pushed the pain and fatigue deep within him and took to the air once more.

Despite Zalinrithe struggling to keep pace, Mesorith would not rest until he quelled his rage.

Soon, Lindamere was beneath them. It was not much of a city—the War of Rescission saw to that—but it would sate his fury. For now. Their true advance would not begin until he allied himself with the Aged One and blights poured forth from the Wistful Timberlands in untold numbers.

Beyond the last of the trees, torchlight flickered against a darkening sky. The dragons circled overhead. Lights danced in the streets.

Mesorith plunged toward the center of the town. A rash course of action, but all he could think about was the taste of flesh.

People screamed and ran as he swooped low and breathed acid across the city's main square. Acrid smoke billowed into the air as flesh dissolved in the acid's path.

Zalinrithe careened into a building and sent a shower of rock through the frantic crowd. A torch bounced off Zalinrithe's chest. She plucked a young Evenese guard in glinting armor from the ground and swallowed him whole.

Mesorith thundered forward, paying no care of the surrounding structures. Trees snapped like twigs and buildings crumbled as he charged. He snatched a young Evenese woman from the cobblestone street and gnashed her between his teeth. Ah. The intoxicating taste of Pureblood meat.

A horn bellowed. Their surprise was laid bare.

An arrow ricocheted off Mesorith's scales and sailed into the night.

Armor clanked as soldiers rushed into the square. A hail of arrows crashed into Zalinrithe. She replied with a deluge of ice that encased a throng of bowmen in a frigid tomb.

Mesorith tore a hole in the corner of a stone building and plucked a man with stark white hair from within. He tossed the screaming man down his gullet. "At night, these vermin prefer to hide within their lairs."

Zalinrithe lashed a building with her tail. The façade shattered and people ran into the streets. She grabbed mouthfuls of them and gulped them down.

More soldiers poured into the square. Unlike the first to arrive, who carried little more than short swords and bows, these soldiers carried sturdy tridents and were accompanied by horse-drawn ballistae.

The dragons came together at the center of the square. A ballista bolt whirred inches away from Mesorith's face and tore a hole through his wing. A trident lodged in Zalinrithe's chest, sending her to flight.

Mesorith surveyed the field before him. More soldiers filed into the square from his left. Patience. He must have patience. Tonight was merely the first salvo in his war to rule Tyveriel. In time, it would be his.

He unleashed his acid breath across the square. Soldiers scattered for cover like mice from a toppled barrel. Before they could recover, he beat his powerful wings and lifted into the air.

He aimed for the Wistful Timberlands as the crowd cheered below him.

A smile crept across his face. Evelium did not know what awaited it.

CHAPTER 1

We have seen the sands of Kalmindon. The mortal mind cannot contemplate their beauty.

- The Tome of Mystics
Unknown Origin. Unearthed from the Ruins of Oda Norde, month of Bracken, 1320 AT

— ▲ —

U mhra the Peacebreaker shielded his eyes from the blinding light that bombarded him from all sides. As the light faded, an idyllic landscape of endless beaches and gently lapping azure waters revealed itself. Kalmindon.

He stepped from the edge of the Waystone that brought him here, and innumerable glass beads shifted under foot. The warmth they imparted crept up his legs and flooded his entire form.

Countless whispers greeted him. *Peacebreaker.*

He kneeled and gathered a handful of the beads in his hand. They clinked gently as they rolled over each other in his palm. Each of them contained at its core a vortex of amber energy that swirled contentedly. It was remarkable to think that everything one was in life could be contained in such an unassuming vessel in death. It seemed so trivial, so insignificant.

Like sand through an hourglass, he let the souls cascade back to their resting place and gritted his teeth. The tusks in his lower jaw jabbing at his upper lip, he stood and focused on what he came here for.

There was no sign of Spara who ascended only a couple days prior. She knew little more about Kalmindon's secrets than Umhra did, since she hadn't ascended with the other Mystics at the end of the Age of Grace. She could not have gotten far.

Umhra scrambled to the crest of a nearby dune and surveyed the landscape. Rolling sands gave way to lush gardens. Beyond, a crystalline tower breached the horizon, beckoning to him from open grasslands.

Umhra drew a deep breath of sweet air to settle his racing mind. He thought of the path that brought him here—to Kalmindon. A lowly half-Orc orphan becomes a Paladin, of which there were supposed to be none. In banishing Naur to the hells of Pragarus, the gods deemed the Paladin worthy to become a Mystic. Now, he walked the land of the Creator Gods. How unlikely.

He set off toward the tower on foot, hoping to maintain some element of modesty on such hallowed grounds. Who was he to soar brazenly through the heavens on angelic wings?

Soon, lush foliage overcame the beaches and the shifting sands narrowed to a path that led into a garden. Umhra marveled at the mysterious creatures that floated from flower to flower like so many ethereal butterflies. Trails of chartreuse mist streamed from the tips of their pointed wings as they hovered over each bloom they probed with an oblong proboscis.

He continued through the garden, its tranquility nearly erasing purpose from his mind.

Umhra came to a circular gate of gleaming metal embedded within a stone arch. The arch was covered in purple flowers that matched the delicate metalwork of the gate, which was carelessly left open. Possibly, this was the first sign he was on the right track.

He passed beneath the arch, and serenity abruptly yielded to despair. A short distance along the path of souls that led him through the gardens, the vibrant foliage withered to brittle black husks. Umhra kneeled at the edge of the corruption and rubbed a narrow leaf between his fingers. It crumbled to dust. Beneath it laid the tip of a sickly crimson tendril. Umhra followed the tendril's trail, the warmth from the beads underfoot intensifying to a searing heat. The gentle whispers that welcomed Umhra since his arrival twisted into screams of torment.

Along the path before him, specters roamed, their ghostly forms having emerged from shattered beads within the corruption's reach. The lurid purple apparitions bore smoky black eyes and mouths of pointed teeth. Long strands of ebony hair undulated from their scalps, like fronds of kelp swaying in the sea.

While some specters staggered about the path aimlessly, others tore at the earth with purpose. With each rake of their elongated claws, more beads fractured.

The broken beads sparked—purple wisps of smoke coalesced into newly formed specters. Each of the newborns was greeted with a chorus of raspy squawks from their brethren who huddled over the burgeoning spirits.

Umhra took another step along the path and the first of the specters turned its attention toward him. It moaned hauntingly, and others of its kind heeded its call. The corrupted spirits gathered and approached Umhra—hissing as they neared.

Umhra's stomach sank at the depths of Spara's depravity. Was there no length she was willing to go to in her quest for revenge? Was there nothing sacrosanct?

He summoned Forsetae to his hand, the blade humming as it took form amongst wisps of blue ether. His armor materialized as a series of overlapping diamond-shaped rhodium shards that locked into place one after the other, encasing him in gleaming plates of the rare metal.

The first of the specters upon him, he slashed Forsetae through its form and sent the soul dissipating in a cloud of inky vapor. A second specter's claws screeched against Umhra's armor, sparks dancing across his chest. He beat the apparition away with the back of his fist. As the specter staggard backward, Umhra noticed the mark of his fist across its neck. It glowed like a vibrant amber brand against the heliotrope of its incorporeal form.

The specter shuddered. For a moment, it clawed furiously at the brand and then its arms went slack, its angry hisses quelled. The amber spread across its form and, slowly, it took the visage of an elderly Zeristar man. The spirit smiled, looked over itself with obvious satisfaction, and bowed to Umhra. With a sigh, the spirit returned to its bead, which absorbed it and fused shut in a flash of light.

"There is another way," Umhra said, astonished by what he just witnessed. "I can save them."

Forsetae's voice resonated in Umhra's mind. *Yes, it seems the Ascended's touch can restore their true nature. Possibly, if you heal this corrupted land, they shall reward you with their peace.*

Umhra thrust Forsetae into the ground beside him and clasped the pyramid icon he wore around his neck. The blue glow emanating from the wind currents etched into the icon's facets intensified. Umhra held an open palm toward the rest of the attacking specters. A vibrant celestial light radiated from his form.

"Stop," he said, his tone resolute.

The specters halted their advance inches from Umhra. The mist wafting from their forms intertwined with Umhra's and drifted into the sky.

Umhra's gaze met the matte black eyes of the incorporeal beings before him. He held their attention. "Brothers and sisters, I mean you no harm. A poison is spreading through the gardens of Kalmindon that befouls each of you. Give me but a moment, and I hope you shall find your way back to your respite."

The specters held their place. They affixed their blank glares on Umhra as if locked in a trance. Umhra kneeled, keeping one hand facing the specters and pushing his other into the scorched and cracked beads beneath him. The anguish of the afflicted surged through him. He withdrew his hand and shook his head—gripped the handle of his sword. *No. I can do this. They deserve better.* He thrust his hand back into the corruption and fought the cacophony that tore at his mind.

Umhra focused his energy on the tormented souls. "Find calm in my presence," he said. There was no discernible response, only the continued discord of the spirits. Umhra bore down, gritting his teeth. "With your help, I shall return you to the tranquil rest the gods have promised you." The screams abated, and the specters edged away.

The corruption's tendrils spread up Umhra's arm, an unrelenting pain grew in concert. He fought the pain and imposed his will on the landscape. He envisioned the corruption fading, the gardens of Kalmindon once again serene, unspoiled.

Umhra's aura flowed through the tendrils, and their color slowly shifted from red to vibrant blue. Umhra persisted until his essence pervaded the entirety of the corrupted space. The tendrils quivered, struggling against Umhra's celestial power. Overwhelmed, they recoiled upon themselves and withered.

The specters surrounding Umhra bowed their heads and drifted back to the scorched patches where their respective beads lay cracked, and still smoldered with fiery embers. As they approached their eternal resting places, the specters grew calm, the color fading from their forms like that of a week-old bruise until they were a pale shade of ochre.

They took on their true forms. There were Evenese, Iminti, Farestere, and humans among them. To Umhra's surprise, there were even a few Ryzarin and Orcs. It would seem that all were welcomed by the gods. All equally worthy of the gods' love. Among the sands of Kalmindon, there was no difference between the races of men—between Pureblood and mongrel. Each soul was weighed by the way it held itself in life, not by the color of its skin or the shape of its ears.

"Peacebreaker," the souls said in unison, their individual voices little more than a whisper.

"I bid you return to your eternal serenity," Umhra said.

Their whispers of his name continuing, the spirits returned to their beads, the fractures that released them sealing with a flash of light. As their presence faded, so did Umhra's aura—the corruption gone.

Quiet prevailed for a moment. Umhra stood and looked for any remnants of the corruption that might enable its return. His head ached with echoes of the tortured. He rubbed his temple and pulled Forsetae free of the ground.

A more equitable outcome.

"Thank you, as always, for your sound counsel."

If you are to walk among the gods, your grace must touch every soul with equal love. You must see all creatures' intrinsic worth as comparable to your own. There can be no favorites, none overlooked. Otherwise, you are no better than the least of them. We are now all your children, Ascended One.

Umhra nodded. It was, frankly, all a little too much. He never strived for exaltation. In fact, he spent much of his life actively avoiding attention, willing to trade his unique skill set for the money he needed to eke out a meager lifestyle and keep his secret hidden. Ascended One—how ridiculous. He failed to protect the Bloodbound, failed to recognize Spara's deception, failed to defeat the Grey Queen. What made him worthy of such reverence? Nothing came to mind. The totality of his power was but a fragment of Vaila's which she saw fit to share. Without her, he was nothing.

"Shall we see which of my children heeds my call?" Umhra

asked, willing Forsetae and his armor to dissipate.

He removed the pyramid icon from around his neck and ran his fingers over its sharp edges and the patterns etched in its sides. He sat, crossed his legs, and set the icon gently on the ground before him. Drawing in a deep breath, he filled his senses with this strange world around him. The sweet, unfamiliar scent of the air calmed his mind. The warmth emanating from the beads upon which he sat soothed his body. He closed his eyes and focused on the rhythm of his breathing.

After a moment, he placed his hands on the beads and spread his fingers out among them. Countless voices pervaded his mind...an unintelligible clamor. *Be still. Who among you will tell me what happened here so I may better serve you?*

Umhra opened his eyes. He plucked a single bead that now shown brighter than the rest from among Kalmindon's masses and held it between his thumb and index finger. He smiled.

"Come. Talk with me."

The mote of amber energy swirling at the bead's core intensified until beams of light broke through its surface. The light coalesced into the visage of a fox.

Freed from its resting place, the brilliant golden spirit stretched its legs and bound through the gardens. Umhra climbed to his feet and followed the fox as it scurried. Coming to the edge of a deep crater in the earth, the fox pounced on a shard of pink stone and looked at Umhra.

Beyond the crater's far edge, a path of scorched earth led to the glimmering tower in the distance. A beam of light now escaped from a fracture in the building's façade and cast an amber scar across the pale pink sky.

Umhra squatted, the spirit coming to his side and pressing its head into his hand. Umhra scratched the fox's head and peered down at the fractured stone. It was Spara's Eye of Eminus, which they had retrieved from Aldresor's vault. It lay broken in the garden, the origin of the scorched earth that stretched to the tower on the distant horizon.

Umhra shook his head. Spara told him it was a sending stone so she could locate her mother's soul upon ascending to Kalmindon. What a web of lies she spun. And every one of them ensnared him like an unsuspecting fly on a black widow's tangled strands.

"Are you able to tell me what happened here?"

The fox glanced up at Umhra. "The Ascended One with anger in her eyes came to this place. She planted her egg in Kalmindon's gardens, and a monstrosity emerged, corrupting the land, and leaving a trail of fire in its wake. She called it, God Slayer."

Umhra snarled. Not only had Spara fooled him with her ruse, but he helped her acquire the very thing she needed to bring the pantheon to its knees.

He picked up a shard of the egg and turned it over in his hand as he looked at the tower. "And that?"

"She said, to become a god, one must kill a god. She directed her God Slayer there, to Vaila's Grace. A rash choice to my simple mind."

Rash indeed. Umhra couldn't fathom what kind of abomination Spara could have at her side that would enable her to kill a god, but surely Vaila was a poor place to begin such a quest. Considering the depths of Spara's fury, it was not surprising that logic may elude her.

"Thank you, my friend. You may return to your slumber if you choose."

"I will. But maybe just a few moments in this place...if you should permit it."

"The least I can do," Umhra said. "Be well."

Umhra took off running along the discolored path Spara and her God Slayer had forged. With every footfall, life blossomed, overcoming the corruption and restoring Kalmindon to its natural state of beauty.

CHAPTER 2

I do not concern myself with the folly of witches. Let them curse what they will. The Forene bloodline is unassailable.

- The Collected Letters of Modig Forene
Letter to Her Holiness Tahira Rhys dated 11th of Prien, 1 AF.
Unearthed from the Ruins of Vanyareign, month of Ocken, 1301 AT

—▲—

Anaris lay in ruin. Even the Kormaic temple had been destroyed by the blights and their titans. Turin Forene crouched at the base of a sundered statue amidst the overgrown cloisters whose bluestone walls remained reasonably intact. A bead of sweat ran down her face as she hid from the afternoon sun. She took a bite of a pale green pear she had picked from a nearby tree, admiring the contrast of its lush flesh with the grey of her own. She read the patinated copper plaque on the statue's base. *Balris Silentread. A man of unrivaled selflessness and honor.*

"Where'd your selflessness get you?" she asked the white marble face that stared back at her, half buried in the earth.

"He was a great man," a voice said from behind her. "One of the best."

She glanced over her shoulder to see a hooded Ryzarin man with long white hair and piercing lavender eyes. His graphite skin was only slightly darker than hers. He bore a jagged scar on his neck. Turin was there the day he had earned it. A blight burst out of the woods and Shadow was the first to leap to the group's defense. Before she knew it, both he and the blight were on the ground—one with a dagger sticking from its chest, the other hemorrhaging from his neck. They would have lost him if it weren't for Nicholas interceding.

He smiled.

"You knew him?" Turin asked.

"Yes." Shadow crouched beside his young queen. "He fell in Meriden when we fought the devils of Pragarus. He was like a father to us."

"Sorry. I had no idea."

"No need for apologies. There has been little occasion to tell you about him. Besides, that was a long time ago, and we have more important things to worry about now. Where are Sena and Aridon?"

"Scouting—the place is crawling with blights. I told them to meet us here at dusk so we can enter the city at nightfall and be back to Peacebreaker Keep before the sun rises. Hopefully, they'll have some semblance of an account of how many civilians are still in the city."

"Sounds like as good a plan as any." Shadow rubbed the back of his neck. "Laudin and Naivara are keeping watch outside the north gate. I'll gather them and we'll meet back up here within the hour."

Turin nodded. She grew up with the Barrow's Pact. They'd taught her everything they knew, and she had learned to trust them implicitly. But they were not her friends. They were—well, they were the Barrow's Pact. Heros of great renown. They had fought alongside the Peacebreaker and had led the resistance against the Grey Queen and the blights ever since. Evelium owed them more than could ever be repaid, and yet she found their presence stifling. In their company, she felt like a child with overbearing parents.

With Sena and Aridon, she could be herself. For that reason alone, she insisted on including them whenever she led these search and rescue missions. They'd grown up together in Ruari, trained together since they could walk, and grew to be the best of friends. She found their company a calming influence on her disquieted mind, despite Sena's antics.

She climbed to her feet and pushed a few errant strands of raven blue hair from her eyes. "Here at dusk, then."

As silently as he'd arrived, Shadow darted across the overgrown courtyard, leaped over the temple's crumbling wall, and fell from sight.

Turin shifted her attention back to the center of the city, knowing that her friends would be returning soon. She took another bite of her pear, a rivulet of its sweet juice dribbling down her chin. A bush rustled behind her. "Is there something else, Shadow? We need to get on with things."

Instead of Shadow's disarming timbre, the reply came in a series of clicks and chitters.

Turin looked over her shoulder to see a blight sentry. The creature stood twice her height, its arboreal form reminiscent of ancient cedar. Long scales of red bark peeled from its trunk-like body and its cylindrical head boasted drooping bows covered with pine needles and cones.

The blight's eyes glowed amber like autumn leaves, the matching orb within its chest swirling with discontent. With a grunt, it swung a great club.

Turin ducked, and the club whirred over her head, taking a chunk of white marble from the remnants of Balris's robes.

Turin rolled. She came to her knees in the high grass and pushed a hand into the loamy soil. She needed no god to wield her magic, no icon to store their gifts. As the cool earth cascaded over her fingers, she felt Tyveriel's life force from which she drew her power, and a chill ran up her arm.

The massive blight sentry lumbered forward, sending a shudder through the ground as though Tyveriel, too, ran cold. Its eyes flared, and it hoisted its club overhead.

Turin thrust her free hand into the air and a stone spike pierced the surface soil, sending a shower of dirt and debris into the air. The spike impaled the blight, lifting it from its feet, the creature's root-like digits reaching out for the earth that proved out of reach.

The blight unleashed a horrid squeal. Its body shook, and it dropped its club on the ground at Turin's knees. The light in its eyes and core faded. The blight fell limp.

Turin climbed to her feet and inspected her foe with a cocked head. Rarely did she have the opportunity to get so close to one when it wasn't trying to take her life. It was beautiful. As much a part of Tyveriel as she. It had every right to live on this land, but there was no means by which to negotiate with its kind. They simply poured forth from the Wistful Timberlands in endless waves and laid waste to the constructs of mankind. No, the blights would not be satisfied until they completely eradicated the last trace of humanity from Evelium.

As unfortunate as it was, the remnants of mankind had no choice but to fight. They had been given no quarter since that fateful night when the Grey Queen led the blights in their unprovoked attack on Vanyareign. Of course, she was only an infant at the time, and all she knew of the events that fractured the hallowed kingdom she had been meant to rule, she'd learned from the stories of those lucky enough to survive.

A twig snapped across the cloisters. With ice in her veins, Turin spun to meet another foe. Instead, a dog appeared from behind the cloister wall. She was lean, with a solid brown head and a speckled body with another patch of brown at the base of her cropped tail. A long, pink tongue lolled from her open mouth. When she saw Turin, she ran for her and leaped up into her face and licked, nearly knocking Turin over.

"Alright. Down, Neela. Good to see you too."

The dog jumped again, but met Turin's hand, which guided her back to the ground. Turin kneeled and scratched Neela behind her ear. "I knew you were going to do that. No jumping."

Neela licked Turin's face again.

"Everything okay?" A voice asked from behind Neela.

Turin looked up into the friendly face of her best friend, Senahrin Riora. Sena's smile betrayed her mischievous personality and her eyes—well, her eyes were like pools of green water that set the boys and girls of Ruari to fits of stupidity. Her Iminti skin was as fair as she was tough, and the tangle of wavy blond hair cropped just above her shoulder made her look like she had always just rolled out of bed.

Sena wore auburn leathers and a low-slung belt that carried a machete at each hip. Turin looked down at herself and sighed. She would never match up—queen or not.

Behind Sena lumbered a broad-shouldered human man, with dark features but for his pale-blue eyes. Aridon Ketch had a youthful face—despite being a year older than Turin and Sena—which now dripped with sweat at the exertion of keeping pace with his partner. He carried a steel halberd, which bore an increasing amount of his weight with each stride.

Turin smiled. "Just the usual overzealous greeting."

"I meant our friend behind you." Sena nodded at the impaled blight behind Turin.

"This?" Turin waved dismissively at the blight. "I had it under control."

"I can see that," Sena said. "All the same, we probably shouldn't be leaving anyone alone out here anymore."

"*Weeds* everywhere," Aridon agreed.

"That bad?"

"We were able to get a look at most of the city," Sena said. "There were several patrols. Some signs of skirmishes as well. The reports of people about the few remaining buildings seem to be accurate. We noticed two doors with fresh blue triangles painted on them—both in the inner district. The outer rings seem completely overrun. This bumbling oaf nearly got us noticed several times. We shouldn't go tonight."

Aridon frowned, gave Sena a playful shove. "I'm not good at being quiet, but I help in other ways."

"You certainly do." Turin put a hand on Aridon's broad shoulder and gave it a squeeze. "Tonight, we focus on the painted homes. They openly signal a desire for extraction. I only hope there aren't too many of them. Indrisor likes to limit the number of civilians in the portal at any given time."

Aridon nodded.

Sena grimaced. "Are the others ready?"

"Yes. Shadow, Naivara, and Laudin monitor the road north. They will be here shortly. Nicholas and Indrisor wait for us at the keep."

"Good." Aridon slumped down on the plinth of Balris's statue and laid back against its legs, his arms folded behind his head. "Time for a little nap before a long night." He closed his eyes, Neela curling up at his feet.

Sena shrugged, her green eyes flashing in the setting sun. "I guess we're on watch."

"We're better off with him well rested," Turin said. "He gets so cranky when he's tired."

Aridon opened an eye and batted the two of them away with an exaggerated swat of his hand.

Turin and Sena found a shady spot along the cloister wall where a fountain once babbled. They sat against the wall, shoulder-to-shoulder, so they had a view of the entire garden.

"This place must have been beautiful in its day," Sena said. "Do you ever wonder what it was like to live in a city like this?"

"Sure. Nicholas told me a story about his brother once. He was apparently a brewer of some renown. People throughout Evelium knew and drank Barnswallow Ales. There were places called taverns where people would gather and make merry over pints of his brews. They played music and games and got into fights."

Sena's eyes went wide. "That sounds like too much fun. Maybe someday we'll be able to go to a tavern and get in a fight."

"Maybe someday." A hole as wide as the Spire Rift filled Turin's chest. These people—her people—deserved better than she could give them. They deserved to enjoy their lives, stumbling out of taverns, and returning to warm, comfortable homes with their loved ones. And yet, the Grey Queen, her abomination of a father, and the endless waves of blights, had kept them in this stalemate for the better part of two decades.

Most of what remained of humanity lived in caves like animals, while the less fortunate struggled to survive among the ruins of Evelium's once idyllic cities and towns. These rescue missions were not enough. Turin knew, at some point, she would have to do something drastic if she were to turn the tide— if she were to find herself worthy of being their queen. She just didn't know what that something was.

Sena rubbed Turin's shoulder. "Are you okay?"

Turin's thoughts snapped back to the present. "Yeah. Sure. I just want to get this over with."

Sena nodded and bit her bottom lip. "There can't be many of them left. Hopefully, this will be our last sweep of Anaris. The rest of the old cities are already empty."

An airy whistle sounded from beyond the crumbling wall of the temple grounds, alerting Turin and Sena of Shadow's approach. Neela's short tail wagged frenetically, but she maintained her position at Aridon's crossed feet.

Shadow rounded the corner, his black cloak flapping in the breeze. Laudin and Naivara followed.

Laudin's stride was effortless, as though he barely made contact with the earth. The Iminti ranger had dark hair which he wore short, and ice-blue eyes. Despite being into his second century, he maintained a youthful appearance with nothing more than a few age lines at the corners of his eyes. He slung his bow over his shoulder and eyed the impaled blight beside the remnants of Balris's statue as he stretched his back.

Naivara's green eyes glistened in the light of the setting sun as she came to his side and blew an errant lock of flame red hair from her freckled face. "It's quiet along the road north. We shouldn't have much trouble getting everyone to Peacebreaker Keep if we can get them out of the city."

"Therein lies the rub." Sena nodded over her shoulder. "The place is crawling with weeds. It seems like there's more each time we attempt one of these insane rescue missions."

Naivara extended a hand to Sena and helped her up. "Their numbers do continue to grow. It won't be long before even the caves aren't safe for our people."

"Don't remind me," Turin said, waving off Naivara's offer of help and climbing to her feet. "We need to catch a break." She gestured wildly with her hands. "All this is pointless if we don't turn the tide."

"It's never pointless to save lives," Aridon said, twisting his back until it popped like a chain of minor explosions.

Sena cringed. "Gross."

"You try carrying this thing all day," Aridon said, lifting his halberd from its resting place against the plinth of Balris's sundered statue. "Your back would hurt too."

Shadow guarded his eyes against the setting sun, his graphite skin glistening in what remained of its presence. "Where are the homes we are targeting?"

"There are two of them," Sena said. "Both in the inner circle."

"Of course. We should get going then. Whatever advantage darkness gives us will arrive shortly."

With a bloodied sky in the west fading to deep purple overhead, the party slipped past crumbling stone buildings the color of storm clouds. Lush shrubs and tall clumps of switchgrass overgrew what remained of the cobblestone streets.

A deer grazed beyond the first bridge. As the party approached, the deer froze. Its ears twitched, and it bound off toward the center of the city.

Heavy footfalls clapped against stone. Shadow waved the party off the street to the corner of what was once a tavern or inn.

Neela growled.

Turin pressed her back up against the wall. She ran her palms across the stone and welcomed the cold, rough surface as it abraded her skin. She imagined the streets of Anaris teeming with life. Children chased each other in a game of tag. Shop owners hurried about to close their stores for the night. Lovers ducked into the shadowed alleyways. The way life should be. The way her mother and Talus described what it was like before the razing of Vanyareign and the rise of the Grey Queen.

Turin peered around the corner of the building through a clump of tangled vines. A warm golden glow lit the chest of a sturdy blight that lumbered into the intersection. Its bark-like skin was white and marked with dark scars like an aspen. It stood no less than twenty feet tall and sawtooth leaves topped the branches that jutted haphazardly from its shoulders and head. It scanned the streets with discerning yellow eyes.

Having inherited her forefather's brazenness, Turin took a step from behind the building. The slightest brush of her thigh against the tall grass and the blight swung in her direction.

Shadow grabbed Turin's arm and pulled her to his side. "No need to draw attention to ourselves just yet. There will be plenty of time for that once we have the others in tow."

Turin nodded.

The blight's footfalls grew closer as the beast crossed the bridge toward the corner where the party hid.

"Quickly, around the other side," Shadow said.

Laudin led the others around the corner and into a tight alleyway between the inn and what used to be an apothecary. Out into the open street, they dashed across the bridge and ducked into a vacant building, its door long since torn from its hinges. Turin peaked over her shoulder as she crossed beneath the lintel. All clear.

"From here, the marked houses are three blocks to the east." Sena rubbed at the grimy north-facing window and peered out into the street, kinking her neck to look as far in the direction they would head as she could. "One is on the north corner, the other is two buildings down on the south side."

Laudin nodded. "We take the far one first and address the other on our return. Any sense for how many there are?"

"Not many. I can't imagine each of the buildings could hold much more than a half-dozen. We didn't see any activity when we were scouting."

"Hopefully, some then. It would be a shame to be doing this for nothing."

"They'll be there," Turin said. "Let's go. No sense in waiting."

CHAPTER 3

Vaila's love endures. She stands by your side through trial and tribulation. She holds your hand through hardship and despair. Praise be her name.

- *The Book of Korma*
Unknown Origin. Unearthed from the Ruins of Travesty, month of Riet, 1287 AT

— ▲ —

U mhra burst from the gardens into an open field of delicate pink grass and stopped dead in his tracks at the sight before him. The path of scorched earth he followed from the crater wherein the God Slayer hatched continued, sweeping across the plains in wide arcs.

The remnants of magnificent marble statues littered the landscape. At one time, there must have been hundreds of pristine sculptures gracing these fields. Now, they were little more than rubble. Fragments of charred stone crunched underfoot, plinths supporting bodiless legs poked out from the grass. Where faces remained, blood streamed from vacant stone eyes.

He approached the alabaster face of an angelic figure that lay at the side of the path, having been shorn from the rest of its head. He kneeled beside it and inspected its expressionless features, and dabbed the fresh blood on its cheek with a finger. It was warm, and the stone was surprisingly supple.

The face's mouth opened wide. The statue screamed.

Umhra fell back on his rear and shuffled away from the bellowing face. His heart raced at the notion these things were alive. How terrible a fate to live as a shattered vestige of yourself. Forgotten, like an egg carelessly knocked from the nest. For now, all he could think of doing was to not disturb them any further.

He climbed to his feet and wove through the weeping statues. Leaving them behind, he came to a moat of azure water, Vaila's Grace looming beyond. He leaped across the moat and landed on the scorched earth before the crystalline tower. Here, the bodies of Vaila's empyrean guard lay strewn across the field, their teal skin singed and torn, their white tunics and angelic wings tattered and blood-stained. Feathers fluttered in the gentle breeze. Each corpse was no less than twice Umhra's size, the gilded swords that lay beside them longer than a lance.

Umhra had seen plenty of death in his life—much of it at his own hands—but the scene before him brought a sense of sorrow and panic with which he was inexperienced. He ran to the first of the empyreans and kneeled at its head. Platinum hair caked to a flawless face with a powerful jaw, a series of puncture wounds stretched from the angel's shoulder, across its bare torso, and along its right thigh.

Bright crimson blood pooled beneath the angel, soaking into the cherry blossom pink grasses around them. The empyrean coughed. Blood poured from its mouth. There was a remnant of life in the noble warrior yet.

Umhra prayed to Vaila, and his icon lit up with blue ether. He placed his hands over the empyrean's wounds and offered the celestial being a portion of his life force. The wounds remained—his efforts unsuccessful.

The empyrean coughed again. "There is no magic that can

heal my wounds, Ascended One. My soul shall rest knowing your good deed."

"Tell me what befell you," Umhra said. "So, I may better know what awaits me in avenging this horror."

The empyrean's gaze fell on Umhra, its opalescent, pupilless eyes tinged with blood. Their eyelids fluttered, and the angel reached for Umhra's icon. It clutched the rhodium pyramid in its enormous hand. The chain bit into Umhra's neck at the force of the empyrean's grasp.

Images of a great battle flashed through Umhra's mind, the empyrean guard streaming forth from Vaila's diamond tower on majestic wings, gilded great swords held high. Spara stood in the field, her celadon gown flowing as a massive worm barreled past her. The worm's pulpy body was the color of rust but for an armored plate of bone around the three eyes on its head. Six pincers protruded from a mouth ringed with dagger-like teeth. The creature's body pulsed, starting at its hind-most segment, and lit a chartreuse eye atop each segment as it progressed forward.

When the pulse reached the worm's head, the three eyes on its face came to light and a shockwave of force burst forth. The nearest of the empyreans were incinerated, their bodies set aflame and cinders scattering on the wind. The force of the blast knocked those behind the vanguard from the sky.

Spara smiled as the worm lurched forward and weaved its way through the field of fallen empyreans. It gnashed them in eager jaws and cast them aside. The God Slayer barreled on toward Vaila's tower.

Another wave of empyreans poured forth, and Umhra's god came to the edge of a balcony high above. Her flawless blue skin glowed in the sun. She looked down upon her adversary with contempt. Her lip quivered as she held Spara's gaze, then she flourished a rhodium sword in each hand.

Umhra snapped back to the present. His focus turned to the tower, and the shattered balcony where Vaila once stood. The empyrean's hand released Umhra's icon and dropped to the ground. Its body shuddered and fell limp.

Umhra jumped to his feet and took off in a full sprint, throwing the caution with which he had approached this strange and new situation to the wind. All he could think about was Vaila.

He hurdled the fallen empyreans, leaped over the final two of the tower's concentric moats in a single bound, and came to the base of a grand staircase as wide as a fallen tree and nearly as tall as one still standing. The building at the top of the staircase, and all its adornments, were entirely constructed of diamond. A soft internal glow refracted through its countless facets and showered the grounds in prismatic light.

Diamond shards littered the scorched landscape, a great fissure in the tower's façade throwing a beam of the purest light into the sky. The vast archway of the entrance lay shattered, something too large for its opening having forced itself within. No doubt, the God Slayer.

Umhra took the stairs in a few effortless bounds and charged into the collapsed portal. Toppled pillars and haphazard shards of diamond littered the hallway within, creating a crisscross pattern like enormous daggers that had fallen from the walls and ceiling. Umhra crept among the destruction, ducking under felled spikes, clambering over others. All the while, he hoped he wasn't too late.

The hall opened into an expansive room that glowed with a nearly blinding light of no discernable source. It reminded Umhra of Aldresor's Vault where he and Spara found the Eye of Eminus which could now be his god's ruin.

At the center of the room, beneath the shattered ceiling, a crimson sigil was burned into the crystalline floor, smoke still rising from its pattern of crisscrossed lines. Beyond the sigil was a throne of flawless diamond, angelic wings stretching from its back and two familiar rhodium swords resting against its left arm.

At the chair's base sat Vaila, her long, ebony hair draped over one shoulder, her fair blue cheeks smeared with blood and soot. She looked up, her gaze meeting Umhra's, and she smiled through streaking tears. Umhra ran to her side.

"I knew you would come," Vaila said. "I expected Spara to ascend with vengeance in her heart, but I did not know she was in possession of an Eketar. Frankly, I was lucky to escape with my life. What is left of it."

Her glimmering gown was rent across her stomach, a deep gash running beneath her ribs. The skin around the wound was black with necrosis. She was paler than Umhra remembered. She looked fragile. Defeated.

"I'm afraid that is my fault," Umhra said, kneeling beside her and placing his hands over her wound. "Along with helping her destroy the Waystones she needed to ascend, I was also instrumental in her recovering the creature's egg from a wizard's lair on Tyveriel. I had no idea what it was, or how she would use it."

Vaila feigned a smile. "The power of the gods has been waning for ages. It was only a matter of time until she ascended—with or without your help. The burden of assuring her failure, however, now falls on you."

Umhra didn't answer, focused on his icon. A radiant light grew from his pyramid as he clutched his hands over Vaila's wound. The light faded. Umhra kept his hands on Vaila for a moment and then withdrew. His efforts had sealed her wound, but a deep purple scar remained. Umhra frowned.

"It is the most you can do," Vaila said. "Alas, this wound shall fester until I meet my end."

"How do I find her? I can stop this. I *will* stop this."

"I still sense her presence in Kalmindon." Vaila struggled to push herself upright, winced. "Having failed in killing me, she would have likely gone to the Mystics, the others of her kind. The others of *your* kind. She will garner their power and then try her hand at another god. Likely one less formidable."

"So, it's true? One must kill a god to become a god, and that is her goal?"

"She doesn't want to become a god, Umhra. She wants to become God. With the Eketar at her side, she will bring ruin to the pantheon and claim Kalmindon as her own."

Umhra pounded the diamond floor beneath him—its flawless surface cracked. "I won't let that happen. I can stop her and her rancid worm."

"Then listen for the other Mystics. Go to them and rid us of this scourge."

Umhra stood and helped Vaila to her feet. "You will be alright?"

"For now, yes. I am weak, but not without recourse. I will help where I can."

"Can you help me contact my friends back on Tyveriel? I left them abruptly, and in a precarious situation. I would like to know if they made it to safety."

Vaila smiled. "Your heart knows no bounds, does it? Of course, I can help if it troubles you so. Now that you have ascended, you can project yourself through the veil between the realms as I have done with you so many times. But to do this, you must share a connection with the one you wish to contact, and they must seek to commune with you."

"Gromley," Umhra whispered. "When I brought him back from the brink of death, I shared with him a piece of my life force."

"Yes. The Cleric of Anar will act as your conduit, as you act as mine."

Umhra recalled Vaila saying these exact words in the Burning Wood after he dispatched Mesorith. She knew all along that he would ascend and need Gromley to tether him to Tyveriel. She knew before he had even considered the notion. Was he really that predictable? Or was this all preordained? He had so many questions, but now was not the time. He had already ceded Spara too much of a head start. A few moments to contact Gromley was all he would spare. Then, he would find the other Mystics.

Vaila drew him from his ruminations. "Between here and the Tower of Mystics, you will find a suitable place from which to commune. Know that while for you only a matter of days has passed since your arrival in Kalmindon, nearly two decades have come and gone for Tyveriel. It is one of the costs of Ascension."

Umhra nodded, his mind racing. "They must think I have abandoned them."

Vaila's eyes welled with tears. "I have taken much from you. More than any man should bear. But know that you are more than merely a tool to manifest my bidding. I am less without you—a shell without a heart. You have given me as much purpose as I have for you. I hope you realize that."

Umhra took Vaila's hand. It was cool to the touch. As soft and fragile as his own was sturdy and calloused. He admired the pale blue of her skin. "I won't let you down."

He looked up to the fracture in the roof high overhead and summoned his wings. In his god's presence, grey feathers sprouted from this back, his wings blossoming around him. "I'll make this right," he said, crouching. He burst into the air and welcomed the familiar thrumming in his right ear.

CHAPTER 4

We observed them from outside the city's perimeter. We dare not step foot within Oda Norde.

A Traveler's Guide to the Odd and Obscure by Sentina Vake
Chapter 1 – Unearthed from the Homestead in Maryk's Cay, month of Riet, 1407 AT

— ▲ —

The house had seen better days. A shattered window was the least of its worries, with the roof having partially caved in and a chunk of the stone façade shorn from one of its corners so that moonlight streamed through unabated.

Blue paint clung to the door like dried blood to a corpse. The crude brush strokes formed a triangle, its asymmetric angles making for a poor representation of the pyramid icon worn by the Peacebreaker, whose ascension to Kalmindon was promised to reset the balance of things. At least, that's what Turin had been told. She often wondered during the long days spent in damp caverns what was taking him so damn long.

The Peacebreaker—it was an odd name for a god or a man or whatever he was. Talus had shared the stories of Umhra's exploits. He'd jumped into the hells of Pragarus to battle gods, he'd fought and temporarily defeated the dracolich known as

Mesorith, he'd broken the ground outside Vanyareign to give mankind a chance at survival before ascending to Kalmindon in pursuit of a vengeful Mystic.

As a child, she would sit outside and watch the night sky, hoping one of the shooting stars she saw marked his return. Now, she wanted more than just rescuing those too weak, stubborn, or dumb to make their way to Ruari on their own. Not that it wasn't rewarding. As her powers grew, so did her desire to lead her people into battle against the blights—against the Grey Queen.

Laudin peered through a fractured windowpane. "Looks empty."

"No. We saw them earlier." Aridon strode forward and rattled the door by its pitted iron handle.

The door didn't budge.

"May I?" Shadow asked, sidling to the front of the party.

Aridon swept his hand wide and bowed in deference.

Shadow inspected the keyhole, slipped a leather roll from within his cloak, and unfurled it on the ground, exposing a set of picks that glinted in the moonlight. He rubbed his hands together and selected two. The tension wrench was sturdy and L-shaped, while the rake had the curves of a slithering snake.

With one effortless motion, Shadow slid the picks into the keyhole and sprung the lock.

Aridon nudged the door open with the butt of his halberd and peered over his shoulder at Turin.

"Let's go," Turin said, striding past the party and into the building.

Wide-planked floors creaked beneath her feet as she crossed what was once a modest living room. The air was musty, as though Turin was the first to breathe it in ages. As the others filed in behind her, she walked the perimeter of the room and noted the furniture lining its walls.

"Dammit," Sena said. "We're too late. They're gone."

Laudin walked across the rug at the center of the room and

stopped in his tracks. He tapped his foot over the space where he stepped last and waved Turin over to him. "There's something beneath the rug," he said. "Possibly a hinge."

Turin looked the rug over. It was the color of rust, with pale yellow flowers woven into its border. Once, maybe it was beautiful, but now it was stained and nearly threadbare. She turned to Aridon. "Pull it up."

Aridon shrugged and placed his halberd on a rough-hewn table beside him. Turin and Laudin retreated from the rug and Aridon and Sena each grabbed one of its corners. They pulled it back, dust billowing into the air.

Beneath the rug, someone had cut the planks of the floor free and replaced them with a hatch of unstained wood. Opposite the hinges were two iron handles.

Laudin and Shadow each grabbed a handle and pulled. The hatch groaned as they hoisted it open and revealed a hole in the earth below.

"Shall we see where it goes?" asked Naivara, stepping to the hole's edge.

Turin joined her at the precipice. "I believe we should. I'll lead."

Turin dropped into the hole and pushed her hands into its loose dirt flooring. A familiar chill ran up her arms and flooded her body to its very core. She stared into the darkness. Slowly, her eyes adjusted. The pitch black of the tunnel ahead gave way to muted shades of amber. Soon she saw without hindrance.

The tunnel seemed to be carved by hand, the light, chalky stone walls pockmarked by tools. It snaked away from Turin, leading north.

"It's clear. Come on down."

Laudin dropped down first, landing gracefully at Turin's side. Naivara followed, then Shadow and Sena. Aridon crashed down with Neela in his arms. The giant of a man placed the squirming dog on the ground, stood upright, and banged his head against the roof of the tunnel.

"Dammit," he muttered as he rubbed the spot with a meaty palm and a scornful look on his face.

"This must have taken years to build." Naivara brushed her fingers against the tunnel wall. "And taken more than a few people."

"Well, I can't see a god forsaken thing," Sena said.

"Yes. Dark." Aridon said, still rubbing his head.

"Naivara, can you do something about that?" Turin asked.

"Hold on." Sena put a hand out in protest.

Aridon clapped his hands with child-like enthusiasm.

Naivara closed her eyes. Green wisps of ether wafted from her platinum circlet along the tunnel roof. She tilted her head to the side, and Sena and Aridon took the form of ferrets. She opened her eyes and kneeled with an inviting smile. "Come on, you two."

The ferret that was Aridon bound forward and hopped into Naivara's satchel. Sena backed up, her lithe body scrunching in a high arch. "Don't be ridiculous, Sena." Naivara grabbed Sena by the scruff of her neck and dropped her into the satchel with Aridon.

Naivara stood, dusted herself off. Aridon poked his head out from the top of the bag, his speckled nose twitching with excitement. Naivara scratched his head. "Let's go."

Turin set off down the tunnel at a hurried pace. It was unlikely there would be any blights down here, and she had little else to fear. Besides, with Sena and Aridon no longer a hindrance, the rest would have no problem keeping up.

The tunnel wove through the earth like thread on a loom until terminating beneath another hatch like the one through which they'd entered. From above, she heard muted voices.

"I guess we knock?" Turin asked as Laudin, Shadow, Naivara, and Neela came to her side.

Shadow flourished a dagger in each hand. "We'll be ready should we be met with hostility."

"We won't be needing those," Turin said. "These are our

people, Shadow. We will bring them home to Ruari. All of them."

Shadow shrugged, spun the daggers in his hands, and returned them to their sheaths. "Fine. Nobody dies, but you give *our* people too much credit."

"Naivara?" Turin asked. "Aridon, please."

Aridon's whiskered face popped out of the satchel. Naivara cupped him under his front legs and placed him on the ground. Then she retrieved Sena.

Naivara took a deep breath to focus her mind, and Aridon and Sena returned to their normal forms.

"So soon?" Aridon asked, his tone wreaking of disappointment. "I was taking a good nap."

"I hate it when you do that," Sena said. "Can you at least ask for permission next time?"

Turin pointed to the ceiling above them. "Sorry. Aridon, mind knocking on this hatch for me?"

Aridon took the butt of his halberd and thumped it on the hatch door high above. Dust rained down and the voices above hushed. After a moment, Aridon struck the hatch again. This time, heavy footfalls crossed the floor above until right over them.

"Who's down there?" A gruff voice bellowed.

Turin stepped forward, staring up at the hatch. "It is Turin Forene, your Queen. We are here to see you safely to Ruari."

"Yeah, and I'm Artemis Telsidor, slayer of the mighty Mesorith." Stifled laughter came from above.

Sena rolled her eyes. "Are you sure we want to save them?"

Turin ignored the question. "We saw the sign of the Peacebreaker painted on your door. You call for help, do you not?"

The room above was silent, as though the question had no answer. More heavy footsteps. The grinding of metal. The creaking of wood. The hatch door swung open.

Turin waved away the dust that rained down upon them.

She peered up into the warmly lit room; a sea of grimy, unshaven faces staring back at her from above. Each of the men had a weapon at the ready.

One of the men put his hand to his forehead. "Well, I'll be— her eyes do glow gold, like the stories say."

The other man reached his hand into the hole and offered it to Turin.

She went to grasp it, but Shadow interceded. "I'll go first. I don't want you taking any more risk than necessary."

"Alright," Turin conceded. "After you."

Shadow took the man's hand and slid up into the room. A moment later, he returned and poked his head back through the doorway, so he hung upside down. "Come on up. You'll want to see this."

The man who had hoisted Shadow up into the room again reached down for the queen. She grasped his calloused palm and clambered through the hatch.

Aridon hoisted Neela up after her and followed, unassisted. He then helped the rest of the party up into the room.

Turin appraised the chamber, the faces of no fewer than twenty haggard peasants staring back at her. Children sat huddled in their mothers' laps, and an elderly Farestere woman darned a pair of pants. There were more than she expected— more than Indrisor would want in the pocket dimension at one time. Some mistakes have a way of never letting go.

"Are you really her?" a young Iminti woman asked from a shadowy corner of the room.

"I am."

Most of the people gathered in the room dropped to their knees and genuflected in their queen's presence.

"Please, I haven't earned such respect. Maybe there will be a day when I am worthy of your admiration. Today, I merely seek to see you to safety. To reunite you with the rest of our people. If we are to be successful, we must get moving. Gather only what you can carry. We will provide everything you need when we reach Ruari.

The room broke into a frenzy as people gathered their belongings. Turin approached the man who helped her through the hatch. "What of the other building marked with the pyramid?" she asked.

The man threw a burlap sack over his shoulder. "Empty. Some weeds caught them in the streets a few months back. Didn't end well. Those that survived live among us now. I'm afraid we're all that's left of Anaris."

"And we're further north in the city here than the other end of the tunnel?"

"Aye."

"Good. We make our way north to Peacebreaker Keep. There we have a means of travel to Ruari."

The man nodded and scratched at his scruffy beard. He was gaunt, with sunken cheeks, and puffy bags beneath his eyes. He looked so tired. Not the kind of tiredness you feel after a poor night's sleep, but the kind you feel at the end of a war. The kind of tiredness you never truly recover from. If he was lucky, one day he would no longer notice it. It would just be a part of him, like the scar that ran along his jawline.

"Then it's best we leave from here," he said. "The quicker we get out of the city, the better off we'll be. The weeds seem to have taken a liking to our streets."

Turin held her hands in the air, and the people focused on her. "We will exit the city through the north gate. If we get separated, take Atalan's Way to Peacebreaker Keep. We must move quickly and quietly to avoid as many blights as we can. Inevitably, we will run into at least a few along the way. When this happens, you are to seek cover together and let us take care of them. We have the necessary equipment and training for these situations."

"And what happens when we get to this Peacebreaker Keep?" an Iminti woman with sandy hair and dark eyes asked. "How do we get to Ruari safely? It's on the other side of

Evelium."

"We have means of quick passage to Ruari from the keep that will allow us to travel the vast distance in under an hour."

"Witchcraft," the woman said, pointing a shaking finger at Turin.

"Wizardry, actually." An older Evenese man stepped forth from the rear of the room. He was tall and gaunt and wore his salt and pepper hair neatly trimmed. His green velvet waistcoat was missing a button, and his soiled shirt and pants hung on his thin frame as they would on a scarecrow.

"Xavier Pell?" Laudin asked. "Is it really you?"

"What's left of me, my dear Laudin."

Laudin wrapped his arms around the man, whose name held no meaning to Turin. He held the embrace for a moment and then looked Pell over. "It is wonderful to see you."

"And you as well." His voice choked. "I never gave up hope that Umhra and the Barrow's Pact would save us. I never imagined Queen Turin, herself, would come for us."

He turned to Turin and smiled. "Thank you, you are every bit a Forene."

Turin had grown accustomed to the odd glares and misguided accusations from even those whose lives she'd saved. She knew she was different. Looked different. No matter what she did, there would always be those who believed she was cursed because of the grey color of her skin and the yellow hue of her eyes. But Xavier Pell was different. She could see it in his eyes. "Of course, Lord Pell." She returned her attention to the woman. "I promise, it's the safest way to Ruari. Unless, of course, you'd rather stay here."

The woman averted her eyes. "No, my lady."

"Then we move out at once," Turin said, her tone resolute.

The room broke into a frenzy of final preparations. When everyone was ready, Shadow cracked the door open and peered outside.

"Looks clear."

"Alright," Turin said. "You lead the way. Sena and I will pick up the rear. Nobody falls behind."

Shadow nodded, pushed the door open, and slipped into the night.

In small groups of two or three, the townsfolk followed him, Laudin and Naivara joining after a third had left the building. More peasants streamed from the hovel, followed by Aridon and Neela. Finally, the rest crept after them. Sena raised an eyebrow and offered a deep anticipatory breath to Turin as the oldest of the group made for the streets helped by Xavier Pell.

Turin shared the concern Sena expressed with not so much as a word. The group was too large—too frail. Even with half the Barrow's Pact assisting, she wasn't sure all of them would make it to Peacebreaker Keep alive.

She shook her head, trying to rid her mind of such negative thoughts, and followed Sena out the door.

A half-moon hung in the sky and the air this far south was warm and humid despite the late hour. It was Turin's favorite time of year, these hot days and nights as the moon slowly waned. There was something about how the heat countered the inner chill she bore in her connection to Tyveriel. But this was not the time to admire the chirp of summer crickets or the fragrant scent of lilies in bloom. She focused her senses on searching for potential threats around them.

Shadow came to a halt at the corner of what once was a haberdashery and threw his back against the stone façade. As the others fell in behind him, he signaled down the line to Turin with four fingers held in the air. The chittering of blights that echoed through the abandoned city streets interrupted the quiet night.

Turin crept along the line of nervous faces. A loose shutter clapped against a stone wall. She crouched and stared into a puddle held within an indentation among the cobblestones. It reflected the moon overhead as clearly as if she gazed upon the heavens directly.

The puddle trembled, the moon's image rippling. They were close. She held her fist up and froze the party in its tracks.

As she crossed beneath the sill of a shattered window, sturdy, branch-like appendages lashed out from within the building and batted her into the open street. A pain shot through her chest as she tumbled over worn cobblestones and through clumps of switchgrass. She wheezed for air.

Pushing herself to her knees, she saw a large blight with the dark, twisted bark of an elm tree crash through the window and roar with abject rage. Frightened people screamed and scattered as the monstrosity thundered toward her.

Laudin drew his bow and loosed an arrow into the blight's back as Naivara led the young and old alike into an alley between the buildings.

Sena drew her machetes, the steel blades glinting in the moonlight. She ran in pursuit of the blight.

Shadow rolled from the corner of the wall as another blight with smooth tan bark crashed into the corner of the building and sent a shower of stone into the air. Three more blights were behind it.

Turin thrust her hands into a clump of grass and welcomed Tyveriel's power to flood her body. As the familiar chill coalesced, she scrambled to her feet and ducked beneath a swipe of the elm blight's arm.

Shadow let a dagger fly and pierced the chest of the blight nearest him. The vibrant green light at the center of its torso flickered erratically, and the creature unleashed an earsplitting screech. Shadow's dagger reappeared in his hand as he flung his other blade into the same spot.

The blight reeled as the second dagger pierced its core. The light emanating from within snuffed out, and the blight crashed into the side of the haberdashery, toppling through the sundered window with a thunderous crash.

Another screech echoed through the city, this one from a block or more away. More blights were answering their brethren's call.

Aridon charged the three remaining blights that barreled toward Shadow, swinging his polearm in wide arcs. The blade hacked into the side of a short, thick blight. Aridon wrenched it free as Neela leaped at the blight's face and bit into the wood around its eyes, thrashing her head from side to side.

Another group of blights, three the size of shrubs and four as tall as a mature pine, shambled into the intersection. One of the larger among them trod on a man as he scrambled for cover. The man's body burst, a spray of gore thrown across the street.

In rapid succession, Sena hacked into the back of the elm blight's legs and brought it to its knees. "Take care of the others. I've got this one."

Turin spun to the pine blights. A trail of gore sloughed off the foot of the largest among them as it lumbered toward her. Taking a wide stance, Turin held her hands out at her hips. Her fingers flexed as though she were squeezing an unseen object that resisted her grasp. A surge of cold ran through her body and she thrust her hands overhead, so her arms crossed.

Two stone spikes broke through the earth. One impaled the blight with the sullied foot through the chest, the other severed a second at the waist. She charged the rest of them.

Arrows flew over Turin's head as she ran, each of them bursting aflame as they neared their quarry. They struck true and lit the two remaining pine blights on fire.

The pigment faded from Turin's hands, the deep grey turning a milky white. One of the smaller blights, a tangle of thorny briars, leaped at her with outstretched claws. She grabbed it out of the air and felt a pulse of energy flow through her body and out of her hands. Ice encased the blight. Turin spun and threw it at the others of its kind.

One dove from its path and rolled across the ground like a tumbleweed. The ice ball hit the other with full force. Both blights shattered on impact in an explosion of ice and wood.

Still more blights responded to the call of their kin. The

Sentinels among their ranks carried great clubs and spears, their bark marred with soot and scars.

Turin backed away from them, considering retreat, when she noticed a cloaked figure crouched along the roofline of a nearby inn. Little more than a silhouette against the night sky, the figure stood and flourished a scythe in each hand. Its cloak caught the wind with the sound of a sail unfurling at sea.

The stranger ran along the ridge of the roof with preternatural speed and leaped for the Sentinels. They swung their scythes in wide arcs as they passed the largest of them. The stranger hit the ground, shoulder rolled across the cobblestone, and came to their feet. In one fluid motion, they swung a scythe upward and took the leg from a second Sentinel.

The dismembered blight toppled sideways into the corner of a nearby building. It dropped its club and clawed at the eaves in a vain attempt to stay upright. The rotted rafters pulled free, and the blight rolled off the side of the building and hit the ground. The largest of the Sentinels took one step further and its torso slid from its lower half at a sharp angle. Life faded from its eyes and chest as its two halves crashed onto the street.

The stranger looked over their shoulder at Turin, their eyes glowing from beneath a black cowl like embers in a bonfire. "What are you waiting for? Gather those you hid in the alley and run."

The voice sent a shiver up Turin's spine. Countless whispers accompanied every word the stranger spoke and swirled around in Turin's ears like they were trying to tear the words apart. "We're heading north to Peacebreaker Keep and then home to Ruari. Come with us."

The stranger ducked beneath a club as the Sentinels surrounded him. "Do not delay. There is no home for me among your kind."

"Try us. You might be surprised."

The stranger embedded a hooked blade in the torso of another blight, eliciting an agonized wail. "Go."

"If you change your mind, ask for Turin Forene. I owe you for your help today."

"Forene?" The stranger asked.

"Yes."

Turin ran to the mouth of the alley and found Naivara within, standing in front of the huddled townsfolk, her hands ablaze and a pile of ash at her feet. "Time to move. Hurry."

The party dashed for the north gate. Turin stopped and looked over her shoulder as enraged blights engulfed the stranger. She bit her lip and ran after the others.

CHAPTER 5

He was thinner than I recalled—gaunt. It will take some time for him to find his former strength. My concern is the emotional toll was even greater.

- Entry from Xavier Pell's Journal
Dated 17th of Anar, 903 AF. Unearthed from the ruins of Anaris, month of Vasa, 1152 AT

— ▲ —

Umhra soared over the endless beaches of Kalmindon. He thought of those who came before him that now rested among the idyllic sands. He thought of his mother and father, of Ivory, the Bloodbound, and Balris, and wondered if, someday, he might reunite with them in some way. No doubt, they were all here somewhere, within this veritable desert of souls. Could they sense his proximity? Did they long for such a reunion, or were they truly at peace and unburdened by such desires?

An oasis appeared on the horizon and drew Umhra's attention, a plot of green amidst the endless sands. He was certain this was the place Vaila directed him toward. The thrumming in his ear confirmed as much.

Umhra collapsed his wings and dove for the verdant spring, the air whistling past him as his descent hastened.

As he neared the treetops, he spread his wings, his fall arrested in a flurry of grey feathers. He landed amongst lush foliage, the sweet smell of unfamiliar blossoms greeting him.

He followed a narrow path of beads that wove between the dense and colorful garden.

At the center of the oasis, beneath a tree with drooping branches covered in soft yellow leaves, was a platform made of pale blue stone. The oval pedestal, which rose to Umhra's knee, had been worn smooth by what Umhra could only imagine was an eternity of exposure and use. This place was ancient—no, timeless.

As Umhra approached, the stone emitted a low hum that drew him forward. He walked its perimeter and squinted into the pink sky. Timeless and perfect. No wonder Vaila deemed it worthy to send him here.

He sat upon the stone and took a moment to enjoy his surroundings. The gentle breeze, the fragrant air. He couldn't recall a place more peaceful.

Satisfied, Umhra closed his eyes and thought of Gromley. Despite it having only been days since he rescued his Zeristar friend from the brink of death, it somehow felt like ages since they'd been together. His mind drifted to Nicholas. Oh, how he missed Nicholas. He chuckled under his breath at the notion of the unlikely pairing of him and the Farestere as closest of friends.

Back to Gromley. He was never good at maintaining focus when his mind was calm.

Umhra thought of the sun-shaped amulet the cleric wore around his neck and used it as his focus. He recalled the brilliant platinum surface he imbued it with when he shared his own life force with Gromley to spare him from death's cold embrace.

A chill ran through his body, and he thought of a moment he and Gromley shared the night before the Barrow's Pact helped him find Spara's icon at Ember's Watch. Together, they sat by a waning campfire, the cold winter wind at their backs, their friends already asleep. Umhra had asked him if his quest to find Spara and to learn what it meant to be a Mystic was worthy, or rather merely self-aggrandizing folly. Gromley was silent for a moment and then offered that the worth of any quest resides in the heart of he who embarks upon it. And that he always knew Umhra's heart to be true.

Umhra's head spun, his stomach churned. He felt the grip of a powerful force tear him from his perch and thrust him through space and time. Tyveriel called him home.

He opened his eyes to find he was no longer in the tranquil garden of Kalmindon, but in a cavern lit by raging braziers. He repressed the urge to vomit as bile bit at the back of his throat and tried to focus his vision.

At first, the image was a blur—as though he observed life through a gossamer veil. He shook his head, and his vision improved enough so he could see Gromley sitting at a table at the center of the room. Gromley laughed, waving a turkey leg around in the air like he would his war hammer.

Umhra could not discern the face of Gromley's companion, but from the figure's diminutive proportions, he deemed it was Nicholas.

Umhra approached the table. "Gromley."

Gromley threw his chair back from the table and stared at Umhra with wild eyes. The other figure in the room, their face obscured in shadow, rushed to his side, but Gromley held them at bay with an open palm.

"Umhra? Is it really you?"

The air rippled between them, so Gromley's form undulated, like Umhra was looking through the heat of the desert.

"It is. I come to you from Kalmindon where a great threat looms. How do you fair?"

"Umhra, it's been nearly twenty years since you left us during the assault on Vanyareign. We've amassed the remnants of our people in the Caves of Ruari and have rebuilt some semblance of society here. We continue to fight the Grey Queen and her blights, but our prospects remain bleak."

"Twenty years?" Umhra's mind raced at the discrepancy. "It's been but a few days for me as near as I can tell. I'm sorry. You must feel as though I've abandoned you."

"Nay. I sensed your ascension. I feel your presence every waking moment. I dream of you nightly. I've kept the others informed. They know you fight for us still."

"With every bit of my being." Umhra reached out and placed a hand on Gromley's shoulder. Warmth surged up his arm and Gromley's icon lit with blue ether.

"It's good to see you," Umhra continued. He looked upon his friend with a lump in his throat. "It's good to see you as well, Nicholas." He nodded to the tiny, veiled figure that now stood beside Gromley. "I've missed you."

"But now is not the time for pleasantries, as I don't know how long I have. I can already feel Kalmindon pulling me away from you. I need you to listen carefully, Gromley. I must stop Spara from destroying the gods. If I fail, there's no saying what she will do with Tyveriel. Her anger knows no end."

Gromley clasped his icon. "Of course, we understand."

"For now, you must go on without me. I do, however, know of something that may help in turning the tide for your cause."

Umhra felt himself get yanked back by a force too strong to resist. He gritted his teeth and strained to remain with Gromley a moment longer.

"Antiikin. You will find what you need in the forge beneath the central tower of Antiikin."

Again, the force tore at Umhra, intense cold shooting through his body.

"Eleazar will be expecting you. Go to Antiikin. Tell Nicholas—"

Like a blow to the back of his head, Umhra lost the connection and found himself in utter darkness. He once again hurtled through the cosmos and the darkness gave way to the dappled light of the garden.

He sat on the stone as though he had never left. Was it real? Had he visited Tyveriel? Or was it just a dream? No, it was real. He felt Gromley—knew he was in his friends' presence. It was good to be back with the Barrow's Pact, if only for a fleeting moment. Hopefully, Gromley was able to understand his message and would relay it to the rest. Hopefully, it would be enough to change their fortunes until he could shift his attention to their plight. But, alas, there was more to do here first. Tyveriel would have to wait.

Feeling hopeful for the first time in what seemed like ages, Umhra left the oasis in peace.

— ▲ —

"Visited by Umhra?" Regent Avrette asked, leaning forward on her elbows and appraising Gromley and Nicholas, who sat with her at the circular stone table. "From Kalmindon?"

Candlelight flickered between them, illuminating the cavern walls that were engraved with images of great battles from the War of Dominion. Jenta wore her disbelief plainly. Gromley could only imagine what she thought of him. Likely that he'd gone mad and dragged poor Nicholas along with him. He stroked his beard. "Well, some sort of projection of him. But yes. He said he was in Kalmindon trying to stop Spara from killing the gods."

"It sounds like he got more than he bargained for with his Mystic friend," Regent Avrette said. "Isn't it always the case that the best of us are so easily taken advantage of?"

Gromley frowned. "There's more. It sounded as though only days had passed for him since he ascended. He had no idea he's been away from us for nearly two decades."

"Interesting. Did you also see this, Nicholas?" Regent Avrette asked.

"No, Jenta," Nicholas offered. "All I saw was Gromley

entranced and mumbling to himself. It was only after that I learned of Umhra's visit."

"And what of his message? I'm sure he brought you more than good tidings from heaven."

Gromley didn't like the accusatory tone in Jenta's voice. He stood and rested his hands atop the back of Nicholas's chair. "Indeed. He told me there is something waiting for us in a forge in the undercrofts of Antiikin. That King Eleazar would be expecting us. He also said hello to Nicholas and that he fights for us still."

Nicholas smiled.

"Getting to Antiikin could prove treacherous," Regent Avrette said. "The blights and their titans maintain a constant presence on the outskirts of the Wistful Timberlands."

"Yes, and Indrisor's pocket dimension won't be able to get us any closer than Vanyareign." Nicholas agreed. "From there, the journey would likely have to be on foot."

"If whatever waits for us in Antiikin can change our fortunes, as Umhra suggests, it's a chance worth taking. Wouldn't you both agree?"

"Of course, Gromley," Regent Avrette said. "I just don't want you running off into harm's way in search of the unknown. I suggest we await Turin's return and decide who should go to Antiikin when we are all here to weigh in."

Gromley bowed reverently. "As always, Jenta, you offer sage advice."

Regent Avrette exhaled heavily. "I'm hopeful. Please don't get me wrong. If what you say is true, we could be at a turning point. But I'd like you to see a Cleric, nonetheless."

"Jenta, I am a Cleric. I know what I experienced. I am of sound mind."

"Then there's no need for you to object to an objective opinion on your health. I do not want to risk sending anyone to Antiikin if there is even the slightest chance this vision is merely a new symptom of the fits you've been having since Umhra ascended."

Gromley huffed. "Very well. I'll see a Cleric if it will ease your mind."

"It would."

Gromley took Regent Avrette's hand and kissed it. He sighed. "Come, Nicholas. We have a Cleric to find. I would like you there as a witness to their opinion."

Nicholas hopped up from his chair and bowed. "It would be my pleasure. I have some time before I must return to Peacebreaker Keep. Thank you for hearing us out, Jenta."

"Yes, thank you." Gromley released Jenta's hand and followed Nicholas from the room.

CHAPTER 6

Not even Vaila foresaw another of us. We are all adjusting to Spara's ascension.

- The Tome of Mystics
Unknown Origin. Unearthed from the Ruins of Oda Norde, month of Bracken, 1320 AT

— ▲ —

"The Tower of Mystics," Umhra whispered in awe.

Constructed of pure rhodium, the building gleamed on the horizon. In stark contrast to Vaila's residence, the tower was conical, bulging toward its center and coming to a rounded peak. Twenty concentric moats of calm cerulean waters surrounded it.

The pulsing in Umhra's ear intensified with each beat of his wings. He dove, coming to rest within the confines of the innermost moat. There were no signs of any disturbance, no scorched earth or perceptible damage to the building. Maybe Vaila was wrong, and Spara didn't come to exact her revenge on the other Mystics first. Maybe she was saving them for last when they would pose no threat. Regardless, the thrumming in his ear led him within.

Umhra warily approached the building's open doorway. He

peered inside. A yawning metallic atrium stretched up to the heavens, lit by an unseen source. Dispersed throughout the vast room were six rhodium orbs, each taller than Umhra.

Summoning Forsetae to his hand, he entered the Tower of Mystics and crossed the atrium. Another sigil—identical to the one he saw that caused the corruption in the gardens—had been burned into the floor at the center of the room. A pang of nerves washed over him. On the floor beyond the sigil was a pool of opalescent liquid from which a trail smeared to a doorway on the far side of the room.

Umhra kneeled and dabbed his fingers into the puddle. It was warm to the touch. He rubbed the viscous fluid between his fingers and sniffed it. Blood.

He grimaced and climbed to his feet, following the shimmering trail across the room. The smear continued through the doorway and down a long corridor.

Umhra crept along the hallway, the smooth walls solid and unyielding. The passage ended at a massive dining room arranged in a macabre spectacle.

A grand banquet table made of the purest white stone acted as the room's centerpiece. In each chair, a body lay slumped over, but for the head of the table where Spara sat beside a brute of a bald-headed man dressed in saffron robes. In her hand, she held six rhodium orbs, each dangling from an unbreakable chain identical to her own.

"Leave it to that self-righteous dragon to let you go," Spara said, shaking her head. She wore her glossy black hair draped across one shoulder, her skin the color of warm bronze. Her eyes were grey and a raging storm swirled within each. "Why is it that *everyone*," she motioned wildly to the bodies around her, "disappoints you in the end? I should have just killed you myself."

Umhra strode forward despite his stomach souring as he eyed the pallid bodies. "There's an Orcish saying I remember my father quoting often when I was a young boy. It went something like, the line between majesty and lunacy is finer than a blade's edge. If I am to be honest, this looks a little like the latter."

Spara smiled, tittered to herself, and tossed the rhodium orbs onto the table before her. "This?" She stood and put a hand on the man's bald dome. He grunted but was otherwise motionless. "How rude of me. Umhra, this is Atalan, the last of the original Mystics and my former love." She gestured to the other bodies around the table. "These were the rest of them. Useless turncoats."

Umhra's gaze left Atalan and scanned the bodies arranged at the table. A shock of auburn hair, a stark white beard. A red flowing gown, dark almond eyes with an empty glare. Blue tattoos. Maybe they deserved their fate. That was beside the point. Spara had her revenge on those who betrayed her. Now, he had to stop her from gaining the power she needed to topple the pantheon.

"Atalan and I were just discussing how he abandoned me on Tyveriel to live for an eternity in a cage while he enjoyed the bliss of Kalmindon. With a little encouragement from Pyra, of course. What was it she promised you, my dear? Herself in my stead?"

Spara lifted the head of the woman next to Atalan by the tangle of chestnut hair streaked with gold and let it drop back to the table with a thud. "How easily he accepted her into his bed as my replacement. I honestly don't know what he saw in her. But you aren't interested in this petty lover's quarrel. You came here to stop me from becoming a god." She stood behind Atalan and drew a diamond shard from her belt. It was a half-foot long and as thin as a porcupine quill, coming to a fine point. The shard refracted light across the room as she held it to Atalan's neck, dimpling his skin.

"No!" Umhra charged toward the table.

Spara held up her free hand and froze Umhra in place.

The air rippling between them, every muscle in his body

burned from the intense cold. He struggled to free himself from Spara's spell, but no matter how hard he strained, he couldn't move. Ivory's Nameless Tome, the book his adoptive father had left him, told of a Mystic's ability to perform such magic, and provided instruction on how one might counter its effects if caught unprepared.

Spara smiled and slipped the diamond shard into Atalan's neck. "Goodbye, my dear. Our story could have ended so differently."

She pulled the shard free and a stream of the same opalescent blood Umhra followed from the atrium poured from the wound. An unseen force lifted Atalan's body from his chair and amber ether drifted from his muscular form into the air. Atalan's energy coalesced before Spara and then entered her body. She closed her eyes and allowed Atalan's corpse to fall to the table, his head cracking against its unforgiving surface. Spara walked from behind the table toward Umhra, rolling the clean diamond shard between her fingers, and pursed her lips. "Now, what do I do with you? It seems I'm having no luck with the boys today."

With one hand, Spara lifted the body of the woman with the short red hair from the table. She had delicate features and wore a pale-yellow gown, now stained with dried opalescent blood. Spara tossed her aside with a sneer. She then came to the bearded man seated next to her at the table. Spara tipped the chair aside, the body falling to the floor beside her.

"Come. Sit," she said.

Umhra's muscles unlocked, and he stumbled forward a step. He growled but then thought better and took the seat Spara offered, nudging a fallen Mystic's body out of the way with his boot.

"Thank you." Spara sat in the other free chair, crossed her legs, and smiled. "Now, how can we come to common ground? I have no interest in killing you like the others. You've been nothing but a loyal friend and useful to my cause. I regret having fooled you into helping me with the Waystones and in finding the Eketar egg. There was simply no other way for me to ascend and have my revenge on these worthless fools."

Umhra worked his lip over the tusks in his lower jaw. "Look at this." He waved his hand across the table, gesturing to the bodies now strewn across the room. "You have clearly made your point by serving such grim justice for the misdeeds against you. It's time for you to put the past behind you and move forward. You will not find peace through these violent ways. I know this all too well."

Spara's face twisted. "You're right, I don't feel any better." She pointed to her eyes, the storms within swirling with discontent. "*They* might have left me on Tyveriel, which was fault enough to meet this end, but it was Vaila who took my eyes when she banished her wicked brother to the hells of Pragarus."

Umhra shifted in his chair at the threat against his god. "I'm not discounting what you've been through. I can't fathom being locked in a cell for two millennia. I hid within myself for the better part of a decade, and it nearly cost me everything. No doubt, you paid a great price for serving your gods that day, but we all pay a price in service of the gods. Some live a life of solitude and chastity in their temples, some risk life and limb in their names, and others suffer loss never to be reclaimed. They ask only what we can bear."

Spara placed her hand on Umhra's knee and smiled. "Join me. We could rule Kalmindon together. We do make a good team. There is no greater testimony to that than our presence here today."

"You know I can't do that. Too much iniquity has passed between us. Either you stop here and now, or I will stop you, or die trying."

Spara withdrew her hand, her smile fading. "That's too bad." She thrust her other hand forward, driving her diamond spike toward Umhra.

He summoned his armor, the spike screeching off the

rhodium of his chest plate and lodging itself in the edge of his pauldron. Umhra swept Spara's hand aside and threw his chair back, coming to his feet. He plucked the spike from his armor and tossed it clattering to the floor.

Spara held out a hand, but Umhra anticipated her spell and forced his will outward against her as the lesson in Ivory's Nameless Tome suggested. The icy grasp of Spara's spell dissipated. Umhra shook off the chill.

Spara scowled and drew Shatter and Quake from her belt. "I suppose this was inevitable," she said. "I'll take no joy in destroying you."

Umhra summoned Forsetae to his hand, the sword gleaming. "I'm sure you won't mourn me long."

Spara shrugged and advanced with a speed Umhra had not expected. He narrowly parried the first of her attacks, Quake ringing off the base of Forsetae's blade. She followed with Shatter. The axe whirred just shy of Umhra's face.

Umhra countered, thrusting Forsetae at Spara.

Spara's form vanished, Umhra's blade left unmet.

Spara reappeared a few feet away, beyond Umhra's immediate reach. "That's new." She smiled. "There was a time I would have relished these games, Umhra. But the time for games has passed. I have pressing matters to see to." Spara held up her hand, the light of her rhodium orb glowed vibrantly.

Umhra tried to close the gap between them before she could cast another spell, but was again bound by Spara's magic. He forced a snarl and thought of Vaila.

"I'll make this quick," Spara said, ambling forward. "I owe you that much. You understand, I can't let you get in my way. This is too important, and you've already come farther than I ever would have imagined."

Spara tucked her axes into her belt and retrieved her diamond shard from the floor. She wiped the spike against her gown and tilted her head. She pressed the shard's fine point against the flesh of Umhra's neck.

The ground shook. Spara staggered back a few steps. The ceiling high overhead shattered, and chunks of rhodium rained down upon them. Spara's gaze darted about the room wildly as she searched for the source of the commotion.

"You're going to ruin my fun, aren't you?" she yelled.

The cascading metal slowed and then hung in the air, suspended. Within the beams of light bouncing off its pure surface, Vaila's form took shape between Spara and Umhra. She held a sword in each hand, her gown as radiant as Umhra could remember, but for a bloodied tear at her waist.

"Child, you have lost your way." Vaila surveyed the room, noting the Mystics' bodies. "I know what they put you through in their haste to reach the heaven I promised them. I know what I put you through in sharing the secrets of Tyveriel's future. But your anger is misplaced. I've tried to tell you this time and time again."

"Misplaced?" Spara grimaced. "Is it misplaced to feel anger toward the god who burned your eyes from your face and the family that traded you so easily for their own redemption?"

"No. It is misplaced because all the pain and anguish that sent you on this course has led you exactly where you were meant to be. You serve a higher purpose than you know. Go about your business, but go about it with a pure heart."

Spara tilted her head, the rage fading from her face. "You mean...I'm still part of your plan? I'm still playing your game?"

"What I mean is, I will allow you to leave if you leave now. Otherwise, I will carry your soul to Pragarus myself."

"Another time, then." Spara released a soft, fluttering whistle. "I'll see you both again soon."

The Eketar burst into the room, reducing a wall to twisted metal. The behemoth coiled around Spara and released a deafening roar, showering the room with stained saliva and acidic foam.

Vaila spun, guarding herself and Umhra from the onslaught.

The lights on the Eketar's back lit up in unison, and Spara and the creature vanished, leaving a sigil burned into the floor where they had stood. The room fell quiet.

Umhra's muscles relaxed, his knees buckling. Vaila caught him in her arms.

"What was that?" Umhra asked, his lungs burning, his muscles tingling as they gradually regained their feeling.

"That was her god killer. Luckily, they are yet to possess the strength to defeat me."

"No, the part about her being exactly where she was supposed to be. That she was serving a higher purpose."

Vaila brushed the hair from Umhra's face. "I told her what she wanted to hear. I told her what was necessary to save our lives. But I only bought us time, and I'm uncertain how much. She will set her sights on one of the lesser gods first—become a god herself—and then work her way up through the pantheon, consolidating her power so she may face me."

"Then, let's stop her."

"We can't." Vaila pointed to the wound in her stomach. "You are not yet strong enough to face her, and my time and power wane. Our only chance of stopping her now is for you to amass more power than her. You must become a god and put an end to her ambitions."

"Become a god?"

"Yes, Umhra." Vaila smiled. "The pantheon's time as we know it has come to an end. You must go to my brothers and take possession of their souls before Spara is capable of doing it herself."

"And how do I do that?"

Vaila produced a shard of diamond identical to the one Spara used in dispatching the other Mystics. She held it vertically between her index finger and thumb, a glint of light catching Umhra's eye. "With this." She held the shard out for Umhra.

He took the spike and examined it. "I can't imagine they will be happy about this. Go willingly."

"Kemyn and Brinthor will do what's right. And Naur—we left him bound in Pragarus. I doubt he will protest an end to his punishment."

Umhra nodded, rubbed his forehead. "So, I'll start with Naur. If I'm to become a god at another's expense, it might as well be him."

"Then I leave you to your task. I will return to my tower and store what strength I have left. Think of my brothers and you shall find them—your ascension lifts the veil between the realms. It is time for you to believe in yourself, Umhra. I can no longer be the crutch you don't require."

Vaila's form rippled and then faded, leaving Umhra alone in what remained of the Tower of Mystics. He closed his eyes and thought of Naur, pinned forever against the red cliff side of Pragarus where Umhra had bound him for eternity. He thought of the portal he had jumped through in his escape, of the burned sky, of the searing winds. Umhra welcomed a second visit to hell.

CHAPTER 7

The blights poured forth from the Wistful Timberlands unabated.

- The Gatekeeper's Abridged History of Tyveriel
Vol. 2, Chapter 1 – Unearthed from the Ruins of Meriden, the
month of Ocken, 1240 AT

— ▲ —

Turin rubbed her aching ribs. The intense pain, however, was trivial compared to the guilt she felt for getting an innocent man killed. Her ribs would heal, but his horrid death would stick with her forever.

Letting her self-pity get the best of her, she lagged behind with the children as the party coursed along Atalan's Way. The early morning sun dappled what remained of the dirt road. Birds chirped from the dense undergrowth that encroached on either side.

"Naivara, can you do something about this? We need to get to Peacebreaker Keep by sunset." Turin gestured to a young boy who had stopped and laid down in the middle of the narrow path. "I'd carry him myself, but I think I broke a few of my ribs."

Naivara dropped back from alongside Laudin toward the front of the procession. "Of course. I'd be happy to." She stood over the exhausted child, his blue eyes glinting from a face covered in grime.

"Bear or bunny?" She asked.

The boy smiled through gaps where his bottom front teeth once were.

"Come on, we must keep moving. Bear or bunny?"

"Bear," the boy said.

"Very well. Bear it is."

Naivara's circlet lit with green ether, and she morphed into a brown bear.

The boy jumped to his feet; his exhaustion apparently forgotten. The rest of the children came running in search of a ride.

Turin scooped the boy up under his armpits and placed him on Naivara's broad ursine shoulders. She winced. "The rest of you are going to have to get up there on your own, I'm afraid."

Sena hurried to Naivara's side and lifted the eager would-be passengers onto her back.

To cheers and squeals, Naivara lumbered forward, leaving Turin and Sena alone.

"Are you okay?" Sena asked, her gaze still affixed on the bear walking away from them. "You took quite a shot back there."

"I've taken worse sparring with Aridon. I'll be fine."

"Who in Vaila's name was the guy that bailed us out? He came out of nowhere."

Turin shook her head. She didn't feel right, leaving the stranger to fend for himself despite his obvious lack of concern. "I don't know, but there was something about him that made my skin crawl. He said he didn't belong in Ruari with *our kind*, as though he wasn't one of us—wasn't a man."

"I don't care if he is a devil. He saved us back there. We were in over our heads. Even you couldn't handle all those weeds."

"Maybe. Maybe not. I still haven't found my limits. I'd like to think we would have worked it out."

Sena ran a hand through her tangled blond hair. "We got

lucky. These missions have been getting more and more dangerous. I know we've saved lives and all that, but the last few we've cut a little close."

"Well, I can't stop," Turin said. "It isn't enough for me to offer them a life in the caves. They deserve more—*we* deserve more. I won't stop until cities like Anaris are thriving again. If you don't want to help, then don't help. Of course, there are risks. Nothing worthwhile ever comes without risks."

"That's not fair." Sena's brow furrowed. "I never said that I didn't want to help. That doesn't mean that I want to get us all killed in the process. If you send me to act as your scout, then listen to my report and heed my advice. I know we must take risks, but that was foolish."

"I think you should return to your post. We're not yet out of the mess *I* created." Turin regretted the words as soon as they left her lips.

Sena stared into Turin's eyes. Her lips quivered, but she swallowed hard and buried the jab. Then she nodded and returned to her position along the periphery of the party, leaving Turin alone.

Turin kicked at the dirt, a warbler darting between the undergrowth that encroached on the road from either side. She looked up at the branches overhead. Sunlight streamed between them. Leaves rustled in a gentle breeze.

She half-expected the branches to curl in on themselves and the sturdy oak they were part of to pull its roots free from the earth and attack. These woods, alas, were not the Wistful Timberlands, and rarely harbored the enemy. Her gaze fell to Sena who crossed her arms as she trudged beside Aridon.

Aridon placed an arm around Sena's shoulders. Sena responded with an arm around his waist.

Turin huffed and followed them.

There were little more than whispers from the townsfolk on the long march to Peacebreaker Keep. Keen eyes scanned the woods for any indications of trouble, but the day brought no threats. By sunset, the gates of the keep came into sight and Turin felt the stress of the last few days melt away.

Shadow and Laudin held the gates wide for the rest to pass through onto the property. The pea stone drive was pristine, as was the courtyard, with statues of the Bloodbound laced throughout lush, manicured gardens.

"It's exactly how I remember it," Xavier Pell said in astonishment. "Why is the keep not overgrown like the rest of the land? I haven't seen grounds like this since before the Cataclysm."

"The property is warded," Turin said. "No blights can enter. No harm can come to it."

"Are there others like it?"

"One in Ruari and one in Ohteira. Indrisor's dimension has many nodes, but only three are protected. Think of it as a constellation of points in space."

Pell knit his brow. "And, you said it belongs to a man named Indrisor?"

"You'll meet him soon enough. I would hate to spoil the fun."

Pell nodded and walked with Turin across the courtyard and through the gardens. He stopped before a statue of Gori. "I had the pleasure of knowing these men for a brief time. They gave their lives to save Anaris."

"You knew the Peacebreaker, then?" Turin asked.

Pell chuckled. "My, he would hate being called that. Yes, I knew Umhra quite well. The Barrow's Pact also."

Turin looked up at Gori's perfectly carved, disfigured face. "He left when I was an infant. Some believe he will return and put an end to this terrible nightmare. Do you believe that?"

"I do. Do you feel otherwise?"

"I don't know what to believe. All I know is that we can't wait around for someone to save us. We must save ourselves, and I aim to do just that."

Pell nodded contemplatively. "Maybe if you had the

opportunity to know him as I did, you would feel differently. He is a truly remarkable man. As you seem to be a truly remarkable young woman. You remind me of him—selfless and insecure."

Turin could not have disagreed more. She was anything but selfless. *She* wanted a better world for everyone, including herself. *She* wanted all those things she spoke with Sena about in the shade of the crumbling cloisters of Anaris. No, she wasn't selfless. And, insecure, she wondered how Pell could mean that as a compliment. She loathed her insecurity more than anything. A great leader cannot afford to be insecure. Until she left her self-doubt behind, she would never be the leader her people needed.

She gave Gori's statue one last look. "Come on. Indrisor is waiting for us. I'm afraid he's going to be quite annoyed when he sees how many of you there are."

They continued around the back of the keep to an unassuming stone building with an iron yett. Aridon held the gate open for them, the others having already descended the steps that led deep below the surface. Aridon slammed the gate closed and locked it, then a heavy inner door of thick iron.

The stairwell wound downward in a gentle spiral and was lit by arcane globules of light that hovered near the ceiling. Each footfall echoed off the walls. At the base of the stairs, a hallway led to another heavy iron door where Laudin waited for them.

"He's a bit upset."

Turin smiled. "I thought he would be. He'll get over it. He enjoys helping others, but only if he can complain about it first."

"All the same, we best not keep him waiting any longer. He's ranting and raving about temporal something or other."

They entered the next room and found the rest of the group waiting for them, along with Nicholas Barnswallow and Indrisor. Nicholas was locked in conversation with Naivara, his youthful, spry look in stark contrast to Indrisor who was notably shorter and ancient. Despite his advanced age, Indrisor exuded an infectious energy and now, was quite animated.

Seeing the others enter the room, the older of the Farestere hurried over to Turin, the top of his head as high as her hip.

Wild tufts of stark white hair protruded from the sides of Indrisor's head, and he wore thick glasses that made his eyes look too big for his face. On his shoulder sat a small lizard with orange and black striped skin. "To say this is unsettling is an understatement, Little One. I've told you time and time again that we must limit the number of travelers in the pocket, yes."

Little One. He'd called her that for as long as she could remember. Indrisor had a penchant for nicknames. In fact, he preferred them to one's given name, which he would seldom use. At one time, Little One was a fitting nickname for Turin, but at her ample height, it would have seemed ridiculous coming from anyone other than the quirky little wizard.

"What was I to do, Indrisor? Leave the children and elderly behind?"

He put his hands on his hips and shot Turin a stern look. "Of course not. Don't be ridiculous. You know how hard it is to keep track of so many in my pocket dimension. One false move, and we could be dealing with a temporal anomaly of unknown proportions."

"See? I told you he was on about some nonsense," Laudin said with a prodding tone.

"Nonsense?" Indrisor threw his hands in the air, his lizard scrambling for safety in the collar of his purple waistcoat. "Nonsense? You call being sucked out into the vacuous depths of space nonsense? You call tearing a hole in the fabric of time itself nonsense? We are not playing with a toy here, ranger. This is a finely tuned machine and my life's work. Nonsense, indeed. And, coming from one that shoots things with pointy sticks, no less." He flashed a toothy grin at Laudin, as though appreciating the jousting session.

"We will make it work, Little One." Indrisor spun from the conversation. "Just keep them on a short leash, yes. We all remember what happened to that lovely Iminti gentleman."

Xavier Pell looked at Turin with a raised eyebrow. She waved the comment off dismissively. "He's joking. He has a macabre sense of humor. Nothing has ever gone wrong on these trips. It's just important to stay together."

Pell nodded.

Indrisor beckoned everyone to join him in a far corner of the room. The party gathered around him as he stood next to a nearly indiscernible mote of light.

"This is a gate to my personal pocket dimension, yes. Its construction has taken me hundreds of years, a dedication few of you can fathom, no doubt. I created it for my personal use, not for tours across Evelium. As such, it is fragile and potentially dangerous. For this reason, yes, I request you follow a single rule—stay with me at all times. If anyone wanders from my path, I cannot and will not be held accountable. As long as you remain by my side, we will see you to Ruari safely."

Murmurs echoed throughout the room.

Nicholas stepped to Indrisor's side. "Well, now that Indrisor has succeeded in scaring all of you, I will say, I've used his pocket dimension several times, and I've always navigated it without getting lost or harmed. In fact, I just arrived from Ruari this very afternoon. Such travel can leave you a bit queasy at times, but it is a small price to pay for such a service. I'll see you within."

Nicholas touched the mote of energy with his finger and vanished from the room.

The townsfolk released a collective gasp at the young Farestere's abrupt exit.

"Can I go next?" a young girl asked with hopeful brown eyes and a freckled nose.

Indrisor looked her over from beneath bushy eyebrows. "Certainly not. You will stay with your mother or whomever you came here with."

The girl frowned. "I don't have a mother."

Naivara stepped forward. "You are welcome to come with

me if it should please our curmudgeonly host."

The girl chuckled.

"Very well," Indrisor said. "You may go along with the shapeshifter. She's never been a cause of any trouble. But only after I have entered."

Indrisor walked into the light and disappeared. Naivara smiled and extended her hand to the girl. The girl accepted and, together, they touched the light and followed Indrisor.

Laudin and Shadow were next, followed by a group of townsfolk. Then, Aridon and Neela and the rest of the citizens, leaving Turin and Sena alone in the depths of the keep.

Sena walked to the light.

Turin stared at her shoes like a child being scolded by their parents. "I'm sorry for what I said earlier." She winced, feeling that her words didn't come out right—didn't do the hurt she caused Sena justice. "You were right. I took too great a risk. We all could have died."

There was no reply.

Turin looked up to find herself alone in the room. She was too late. Sena had already entered the portal.

There was nothing to do now but head home. She'd have to wait for another opportunity to make her apology. She would take her time and make sure Sena knew how important she was. Why was saying you are sorry so hard even when you know you were wrong?

Turin's stomach churned. She wasn't sure if she was more anxious about her inevitable conversation with Sena or the pending trip through Indrisor's dimension, which always left her feeling ill. She took a deep breath and touched the mote of light.

CHAPTER 8

*I always thought one must be willing to sacrifice everything
to achieve greatness. Yet, I feel as though I may have given
too much.*

- Entry from Aldresor's Journal
Undated. Discovered: The Tower of Is' Savon, month of Riet,
1444 AT

— ▲ —

Turin found herself in total darkness. A familiar force
grabbed hold of her and ripped her forward at great speed.
Wind buffeted her face as a light appeared in the distance. What
at one moment was impossibly far away, the next was upon her.
A blinding white light enveloped her. Its welcoming glow held
her for a moment and then faded, revealing a banquet hall with
backlit walls of honey onyx stone.

At the center of the room hung a crystal chandelier over an
oval table with seating for thirty-two—exactly the number of
those traveling. Indrisor had a penchant for such detail. The
table was set with fine silverware, glistening as if just polished,
and stemware so delicate one wrong look could shatter it into a
thousand shards. Beyond the table there were three pewter
doors, one offset from the others, so the room felt somewhat off

balance.

"Sit, yes," Indrisor said from the head of the table. "Many of you have not had the opportunity to eat a fine meal in some time and from the looks of many of you, you wouldn't know a fine meal no matter the time." He shot a sideways glance at the girl who held Naivara's hand.

Turin took the seat at the opposite head of the table. She always found it uncomfortable, but Indrisor insisted it was hers and hers alone ever since she was old enough to feed herself. Sena and Aridon flanked her. Neela curled up at Aridon's feet.

The townsfolk exchanged awkward glances, but dispersed around the table, and each took a seat. Laudin, Shadow, and Nicholas filled in the gaps.

Once everyone was settled, Indrisor clapped his hands twice. "Let the feast begin, yes."

The rag-tag group sat at the resplendent table before their empty plates.

"Well, napkins on your laps, yes, or they'll never come."

The napkins were of fine white silk, each embroidered with a gold skull at the corner. Turin had asked Indrisor about the recurring skeletal imagery throughout his pocket dimension over the years. His answer was always the same. "Some day when she had cheated death as long as he had, she would understand the appeal."

The rest of the room waited. Turin placed her napkin on her lap.

From the soft glow of the walls, golden apparitions emerged. Barely visible, their shimmering ghostly forms faded into nothing below their waists, so they appeared to float above the floor. Each carried a platter of food or a jug of drink. They swirled around the table at a slow, even pace and then approached and placed their offerings before Indrisor's guests. The food materialized, one succulent delicacy after another.

The apparitions filled stemware with wine and sage water. They served venison, lamb, and roasted vegetables. They offered trays piled high with apple tarts and baked pears—bowls filled with dried fruit and nuts.

With the feast delivered, the apparitions bowed to their guests and then to Indrisor. The wizard clapped his hands twice, and his servants receded into the walls from which they came.

Quiet reigned as the townsfolk sat in awe of what they had just seen.

Indrisor waved his hands across the table with his palms up. "Eat, yes. Celebrate."

The room broke into an uproar. The townsfolk eagerly emptied and refilled their glasses, wine sloshing onto the table with every overzealous pour. They loaded their plates full and scraped them clean.

Turin and Sena sat in awkward silence as they ate. Every so often, Aridon would look up from his plate and eye the two of them. With a furrow of his heavy brow, he would return to his meal.

After nearly an hour of unbridled gluttony, Xavier Pell leaned back in his chair. He hung a thumb on his belt and raised a glass in the air. "To our host, Indrisor, and our savior, Queen Turin."

"To Indrisor and Queen Turin." The cheer rang off the walls.

Indrisor clapped and two ethereal servants appeared beside him and pulled his chair from the table. He stood on his seat and gently tapped his fork against the edge of his glass. The ring reverberated through the room and hung in the air.

"It is time we make our way to Ruari. The path is specific, so I need everyone's attention, yes?" He snapped a wary glare at the girl at Naivara's side. "Especially you. I have decided we shall rely on you to lead us along the correct path."

"Me?" the girl asked as she chewed a mouth full of apple tart.

"Yes you, Lionheart. Do you rise to the challenge?"

"I do. But my name isn't—"

"Lionheart," Indrisor insisted. "Listen up. What I say next is of utmost importance."

Lionheart leaned forward, her elbows on the table, her chin in her hands.

"From Anaris to Ruari, take the door of gold through the sea, then the door of old, then through the tree. Can you remember that Lionheart?"

"From Anaris to Ruari, take the door of gold through the sea, then the door of old, then through the tree. I have no idea what it means."

Indrisor smiled a crooked, toothy grin. "It matters not that you understand it, just that you follow it."

Lionheart nodded. "I will. I promise."

"Very good. Then we are on our way. Follow me, yes."

Indrisor hopped down from his seat and scurried around to where Lionheart was seated. "Pick a door Lionheart. Lead us to Ruari."

Lionheart wrapped an apple tart in her napkin and stood. She walked past the three doors and inspected them each closely. She shook her head as though displeased with her options. "The door of gold," she whispered.

She turned from the doors and stood before the gap between them. With the caution of one walking in a strange room in the dark of night, she held a hand out before her and walked to the onyx wall. Instead of meeting firm stone, her hand pushed through the membranous surface. Lionheart looked over her shoulder at Indrisor and smiled. "The door of gold."

Indrisor returned her smile. "Oh, we are in good hands. Yes, trustworthy hands. We follow Lionheart through the door of gold."

Turin watched and remembered how Indrisor played these same games with her when she was a spirited child. He had the ability to break you down, only to build you up to heights you never saw in yourself.

Lionheart pushed through the membrane—Indrisor

followed closely behind. Turin waited for everyone to cross over and then followed.

She emerged on the other side and fought her churning stomach. The townsfolk paid her no mind as they walked the length of a translucent hallway in astonishment.

Outside the clear walls swam countless fish only found in the depths of the Sea of Widows. Angler fish with long fangs jutting from their jaws sat on the sea floor with lures that glowed overhead. A goblin shark wrestled with a formidable crab with absurdly long legs and thin, dagger-like pincers. Comb jellies flashed with bioluminescence as they drifted in the current, their blue, green, and red flashes adorning the passage in a display of prismatic light.

Despite having been in this tunnel many times before, Turin still admired their beauty as she caught up with the rest of the group.

"Don't touch the walls, yes," Indrisor said from upfront alongside Lionheart. "One mistake and the tunnel collapses and we are all crushed by the relentless pressure of the sea. It would be quick, but less than ideal."

At the far end of the tunnel was another membrane like the one they had entered in the dining hall. Indrisor gestured for Lionheart to lead the way and the girl pushed through the membrane without hesitation.

"A fine child, that girl," Indrisor said, his tone filled with admiration. "Reminds me of you, Little One, when you were that age."

Turin smiled. She would have agreed, but she was preoccupied with the trepidation of having to cross another gate. Her stomach had just settled. She watched the others follow Lionheart and then pushed through, herself.

The gate emptied into an expansive room with dark stone walls and a large hearth set with a blazing fire. The room was staged with a quaint sitting area complete with matching leather settees and rich mahogany tables on a burgundy rug.

The room stretched out beyond the sitting area lit by iron candelabras held aloft by heavy ropes. Below each candelabra was the skeleton of a great dragon, each posed as though striking out at an enemy.

Lionheart wandered the room, inspecting the myriad of doors that pocked the walls. After a few moments, she came running back to Indrisor. "I've found the next door. The door of old."

"Oh, have you?" Indrisor stroked the lizard on his shoulder.

"Yes. I'm certain of it. Come."

"We follow Lionheart to the next door, yes."

The girl hurried to the far end of the room with the rest of the group in tow.

Turin ambled behind them, eager to get home but willing to allow Indrisor his little game. Not that she could stop him if she tried. He had a fierce independent streak.

She paused before one dragon with a claw outstretched and mouth agape. The placard before her read, *Oredwrithe, Matron of Flame.*

"This is it." Lionheart pointed at a door. The door, not unlike the others, was fashioned from heavy wood and banded with iron.

Indrisor removed his glasses and rubbed the thick lenses between the folds of his shirt. "Why this door?"

"Every door has a name engraved above it in Evenese," Lionheart said. "This one is different. Its name is written in the old tongue. The door of old."

Indrisor glowed with pride. "Remarkable child. We continue to follow the sage advice of Lionheart."

The door opened into a rolling field of high golden grass that stretched out as far as Turin's eye could see. A lone ancient beech tree stood on the horizon, its twisted branches raking the pastel sky.

"The tree," Lionheart marveled.

"I planted its seed in this place four-hundred-twenty-six

years ago. It has grown to be a marvelous specimen, yes." Indrisor strode toward the tree. "Ruari awaits."

They crossed the field, Indrisor nearly disappearing as he wove a path through the high grass. As they approached the tree, the wizard uttered a few words beneath his breath and the rough grey bark of the tree split wide. A warm amber glow emanated from within.

Indrisor stepped aside and swept his arm toward the tree with a grandiose bow. "Through we go, yes. This one I can't hold open for long."

Lionheart crossed over first, along with Laudin and Naivara. The rest of the group followed and left Turin and Indrisor alone in the pocket dimension.

"Thank you, Indrisor. As always, I appreciate you allowing us use of this marvel of yours."

"For you Little One, anything. Yes, anything."

Turin smiled. "She needs you—Lionheart. She has no family left, and she's too young to be on her own in Ruari."

Indrisor pushed his glasses up on his nose. "If you think such a relationship would be of value, Little One, I will inquire whether Lionheart is amenable to it."

"Good. Let's go home."

Together, Indrisor and Turin stepped within the tree and emerged in a cavern ringed with torches. They stood before a mote of energy that glowed like a white-hot star.

The cavern was bustling with activity. A greeting party whirred about the room, documenting the newcomers' arrival and seeing to their immediate needs. Shadow, Laudin, and Naivara spoke with Turin's adoptive father, Talus Jochen, around a table beyond the frenzy.

Talus's gaze met Turin's, and he smiled. It was rare that he wore such a disarming expression, but he let one sneak through his austere façade whenever Turin entered the room. He was tall, with broad shoulders and blond hair, and kept himself quite fit despite being well into his forties. When they sparred, he would often complain about having lost a step over the years, despite Turin struggling to see where. After securing his inevitable victory, he would remind her that a sharp mind would always best a sharp sword.

Talus weaved his way through the mayhem to greet Turin. He put his arm around her shoulders and squeezed her tight. "A little dicey, I hear."

"I know they're your friends, but do they have to tell you *everything*?"

Talus smiled. "Yes. Yes, they do. But I'm not here to chastise you, and your mother won't hear about any of it from me. There have been some developments while you were gone. We've received a report from our scouting party in Travesty. They spotted the Grey Queen heading toward Orrat Skag just days ago."

"What could she want with the Orcs? She has no quarrel with them."

"I don't know. Maybe she rallies them to her cause. Maybe she searches for a body suitable to resurrect her father. Regardless, she is as far from Mount Anvil as possible."

Turin had been waiting for such an opportunity. Since the Peacebreaker destroyed the dracolich that was once the mighty Mesorith, the Grey Queen had been reticent to engage the armies of men in direct combat. Instead, she favored attacking the remnants of once great cities and villages in the dark of night, while spending her days searching for something. That something was presumably a suitable host for her father's soul.

Indrisor gave council that the only way to destroy Mesorith once and for all was to first retrieve the phylactery that housed the dracolich's soul and enabled his return. Jenta had nonetheless forbidden any mission to the Isle of the Twelve Mines in search of the artifact as she deemed it too risky to delve into the dragons' lair beneath Mount Anvil, should the Grey Queen be protecting her hoard.

Turin rubbed the back of her neck. "I need to speak with

Aunt Jenta. Can you please have Indrisor, the Barrow's Pact, Sena, and Aridon meet us in the royal chambers? We can speak privately there."

"There's more. Gromley also has important news to share."

"We can kill two birds with one stone, then."

"As you wish, My Queen."

"I wish you wouldn't call me that."

Talus frowned. "But you are, in fact, my queen. And we are in a public setting, are we not? You must get comfortable with it at some point."

"Things don't work like that anymore, General Jochen. I will not be the queen of a homeless nation living in squalor. You may call me your queen when we reclaim that which is ours, and I earn such a title. Until then, I am simply Turin."

"My dear, there is nothing simple about you. You are Turin Forene, the last of a bloodline these people have looked to for leadership for over a thousand years. Now that you are of age, they turn to you for the same."

Turin nodded. "When I earn it."

"As you wish."

Turin slipped through the throng of newcomers and out of the cavern into a passageway lined with wooden doors, an oil lantern lit over each. People gave her a wide berth as she hurried through the bustling hallway. She was unsure whether their actions were out of reverence or fear but, at the moment, it didn't matter.

The passage opened into the Iris—a vast circular cavern with similar tunnels dispersed across its perimeter, like the spokes on a great wheel. The Iris had a hole in its floor and was rimmed with a wide pathway that spiraled downward into the depths of Ruari. People traveled the path between the many levels of the caves. Some were on foot, burdened with bundles or towing children behind them. Others rode bahtreigs—large amphibians that resembled salamanders but had three sets of legs.

Turin approached the bahtreig stable at the top of the pathway. A middle-aged human woman sat on a wooden stool beside a pen holding two dozen of the beasts, each a deep teal in color, like the barbs of a peacock's plumage. The bahtreigs lounged on the cool stone floor, curled in tight balls with their tails covering their eyes.

Upon seeing Turin approach, the woman stood and straightened her grimy clothing. "Are you in need of a mount to the lower rings, Queen Turin?"

"I am, thank you. Any will do."

The woman nodded and entered the pen. The bahtreigs didn't acknowledge the intrusion. She grabbed one of the beasts by the handles of the thick leather harness around its chest and hauled it to its feet.

The bahtreig's body flashed with bioluminescence for a moment and then returned to its normal color. It yawned and released a shrill whine but followed without protest.

The woman led the bahtreig through the gate and passed it off to Turin, who offered the woman the customary ten sovereigns in return.

"That won't be necessary. I'm happy to serve the crown."

"Nonsense." Turin gripped the handle and climbed upon the bahtreig's back. "Besides, I'll need two hands free for the ride."

She forced the sovereigns into the woman's hand with a smile. "I insist."

"Most kind of you," the woman said. "Have a safe trip."

Turin nudged the bahtreig forward with a pat on the side of its neck and the beast burst into a sprint.

They coursed down the winding road, level after level, until they reached a set of great iron doors with a guard on each side.

The men wore yellow tunics over black leathers and held flails slung over their shoulders. Each with one hand on the wooden handles of their weapons, the guards placed their other hands over their hearts at the sight of their queen approaching.

Turin reared the bahtreig to a halt before the guards. "Do

either of you know where the regent is?"

"She is in the great hall, my lady. Should we call for her on your behalf?"

"That won't be necessary. I will go to her myself."

"As you wish." The guards pulled on the doors, which groaned in objection.

They opened into a well-lit cavern of purple stone with walls carved to emulate a hemlock forest. As she rode her bahtreig across the cavern, Turin recalled being told that Modig Forene commissioned the carvings to remind him that his enemies were vigilant and to never grow content with life in the caves. She found it quite striking, herself, and struggled with the widely held belief of her forefathers that nature was meant to be dominated—that it was the enemy. She understood all too well the war her people waged against the blights, but thought that, possibly, there was room for all in Evelium. All but for the Grey Queen and her undead father, that is.

She patted the bahtreig on the neck and it picked up its pace. The cavern opened wide, and the stone forest gave way to a subterranean keep sculpted from the natural rock with meticulous care.

Carved birds of prey perched above the enormous portcullis, their keen eyes forever on watch for the enemy. Mosaics of great battles between man and dragon graced the façade.

Turin brought her bahtreig to a stop and hopped off its back. She passed the beast off to a guard who came to greet her and bound up the stairs and through the portcullis.

CHAPTER 9

Through his grace, he will rid Tyveriel of corruption and decadence. Praise be to the God of Fire. For his flame cleanses all.

- The Elevation of Naur by Alabaster Beryl
Unearthed from the Ruins of Meriden, month of Mela, 1399
AT

—▲—

The blistering winds of Pragarus buffeted Umhra's face. He guarded his eyes against the relentless dust and debris. Behind him, Naur's portal lay dormant, shattered by a deep fissure in the red earth that caused a portion of the gate to jut up at an awkward angle. Memories of his last visit to this hellscape came rushing back—Balris and the cloud of souls racing about the portal holding the devils at bay, the battle waged between Naur and Vaila, pinning Naur to the escarpment before him by the blades of Vaila's swords and his own Forsetae. Now, he returned as a Mystic, his form glowing with celestial light.

He turned his attention to the cliff face. Naur was nowhere to be seen. Umhra rushed over to where the God of Fire had been bound. All that remained were three holes where the swords had penetrated the rock face, which now bled a thick, black ichor that pooled on the ground at his feet.

Umhra clenched his jaw. This would not be as easy as he had hoped. He closed his eyes and imagined Naur. No image came to him. He didn't teleport to the God of Fire's location. It would seem such powers didn't work in this realm of the damned, or Naur took precautions against being found.

He sighed and turned from the wall, peering out over the desolate wasteland, and summoned his wings. Instead of the grey angelic wings he had grown accustomed to, black, bonelike protrusions grew from his back as though the feathers and flesh had been burned from them. Useless.

He snarled in disgust. Allowing the vestigial appendages to dissipate, Umhra set to walking across the arid landscape. Coursing between the toppled cliffs, Umhra navigated the felled bodies of Naur's minions. What possibly could be the need for so many types of devils? One would suffice in bringing terror to the souls of men.

Umhra slid down a ridge of singed red stone and paused. A rustling sound emanated from a pile of boulders before him. He summoned Forsetae to his hand.

And so, we have returned to this wretched realm.

"I don't like it any more than you do," Umhra whispered. "There's something down there."

I hear it as well.

Umhra crept along the ridge to get a different angle on the noise. A creature came into view, hunched over the corpse of a devil, picking it over with oversized claws. The creature was short and bulbous, with trunk-like legs and long, thin arms. Its skin was grey and purple, and plagued with lesions and rot.

"A devil," Umhra said, coming behind the unsuspecting monstrosity.

No. A demon. From the inner realms of Pragarus. The devils are few since this massacre. The culling must have emboldened the demons to venture into contested territories.

Umhra approached the demon and placed Forsetae's cold

blade on its neck.

The demon's skin smoked as it entered Umhra's aura. The smell of burning flesh filled the air. The demon screeched in terror, stumbled over the corpse it was looting, and fell upon a jagged rock. It gurgled and retched. "No—no," it said in a guttural tone. Yellow teeth and black gums filled its lipless, decaying mouth. It glared at Umhra through wide-set black eyes. "Please, don't kill me, Ascended One."

Umhra approached, looming over the hapless demon. He raised Forsetae overhead.

This one could be of value.

Umhra allowed Forsetae to vanish in a cloud of blue ether. Perhaps this pathetic creature could serve a higher purpose. Perhaps they could serve as a guide. He held his hands out to the demon, his icon glowing.

"I mean you no harm," he said, crouching to the ground before the retching creature. "I'm sorry to have scared you so. As you can tell, I don't belong here. Please, try to consider me a friend."

The demon scrambled forward on hand and knee to the edge of Umhra's aura. Its serpentine tongue flicked out of a fetid hole where its cheek should have been. The smell of death and decay accompanied it. The demon prostrated itself before Umhra.

"Ascended One. I am your humble servant. Please, tell me what you seek from Trogon Podion."

"I seek the demon-god, Naur. I left him here some time ago, and he seems to have once again found some modicum of freedom."

Trogon Podion retched again. "Do you know what you ask? This is not of sound mind."

Umhra chuckled. "I assure you I know what I ask. It is of utmost importance I find the God of Fire at once. Can you help me?"

"Yes. Yes. I can lead you as far as the hells allow. I know

where the God of Fire resides, but the path is arduous even for one that belongs to Pragarus. You. You will be a celestial beacon to my brethren. A trophy."

"I understand the risks." Umhra stood and offered a hand.

Trogon Podion recoiled, hissed. Refusing help, the demon climbed to its feet, rising only to Umhra's chest.

"Follow me, Ascended One. We have a long journey ahead of us."

"Lead the way. And, please, call me Umhra."

Umhra watched as Trogon Podion shuffled down a narrow path between two towering crags.

"Come, Ascended One. I shall guide you through Pragarus."

Umhra followed, loose rubble shifting underfoot. He gave Trogon Podion a wide berth, keeping his discerning gaze trained overhead as hellish creatures skittered across the escarpments. The devils did not attack, nor did they screech in alarm. They simply watched with curious eyes, careful not to expose themselves any more than necessary to this Mystic who dared to walk among them.

They traversed the wastes of Phit until they came to the jagged spur of a towering mountain. The surface of the mountain undulated as though itself were alive.

Umhra squinted, trying to discern the nature of the anomaly. "What is this place?"

Trogon Podion stopped and turned to Umhra. "This? This is the Slopes of Phit. It is where the devils torture those avarice mortals who prized wealth above all in life. They climb the mountain burdened by the weight of their worldly fortunes with the promise that, if they reach the summit, the gods will absolve them of their sins and allow them to ascend to Kalmindon.

"I see no summit."

Trogon Podion retched. "Therein lies the farce. Devils do enjoy their petty games. Come. We must continue."

Skirting the base of the mountain, Umhra got a closer look at the masses on the Slopes of Phit. The damned lumbered, scree giving way underfoot, belaboring their progress. The figures carried heavy iron yokes secured to their necks and wrists. From each end of the restraint hung a large iron box on thick chains.

Umhra paused. He watched the poor souls struggle under the weight, their progress inevitably giving way to exhaustion and a painful slide back to the mountain's base. Some wailed as they stared at their wounds. Others cursed the insurmountable peak. Devils scattered among them shouted, dragged the fallen to their feet, and lashed their exposed backs with terrible whips for added motivation.

Umhra wondered if it had all been worth it—amassing untold fortunes in a fleeting mortal life in exchange for an eternity of fruitless labor. Would they have chosen a different path if they had known the consequences? He took a step toward the masses, intent on knowing more about their plight.

"Best you leave them be," Trogon Podion said from farther down the path. "The devils will not take kindly to being interrupted."

"Wait here." Umhra found the urge to explore the condition of man's eternal soul unrelenting.

Trogon Podion waved Umhra off like a disapproving parent and huddled against a rust-colored boulder.

Umhra strayed from the rock-strewn path toward the base of the mountain, where a group of battered and bloodied souls in tattered rags prepared for their long march back up the steep slope. The Mystic's approach garnered the attention of the hulking devil guarding them.

The fiend towered over Umhra, with a thick muscular frame and heavily scarred bronze skin. Its skeletal head boasted two enormous tusks at the crest of each jaw. It wore heavy iron plates, bolted to its body, and a crimson sash across its chest.

The devil took a brazen step forward, drawing a tarnished falchion from its hip. The weapon had a distinctive chip in its blade, the imperfection somehow making it even more threatening.

Umhra focused on his icon, eliciting the blue wisps of ether that drifted lazily from its engravings to intensify. "There will be no need for confrontation," he said to the devil. "I will take but a fleeting moment in an eternity of torture." He held an open palm toward the devil and envisioned the fiend pacified.

The devil sheathed its blade and stood down, allowing Umhra to approach the damned.

"You." Umhra singled out a thin Evenese man with narrow dark eyes and a long chin. "Tell me who you are."

The man eyed the devil. Noting the fiend's disinterest in the intrusion and the lack of progress its prisoners were making, he halted his advance up the mountain and allowed Umhra's approach. "Angel, have you come from Kalmindon to deliver us from this toilsome punishment?"

"No. I have no such power or authorization. I am able to offer you a moment of rest should you wish to speak with me, though."

The Evenese man frowned, his face caked with soot. "Very well. What should you want to know?"

"Who were you in life?"

The man paused, rubbed his ample chin. Then he stood up as tall as the heavy burden hanging from his yoke would allow. He stuck his nose in the air and gazed into the distance, wistfully. "It's been so long. I dare say I've nearly forgotten. The name was...Chronivur Massik of House Balyxx."

The name sounded important enough but meant nothing to Umhra. "What brought you here? To this end?"

"Before the Whispered Death, I was Lord of Fellboro. When the plague took hold, I told the townsfolk I would levy a tax in order to guarantee their safety—to cleanse the town of the curse that befell us. They paid. They put their faith in me. And I took it all. I took their sovereigns and their trust. Then, I provisioned my keep with enough supplies for years, hired a band of mercenaries, and left the people of Fellboro to fend for themselves."

Umhra now understood the depravity of those bound to this mountain. These were not people that aspired to live better lives, to better their families through hard work and effort. These were not people who stole in the name of the common good. No, Chronivur Massik and his companions were truly loathsome—amoral.

"And what became of you?"

"Many months later, after the Whispered Death had claimed most of those townsfolk I defrauded, death visited me. One night, a long-dead warrior—little more than the skeletal remains of his mortal form—came to my keep proclaiming the town had changed its name to Retribution, and that I was to be the first sacrifice in earning its name.

"This undead warrior carved his way through my ample guard with merciless efficiency. I tried to escape, but he caught up with me in my stable. The very sight of him sent my blood running cold. His eyes glowed red with arcane fury, and there was a black void where his nose should have been.

"He grabbed me with preternatural force and dragged me before those few survivors and held me as a young man drove a dagger into my heart. Tell me, angel, how long has it been since I came to this place of the forsaken?"

"Well over eight-hundred years."

Chronivur Massik frowned. "That is a terribly long time. What became of Retribution?"

"It thrives in your absence. A city of strong, hard-working people. Do you regret the path you chose?"

"A path of wealth, power, and countless women? Please, I'm only sorry I didn't take more from Evelium in my one-hundred-seventy-four years. You've taken enough of my time. I must reach the summit. It is my only means of salvation."

Chronivur Massik turned away from Umhra, his heavy burden groaning as he steadied himself at the base of the mountain. Umhra watched as he took his first few precarious steps on the rocky slope. Shaking his head, Umhra strode past the hapless devil and returned to the path where his guide waited for him.

"Did you get what you sought from that encounter?" The demon asked, emerging from behind a boulder.

"To be honest, I'm not sure what I sought other than education. I've known many men like him and never understood their motivation. Now, while I cannot fathom how they justify their ways, I do better understand how they think."

Trogon Podion wiped a string of putrid sputum from their chin. "I suspect you will find much that will intrigue you on our journey. Come, we must keep moving."

CHAPTER 10

*Emboldened by the Creator Gods' abdication, the dragons
wreaked havoc across Evelium.*

- The Gatekeeper's Abridged History of Tyveriel
Vol. 2, Chapter 1 – Unearthed from the Ruins of Meriden, the
month of Ocken, 1240 AT

— ▲ —

Silyarithe soared over the Orc settlement of Bessik Uk, the
inhabitants below scrambling about like ants defending a
trampled nest. She lit the sky ablaze with a blast of purple
plasma to make her presence known and spiraled down toward
the vast encampment. How she preferred the Orcs to the other
races of man. They harbored nearly as great a disdain for the
Creator Gods as her own and held unwavering respect for true
power.

Makeshift pens housing emaciated livestock separated
longhouses made of scarred tree trunks and thatched roofs. At
the center of the village was a vast yard of baron earth. A
veritable mountain of amber, marred by a dark occlusion, stood
at one end of the lot, and loomed over a stone altar ringed by
bonfires. Sacred ground.

If this were an Evenese shrine, she would have been all too

happy to land in its midst and burn it to the ground. The Orcs, perhaps, deserved a more tactful approach. After all, she required something dear to them. For that, and their hatred of the gods who abandoned them, she would honor them with restraint.

Silyarithe swept over the infertile land and dropped two mammoth carcasses beside the masses below. Circling the encampment one more time, she landed in the courtyard. The last beat of her wings sent a plume of earth into the air. She roared, as if her arrival had gone unnoticed.

A sea of green skin clothed in leather and fur gathered around their unexpected visitor. Some stood with weapons drawn over their shoulders, others chattered between themselves. Even the children among them could not suppress their curiosity and peaked out from between their elders' shields and armor.

An Orc shaman with deep set wrinkles and who wore heavy leather robes emerged from the largest of the longhouses. Despite maintaining a sturdy frame, he hobbled in his gait, which required him to carry a gnarled staff topped with the skull of a dire wolf. The shaman kept his stark white hair bound in a single plait and wore a silver icon in the shape of dragon's tooth around his neck.

The crowd split as he hobbled forward, the bones and teeth affixed to his robes clacking together as he progressed with two dire wolves trailing behind him.

Silyarithe drew in a deep breath through her nostrils, searching for the scent of fear in her counterpart. She detected nothing other than his musk, which he wore proudly. She bowed her head in respect.

The Orc shaman stopped before Silyarithe and slammed his staff against the earth. The dire wolves sat beside him, and his clan grew quiet. "What brings the Grey Queen to our settlement?" His voice was coarse and unwavering. "We do not seek a part in your war against the Evenese, even though we wish the usurpers gone from our lands as much as you."

"I bring you gifts." Silyarithe nodded to the mammoth bodies. "These will feed the lot of you for months."

"We thank you for your offering. But surely, you didn't come all this way only to bring us meat."

Silyarithe surveyed the gathering. There weren't as many of them as she would have thought—not that she came for their numbers. It was a shame to see how a once mighty race had been whittled down to a few settlements after ages of being relegated to live in such inhospitable lands. "I do not call upon you to bear arms in my cause, though you shall benefit from my inevitable victory. I do, however, come to ask a favor of some significance instead."

The Orc shaman pointed at the mountain of amber. "I assume you refer to Nezenrith, the Red Fury."

Silyarithe glanced over her shoulder at the perfectly preserved body of an ancient red dragon encased within the amber mountain. "I do. My father requires a—suitable vessel. Since his own corporeal form was destroyed, we have gone through several lesser hosts. With Nezenrith at my side, I could hasten the downfall of my enemy. I could bring lasting peace to Evelium and then to the rest of Tyveriel."

The crowd broke into an uproar. The shaman slammed his staff into the ground once more, and they heeded his unspoken command.

"You ask us to give you our most prized possession. The very symbol of our strength—the focus of our faith. For millennia, Orcs have come from the wide reaches of Orrat Skag to bear witness to Nezenrith's greatness, and you ask us to part with this holy relic so you may further pursue your already depleted enemy."

Rage welled up within Silyarithe's gut. It would be all too easy to burn them all, but she found the idea distasteful. Such a rash response would make her no better than those she sought to destroy—those who subjugated the Orcs to this miserable existence. No, they would have a part in her world should she have her way. They deserved as much.

She exhaled slowly, and let the rage disperse. Her heartbeat slowed. "I understand the significance of my request, as I have seen the memories of my ancestors. I know of Nezenrith's admiration for your people—that he bequeathed himself unto you for eternity in exchange for your devotion. Imagine, though, the great Nezenrith taking to the sky once more."

"You do not talk of Nezenrith's return but rather, your father's, in the Red Fury's body. You ask that we break a sacred vow for your gain."

Silyarithe turned to the ancient dragon encased in its honey-yellow shell. Its wings were spread wide, its lips curled into a snarl. Every tooth and talon, razor sharp. Perfection. As her father would want to be seen.

"I don't want to take it from you," she said remorsefully, "But it's my only choice. I have searched the minds of my ancestors and know of none other than Nezenrith who prepared such a spectacular death."

"You are free to do what you deem necessary."

Silyarithe turned back to the shaman. "I would prefer you give it to me freely. Maybe in trade. I would gladly give you all Evelium to share with the blights. Think of how your people could thrive."

The shaman looked over his clan with a furrowed brow. The group stared back at him expectantly. "What say you? Is the betterment of all Orc-kind worthy of such a great sacrifice?"

A young, muscular Orc, bare-chested but for a leather strap that bound a massive cleaver to his back, stepped forward from the crowd. He had a broken tusk and bore a deep scar at the base of his neck.

"We have lived in the shadow of the Evenese for too long. It is time we reclaim what is rightfully ours. I say we give the Grey Queen what she wants and return to our homeland as the sages have foretold is our destiny."

The rest of the clan roared in agreement.

"And what of the other clans?" the Shaman asked. "Should they not have a say in the matter?"

"The other clans will follow the Wolfsbane as they always have."

The shaman turned to Silyarithe, a grave expression on his face.

"Then, we have an accord with the Grey Queen. You may let your lich father possess the body of Nezenrith. In exchange, the Orcs of Goshur Uk shall return to Evelium."

Silyarithe bowed appreciatively.

"You had better start preparing one of those mammoths. Tonight, you feast to celebrate our union. My father and I are forever in your debt. I will return with his phylactery, and you shall bear witness to Nezenrith's resurrection. Then you may return to Evelium under my protection when you are ready."

"We await your return."

Silyarithe looked at the sky. She beat her wings, buffeting the Orcs in dust and debris. Lifting into the air, she narrowly cleared the nearest longhouse and spiraled over Bessik Uk. Satisfied with the deal she struck with the Orcs, she looked down upon the mountain of amber that would be her father's salvation and flew toward Mount Anvil.

CHAPTER 11

I watched as they walked into the woods. Brave souls. I hope
they return safely and with answers.

- Entry from Xavier Pell's Journal
Dated 6th of Vasa, 903 AF. Unearthed from the ruins of Anaris,
month of Vasa, 1152 AT

— ▲ —

Other than the vast mountain at its very center, Phit proved
every bit the desolate and unwelcoming wasteland Umhra
had assumed during his prior visit. At the time, he had no sense
as to the enormity of the Hells of Pragarus, but now, the notion
dawned in his mind. If the purpose of Phit was to hold the
countless souls he witnessed on the Slopes, the journey to find
Naur would take more time than he had assumed—more time
than he had to spare.

Possibly, Spara's approach to achieving deification was
the path of least resistance. Umhra thought. *Maybe amassing*
the combined power of numerous lesser gods was more
efficient than assuming the superior power of the Creators.

Trogon Podion stumbled along the rock-strewn path,
retching every so often as it was prone to do, but otherwise
keeping to itself. Umhra followed his guide, and no longer

strayed from the path.

They entered a narrow chasm with steep walls of red stone. Pebbles and dust occasionally showered down upon them as spined devils skittered along the crags on spindly legs. The air grew damp as they progressed. Before long, a thick mist hung in the air and the devils stopped making themselves known.

"We are soon to enter Blor," Trogon Podion said. "It is a land of endless storms."

"And what deplorable souls will we encounter here?"

"Those whose lives were defined by lust. I am assuming you should want to speak with one of them as well?"

"If the opportunity arises, possibly."

"I am certain they will want to speak with you."

Umhra stopped momentarily. "Why would they?"

"We'll be there soon enough. You will see."

The ravine gradually widened, the mist turning to rain. Every footfall soon became a squelch in the thick mud. Foreboding clouds blanketed the sky, with lightning flashing and illuminating the landscape in an eerie green glow.

With each clap of thunder, Trogon Podion shuddered.

Here, the only signs of life were large insect-like creatures, with sturdy carapaces impervious to the constant deluge. Their ruddy forms effortlessly scrambled over slick rock and mud as they chattered to each other in something resembling an ancient dialect of the infernal tongue.

The rain poured, sending a chill through Umhra's body. Disheartened by the relentless onslaught, Umhra trudged after Trogon Podion, to the edge of a vast open field of mud. Dispersed throughout the field were an endless number of souls. Each of them was naked but for the iron manacles that bound their hands behind their back and another set barring their ankles. Sturdy iron chains tethered the manacles to anchors embedded in the earth so they could pull to within inches of each other but never come into contact.

As Umhra neared, the enraged screams of the bound cut

through the din of the storm. Some strained against their chains in a futile effort at physical contact with the soul next to them. Others kicked at the anchors that bound them with mud-caked feet. Others still sat in the mud within the confines of their trodden circles, rocking back and forth and muttering to themselves.

Trogon Podion slid down an embankment into the field below. The demon grimaced and peered through the storm.

"What's the matter?" Umhra asked.

"There is but one path through this field and the storm renders it unclear to me. If we stray from that path, we risk touching one of these wretched beasts. Any interference with them will be met with severe punishment, as they are cursed to never again experience the contact of another despite it being their sole desire."

"Understood. We progress slowly and deliberately."

They proceeded along the narrow path that weaved through the morass of souls.

The storm raged around them, soaking Umhra to the bone and sending Trogon Podion jolting with each crack of thunder. The pair fought howling winds and calf-deep mud.

A Ryzarin woman with deep violet skin lunged at Umhra. Her chains snapped taut inches from his arm. "Touch me," she begged. Her mane of drenched white hair clung to her face and neck, her lavender eyes wild and desperate.

Umhra shook his head, unsure how to respond.

Another chain clanked behind him and a grimy human man with yellow teeth strained against his restraints. The sinewy muscles in his neck bulged like strands of rope about to snap. "What's wrong with you, boy? Touch her...I need you to touch her."

Umhra spun from the man. His head was woozy, his stomach churning.

Another man leaped to his feet and joined in the taunting. "Lick her. She won't mind. None of us will."

"Yes," shouted another through the storm. "What are you waiting for? Take her!"

"What's wrong with you?" the woman screamed. "Are you a eunuch?"

Umhra's throat suppressed the urge to vomit, his mouth a veritable desert, his heart racing. Never had he encountered someone so depraved. At first, he felt disgusted, but then he considered the horrifying prospect of being trapped in this place. He already noticed his mind being overwhelmed, despite having only been here for a matter of moments. How could one not descend into madness in a matter of weeks, months, or years? How broken they all must be.

"I don't think you should want to stop and talk to any of these." Trogon Podion retched. "I suggest we continue."

Umhra nodded, unable to muster the words. He took a step along the path and the grimy man spat in his face. The rain washed the thick, yellow sputum from his cheek. He took a half step toward the man and loomed over him. He raised a fist in the air.

The man stood tall and closed his eyes. A welcoming smile spread across his face.

"No contact," Trogon Podion said. "They will take pleasure in anything. Even you beating their head into a pulp. It will end in disaster."

Umhra's shoulders slumped. He was ashamed of letting the man get the better of him. He lowered his fist and took a step back to the path.

"You're no man," the grimy man said with a hiss. "Come back here and I'll teach you how to be one."

Umhra ignored the added insult and followed his guide.

The Ryzarin woman screamed after him in a plea for him to return. With a sickening thud, the third man bashed his own head into his iron anchor, splitting his skull. He fell limp to the ground.

The hair on the back of Umhra's neck stood on end. The

smell of ozone filled the air. Then lightning struck the limp man. The nearly simultaneous clap of thunder sent a sharp pain shooting through Umhra's ear.

Umhra clasped the ear with his hand, and he felt warm blood on his palm. The ear rang. Umhra took two awkward steps toward the Ryzarin woman before shaking his head clear.

Smoke rose from the limp man's body. The smell of charred flesh filled the air. The rain washed both away, and the limp man sat up with a start, his eyes darting about in terror, his face smeared with blood and his body covered in burns.

Umhra turned from the scene and urged Trogon Podion onward with a wave of his hand.

They continued through the cold rain, sticking to the narrow path between the damned, all the while being taunted and propositioned with untoward acts. Umhra kept his eyes trained on the path before him, only glancing from time-to-time toward the lost souls on either side of him.

Anger swelled within him at each lewd comment. Time and time again, Umhra had to remind himself that he was above it all. That he was a Mystic and had more important matters that beckoned him than the jeers of these poor souls.

He found himself losing track of time as they traveled. There was no sunrise or sunset by which to mark the passing of the day. There were no stars in the cloud-filled sky. Distance was equally difficult to estimate as the path meandered back and forth through the field. Regardless, crossing Blor was an arduous task by both physical and mental measurement.

The rain eventually slowed, and the thunder's clamber grew distant and fell behind the flashes of lightning to which they were inextricably bound. Umhra welcomed the growing warmth of the air. He unbound his ponytail and shook out his long black hair.

"We approach Thyyg," Trogon Podion said, seemingly unaffected by the storm or taking any pleasure in it ceasing. "Home of the gluttonous."

"Sounds glorious."

Trogon Podion shrugged. "It is as far as I've traveled through the realm of devils. Beyond Thyyg, beyond its gates, I have only heard tales of what to expect. I'm afraid I will be of little use to you."

"You aren't my captive. You may go your own way at any time. If you decide to stay with me, I will see you to Syf safely."

"It remains a better choice than staying among the devils."

"Then we shall see these new lands for the first time together. How do we enter Thyyg?"

"There is a set of caverns ahead. Come, Ascended One, I will show you the way."

CHAPTER 12

Laudin of Farathyr often felt misunderstood as a child. Poorly suited to follow in his father's footsteps, he left home at an early age and explored the wilds of Evelium.

- *The Legend of the Barrow's Pact by Nicholas Barnswallow*
Chapter 1 – Unearthed from the depths of Peacebreaker Keep, month of Jai, 1422 AT

— ▲ —

Jenta's frown bore wrinkles Turin was not accustomed to seeing on her aunt's flawless Evenese face. Even with all she had been through...all the destruction and death she had witnessed under her stewardship, the stress didn't seem to weigh on her as it would so many. At least, she usually never let Turin know if it did. Right now, however, she wore her disdain for Turin's idea plainly.

Turin often thought of abdicating in favor of Jenta being renamed queen. She made it look so easy, and people didn't recoil when they first met her. In fact, people gravitated toward her wisdom and refined personality. Of course, the flowing blond hair, her high cheekbones, and the skin of a porcelain doll didn't hurt. Maybe Turin would find it easy to rule with those assets as well.

"I think it sounds insane." Jenta rose from her seat at the table and flashed Turin a worried glare. "We are not sending the last of the Forene bloodline into the Grey Queen's lair. Why can't Shadow lead the party? He's more than capable."

"Aunt Jenta—Regent. When the army of Winterashe descended upon Vanyareign, did you send your generals out to parley on your behalf? If there is one thing I've learned from you, it's that you must lead by example. I cannot in good conscience send others to complete a task I am unwilling to do myself. This is the closest we've had to surety that the Grey Queen has left her lair exposed and the phylactery unprotected. We will be in and out before she's able to return from Orrat Skag. All I ask is for you to hear me out.

"Besides, is it more insane than delving into the undercrofts of an ancient ruin based on the word of a man who claims the Peacebreaker visited him from Kalmindon?"

Gromley stood in protest. "I—"

"Gromley, please. Not now." The regent bade him to go no further with a flash of her palm.

Without another word, Gromley retook his seat.

Jenta glanced around the table at each of the Barrow's Pact, Indrisor, and Talus. She sighed and returned to her seat. "I will hear you out, but I give no promise that I will support whatever plan it is you've concocted."

"That's all I ask." Turin cracked her knuckles. "The way I see it, we cannot afford to ignore either of the potential gifts that have been presented to us. As such, I say we send Talus, Laudin, Naivara, and Nicholas to Antiikin to find out what lies in wait for us in the forge room beneath its ruins. While they head north, Gromley and I will lead a small party using Indrisor's pocket dimension to Mount Anvil and search for the phylactery among the dragon's hoard. If we are lucky enough to find the artifact, we steal it and ensure that Mesorith can never again return and aid the Grey Queen in her conquest. That is, if it's okay with you, Indrisor."

Indrisor grimaced. "I have not had use of the node within Mount Anvil in ages, yes, but it is viable."

"How will you locate the phylactery with all of Mount Anvil as your hunting ground?" Jenta asked. "You don't know what it looks like, nor where Mesorith keeps it."

Indrisor cleared his throat. "I may be able to help the little one with that, yes."

The table's attention turned to the diminutive Farestere. He wriggled uncomfortably in his seat.

"How so?" Turin asked.

"The phylactery is constructed from a shard of deep crystal taken from within the Sepyltyr beneath Mount Anvil. It was imbued with a soul tether of quite unique construction. When in possession of the black wyrm's soul, it undulates with a dark mass at its core. When empty, the shard emanates a deep violet glow."

"You speak as though you've seen it."

"No, Little One, I speak as though I made it." Indrisor smiled sheepishly.

"That's impossible. I know you're old, but Artemis Telsidor slew Mesorith nearly a millennium ago. The phylactery had to be created before then."

"Yes. One thousand two hundred forty-seven years ago, to be exact. You see, yes, back in my earlier days, I was obsessed with understanding the mortal condition and its boundaries. When I went by the name Aldresor, I was well known for experimenting with the necromantic arts. The black wyrm sought me out and held me in his lair against my will for nearly one hundred years as I worked on his request for a phylactery that would house his soul in case he should perish."

"Aldresor?" Nicholas asked. "Umhra mentioned that name in the past. Something to do with the Pell family."

"Don't get me started on those vagabonds." Indrisor scratched his head. "Nothing but trouble, they are.

"I delayed as long as I could, building the beginnings of my

tonight. That would put us in Antiikin in three-day's time."

Turin bit her bottom lip and nodded. "Then the rest of us move out tomorrow morning. I don't care to give the Grey Queen time to return to Mount Anvil."

"We will begin our preparations immediately," Talus said.

Laudin came to Indrisor's side and placed a hand on his shoulder and offered a kind, understanding smile. "We will put an end to Mesorith and his daughter," he promised. He followed Naivara, Nicholas, and Talus from the room.

"Turin, Indrisor, a moment, please?" Jenta asked.

Turin flashed a wide-eyed smirk at Indrisor and elicited a toothy smile in return.

"We will wait for you outside." Gromley bowed. "Jenta."

Jenta nodded. "Gromley. Shadow."

Shadow offered a smile and joined Gromley in his departure.

"Yes, Aunt Jenta?" Turin asked once they were alone.

"Indrisor, thank you for your honesty today."

"Of course, Regent. All in service of the Little One."

"Your story does bring with it a minor concern."

"That being?" Indrisor asked.

"When I was growing up, I was required to read the letters of Modig Forene so I could better understand what it takes to rule a kingdom such as Evelium as well as appreciate what our forefathers sacrificed for our prosperity. In several of the letters, my great grandfather wrote of a wizard by the name of Aldresor and lamented on how letting him escape was one of his greatest regrets."

Indrisor stroked his lizard's back. "Yes. That sounds accurate. Did those letters of the great king also say that, as part of his agreement with the Kormaic church in which it stripped the paladins of old of their power, the great king promised the church to hunt down and execute every last heretic including my brethren because we practiced magic unsanctioned by the gods?"

"Admittedly, they did not."

"Did the letters of the great king say they hunted me across Evelium, but I was too cunning and evaded their pursuit and that the great king feared I would return and avenge my brethren?"

"Again, no."

"Did they say that I disguised myself and offered years of supportive counsel to the great king while not once making any effort to harm him or any member of your family?"

"That's a little creepy," Turin said with a sideways glance.

Jenta sighed. "You made your point, Indrisor. I do not question your commitment to Turin and our cause. Hearing the name Aldresor, I found somewhat disconcerting, however."

"Regent, nobody is more disconcerted than I for having had to bring it up. It is a name, yes, I have spent hundreds of years trying to forget."

"I understand. Thank you for your honesty. I'm sorry to have you rehash such memories. You two have much to do. Please, don't let me hold you any longer. May the gods keep you safe on your mission. Indrisor, if I may have but a moment with the queen."

Indrisor bowed and exited the room.

Jenta approached Turin as gracefully as a swan through still waters. She took Turin's hands in hers. "Please keep yourself safe. If anything goes wrong, get back to the pocket dimension as soon as possible."

"I'm in excellent hands, Aunt Jenta. With Gromley leading us through the halls of his homeland, we'll be in and out in the blink of an eye."

"No doubt you will. And yet, I can't help worrying. But go now and see your mother. Let her know you are home safely from Anaris. She worries about you as well."

"I will. And I'll report back to you as soon as we return. Hopefully, with the phylactery destroyed."

Jenta nodded and released Turin's hand.

Turin gave Jenta a hug and ran to catch up with Indrisor, who waited for her outside.

"Well, that was a lot to process," Turin said as she approached. "Why didn't you tell me sooner? You know I wouldn't have judged you harshly."

"It is not a question of judgement, Little One. I have grown beyond worrying about such things. For all your wisdom, you are but nineteen years of age and have only now begun to feel the weight of the world. I have felt that weight for over three-thousand years and it is a heavy burden. I do not share my failures, my traumas, my losses, because they are so immense, and I cannot bear to acknowledge them. At my age, I must keep looking forward because in my wake travels a horrid monster I care not to confront."

Turin tried to imagine all Indrisor would have experienced in a life that long. He knew Tyveriel during the Age of Grace, witnessed the War of Rescission when gods battled over the fate of the planet they created, the War of Dominion when men wrenched Evelium back from the dragons and blights. She wondered where he had been during the Whispered Death when it took so many lives in Winterashe. These were things she'd read about in books and letters, but he likely saw firsthand.

"Then, let us keep looking forward. Just know, I'm here for you, just as you have always been here for me."

"Thank you, my dear Little One. All this talking about my past has reminded me of something I have been meaning to give you."

Indrisor dug into a vest pocket and retrieved a tarnished silver chain. From the chain hung an oval rough-cut emerald held in a silver setting by four clasps. It looked ancient—as though it, too, could trace its origin back to the Age of Grace. Indrisor held out his hand, allowing the gem to dangle freely between them.

"It was my mother's. The last vestige of my earlier life. I

thought it fitting of a queen."

Turin's throat tightened. Her lips trembled. She accepted the necklace and admired the opaque stone and the rune-engraved setting that clutched it.

"What does it say?"

Indrisor smiled. "Roughly, Love has many forms. All are eternal."

Turin pondered the message. She knew the love of her mother and Talus, and that of Aunt Jenta and Indrisor. And, of course, there were Sena and Aridon. Their forms all seemed similar in nature. Maybe someday she would know another form of love. When she was ready to open herself up to such a notion. If she was lucky enough to meet someone who could see past her ashen skin and other peculiarities. It seemed as remote a possibility as the Peacebreaker returning and setting everything right.

She made to affix the chain around her neck.

Indrisor placed a hand on her arm, stopping her.

"For a queen, Little One. I should not have you wear it until you accept your station. For now, you are only queen by name, not by rite."

Turin nodded. Her heart ached at what felt like a rebuke. Surely, Indrisor understood her apprehension in claiming the Circlet of Everlife—her desire to earn the right to lead her people rather than have it handed to her by blood.

The wizard smiled. "For now, I trust you will keep it safe. I look forward to one day seeing it around your neck. When you are ready."

Turin fought back the tears. "Thank you."

"You do me a great honor by accepting it. Now, it is time we get ready for our trip to the Isle of the Twelve Mines. I haven't used that portal in ages and need to refresh my memory on how we are to get there. One wrong turn and—"

"And we could be dealing with a temporal anomaly of unknown proportions."

"Yes. Yes. See, you've learned well. I don't see why they all think you are so difficult."

"Difficult," Turin asked. "Who?"

"Never mind, Little One. We have more important things to concern ourselves with. Come, I must remember the way to Mount Anvil. I may need to meditate on this."

CHAPTER 13

Ours is the work of the One God. By returning Naur to the mortal plane, we shall set Tyveriel on its rightful path.

- The Elevation of Naur by Alabaster Beryl
Unearthed from the Ruins of Meriden, month of Mela, 1399
AT

— ▲ —

The pair trudged until coming to the yawning mouth of a dark cave. Trogon Podion pointed into the void.

"The caverns of Thyyg." The demon retched. "The gates beyond lead us into Gresh, the fourth realm of Pragarus."

"And that is where we will find Naur?"

"No. He has not made it so easy to find him. Naur lives in the recesses of Syf beyond the Bridge of Tears. You should not come to hell so unprepared."

"It should be obvious that I wasn't expecting such a journey. I fully expected to find Naur bound to the rock face where I had left him. Otherwise, I would have focused on his location rather than on the cliffs. Now that I'm here, I seem out of sync with some of my powers."

Trogon Podion looked up at Umhra, shrugged their hunched shoulders, and entered the caverns.

Umhra summoned Forsetae to his hand and followed, ducking under one of several sharp stalactites that hung from the lip of the entrance.

The cave within was small, with a dank pool of green liquid at its center. The odor was abhorrent—the combination of rotting flesh and decay forcing Umhra to bury his face in his sleeve. His stomach churned. The floor of the cavern had a spongy texture and compressed under each footfall with a squelch.

Trogon Podion led Umhra along the wall of the cave, careful to avoid the pool of sludge at the room's center. Deep gouges scarred the walls—claw marks left behind by some unholy abomination.

The light faded as they progressed, leaving them in darkness but for Umhra's and Forsetae's soft glow. Trogon Podion found the entrance to a tunnel at the far end of the cavern and led Umhra within.

The cramped passage barely deserved to be called a tunnel. Umhra's leathers scraped against the walls, forcing him to hunch over, and giving him a similar posture to his guide. The tunnel sloped downward for a long while. The sour stench of rotted flesh intensified with each step—an unforgettable smell Umhra had regrettably encountered too many times in his life. Now, however, he wondered if the source of the noxious odor was the company he kept or something more ominous that lay ahead.

Giving way to the expanse of a massive cavern, the two travelers poured out of the tunnel. Umhra stretched his back and held Forsetae up against the darkness. White tendrils hung from the ceiling high overhead, glistening with a gelatinous slime that dripped to the cavern floor in a sickening chorus of splats.

Innumerable bodies lay coiled in the bramble formed by the intertwined tendrils, with all the races of Tyveriel represented, interspersed among embroiled devils and other horrid creatures with which Umhra was unfamiliar.

"Don't stand too tall, Ascended One," Trogon Podion said, "Lest you end up among them. The Threads would welcome you. The Threads devour all."

Umhra nodded, returned to his crouch.

For some time, they crept beneath the Threads which probed the floor of their cavern in irregular intervals in search of the errant souls that disturbed them.

"One last passage and we will come to the Gluttons' Gates." Trogon Podion pointed across the cavern to a hole in the wall lit by a flickering light deep within. He continued onward, unaffected by the display above.

Umhra glanced up at the ensnared souls and grimaced. In unison, their eyes all snapped open to garner him in their hollow glare.

"Help us," whispered the nearest of the bodies.

"Help us," another said. Then more joined in, until the grim pleas of the dead filled the room.

The Threads writhed, raising some of the bodies closer to the ceiling, and tightening their grasp around whatever body part was available to them. Rancid flesh burst, brittle bones crunched.

Umhra hurried after Trogon Podion. He hoped to put this macabre display behind him but knew all too well it would haunt his memories for the rest of his days. He resigned himself to the notion this would not be the last horror Pragarus would have him witness.

"Tell me," Umhra said, entering the tunnel on the far side of the cavern all too eagerly. "What did they do? Those in the threads."

Trogon Podion shrugged. "Not all who find their way here are so easily categorized. Their sins remain hidden."

Umhra's heart sank at the thought that if he had chosen a different path, he too could be tangled in the Threads with those hapless souls. Maybe he deserved it. He'd killed. He'd lied. He'd disavowed his own god. He was far from faultless and yet he stood here on the door of deification, and they languished in endless pain.

Umhra shook his head clear of the notion.

"Where do those of your kind come from and why are they among the devils?"

Trogon Podion stopped, waddled about to face Umhra. "This question has never been asked of me before." He picked at a patch of rotten flesh on his chin. "Pragarus is not one hell, but many hells. You have witnessed Phit, which is the closest to the mortal plane. From there, we descend through the various realms of the devils until we reach the city of Debreth and the Flesh Gate." The demon tried to spit on the ground, but the stained saliva just ran down his chin and settled on his bulbous stomach.

"Beyond the Flesh Gate is my homeland, Syf. The demons control those hells beyond the gate. We have lived there for ages, trapped by the devils, and unable to influence the mortal plane as we would like.

"Our war found a regrettable stalemate ages ago, before the God of Fire came to us. Naur was eager to return to the mortal plane and promised us free rein of the lands of Tyveriel outside the one he called Evelium. He chose the devils to lead his assault on the mortals, knowing many would not survive the gate and many others still would fall to the weapons of man.

"This culling would weaken the devils enough for the demons to push into the upper hells and assert their destined dominance." Trogon Podion retched. "This is how you came to find me."

"Your superiors sent you to Phit as a scout?"

Trogon Podion turned his back on Umhra and started back down the pathway. "No, Ascended One. A scout has value in the information it brings to its army. They sent me to Phit as bait, to draw the devils out so the scouts could get a better count of their true numbers. I am the only survivor—left behind to die like the others. It seems I am not even capable of being bait."

Umhra frowned, surprised at the intensity of his empathy for the demon. Surprised that he was enjoying the foul creature's company. "Well, we'll get you home."

"Yes, as the feeble demon that brought a Mystic with him to slay the God of Fire. All is lost for me. I have resigned myself to this fate. I suppose it is better than staying among the devils."

Umhra had not taken the time to consider what he asked of his guide. Framed from Trogon Podion's perspective, he could now see how selfish he had been. But this was a demon he was dealing with. Surely, such a monster deserved every bit of torture that came its way. At least, that's what his studies had led him to believe. Some things are better left learned through experience.

As the undulating surface leveled off, carved stone replaced the sponge they traversed since entering the caverns. The tunnel widened, and the roof sloped up at a steep angle, revealing a massive set of gates constructed of what looked to be wrought iron. Each baluster had a barbed spear that held a body in place. The bodies writhed, trying to pull themselves free of the barbs. No matter how they struggled, their efforts were in vain.

On either side of the gate sat a stone pedestal which carried a morbidly obese devil covered in asymmetric rolls of sickly pink flesh. Twice Umhra's height, the devils lazed on their platforms, disregarding the intrusion.

"Gorgers," Trogon Podion said, "We dared not cross these gates on our way to Phit. The scouts followed another path, but they transported us within chamber gems, and I do not know their secret ways."

"Will they let us pass?"

"I should think not." Trogon Podion retched. "They are known to prefer consuming anything that approaches their precious gate. I assumed you would see to that not happening."

Umhra ran his tongue over one of the tusks in his bottom

jaw so his lip bulged. "Let's at least try to reason with them first."

Trogon Podion plodded into the light thrown from two enormous braziers that raged beside the Gorgers' platforms. "Open the gates." The demon's voice, uncharacteristically resonant and authoritative, echoed through the chamber. "The gods demand it. They have sent an angel and require for him access to Syf."

The Gorgers shifted, one grabbing the edge of their podium with an arm too short for their frame and laboring to pull themselves to face the intruder. The other rolled to its back and tilted itself into a standing position, a layer of skin sloughing off on the edge of its platform.

Their heads were absurdly small in relation to their enormous, corpulent bodies. Their eyes were narrow and grey, as if cataracts clouded them, and heavy leather straps were sewn across their mouths, leaving them open but restrained.

"What is this?" the standing Gorger asked. "A demon in our midst. We shall eat your flesh, trespasser."

A gate slammed down behind Umhra, cutting them off from any path of retreat. Locked in the room with the Gorgers, Umhra came to Trogon Podion's side, blue ether streaming from his icon.

"One for each of us," the other Gorger said, laboring to its feet, "But this one is no demon. Such exotic fare." The Gorger pulled on a body impaled on the gate. It tore off a leg and shoved it between the strapping that bound its mouth. The figure on the gate howled and shuddered violently.

Umhra stepped forward, muttering a prayer in a celestial tongue. The aura cast from his form intensified and spread forth to encompass the Gorgers.

The fiends recoiled and tried to guard their eyes against the glare, but their rotund arms were too short to reach. One stumbled backward, falling over the corner of its podium, which bit into its flesh. It crashed to the ground in a pool of blood. The other took a few determined steps away from Umhra, waving its hands in the air.

Trogon Podion hissed and ran to the gate that had slammed shut behind them, shaking the bars furiously.

"Please," the standing Gorger pleaded, its voice shrill with fear, "come no closer. I beg you for mercy."

Umhra strode forward, flourishing Forsetae in his left hand and keeping the remaining Gorger within his aura. Now in the shadows, Trogon grew calm and released the gate, but kept a safe distance along the stone wall.

"Open the gate." Umhra motioned to the Gorger with the point of his blade. "We will pass whether you live or die. The choice is yours."

Umhra's aura flickered. He stared at his icon, the light emanating from it erratic. He called to Vaila in his mind, but there was no answer. The aura holding the Gorger at bay dissipated.

The Gorger put its hands down and laughed. "You have come too far from your home, Mystic. Your magic withers. It seems you shall not pass through our gates after all."

The Gorger strained to open its mouth further than its leather binding would allow. The strap snapped, and the Gorger flexed its jaw. Like a python about to devour its prey, the Gorger's jaw unhinged, and its mouth opened wide, tearing the flesh of its chest.

Its body streaked with blood—the Gorger charged.

Umhra gripped Forsetae in both hands and held his ground.

As the Gorger lumbered by, Umhra stepped aside and swiped Forsetae across its side, drawing a deep wound. Exposed fat glistened. Gore fell to the floor.

Unaffected, the Gorger turned and reached for Umhra. Its arm extended farther than should have been possible and grabbed hold of his neck.

With a vice like grip, it lifted Umhra off his feet.

Umhra focused on the Gorger and drew upon the space around him. There was no response. He visualized the Gorger blown to pieces. Nothing.

The Gorger opened its mouth wide and drew Umhra close.

Umhra dangled above the devil's maw. Beyond a row of curved teeth was nothing but a black void.

Umhra hacked at the Gorger's meaty wrist, severing its hand. He fell toward the devil's vacuous mouth and drove Forsetae into one of its eyes.

Forsetae burst through the back of its head and the Gorger slumped to the floor, Umhra standing on its face.

He pulled his blade clear in a spray of ichor.

Both Gorgers lay still.

Trogon Podion stepped from the shadows and around the pile of flesh upon which Umhra stood.

"Loathsome creatures," he spat. "They got what they deserved."

Umhra's chest heaved, his lungs burned. He climbed down from his perch and allowed Forsetae to dissipate.

"I had no choice."

Trogon Podion shrugged. "They will not be missed. I suggest we move on, though."

Umhra nodded. While he was tired, this seemed a poor place to rest. He made for the heavy iron chain hanging beside the immense gate. He took hold of the chain and threw his strength against it. The chain snapped taut, and the gate groaned. The bodies speared along its balusters shuddered and twitched and screamed in agony.

Metal scraped against stone, and the gate slid open.

"After you," Umhra said, motioning for Trogon Podion to pass through the opening.

Trogon Podion shuffled ahead and Umhra followed, the gate slamming shut behind them.

"Come, Ascended One," Trogon Podion said, "We have entered Gresh. There still lies a long, treacherous journey ahead."

CHAPTER 14

*It seems it is I who was fooled after all. The black wyrm holds
me prisoner in his lair. I must find a means to escape.*

- Entry from Aldresor's Journal
Undated. Discovered: The Tower of Is' Savon, month of Riet,
1444 AT

— ▲ —

Turin sat upon a rocky outcrop amongst the phlox covered
hills above the Caves of Ruari as Talus, Laudin, Naivara,
and Nicholas fell away on horseback to the east. At this early
hour, the sun had just crested above the horizon and warmed
the sky with soft orange tones. She watched the party dip
behind a grove of trees and wondered what they would meet
along the way to Antiikin. Was whatever the Peacebreaker knew
lay hidden in the bowels of those ancient ruins worth the risk?
Of this, she was still unsure, but if Gromley's vision was real and
the Peacebreaker's gift could turn the tide as he suggested, she
owed it to her subjects to at least try.

She drew in a deep breath of sweet air and closed her eyes.
It was time for her to head back and meet up with the others.
Indrisor would be impatient to get their journey underway.

Turin slipped between the crags and into a steep tunnel that led back down to the caves. A bahtreig waited for her, curled in a ball beside a rock. She kneeled and patted the amphibian's head. "C'mon, buddy. We need to get moving. You'll have plenty of time to nap later."

The bahtreig licked its bulging eyeball with a long, yellow tongue. A wave of bioluminescence washed over it—casting the tunnel awash in blues and greens—and then faded. The beast climbed to its feet and Turin mounted its back. With a gentle tap on its right cheek, the bahtreig bolted down the corridor.

By the time Turin arrived at the portal room, the others were all gathered and ready to depart. She hopped off the bahtreig and tried to garner Sena's attention, but Sena kept her gaze trained on the machete she was sharpening with a filing stone.

"Excellent," Indrisor said, rubbing his hands together fiendishly. "Little One is here and we are free to depart. A moment of your attention before we do, yes?"

Sena sheathed her blade and woke Aridon who napped at a table with Neela at his feet. He smiled at seeing Turin and joined the others as they gathered around the wizard standing before the portal.

Indrisor pushed his crooked glasses up the ridge of his nose. "I have not been to Mount Anvil in ages. As you well know, I would prefer never to return to that place for all my days. Despite the vast length of my absence, yes, I am mostly sure I know the path we need to take."

"Mostly?" Shadow asked.

"Mostly, indeed. I may need a moment here or there to avoid a wrong turn. Be on the ready in case I err."

Turin placed a hand on Gromley's shoulder. "Once we get to Mount Anvil, we follow Gromley, as he knows the layout of the Zeristar stronghold best. Even with the considerable damage the dragons have likely done in reclaiming the mountain, Gromley will know the way. When there last, Mesorith used the former throne room as his lair. I suspect he and the Grey Queen are doing the same today. We get in, Indrisor locates the phylactery, we steal it, and get out. We don't wander from the path; we don't stray from the plan."

The group nodded.

"Then we are on our way, yes." Indrisor spun on his heel and touched the mote of light behind him. He vanished.

Shadow and Gromley followed, then the rest.

They once again found themselves before the great elm tree in open fields of tall grass.

Indrisor turned slowly in a circle, a crooked finger across his lips. "Yes, yes. Come. This way. We must first return to my library." He strode with confidence through the fields in a direction Turin had never been.

"Don't you have a rhyme for getting to Mount Anvil like you do for every other place we've been?" Sena asked as she waded through waist high grass.

"I once did, I'm sure. Do I recall what it was? No. You must understand, I assured myself I would never again have use for it. You have shared a similar sentiment for something in your life, yes?"

"Well, there was Dahlia Thorn." Sena scrunched her face in feigned disgust.

Turin laughed. "Is she the one at the leather works?"

"No. She's the infirmary nurse."

"Nice girl," Aridon said.

"Yeah. I liked her for you." Turin gave Sena a playful shove.

"Well, that makes one of us. She was too serious. I need someone who can make me laugh."

They crossed the fields and came upon a village of thatched huts. There were fires burning in open pits, hides tanning on racks, and kilns firing pottery, but no evidence of people otherwise.

Indrisor led them between the huts to the center of the village where a large communal hut resided, smoke billowing from a hole in its roof.

"This looks exactly like Whitewood Knoll," Shadow said. "I mean, without the surrounding wilderness."

Gromley nodded as he tore into a strip of jerky from his satchel.

Indrisor shook a finger at Shadow. "You have a keen eye, thief. It is a replica of the commune when I started it nearly three hundred years ago."

"You started Whitewood Knoll?" Shadow asked. "Why?"

Indrisor disappeared into the dark interior of the communal hut. "It was a time of great discontent with the establishment. There was a certain excitement in the people I hadn't seen in a very long time. I thought how better to celebrate liberty than to bring that energy together in one community." The wizard's voice suddenly sounded as though it were a great distance away.

The others followed and entered a translucent hallway that passed through a void of deep space. Countless stars dotted the expanse. Not far off, a great planet loomed. Lush green landmasses and vast blue oceans covered the planet's surface. A branch jutted out from the passage toward the planet, but ended abruptly before reaching the haze that surrounded it.

Turin spun in a slow circle, taking it all in. She had never seen anything like it.

"What is it?" Sena asked.

"Iolis," Indrisor said dismissively. "The closest planet to our own, yes. I've been trying for ages to reach it, but my magic does not seem able to coexist within its atmosphere. It is very likely life thrives there. In what form I have only dreamed."

"It's beautiful," Sena said, her eyes wide. "Paradise."

"Sometimes, the most beautiful things are the most dangerous," Shadow said. "Be careful of first impressions."

"Come." Indrisor stood, tapping his foot at the end of the passage. "We cannot afford to linger, yes."

Turin followed Indrisor and the others through the membranous gate at the end of the passage and emerged in Indrisor's library. The room stretched into darkness—the shelves that lined its walls stacked high with countless books. It was warm, welcoming, and Turin loved how it smelled of old leather and yellowed paper.

"The door across from us leads to Vanyareign, that I know. This one in the middle will take us to Maryk's Cay and points south. The one to the left, then, will bring us a step closer to Mount Anvil." Indrisor opened the door and held it wide for the others to pass through.

The room within had arched walls of striated stone, with enormous lanterns hanging from the curved ceiling on black chains. Rows of neatly arranged iron tables adorned the floor. Some were covered with glass retorts that distilled bubbling liquids over open flame, while others held crucibles filled with molten metals. The laden shelves housed jars of herbs and other exotic materials used in alchemical processes.

Indrisor led the party across the room to the far side, where two wooden doors awaited them. "My lab. I haven't gone beyond this point in some time. I believe it's the door on the right that leads us to the west, but do not recall where the other goes, so it's best left alone."

The wizard opened the door and ushered the others within. The room was pitch black—a testament to years of disuse. As the door slammed shut behind them, a preternatural light flickered and then sustained itself, casting a cold blue glow across what looked like a cavern. Water dripped from the ceiling into pools below. The air was musty and warm.

"Well, this is simply not right," Indrisor said. "I may have gotten us into a spot of trouble here."

From the shadows deep within the cavern emerged a hulking monstrosity with a rust-colored carapace. With a hunched posture, it lumbered forward on two legs. The spine of spiked protrusions that ran the length of its back nearly scraped the stone above. The creature had four arms, the top two ending in deadly serrated claws, which it held folded to its chest like a praying mantis. It had bulging insect eyes and jagged mandibles that it gnashed with an unsettling eagerness.

"I used to favor flesh golems for such purposes," Indrisor offered, unsolicited. "These novatids are much more durable, however. True marvels."

"Can you stop it?" Gromley asked. "Let it know we mean no harm?"

The novatid strode forward and shrieked defiantly.

"There is a word that placates it, yes. Unfortunately, it escapes me at the moment."

Aridon turned to the door behind them and pressed against it. He strained, but the door did not give way. "No door."

"Yes," Indrisor said. "The door automatically locks until the perceived threat is neutralized or the correct password provided. A failsafe if you will."

Sena drew her machetes. "Well, you better remember it soon."

Gromley charged forward and slammed his war hammer into the novatid's hardened form. The giant insect staggered backward and struck out with a snap of its fore claw. Gromley tried to parry the attack, but the novatid was too fast and slipped past his guard. The blow connected with a resounding crack and sent Gromley hurtling into the wall. He fell to his knee and glared at the novatid with anger in his eyes.

Indrisor pointed a finger at the novatid. "Restraint."

The novatid kept its aggressive posture and turned to face Shadow and Sena, who swept in to confront it. Sena's blades whirred through the air and cut deep gouges through its chitinous exoskeleton. Shadow let two daggers fly. The first struck true in the novatid's torso, drawing forth a spray of black blood. The novatid deflected the second which clattered across the floor of the cavern and then returned to Shadow's hand.

The novatid screeched. It lunged at Sena with mandibles that dripped with tinged sputum. Sena rolled, and the mandibles snapped closed above her head.

"Slumber," Indrisor said, his voice touched with panic.

Aridon thrust his halberd at the creature's chest. The novatid grabbed the weapon's shaft with the claw of one of its smaller arms and twisted it from Aridon's grasp.

"Not yours," Aridon said, Neela barking at his side.

Turin gave a sideways glance at Indrisor, who rubbed his chin, one eyebrow arched. She put her hand against the stone wall of the cavern and waited for the rush of cold to enter her body. Tyveriel did not answer.

"We are not on Tyveriel, Little One," Indrisor said. "You will not hold sway over this land. Oh. Temperance."

The novatid's shrieks ceased. It collapsed its fore claws to its chest and retreated.

"Yes. It was temperance. How could I have forgotten? The beast will no longer pose a threat. All the same, I do suggest we leave it be."

"You'll get no arguments from me," Sena said, her chest heaving. "Do you think you can remember the rest of the way without running into anymore of your pets?"

"That should be highly probabilistic with my error corrected. Come. Follow."

Indrisor pushed through the doorway and back into his laboratory. Once the others were all gathered, he led them to the door on the left. "With only one choice left, it will be hard for me to be wrong again." He offered a quirky grin that said *I'm sorry, and get over it, and you're lucky I'm sharing my private pocket dimension with you in the first place* at the same time.

Indrisor opened the door and led the party through the portal into a tunnel with opaque walls. The passageway curved in a sweeping arc as though to circumvent some massive obstruction.

Turin came to Indrisor's side. "Why is this tunnel different from the others? I mean, no exotic views and whatnot."

"One of the reasons it took me so long to escape from Mesorith's lair was because tunneling from that wretched place was like forging a path through solid iron. I do not know what it is about the Isle of the Twelve Mines, but it is quite resistant to magic. You may want to remember that when we are within the lair, yes."

Turin nodded. "So, we're getting close, then?"

"I should have remembered it sooner. Through the library, through the lab, the door on the left to the dragon's lair. Yes, Little One, the halls of Mount Anvil lie ahead."

CHAPTER 15

Death, itself, walked among them. There was no safe harbor.
- The Gatekeeper's Abridged History of Tyveriel

Vol. 2, Chapter 17 – Unearthed from the Ruins of Meriden, the
month of Ocken, 1240 AT

— ▲ —

The narrow, winding path from the Gluttons' Gate ended
abruptly at the edge of a vast desert of rolling dunes. The
sky ahead was bleached white, the endless sands nearly as stark.
The intense heat caused the air to ripple between Umhra and
the horizon. He unlaced his leather jacket and stripped down to
his sweat-soaked linen shirt.

"Gresh," Trogon Podion said. "The Wastes of Wrath. I have
only heard stories of its horrors. I must confess to my
excitement."

That was possibly the most human thing the demon had
said in Umhra's midst. Resignation had dominated Trogon
Podion's spirit since Umhra had found them in Phit and here,
on the edge of unknown dangers, they expressed genuine
emotion.

"Well, we better keep moving, then."

With a certain eagerness to their stride, Trogon Podion

shuffled into the sand.

For a long time, they traversed the dunes, scrambling up one side, just to slide down the other. Mirages dotted the landscape, one false promise after another. Otherwise, there was nothing to break up the monotony and, more importantly, no landmarks by which to guide oneself.

Sand shifted underfoot, slowing their progress, but they pressed on through the oppressive heat. Umhra licked his lips, but his dry tongue merely scraped against their chapped surface, offering no relief.

His head swooned. He stopped and doubled over with his hands on his knees, his empty stomach twisted in knots.

Trogon Podion stopped and turned to face him.

"Are you dying?" The demon asked.

Umhra shot them a wry look. "No, I'm not dying. I just need a moment. The heat is taking a toll."

"Will lingering help?"

"No. How much farther?"

The demon shrugged and continued walking.

Umhra sighed and willed himself onward.

His nausea subsiding, they came to the crest of a massive dune. Umhra wiped his brow. Below lay a vast sandstone canyon as though carved by an ancient river long since perished. The field below teemed with warriors engaged in battle. Weapons clanked against armor, men screamed in anger and despair. The injured dragged themselves through the sand, blood running from gaping wounds. The dead lay strewn between them, a sea of severed limbs and still hearts.

"Is this what war looks like in the Realm of Men?" Trogon Podion asked, their eyes wide with amazement.

"I've only seen but a few battles of this size in my life. But, yes, this seems like an accurate portrayal."

"And what reasons do men give for such behavior? What reason could there be to mutilate each other, so?"

"I'm sure the same as those given by the Demon Lords and

Arch Devils of Pragarus. Conquest, greatness, revenge. The true flame that ignites every war, however, is hubris."

As they spoke, the wind picked up, building from a gentle breeze to a torrid gale. A wall of sand swept over the far slopes and raced across the canyon, obscuring the warring factions below.

Umhra covered his face as the sandstorm crashed into the cliff face before them and billowed into the air overhead. The sand abraded his leathers and lashed the skin on his exposed hands like thousands of pinpricks.

The din of the storm was deafening. When Umhra opened his eyes, he could barely make out the form of Trogon Podion beside him. He took a step closer to his guide, leaned down to come to ear level. "We must shelter," he said through a mouthful of sand.

"We are unlikely to," Trogon Podion said. "The best we might do is get off this rim, beneath the worst of the storm. There is a path just to our left. Follow me. Stay close."

Trogon Podion retched and took a careful step toward the cliff's edge. Umhra stalked after them in a deep crouch. The updraft from the storm climbing from the canyon slowed their progress, but they found the narrow trail Trogon Podion had spoken of. Barely wide enough for either of them, the trail worked its way toward the center of the canyon, where they had witnessed the battle before the storm caught them off guard.

Once their heads dipped below the lip of the canyon wall, the storm's strength abated, and they found relative calm against the cliff face. They were cautious in their descent, the footing less than ideal. The rubble their movement cast off the side of the trail fell for a moment, only to be swept upward by the gales.

After hours of tedious travel, they finally found solid footing on the canyon floor. Disoriented, Umhra peered out into the storm. "We should try to avoid the battlefield if possible."

Trogon Podion nodded and pointed to the left, indicating a

direction, and pushed back into the storm. It wasn't long before they came upon the first corpse. It was that of a huge barbarian man with a matted mass of dark hair. His neck was twisted so his grit-smeared face looked over his tattooed shoulder. A spear jutted from his chest, broken at the haft. Fresh blood seeped from the wound.

Umhra kneeled beside the body and inspected the weapon. It was Orcish by design, with a thick black shaft and serrated iron head. Dried sinew bound the head to the shaft, tribal beads adorning the end of each rope.

He climbed back to his feet and motioned for Trogon Podion to continue onward on their current path.

Next, they came upon an Orc and a barbarian twisted together in death, having run each other through with wicked looking blades. Sand caked the pool of blood beneath them, and the Orc's tribal medallion fluttered in the persistent wind. Umhra kneeled and cradled the sacred medallion in his hands.

It was carved from Orc tusk, most likely that of a fallen ancestor known to be a great warrior. This particular tooth was carved to resemble a wolf howling...a sign in Orcish culture of strength, cunning, and leadership. It was the medallion of his father Yargol's tribe. As a young child, he coveted the near identical one his father wore as their tribe's chieftain. How he had wished to earn his own as he grew into a warrior himself. The Tukdari took that life from him in a scene of events closely resembling the one in which they now found themselves.

His heart raced. These were his people. He shared their blood. Maybe there was something he could do to stop their slaughter.

Umhra placed the medallion on the Orc's chest as memories of the terrible day he'd lost everything came racing back. He hurried into the storm, Trogon Podion laboring to keep up. He climbed over beheaded corpses, searching each of them for familiar markings.

Beside a windswept rock, he saw the body of a young Orcish

warrior with dark olive skin and a jagged scar on the back of his left shoulder. He rushed over and kneeled beside the corpse. He rolled the body over to reveal the face of his cousin, Arkut the Liesworn, who died along with the rest of his clan that day so long ago. A deep cut ran across Arkut's throat, nearly decapitating him. His blade lay sundered on the ground, leaving little more than a shard attached to its hilt. Exactly how Umhra remembered finding him as a child.

Now in a near frenzy, Umhra pressed onward, ignoring the Tukdari corpses in favor of the Orcs strewn among them. Then, he came to the pikes. An Orc head on each boasted of the Tukdari's prowess in warfare. He followed them, one grim face after another until he came upon the body of a Tukdari goliath dressed in heavy furs. Upon the goliath's chest sat an equally impressive Orc, one tusk broken halfway to its base, a nose ring of black iron. The Orc's chest heaved with exhaustion, a gaping wound running across his stomach.

"Father?" Umhra collapsed to his knees at the Orc's side.

The Orc looked into Umhra's eyes and cocked his head, confused. "Umhra?"

His voice was deep and powerful. It graced Umhra's ears like that of an angel.

How could it be that his father found himself in Pragarus among such deplorable souls? All Umhra's memories fought the notion. This was a proud warrior, an attentive father, a respected leader of his clan. There had to be some mistake. Umhra fought back the lump in his throat.

"Yes, father, it's me."

"How can this be? How long has it been?"

"Twenty-eight years, almost to the day."

"I told you to stay in the tree."

"I did, father. I stayed in the tree. I stayed there until the raid was over and then made my way to safety in Evelium."

"Of course you did." Yargol smiled. Put a firm hand on Umhra's shoulder. "And look at you now. You're nearly the size of a pure-blood Orc. Not bad for a mongrel. Your mother came from good stock. What a strong woman. She was a worthy conquest."

"You're injured." Umhra nodded to the blood seeping from beneath Yargol's leather cuirass.

Yargol nodded. "Some days I best him, some days he beats me. And so it has gone every day for the last twenty-eight years without rest. Today, it seems we have both lost, just him quicker than me." He coughed.

"Let me heal you."

Yargol ignored the offer. "If only I'd bested him on that day, things would have been so different. The clan may have survived. I may have lived long enough to see Florek rise to my station. Your half-brother would have made a fierce chieftain. Now, I get to watch him die a terrible death every day." He nodded to the nearest pike where the head of another young Orc lay skewered.

Yargol coughed again. Blood ran from his mouth. "Tell me, what has become of my half-breed son? What terrible fate brings him before me on this day?"

"I travel the hells of Pragarus on behalf of the gods. I suppose they saw fit to put you in my path. To what end, I'm admittedly unsure."

"So, you too can pass judgment on me, no doubt. The gods..." He spit blood into the wind. "They forsake our people in favor of the Evenese and now my own son works on their behalf? My failure knows no end."

Yargol struggled to his feet and held his hands out wide. "Cast your dispersions, oh messenger of the gods. Lay waste to your father's name, which your mongrel blood does not deserve to bear."

Umhra stood to meet his father's angry, twisted face. He could not believe what he was hearing. The pain of his father's words coursed through him like poison in his blood.

"To think how I idolized you as a child. How I've lived my

entire life in your shadow, wondering if I would have lived up to your expectations. And here, in our fleeting moments together, all you can do is berate me for being exactly what you intended to create. I did not ask you to bring me into this world, father. I did not ask to be what you so easily call a mongrel. Your ignorance is your true undoing, and I now see that I am better off for your head having been lopped off by this goliath's axe and held aloft on the empty pike next to Florek. I will thank Vaila in my prayers for having treated you so justly."

He regretted the words the moment they left his lips.

Yargol lunged at Umhra but came up short and gripped his lacerated stomach. Gritting his teeth, he swung at his son and struck him with the back of his fist.

Umhra did not flinch. The impact could not do any more damage than his father's words had already done.

Yargol raised his hand again and then dropped to his hands and knees and spit blood into the sand.

"Leave me. You are no Orc, and this is sacred ground fed by our blood."

Umhra swallowed. "Your time is not long now, father. I trust tomorrow will be equally rewarding for you. I regret I will not be here to observe it once more."

Yargol dropped to the canyon floor, his blood soaking the sand beneath him. The sandstorm passed.

Umhra grabbed the medallion that hung around his father's neck and snapped the leather chord that held it with a quick jerk. He held it up to the bleached sky and then tossed it into the sand.

He turned from his father's body to find Trogon Podion wandering among the dead a short way off.

"I could not keep up when you ran off into the storm," the demon said as Umhra approached. "I thought we were to stay together."

"My apologies. I lost myself for a moment—let my emotions get the better of me. Seeing these Orc bodies brought me back to my childhood, and I thought I might find someone I once knew."

"Did you find them—the damned you once knew?"

"No. No, I didn't. It seems I never knew them to begin with. It seems my memories of them were little more than childish idealizations."

"There is clarity in such learnings. To know the truth of things. Demons are unabashed in our lust, our greed, our wrath, but you men of Tyveriel—you bury your true selves beneath a patina of lies. You cannot help but make yourselves seem like something you are not. I ask you, which is the worse offense?"

"You have a wisdom about you, Trogon Podion, far beyond your station. Maybe you should lead the hells of Pragarus."

Trogon Podion retched. "I think you have lost yourself again, Ascended One. My path leads to no such destination. Not that I aspire to it. Come, we near the tunnels to Hephimus. There is still some distance between us and your quarry."

CHAPTER 16

Despite being in line for the throne, Gromley's father bequeathed him to the order of Strongforge Clerics as a symbol of his faith in Anar.

- *The Legend of the Barrow's Pact by Nicholas Barnswallow* Chapter 2 – Unearthed from the depths of Peacebreaker Keep, month of Jai, 1422 AT

— ▲ —

To Turin, Indrisor somehow seemed smaller than before. It was almost as though the weight of returning to this wretched place crushed him. The cavern was oppressively hot and reeked of putrescence. There were remnants of a crude lab like the one in Indrisor's pocket dimension, but everything that remained was heavily corroded, no doubt by the acid breath of an enraged Mesorith all those years ago.

"The black wyrm kept me in this small cavern for the entirety of my sequester. Here, he and his pallid bride watched me with unwavering dedication. I worked tirelessly on the phylactery Mesorith demanded for himself. The blights had faltered as the great king's army pushed into the Wistful Timberlands in its relentless pursuit of their annihilation. They hacked and burned and poisoned the earth to put an end to the

War of Dominion.

"But I digress. I stole moments when I could to work on the enchantments that would be the foundation of my pocket dimension and my ultimate salvation, yes. I knew my work well enough to know the phylactery was indestructible. So, my intent was always to one day escape with it, so it would forever be out of the black wyrm's reach. As soon as I bound his soul, I did just that, and threw the phylactery into the Sea of Widows off the coast of Maryk's Cay."

"I've never seen this place," Gromley said. "And I know every inch of what was once my people's home."

"We are deep within the mountain. Beneath the mines that brought the Zeristar untold wealth. Near the magma that flows within Tyveriel like the blood that flows through our veins. The Zeristar built their new stronghold—the one you are familiar with—atop these ancient caverns to bury the tragic past. Unfortunately, it seems they were not entirely successful."

"And how, exactly, are we to locate this new lair and the phylactery we can only suspect lies within?" Shadow asked.

"I will be able to locate the object once we get close enough. It will call to me as a lost child would its parent." Indrisor rubbed his hands together. "Are you familiar with the Molten Falls, Cleric?"

Gromley frowned. "All these years and you still need to come up with a better name for me than that. Of course, I'm familiar with the falls. We used to throw rocks off them as children. It was as far as we were allowed to go within the mountain."

Indrisor flashed a toothy grin, his glasses cocking at an awkward angle on the bridge of his nose. "I can get you there— to the base of the falls. There is a staircase, narrow and hidden among the rock face. It should lead us to where you speak of."

Gromley stroked his beard. "From there, I can get you wherever you need to go."

"Splendid, yes. Let us be on our way. I abhor the idea of

being in this place a moment longer than necessary."

Indrisor led the party from his former laboratory to an adjoining cavern of considerable enormity. Pitted with pools of fetid, stagnant water and littered with corroded bones, insects swarmed every available surface.

"A foul place, the lair of an ancient black dragon," Indrisor said through the sleeve that covered his face. "And, even after so long a time."

Turin's stomach turned—the tang of bile soured her throat. "Abhorrent. I'm assuming the active lair will be no better."

"No better, indeed." Indrisor skirted the edge of a black pool. "There will be rotting corpses and other atrocities, yes. Although, I am uncertain what living conditions the Grey Queen would find acceptable. There has never before been a grey dragon, to my knowledge. We will be the first in history to step into one's lair."

"Is that supposed to make us feel better?" Sena asked as she tucked a tangle of blond hair behind her ear.

"Doing something that no one has ever done before is one of the great achievements of a lifetime."

"Not if you get eaten in the process."

"I'm hungry," Aridon said, rummaging through his satchel.

"How can you be hungry?" Turin asked, her stomach reeling.

Aridon shrugged and bit into a strip of jerky.

At the far side of the abandoned lair was a broad tunnel that allowed the party to walk abreast. A rich orange glow lit the exit far ahead and waves of heat rippled the air.

Turin wondered which was worse; the sulfurous odor that grew with every step or the stench of Mesorith's old lair they left in their wake. Then she found the perfect combination of the two and turned to the wall and vomited. She braced herself against the wall with a hand and noticed for the first time the deep grooves that marred their black stone. Claw marks.

Aridon lips smacked with satisfaction as he shared his last

scrap of jerky with Neela and then licked his fingers clean. The others waited patiently as Turin wiped her mouth on her sleeve and rejoined them.

"Sorry about that," she said. "Let's keep going."

Gromley came before Turin and held out a hand. She loved how he knew her well enough not to ask if she needed his help, but to offer it with nothing more than a fleeting smile. She accepted the cleric's hand, and he grasped his icon with the other. Vibrant blue ether burst forth from the pyramid etched into the platinum sun he wore around his neck. Turin closed her eyes and welcomed the warmth of Gromley's magic. Her stomach settled—her racing heart slowed.

The party continued and entered a massive cavern that dwarfed that of the abandoned lair. A river of molten rock snaked through it, fed by a crescent-shaped fall that cascaded from an escarpment in the distance. Heat radiated from the earth, licking the bottom of Turin's feet through the soles of her boots.

"We must cross the flow to get to the stairway I spoke of." Indrisor pointed. "It is by far the narrowest toward the far end of the cavern, where it enters a tunnel. I suggest we jump across there, yes."

"No need for that," Turin said. She dropped to her knees and pressed her palms against the cavern floor. She pulled her hands away quickly, as the stone was much hotter than she'd expected. She rubbed her hands together, better prepared for the searing heat, and tried again. Her palms burned but for a moment until her connection with Tyveriel manifest and she welcomed the associated chill.

Turin focused on the stone at the edge of the lava flow and commanded it to rise and arc over the noxious river. The ground tremored and rock groaned as it gave in to her will and formed a natural bridge connecting the two sides of the lava flow. It was imperfect—narrow and thin in places and slanted and thick in others. Turin was left unimpressed, but it looked like it would hold.

Indrisor rubbed his chin and inspected the bridge. "You continue to refine your abilities, Little One. Your power has grown considerably and your control much improved."

"I still struggle with commanding things of this size."

"That is a matter of self-confidence," Indrisor chided. "You think too much and act too little. Do you think the size of the object matters to Tyveriel? That is a limitation you set upon yourself."

He was right. She'd never known him not to be. But how do you gain confidence in yourself when everyone looks to you for salvation and all your best efforts have resulted in failure? How would she come to assure herself she was enough? That she was the savior her people needed her to be? It didn't come easy.

Shadow helped Turin to her feet. "After you."

Turin led the party across the bridge. They turned upstream, keeping a safe distance from the molten river as it widened into a plunge pool at the base of the fall.

"The staircase is over here, yes," Indrisor yelled over the sound of molten rock crashing into the pool. "It is a steep and narrow path but will serve to get us to the dragon's lair."

Turin searched the rock face but could not make out the staircase Indrisor described. It wasn't until she stood upon the first step that the jagged, zig-zagging path revealed itself to her. Calling it steep and narrow was like calling the titans of the Wistful Timberlands large, or the blights numerous. The steps carved into the obsidian cliff were only a foot wide and nearly as high. She followed the path with her gaze until it disappeared into the darkness above.

Indrisor bound up the stairs, undeterred by the blatant danger it presented. The others paused for a moment at the stairway's base. "Come now," the wizard said. "Time is of the essence."

Shadow squeezed past the others and patted Aridon on the shoulder. "The rest of you get started. Aridon and I will pull up the rear. Wait for us at the top."

Gromley, Sena, and Turin began their ascent. Neela bound after them.

"Follow me, big man. I'll help you to the top." Shadow leaped up the first few stairs and waited for Aridon to follow.

"This, I don't like." Aridon grimaced and wedged himself onto the first stair, his back against the obsidian wall. The toes of his boots hung over the edge of the stairs, but the footing looked ample enough from Turin's vantage.

"That's it—just like I showed you in the caves." Shadow ascended a couple more stairs.

The climb was arduous. Each step presented its own challenge. Some steps were sloped, others were slippery, and still others were narrow or missing altogether. It switched back and forth up the obsidian wall, all the while offering an unbroken view of the treacherous fall. Turin's head swooned as she wondered how Aridon fared as he struggled several flights below. No doubt, he'd need rest after such an ordeal. She pressed on, as she had no interest in being on the stairway longer than necessary.

Sweat pouring from her brow, she reached the top where Indrisor, Gromley, Sena, and Neela waited for her. Her lungs burned. "Shadow and Aridon," she said between heaving breaths of acrid air, "are about five flights below. We'll be waiting for some time, I'm afraid." She slumped to the ground beside Sena, who held out a waterskin in invitation.

She slaked her thirst on tepid water, the dust and grime washed from her mouth for at least a few moments. "Thanks."

"You're welcome."

There was no playful nudge, no mischievous smile. It seemed like there was an ocean between them despite their shoulders nearly touching. Now was not the right time to clear the air. As soon as they got home, she would set things right.

"How much farther?" Turin asked.

"From here I know the way," Gromley said. "We are still

several hours from the throne room, depending on how extensive the damage is to the tunnels."

"We can head out once Aridon and Shadow have rested," Turin said.

"And you can locate the phylactery once we are close enough, Indrisor?" Gromley asked.

Indrisor rubbed the lens of his thick glasses with a tattered silk handkerchief. "Get me in the general vicinity and I will locate the object, yes. More importantly, remember the way back here should things sour and we get separated. I will mark the tunnels as we progress to help."

"Not much of a plan," Shadow said as he breached the lip of the clifftop. He smiled as Aridon joined him, notably paler for the effort. "See, I told you I'd get you up here in one piece."

Neela bounded over to Aridon and jumped into his arms. She licked his face mercilessly.

Aridon placed her on the ground and scratched her ear. "I'm proud of you, too." He slumped to the ground beside her.

"Take a few moments," Turin said, "but we really need to keep moving. There's no telling how much time we have. Hopefully, whatever business the Grey Queen has in Orrat Skag is important enough to keep her there until we are through."

"I should hope so," Gromley said. "We are all risking too much for this to fail."

Turin knew what she asked of them. Sneak into a dragon's lair to steal the phylactery of a powerful dracolich having no knowledge of what awaited them. They were all her responsibility. She would have to answer for each life lost. No, failure was not an option.

Turin rubbed her palms over the vitreous surface of the ground. She opened herself to the connection she alone shared with Tyveriel. *I am humbled by our bond. Give me the strength to save my people and I will usher in an age where all creatures have a rightful place—where we no longer take from you more than we give in return. These enemies we face are not of your making, otherwise, they would not be able to harm me, for we are one. Together, we can create a better future for all your children.*

Turin's palms went cold. Her fingers stiffened, went numb. The chill spread up her arms and pervaded her body. Everything burned as though she were trapped below a sheet of ice and freezing water filled her lungs. She gasped for air and went limp.

"Wake up." Sena slapped Turin's face. "Turin, wake up."

Turin's eyes fluttered open, the fury of Tyveriel having ebbed. Gromley and Sena sat beside her, the others peering over their shoulders, their brows furrowed in concern.

"What the hell was that?" Sena asked. "What happened? Even Gromley couldn't bring you back."

"I don't know." Turin pushed herself up with her friends' help. "I was focusing on my tether and Tyveriel answered more forcefully than normal. She spoke to me. I felt her anger. I felt her pain. I saw an ancient black monolith in the depths of a dark forest. Roots grow from its resting place and corrupt everything they touch. It turns Tyveriel against herself in the name of power and revenge. Then everything just went black."

"An ancient monolith, you say?" Indrisor crouched at Turin's side. "Little One, this is most curious. I believe Tyveriel shows you a primordial god, yes."

"What is a primordial god?" Sena asked.

"There is an ancient text called E' Ty'wyl Gol. The name translates from the old language to roughly, The Tyveriel Codex. It is filled with stories from the dawn of time. From the Ur'chea, when the Great Creators forged the first Orcish from Tyveriel's rich soil. It is said in the codex that other entities shared Tyveriel with the Orcs, having struck a bargain with Vaila and her brothers to protect their experiment in exchange for safe harbor from whatever chased them from their home far across the universe. Accounts suggest these entities resembled great stones and from them grew the first trees of Tyveriel's great forests. They came to be known as the primordial gods."

"I've only seen one passing mention of these primordial gods." Gromley said. "And I've never heard of this codex. Why is there so little mention of this in the great historical tomes?"

"History, Cleric, is above all else an account of the victors. A filter by which those who rule want their vassals to experience the past. A pantheon does not consolidate its power by laying bare its worst atrocities. It weaves a fanciful story of good overcoming evil and the pitfalls of impiety."

Gromley grimaced. "And what became of these primordial gods?"

"They revolted against the Creator Gods—tried to take Tyveriel for themselves, yes. They were destroyed. At least they were thought to have been. Not until the Age of Chaos do we see mention of a being that could be construed as one. Most of these accounts are unreliable, to say the least."

Turin climbed to her feet. "Well, whatever it is, Tyveriel wants to be rid of it. Let's get moving. We can talk on the way."

"Are you sure you're alright?" Sena asked, her eyes wide.

"I'm fine." Turin flashed her most convincing smile.

Sena rolled her eyes in reply, obviously unconvinced.

The glow of the magma river fading behind them, Gromley retrieved a glass orb from his satchel and set it adrift before him. It came to light, casting a warm amber glow that lit their way. He led the group through a labyrinth of lava tubes that wove up through Mount Anvil. As they progressed, Indrisor stopped periodically and dropped a handful of linum seeds and crushed them underfoot while muttering under his breath. They left in their place a small ward that emanated a vibrant white light. Turin was certain that without them, they could never find their way back through this maze without Gromley's assistance.

After hours of trudging through winding tunnels, naturally carved stone gave way to a manmade structure. Gromley stopped.

"What is it?" Shadow asked.

GOD ASCENDED | 143

Gromley shook his head. "It's the first time I've returned to Mount Anvil since the dragons destroyed my people. Only now do I wonder if I'm ready for what I'm to see."

"I will not lie to you. It's likely to be difficult, but I'm here for you. *We* are here for you. Stay focused on making them pay for what they did to your home and your people."

Gromley nodded and ran his fingers along the ancient glyphs that marked the threshold to the Zeristar stronghold. "You're right. Let's find the phylactery and put an end to Mesorith once and for all." He hoisted his war hammer over his shoulder and continued on with Shadow at his side.

The passage opened into the first of the great halls, an expansive room of ebony stone with oval pillars that stretched up into darkness. Many of the pillars were cracked, and some had toppled to the floor, reducing their intricate carvings depicting the history of Gromley's people to little more than rubble.

The resonant sounds of fracturing rock echoed through the chamber from the shadowed ceiling. A rat scurried across the room and disappeared behind one of the sundered pillars. Shadow drew his daggers, Sena her machetes.

Gromley turned at the sound of the blades scraping free of their sheaths. "I don't expect we'll be needing those just yet. This is a great hall of one of the lesser houses. All reports said the dragons made directly for the halls belonging to my uncle. We are still quite a way beneath where they've likely made their lair."

"Yes," Indrisor agreed. "I am yet to sense the phylactery. We have further to go."

"I'll keep them out, if it's all the same," Shadow said.

Gromley nodded and led the party across the vast room at a cautious pace. On the far side, they found an ascending stairwell that led further into the Zeristar stronghold. After Indrisor marked the entrance with his linum seeds, they climbed the stairs, passing two heavy iron doors along the way.

At the third iron door, Gromley paused and held up his hand. His heavy armor glinted in the light cast by his globe. "This door will lead us into the halls of the Cepryn family, my blood kin. We shall first pass through the Ancestral Hall, where statues of my forefathers, the great Zeristar kings, stand guard. Beyond that, we will cross the Chapel of Anar where I studied to become a cleric and then take the Gilded Corridor to the Royal Hall. That is where we believe the dracholich resides."

Turin made her way to the front of the group. "We are not to stay a moment longer than need be. We get into the lair, find the phylactery, and get out. Should we run into any trouble and get separated, we follow Indrisor's markers back to the magma falls and make for the pocket dimension." She turned to Gromley and placed a hand on his broad shoulder. "If this at all becomes too much for you, return here and we will pick you up on our way out. There is no shame in embracing your loss."

"I appreciate the sentiment, but I am a Strongforge Cleric and a Cepryn. I'll be fine."

If anyone else had made such a claim, Turin would have found it hard to believe, but Gromley was as levelheaded as he was stout. Whether it was his connection with the Peacebreaker, or just his natural demeanor, she was unsure, but he had a way of finding light where others saw only darkness. He was an unsinkable ship, even in the roughest of seas.

Gromley pulled the door open, and the acrid smell of peat and decay affronted their noses.

Turin stepped within the Ancestral Hall and gasped.

Gromley followed her in, and his eyes went wide at the scene before them.

The walls oozed with black ichor, which gathered on the floor in stagnant pools. Red agate statues of Gromley's ancestors lay in ruin, their stoic expressions and fearsome weapons pitted with corrosion. But it was the bodies that were the true horror.

The remains of countless Zeristar men, women, and

children lay strewn between the toppled effigies, their clothes tattered and exposed skin burned away from their detestable dull green flesh. Gromley dropped his war hammer and buried his face in his hands.

The war hammer hit the floor with a clang. A tangled pile of bodies near Turin and Gromley writhed.

As the rest of the party filed into the room, the undead climbed to their feet and set the intruders in their sights. They shambled forward. Some drew weapons, their rusty armor clattering with each uneven step.

Gromley retrieved his war hammer from the floor and focused on his icon. His icon lit with blue ether, and he cast forth celestial light that formed a halo around him.

"Please, remember, these were my kin—my people. I ask we give them an honorable death."

The first wave of revenants hit the edge of Gromley's halo and screeched, their moldered green flesh smoking. Others stirred behind them, rising to meet the agonized calls.

"Stay within Gromley's aura," Turin commanded. "They can't touch us in here."

As Turin finished delivering her orders, a rusted axe whirred past her face like a frigid winter wind. "Maybe we aren't as safe as I thought. We cross the room together. Kill anything within reach. With care."

Shadow threw a dagger. The blade lodged in the putrefied skull of a Zeristar revenant that wielded a glaive. Thick black gore burst from the wound and the abomination fell to the ground. Shadow's blade returned to his hand.

Aridon disemboweled three of the revenants with a sweep of his halberd. Intestines spilled to the floor like rope from a toppled satchel.

More revenants awoke and gathered at the perimeter of Gromley's halo, their long-neglected weapons a constant barrage as the party crossed the room.

A blade destined for Turin's chest stopped short. The

revenant who willed the weapon to its target growled through a lipless mouth of rotten teeth. Sena took the revenant's head with a swipe from her own blade. The revenant's weapon clattered to the floor. Turin kicked the decapitated body aside.

The blue aura that surrounded them flickered. A blade caught Aridon in the shoulder. The halo returned and took the arm from the Zeristar revenant that wielded it.

"What was that?" Shadow asked.

"I don't know," Gromley said.

The halo disappeared again.

"They can't hurt me," Turin said. "Their weapons belong to Tyveriel. I will draw them away. Run for the chapel. I will meet you there."

Before anyone could protest, Turin bounded from the relative safety of the group and out into the morass of shambling corpses. It wasn't long before she could no longer see her friends through the masses that surrounded her.

"Hurry," Gromley said. "I fear her distraction won't give us much time. Stay close."

Surrounded by the undead, Turin saw Shadow dash for the door. He swept through the stray revenants that ambled in his path, his daggers blurs of glinting steel.

As the bodies in his path collapsed to the floor, the rest of the party ran for the door. Indrisor passed into the chapel first as Shadow stood guard at the door. Gromley followed, then Aridon and Neela. Sena stopped shy and spun to look back.

Seeing that everyone was close to the exit, Turin swept her fingers across the pitted surface of a toppled pillar and sought her connection with Tyveriel.

There was no reply.

Not now.

The revenants shambled closer. Turin's heart raced.

She tried to steady her mind, but the horde neared, weapons at the ready. *Please, take them back. They belong to you.*

A rush of cold climbed up her arms.

The stone floor quivered and grew smooth as it shifted from solid to liquid form. The revenants sunk to their ankles while Turin was unaffected. Liquid stone crept up the legs of the undead and enveloped them.

The stone hardened, encasing the revenants in an impenetrable cocoon. Turin threw her hands out wide and the revenants shattered into countless pieces. She ran for Sena and Shadow, who waited for her at the chapel entrance.

As she neared the doorway, one of the remaining Zeristar corpses grabbed her ankle. She spiraled away from the revenant's grasp but lost her balance and fell to the floor. Her knees cracked against cold stone, her hands burned from fresh abrasions, and the knife she kept at her belt came free. The blade clattered across the floor to yet another pile of cadavers.

"Dammit," Turin cursed. She considered retrieving her blade, but the bodies it rested near now writhed, untangling one decrepit limb from another.

Shadow dashed into the room and helped her to her feet. He threw a dagger into the chest of an approaching revenant. "Hurry, now."

Turin nodded, and they ran for Sena.

CHAPTER 17

*My lust for blood knows no bounds. I am compelled to kill by
the very thought of it.*

- Telsidor's Missives
Diary entry dated 12th of Prien, 443 AF. Unearthed from the
Ruins of Anaris, month of Emin, 1156 AT

— ▲ —

The desert gave way to dull grey stone, walls climbing high on
either side. The path narrowed quickly, and Umhra and
Trogon Podion once again found themselves in the cramped
confines of a sweltering tunnel. The passage sloped downward,
its sharp, jagged stone twisting as they progressed.

A repellent stench forced Umhra to bury his nose in the
crook of his arm as he preferred to smell his own foul musk to
the air Hephimus offered. He was growing accustomed to the
malodors of Pragarus but this one—a mix of excrement and
rotten eggs—turned his stomach into a roiling storm.

The source of the smell became apparent as the earth grew
soft and wet, and the tunnel opened into a vast swamp with
green, smoke-filled skies. Dead trees, their trunks thick and
black and their branches gnarled and broken, obscured the path
forward. Pools of oil percolated between mounds of saturated

earth, releasing noxious fumes into the air. Umhra's eyes stung and teared.

He stepped to the mouth of the tunnel and peered down upon the unwelcoming landscape. Bodies were scattered in the muck, hanging from trees on iron chains, skewered on pikes jutting at awkward angles from the ground, and ensnared on large iron hooks. Everywhere, death and decay assaulted Umhra's senses.

"What is this place?" he asked, his voice a husk of its normal self.

"The swamps of Hephimus," Trogon Podion said as a matter of fact. "Eternal home of murderers, rapists, violators of all sorts. I am told they are all quite aware of their condition. Serves them right to end up in such a hopeless place."

Umhra cocked an eyebrow. "Is it not the demons of your ilk that corrupt men, tempting them to become such miscreants?"

"Sometimes, but not very often. We have much less influence on the mortal plane than you might think. Much less than we would like. Men have an uncanny way of corrupting each other without our help. They are weak creatures with no inherent direction. For all our flaws, at least demons are unabashedly true to our nature."

Umhra found truth and logic in Trogon Podion's words. "Will they interfere with our progress?"

"Them? Yes. I'm afraid they will not take kindly to our presence. I would think most of them would have enough sense to avoid you, but, no doubt, others will test us. For here, they are the most unfiltered form of what they were in life."

Umhra grimaced. Detestable. "Maybe it's best we rest here then."

"Rest?"

"Yes." Umhra found a reasonably dry patch of earth at the base of the tunnel. Behind him, a sheer black cliff rose until obscured by dark smoke that blanketed the threatening green sky. "Come, sit down."

Trogon Podion shuffled over to Umhra and looked at the ground curiously. They turned three times, like a dog preparing for a nap, and thumped down in a puddle of muck. "How often do you rest?"

"Less and less these days," Umhra said. "Most mortals need rest daily. Some, a few times a day."

"And you sit in the mud to do this?"

Umhra chuckled. "No. This is far from ideal. At home, we prefer a soft bed. When traveling, we set a campfire to keep us warm and to provide light."

"Warmth and light are things you seek?"

"Yes. I suppose here there is no want for warmth as it comes in ample supply."

"And light is inconsequential. Demons do not search for such comforts. We do not yearn for rest, or warmth, or light. We do as our archdemons command with little concern for other matters. I will say, however, I am not opposed to this rest of yours."

"I welcome your company in this inhospitable land," Umhra said, digging a heel into the peat between them. "I apologize for you getting caught in my aura earlier. I saw no other way to get the Gorgers to open the gate and was careless."

Trogon Podion sat in silence, staring at Umhra, licking their rotting lips with a long, forked tongue.

Umhra looked beyond his companion, a disturbance in the turbid waters of the swamp catching his eye. "I'm afraid our rest is about to be cut short." He stood and summoned Forsetae and his armor. The sword materialized—his armor did not. He huffed. "Hurry, get behind me."

Trogon Podion scrambled on all fours to the cliff face at Umhra's back as three humanoid creatures broke the surface of the mire. Clothed in tattered rags, they shambled forward, their muscular grey bodies covered in leeches and open sores. Two elongated tongues lolled from each fang-filled mouth. The ghouls growled in confrontation.

Umhra took the head of the first, Forsetae humming as it sliced through a sinuous neck. The ghoul's head toppled to the ground, landing in a dank puddle, its tongues still thrashing.

The second ghoul took a swipe at Umhra with an oversized claw. Its black nails tore through his linen shirt but missed his flesh. He threw the ghoul back, slashed Forsetae across the fiend's chest, deep crimson blood spraying from the gaping wound. The ghoul howled, staggered again toward Umhra.

Umhra thrust Forsetae through the ghoul's chest and wrenched the sword up, tearing it clear at the base of its neck. The ghoul slumped to the ground.

The final ghoul had made for Trogon Podion and the two were now locked in a grim embrace—the ghoul forcing the smaller demon to its knees.

Umhra dashed to the pair and careened into the ghoul. His broad shoulder cracked the ghoul's jaw, and it crashed against the cliff face. Gore sprayed from the back of its head.

Trogon Podion scuttled along the base of the cliff. They retched and muttered harsh words in a foreign tongue in their escape.

The ghoul hissed and jumped at Umhra. Forsetae at the ready, Umhra ran the fiend through.

Pulling Forsetae free, the ghoul fell to its knees and then to the ground with a splat. The earth around the ghoul grabbed hold of it, consuming it in a willful act of repossession. Umhra spun. The other two he had dispatched were already gone.

"They will return," Trogon Podion said, climbing to their feet. "They are willed on by this swamp to never rest. It serves as punishment for their transgressions in their mortal lives. They will die countless times and keep coming."

"Then we better get going. I suppose there is no rest until I accomplish my goal."

Trogon Podion trod into the swamp. Umhra took one more look at the indentations in the saturated earth where the ghouls had fallen. Despite the heat and humidity, he put his leather jacket on over his torn linen shirt and hurried after his guide.

Bodies shambled through the swamp—all but the stray few keeping their distance. Those hanged in the trees and held aloft on hooks or pikes writhed and twitched as Umhra passed. They raked the air between them, to no avail. Some screamed in abject horror, others in unfettered rage.

Ebony feathered birds, larger than any Umhra had ever seen, picked at the bodies with curved beaks. Their feathers dripped of glistening oil, and they clung to gnarled branches with hooked talons, each as large as a bison's horn.

The shadows lurking at a distance in the swamp mounted, their footfalls splashing through the fetid waters and peated earth in a thunderous chorus. An army of lost souls driven by their compulsion to ruin others. All the while, Umhra fought the urge to destroy them all in a violent rage. But that is exactly what this place would want—to reduce him to the base level of its inhabitants. He would not give Pragarus the satisfaction.

For countless hours they slogged, untold numbers of the damned biding their time. Umhra stopped, the muck half-way up his calf. He peered through the trees at their shadowed forms. "There are so many of them."

Trogon Podion tripped over a root that jutted from the ground. "Yes. So many. Man is a vile beast. I dare say stopping would be unwise. They seem unable or, at least, unwilling to test you since we've shown purpose."

Umhra nodded and ran his tongue over his teeth beneath his upper lip. It had been close to four days since he'd had food or water. While his surroundings tempered any notion of hunger, his thirst was overwhelming. His mouth was dry and sour, his throat hoarse.

"How much longer will we be in this swamp?" Umhra asked as he pushed his thirst aside and stepped over a half-eaten corpse the swamp was reclaiming.

A geyser erupted behind Trogon Podion, sending a spray of hot oil into the stale air. The demon wiped the unctuous film from their pale face with the back of their hand. "I am uncertain. For those that belong here, the swamps are said to stretch on forever. For us, we shall find the fields of Hyenor and the city of Debreth beyond. There we will go before Qaresdoth and seek passage into Syf."

"Qaresdoth?"

"The arch devil of Debreth. They and only they will decide whether to let you beyond the realm of devils."

Umhra's heart raced at the thought of going before an arch devil. But what choice did he have? If finding Naur meant convincing this Qaresdoth to allow him into Syf, then so be it. Time was fleeting. There was no telling what progress Spara had made in her quest to kill a god, but the power of the other Mystics flowed through her, no doubt giving her the upper hand. "Then Debreth it is."

Trogon Podion continued, a plume of oil again shooting into the air.

Slowly, the earth grew firm beneath their feet as the elevation inclined at a gentle slope. The swamp receded in favor of arid wasteland, the horde of ghouls falling away behind them. Bonfires dotted the expansive landscape before them, each with four charred bodies tied to their center poles. The fires raged to the relentless screams of those bound within.

Between the fires shambled yet more bodies, these lost souls covered by countless festering welts. Wasps the size of hawks swarmed overhead, diving out of the smoke-filled sky on vibrant red wings, their dagger-sized stingers piercing the flesh of the damned.

"The fields of Hyenor," Trogon Podion offered.

"Lovely." Umhra pointed to the jagged cityscape of black iron towers looming on the horizon. "Debreth, I presume?"

"Indeed."

"What can you tell me about Qaresdoth?"

Trogon Podion snorted. "Nothing. I know them only by name. I would have no reason to know them otherwise, as they are an arch devil, and I am but a minor demon. If it were not for you, I would gladly serve out my days without ever crossing their path."

"Does entering Debreth put you at risk?" Umhra asked.

Trogon Podion retched. "Of course. Only having you by my side keeps me alive. I would never survive such a journey alone."

"Then I will not leave your side. You will make it home."

"I do not seek home, for I am doomed. The only question is if my end comes at the hands of a Mystic, a devil, or one of my own as punishment for my failures. I do not delude myself with thoughts of salvation."

"Your demise will not come by my hand. That, I promise you."

"But, once my company no longer suits your goal, you will discard me as you would any of these pathetic sinners before us. There is no difference."

The demon was right. It was an easy decision for Umhra to use some lowly fiend that harbored only evil in its heart and leave them to the whims of Pragarus when their utility waned. Trogon Podion, however, was anything but. Surely, they wouldn't have survived long in the territory of devils, but now Umhra felt responsible for the poor wretch. "I will not discard you, either. I promise. Shall we continue?" He swept his hand out across the fields in a grand gesture for his guide to proceed onward.

The unlikely pair wove through the ambling souls, Trogon Podion dispassionate, Umhra suppressing his disgust at the abhorrent sights, sounds, smells of the condemned burning and the buzzing of giant wasps.

"You can't help your compulsion to deliver them from their sentence," Trogon Podion said after a long while.

"No. It's a problem for me."

"Even these?" Trogon Podion pointed to the body walking past them, a wasp on its back puncturing its torso with a stinger nearly a foot in length. The wasp hissed, flew into the sky. "These are the most deplorable souls from your world. Some of which you put here yourself, no doubt." The demon retched. "And you still feel compassion for them."

"I feel compassion for all things. I see the potential for redemption in all mankind and mourn all those that stray from the path and find themselves here."

"A sentiment my experience does not elicit. But, alas, we reach Debreth." Trogon Podion pointed ahead, where the expanse before them narrowed to a winding path of black stone leading to an unwelcoming portcullis of jagged metal fashioned to resemble the jaws of a terrible beast.

Beyond the sheer blackened-iron walls jutted sharp towers, their windows burning brightly as though each contained a forge within. Not a soul walked the path to or from the great city—none other than Umhra and his guide.

Alone, they approached the portcullis, which went unguarded. They traversed the razor-like teeth that protruded from the gate in all directions. The overt warning disregarded, Umhra entered the devil stronghold and prayed to his god.

CHAPTER 18

Finally. After months of searching, we came upon the elusive Miggins in its natural habitat high in the Ilathril Mountains.

A Traveler's Guide to the Odd and Obscure by Sentina Vake
Chapter 2 – Unearthed from the Homestead in Maryk's Cay, month of Riet, 1407 AT

— ▲ —

Laudin crouched behind the berm, rejoining Talus, Nicholas, and Naivara who awaited his return. It had rained relentlessly for the last day of their journey and a dim sun struggled against a blanket of clouds which seemed intent on snuffing it out. Blights swarmed the vast open fields between them and the ruins of Antiikin which loomed in the distance. He shook his head.

"I couldn't discern any safe path through their ranks. They are literally everywhere."

Talus grimaced. "What are our options?"

Naivara's gaze darted to Laudin, along with a half-cocked smile. He loved her, but he didn't always love her wanton disregard for the humanoid form.

"I can change at least three of us into wolves. Possibly all. In such a form, we could pass into Antiikin without garnering the blights' attention."

Talus turned to Laudin. "Well? It may just be our best chance. I can wait here and back you up if she can't change us all."

Laudin sighed. "I hate to admit it, but I don't know that we have a better choice. I'm in."

Naivara bit her bottom lip, suppressing a grin. "Yes. Let's go."

"This is so exciting," Nicholas said. "I've always wanted to do this."

Naivara closed her eyes and murmured a few words in her druidic tongue. The platinum circlet she wore lit with green ether and all four of them transformed into wolves.

They made for handsome creatures. Talus was larger than the rest, with light grey fur and piercing blue eyes. Nicholas was smaller and had brown fur streaked with tan. Naivara held her head high, obviously pleased with her success. She bounded to the top of the berm and trotted into the open field.

Talus and Nicholas followed, with Laudin picking up the rear. No matter how many times he shape-changed with Naivara, it still made him uneasy to take on a false form. Here, padding to the perimeter of the ancient ruins, however, he was thankful for the disguise.

On mud-caked paws, they trotted through the fields. As they neared the first of the blights, they slowed to a cautious pace. The blight was an unassuming pine, with dark needles covering its head and appendages, and a deep garnet glow in its core.

The wolves slinked by without incident. More confident in their disguise, they coursed through the countless blights that ambled between them and Antiikin.

To the north, the Wistful Timberlands now overgrew the remnants of Mirina's Path and encroached on the jade towers of the Evenese ruins. Thankfully, they hadn't used Indrisor's pocket dimension and gone to Vanyareign. There's no telling what resistance they would have encountered, or to what extent the city still existed. It's possible that the relentless expansion of the timberlands completely overran it.

Blights roamed the perimeter of Antiikin but dared not step foot on its grounds. The wolves proceeded toward the central tower where Umhra told Gromley salvation lied.

Laudin stopped. Held his nose to the air. In the times he had been here prior, he'd not noticed the stench of death. Then again, he'd never been here as a wolf. What an amazing creature. Such delicate senses married with an efficient and enduring form. He pressed on after the others, weaving through toppled statues and sundered buildings until they came to the door of the towering jade structure at the ancient city's heart.

They dropped their ruse, returning to their humanoid forms, and stared into the heavens. The tower gleamed as if new as it stretched into a sky of billowing clouds. Laudin took a deep breath and stepped closer to the door, which was flush with the tower's façade, offering no discernible means of ingress.

He ran his hands over the cold, smooth portal. "The night we met Umhra outside of Ember's Watch to retrieve Spara's icon, he recounted to me his last visit here—when he aimed to return Forsetae to the ghost king Eleazar as he had promised. He could only gain entry when he used Forsetae as a key which allowed him to pass through this door."

"We don't have such a key," Nicholas said, his neck craned as he squinted up at the tower's peak.

"Maybe we do." Talus drew Aquila from its sheath, the blade humming with anticipation. "It doesn't speak to me, but they forged Aquila in this very tower, along with Forsetae." Possibly, the blade will receive an equally warm welcome as its sibling.

Talus stepped forward and held Aquila out before him. He touched the blade to the doorway. The stone rippled like the surface of a still pond when disturbed by an errant pebble. He looked over his shoulder at Laudin and smiled, then continued forward, his hand enveloped by the doorway.

"It looks like we have our key," Laudin said. "Let's go."

Talus pressed through the doorway, followed by Nicholas and Naivara. Laudin paused, surveyed the surroundings for signs of life. Seeing none, he passed into the hall of Antiikin.

He found his friends waiting for him within.

Naivara took his hand. "Is everything alright?"

"Yes. I was just taking a moment to make sure we weren't being watched."

"The only thing watching us here is the dead," Nicholas said, pointing to the interior of the great hall.

Laudin looked past the jade pillars that lined the darkened entryway upon two rows of apparitions adorned in green glass armor. Each ghost held a sword at its side and stared blankly ahead, seemingly unphased by the intruders.

Talus stepped forward to the edge of the ghosts' preternatural glow and held Aquila out before him.

"I am Talus Jochen, and this is Aquila, the very sword of Modig Forene."

There was no discernible response.

"We come before you at the instruction of Umhra the Peacebreaker. He sends us to acquire that which resides in your forge room."

Still, the apparitions did not react.

Talus glanced over his shoulder at Laudin and shrugged. "Shall we?"

Laudin nodded. "We stay together, weapons sheathed. Including Aquila."

Talus turned back to the formation of ghosts and buried Aquila in its scabbard.

In unison, the spirits turned to the far end of the great hall. They pointed their swords toward a wide stairwell that fell away to the undercrofts, where an orange glow greeted them.

Laudin came to Talus's side and led the party across the room, passing the specters two at a time. They maintained their Evenese features, with long, pointed ears and high cheekbones, but their sunken eyes lacked any signs of life, and their weathered skin resembled tanned leather. The apparitions stood at attention and allowed their guests passage through the great hall.

The heat climbed the stairs in relentless waves as Laudin led his friends toward the roaring inferno they sought. They crept down the stairs and followed the forge's light along a corridor of dark stone. At the far end of the hallway, an agape doorway greeted them, offering a clear view of the raging forge for which they came.

The four friends entered the forge room despite the oppressive heat. Rimmed in glowing old-Evenese glyphs, the forge stood beyond a blackened iron anvil. White marble plinths lined both sides of the room, each covered with violet silk. All but two held ancient relics.

"I can only suppose the Mystic sent you. The one who calls himself Umhra the Peacebreaker." King Eleazar's form materialized before the fire within the forge.

The ethereal king floated forward through the anvil to stand face-to-face with his visitors.

"Yes," Laudin said. "We were told this room would hold something for us that could help in our war with the blights."

King Eleazar nodded. "Presumptuous the mongrel is, but no fool. The vestiges in this room are the last remaining examples of pureblood craftsmanship. Forged during the Age of Grace, when the gods shared freely their powers, they are each imbued with old magic akin to Forsetae and the blade that graces this lowblood's hip. But I hesitate to give them to you for such a purpose. I see the blights roaming the fields to the south and the Wistful Timberlands grow unchecked to the north, but I knew the blights as a harmonious creature in my time. They were one with nature and the races of mankind belonged to their mosaic."

"I wish that were still the case," Naivara said. "Now, they seem only to care about the destruction of man."

King Eleazar looked them over. "Not a pureblood among you. Possibly, your strength and conviction come from your

diversity. Sometimes, the differences between us create unbreakable bonds.

"I shall share my gifts with you under one condition."

"Name your price," Talus said. "We only seek to see the races of man survive. We cannot allow the Grey Queen and her blights to continue their aggression toward *our* people."

King Eleazar drifted over to the plinth closest to them. Upon it sat a golden helm with a single horn protruding from its side.

"I care not for the queen, do what you will with that abomination. Like all her kind, her heart knows only evil. The blights, however, have lived on these lands since before the dawn of time and deserve a future just as much as any of you. I ask only that your journey is one of enlightenment. Search out the cause of the blights' rage. Do not slaughter them mindlessly with the power I am about to share with you."

Laudin approached Eleazar. "Great King, you have our word. We will make every effort to quell our enemy's fury and attempt to strike an accord if possible."

"You, Iminti, speak from the heart. I can see why the Mystic has placed his trust in you. I shall as well. Come."

King Eleazar retrieved the helm from its resting place and held it out to the party. "This is Barofyn, helm of Ordyk the Paladin of Mela. It shall grant the pure of heart the strength of body and mind. Choose wisely who wears it."

He passed the helm to Laudin and drifted to the next plinth. Upon it sat a pair of blackened steel bracers, each with two opalescent gems embedded in their surface. The gems swirled as King Eleazar grasped them. A gift from Vaila, herself. The warrior who dons these bracers becomes one with the wind. Whether they choose to be a gentle breeze, or a raging gale is up to them.

Laudin gave the helm to Talus, who strapped it to his satchel, and accepted the bracers from King Eleazar. "Nicholas, will you hold on to these until we determine who best to use them?"

"Of course." Nicholas bounded forward and took the bracers. He studied the gems with curiosity. "It would be an honor."

King Eleazar lifted a green glass dagger from the next stand. "My people favored Savonian glass to the metals preferred by the gods. The process of forming it is now lost to time. This blade is the last of its kind. It is harder than any material known and sharper than any blade created at the hands of man or god."

Laudin slipped the dagger into his belt. "I know someone who will put this to good use and care for it as it deserves."

King Eleazar nodded. "My last gift seems most suited for you, Iminti."

The ghost king retrieved a bow made of black wood from the final plinth and presented it in open hands.

"Fara gave this to me when I was a young bowman in my grandfather's army. It no longer recognizes my touch. Perhaps, in new hands, she will live again."

Laudin had seen nothing like it. The wood, with which he was unfamiliar, twisted around itself from one pointed limb tip to the other. A soft white glow emanated from the ancient runes etched on its surface.

"What do you call her?"

King Eleazar's persistently stern expression fractured into a thin smile that revealed desiccated gums and broken teeth. For a moment, he almost looked alive.

"Her name is Sem'Tora."

"Tiebreaker," Laudin said. "I like it. May I?"

"I give her to you freely."

Laudin lifted the bow from King Eleazar's hands. It was cold to the touch, but otherwise felt comfortable in his grasp. As he inspected the time-honored weapon, its runes flared to a vibrant white, sending ether into the surrounding air.

An odd humming sound nagged in Laudin's ear, reminiscent of an overzealous gnat. Laudin peered over his shoulder as the arrows in his quiver changed color from the natural cedar he'd always preferred to frost white.

"It is good to see Sem'Tora lives on," King Eleazar said. "For me, it is like witnessing a child thrive even as the parent wanes. A legacy assured. Her only limitations are those you impose upon yourself."

Laudin shouldered the bow over his own. "We cannot thank you enough, King Eleazar. You have proven yourself every bit the ally Umhra intimated. We shall not abuse the trust you place in us."

The king's ghostly image faded. "Should you see the Mystic, tell him I still hold him in oath. I have witnessed his ascension to Kalmindon and expect him to keep the promise he made to me."

King Eleazar vanished, leaving the four friends alone in the forge room.

"Umhra is a man of his word," Nicholas whispered.

"Indeed," Talus agreed. "And these vestiges may, in fact, hold the key to our salvation. We should return with them to Ruari at once."

"Agreed, lowblood," Laudin said with a smile. "Let's go home."

Talus frowned. "I thought I did well to maintain my composure."

Naivara put a hand on Talus's shoulder. "No doubt. You've come a long way."

They made their way back through the ancient tower and out into fresh air. No sooner were they outside than Naivara once again transformed them into wolves. Talus tackled Nicholas, and the two rolled through the long grass. Talus leaped into the air with a yelp and ran. Nicholas gave chase.

Laudin was content to hang back with Naivara and trot back to the relative safety of the southern foothills. Together, they weaved through the roaming blights and watched Talus and Nicholas play their game of tag up ahead when they reverted to their normal forms.

Laudin looked at his hands, then at the sentinel blight that lumbered past him. "Naivara, what happened?"

"I'm not sure. I lost my connection."

"Can you fix it?"

"I don't think so. Tayre isn't there."

"Then, run."

The blight sentinel bellowed into the cool evening air and swung its great club at Laudin. Laudin rolled. The club crashed into the earth beside him. The blight tore the club free and sent a shower of dirt and rock into the air.

Defenseless, Naivara ran for Talus and Nicholas, who stood their ground with three smaller blights around them.

Laudin drew Tiebreaker from over his shoulder and nocked an arrow from his quiver. He ducked below another swipe of the blight's club and let the arrow loose into its chest. It struck true to the blight's core and encased the pale green orb in ice.

The blight tore at its chest, but the ice continued to spread until it froze its body in place. The blight shattered; an arm crashing to the ground, followed by its torso sliding from atop its trunk-like legs.

Laudin sprinted after Naivara and nocked another arrow, wishing he had fire rather than ice. Tiebreaker's runes flashed red and Laudin released the arrow. It pierced a blight's back and set it aflame. Laudin stared in awe at the bow's glowing runes and wondered what else his new weapon was capable of.

Nicholas followed Laudin's lead and released a fireball from his ruby ring. The blast instantly incinerated two of the smaller blights that stood between him and Naivara. Talus flourished Aquila and took the head from the third.

The path now clear, Naivara dashed past Nicholas and Talus toward the woods. They joined her in retreat, with Laudin pulling up the rear. As they neared the edge of the copse, Lauding drew another arrow and spun back toward the open field.

The blight he had struck with his flame arrow stumbled

through the tall grass, setting the dry fronds on fire. The others stood back from the blaze, their desire to destroy humanity apparently overwhelmed by their fear of becoming tinder.

Satisfied they were no longer pursued, Laudin returned his arrow to its quiver and followed Talus into the woods.

CHAPTER 19

There are but two of them. I see no excuse for failure.

- The Collected Letters of Modig Forene
Letter to Artemis Telsidor dated 1ˢᵗ of Anar, 985 AC. Unearthed
from the Ruins of Vanyareign, month of Ocken, 1301 AT

— ▲ —

G romley slammed his war hammer into the chapel wall,
sending a crack across the stone and an echo through the
chamber. Shadow came to his side and wrapped an arm around
him as though sheltering him from the entire world. He took
Gromley to the corner of the room and whispered privately.

The others searched the chapel for signs of more revenants.
There were none. Turin wondered if it was because this room
was a place of the gods and the undead were not welcome within
its walls or if the Grey Queen forbade such detritus so close to
her lair.

In the center of the room, there was a pit with a stone altar
covered in Zeristar glyphs. Directly above the pit, a beam of
sunlight entered the room through a hole in the ceiling that
must have extended thousands of feet to the mountain's surface
above. The sunlight hit the ground beside the altar, where
curved, gilded benches sat in rows surrounding the pit.

Turin stepped to the edge of the pit and stared down at the image of the sun carved into the altar's surface.

Gromley rejoined the group, with Shadow at his side. "Once a year, on the afternoon of the Sowing Moon, the sun shines upon our altar and Anar makes himself known to us in the Solaris Rite. Each of the Strongforge Clerics renews their commitment to the Sun God during the ritual. I, myself, came into Anar's light in this very room."

"It sounds beautiful," Turin said. "I hope you are able to begin it anew someday."

Gromley shook his head. "Those days are gone. The Zeristar are gone. Our only hope for salvation lies with Umhra."

"I wish I could have your faith, but I believe we are our only hope. I believe the gods have forsaken us, and your friend, wherever he is, whatever he is, has taken his place in Kalmindon at their side. I will not sit idly by and wait for a miracle."

Gromley smiled, stroked his ebony beard. "I understand your skepticism. But you don't know Umhra. He's not one to take his place beside anyone and idly watch while others suffer. I've witnessed him jump into a portal to Pragarus to confront a god. I've seen him shatter the earth to stop a blight onslaught when all seemed lost. I've seen him leap out of a hole in the side of Castle Forene to meet the Grey Queen in battle, knowing he could not beat her. He will figure out a way to end this nightmare—or die trying."

These were stories Turin had heard many times before. Nothing ever came of them other than more promises of the Peacebreaker's return.

Gromley hopped into the pit and kneeled at his center. He closed his eyes and clasped his hands in prayer.

His face twisted as though he strained under a heavy weight. He looked at Shadow and went pale.

"Nothing."

"What do you mean, nothing?" Shadow asked.

"I reached out to Anar. He always answers—honors our

suffusion. Just now, upon his most-hallowed altar, he did not."

Shadow helped Gromley from the pit.

"You're under a tremendous amount of stress. I can't fathom the weight your heart bears right now."

Gromley clasped his icon and again tried to connect with his god. There was no ethereal glow, no discernible response.

The Zeristar cleric shook his head. "No. He's gone. My suffusion is dormant."

"Dormant?" Turin asked. "How can that be?"

"I'm unsure. Maybe I should try reaching out to Umhra. Maybe that will work."

Turin shrugged. "It's worth a try."

Gromley again closed his eyes and gripped his icon. A moment of quiet passed. Then Gromley's eyes snapped open and rolled back in his head. He held his free hand out as if touching something only he could see before him and mumbled incoherently.

Shadow's brow furrowed as he watched his friend with grave concern. He took a measured step toward Gromley, but Turin held a palm out to stop him.

"Give it a moment. I don't think he's in any harm."

Shadow nodded, but his expression remained unconvinced.

"The room is clear," Sena said. "The Gilded Corridor, or whatever, has seen better days, though. Is he alright?"

"Talking to god," Aridon said from a front-row seat in the pews.

Sena took a seat beside him and rested her back against his broad shoulder. "Oh. Sure."

Gromley faltered, his eyes fluttering open. Shadow swept forward and caught him under his arms. He stooped over and stared into Gromley's eyes.

"Did it work?"

"Yes. Yes, it worked."

Shadow guided Gromley to a seat beside Sena and Aridon.

Gromley rubbed his forehead. "He's in Pragarus, searching

for Naur. It seems that Spara has found some success in killing the gods. Anar must have been among her conquests. He is gone, along with the powers granted me by my suffusion. Umhra seeks to stop her by consolidating the power of the Creator Gods."

Turin's head swam at the notion. She normally did not concern herself with the affairs of the gods, but, for the first time, their machinations impacted her directly. Gromley losing his powers was concerning, to say the least. What if the little magic that remained in Tyveriel were to vanish? What chance would they stand against the Grey Queen and the blights then?

"We should keep going," Gromley said, rising to his feet. "I don't want to delay us any further."

"Are you sure you're alright?" Turin asked.

Gromley hoisted his war hammer onto his shoulder and nodded. "I'm not sure what use I will be, but I am prepared to see this through."

The party crossed the chapel and found Indrisor standing guard at a gaping hole in the wall at the far side.

"Big hole." Aridon grimaced over the wizard's shoulder. "No easy way across."

Turin peered into the crevasse that was once the Gilded Corridor. Deep gouges scarred the rock that fell away into darkness.

"I should be able to form a path across, but I'm not sure how much more stone shaping I can do today."

Indrisor approached the precipice at her side. "I feel as though we are close, yes. I believe the phylactery is not too much farther."

"Then a path across it is," Turin said.

She drew in a deep breath and focused on the stone that crumbled away at her feet. She willed the stone to flow forth across the chasm, forming a path wide enough for the party to cross in single file. Turin gritted her teeth—fighting back the more intense cold than before—until the stone she molded reached the other side.

They crept across the newly formed bridge and reached what remained of the Gilded Corridor on the far side. The truncated hall still boasted walls of gleaming gold and ended at an equally lustrous banded door.

Indrisor placed his hand on the door. "Yes, we are close now. I can sense the phylactery within the adjoining chamber."

"Any chance you can sense a dragon?" Sena asked.

"How, exactly, does one sense a dragon?" Indrisor replied. "Only by their bite or their breath, unfortunately."

Sena frowned.

The party stared at the door. A moment of contemplation passed between them before opening themselves to the unknown.

"We don't know what awaits us within the lair," Turin said. "We find the phylactery and get out as quickly as possible. If anything goes wrong, follow Indrisor's sigils back to the pocket dimension. Does everyone understand?"

The others nodded solemnly.

Turin motioned for Aridon to open the gilded door.

The door groaned. Shadow winced.

"Give me a moment," he whispered. "I'll take a quick look around before we go barging in there."

Turin agreed, and Shadow slipped through the agape doorway.

A pang of nerves gripped Turin's stomach as they waited. Moments seemed an eternity.

Finally, Shadow poked his head back through the crack in the doorway.

"The throne room seems to be clear. There are two vast holes in the floor and there is virtually no light, so be careful. I didn't see any sign of a hoard, but I only gave the place a quick scan. And I didn't pass beyond the toppled pillar at the center of the room."

"That's as good an assurance as we are going to get," Turin

said. "Let's go."

Gromley sent his orb of arcane light over Shadow's head into the throne room.

One-by-one, they squeezed through the doorway and joined Shadow within the once proud center of the Zeristar kingdom. As Shadow had reported, there were two massive holes in the floor, no doubt how the Grey Queen and her dracolich father came and went. Beyond the pits, a fallen pillar blocked their view. All was quiet.

Indrisor came to Turin's side and whispered. "Little One, the phylactery calls to me from the far side of the room."

Turin nodded and called everyone into a huddle. "Aridon and Sena, I need one of you at each of those holes. Let us know if the Grey Queen returns. Gromley, stand guard at the door with Neela. Make sure it stays open in case we need to make a hasty retreat. Shadow, Indrisor, and I will make our way across the room and see if we can locate the phylactery."

As Sena and Aridon crept to the edge of the pits, Turin led Indrisor and Shadow across the narrow passage between them. When they passed beyond the glow of Gromley's drift globe, Indrisor manifested a light globule of his own and sent it overhead.

The pillars on either side of the dais were destroyed. One stood, deep fissures running through its form, while the other lay toppled across the breadth of the room. Turin found a break in the massive stone column and led Indrisor and Shadow through the fracture, her leathers scraping against the sharp edges of stone. On the other side, they found the throne of Gromley's uncle, King Cepryn, which sat undisturbed on its dais. The chair was made from a single piece of flawless red hematite and bore a war hammer carved into its crest. Upon the chair sat a shard of clouded crystal.

Indrisor pointed at the phylactery with a bony finger. "That, Little One, is what we came here for. Remember, the vessel cannot be destroyed. In order to assure the black wyrm's demise, we must hide the phylactery within my pocket dimension, so his soul has nowhere to go."

"Understood." Turin felt a tremor run up her leg from deep within Mount Anvil. She shrugged it off. "We head directly to the pocket."

Indrisor tilted his head and furrowed his brow.

"What is it?" Shadow asked.

The wizard scrambled up the steps of the dais. He dropped to his knees before the throne.

"There's something wrong, yes. Come—look."

Turin and Shadow approached the throne.

The crystal was the length of Indrisor's forearm and was uncut at its base. It tapered to a polished point and was clear around its edges, with a smoky, dull grey interior.

"The soul is not within the phylactery," Indrisor said.

Turin's throat tightened. "What do you mean? The soul is not in the phylactery?"

Indrisor looked up at Turin, his eyes panicked behind his thick goggles. "When in possession of the tethered soul, the phylactery would contain a vortex of energy at its core."

"What are you saying?" Shadow asked.

"I am saying that Mesorith lives."

Turin's heart leaped in her chest. How could this be? Mesorith had not been seen since Umhra destroyed his physical form. It was always thought Silyarithe had failed to secure a suitable host for her father's return.

"Grab the phylactery. Let's get out of here."

Indrisor snatched up the crystal and passed it to Turin. "You take it. Yes, yes. Let us go."

Turin helped Indrisor to his feet. The room shuddered with the force of an earthquake.

"Hurry," Sena yelled from beyond the fallen pillar.

Indrisor and Turin stared at each other, then at Shadow. They spun to see a cloud of noxious gas blast forth from the hole by which Sena stood guard.

Turin ran, weaving her way between chunks of shattered pillar, Indrisor's rapid footfalls close behind. Her leathers snagged on sharp stone. She tore herself free. As she slipped from the pillar's grasp, she saw Aridon running to Sena's aid with his halberd at the ready.

Sena scrabbled back from the pit's edge, choking on the poisonous cloud, as an enormous green dragon emerged from the depths. Its claws dug into the stone floor, and it released a deafening roar.

"I shall consume you all," Mesorith bellowed as one of Shadow's daggers whirred past Turin's ear and glanced off an emerald scale.

As Turin ran for the door, she noticed that despite his grand stature, the dracolich's new form looked as though it had been exhumed from a grave. He had only one wing, and it was tattered beyond use. The rest of the body was heavily decayed, and its eyes were milky white.

Mesorith snapped at Sena but missed. He drew in a deep breath in search of his quarry. "I smell your filth. How dare you enter my lair."

Aridon leaped and buried his halberd in Mesorith's chest. The dracolich snarled and flicked Aridon from his form like an errant fly. Aridon careened across the room and tumbled to Gromley's feet.

With a thrash of his decrepit tail, Mesorith pounded Sena to the ground.

Turin slid to Sena's side and reached out for her connection with Tyveriel. There was no answer. She tried again, willing the stone floor to rise, and put a wall between them and the dracolich. Again, Tyveriel did not heed her call.

"No, no, no."

Mesorith stepped forward, putting Turin and Sena squarely between his fore claws. He looked down upon them and grinned, toxic fumes billowing from the gaps between his rotted teeth. He opened his mouth wide.

Turin felt the hair stand up on the back of her neck—a static charge building in the air.

"I think it's me you want, Black Wyrm." Indrisor sent a bolt of lightning crashing into Mesorith's putrescent neck.

The dracolich turned to face Indrisor. "I know this voice. It has been too long, wizard. I thought you would have died by now."

"We aren't all as careless with our time as you are."

"Nevertheless, I will take great pleasure in stripping the skin from your body."

Indrisor sent another bolt of lightning forth and struck Mesorith in the jaw. "I invite you to try, yes."

As Mesorith lumbered toward him, Indrisor looked to Turin, who was still huddled on the floor with Sena. "Go, Little One. I have a score to settle and will buy you the time you need to escape."

Mesorith again thrashed his tail. The serrated scales at its tip crashed down beside Turin and shattered the stone floor. "I think I would rather kill you all. This fetid form almost makes it sport."

Indrisor reached into his satchel and conjured a false image of the crystal Turin now possessed. He held it up to his enemy. "I hold in my hands your phylactery, Black Wyrm. I am certain it is of more value to you than the death of a few insignificant mortals."

Mesorith roared and charged blindly at Indrisor.

Turin climbed to her feet and hoisted an unconscious Sena over her shoulder while staring at the blasts of lightning and poison that fell away to the far side of the throne room.

"Come on, Turin," Shadow said as he came to her side. "It does our cause no good for us all to die here today. Indrisor knows what he's doing."

Turin held her gaze on the burgeoning battle before her. "Yes, we stick to the plan. We return to the pocket dimension, stow the phylactery, and head home. He will find a way to catch up."

Shadow dragged Turin to the doorway where Gromley and Aridon waited.

"I will try to heal her when we get to safety, if you can manage until then," Gromley said.

Aridon held out his brawny arms, blood streaming down his face from a gash on his forehead. "I'll carry. She's tiny."

He lifted Sena from Turin's shoulder as Gromley pushed the door wide to hasten their escape. The party funneled out of the throne room in retreat.

Indrisor had imagined this day for over a thousand years. Not even in his wildest dreams—of which there were many—did he expect to have the opportunity to come before his former captor and strike him down. Stealing the phylactery would have been sufficient revenge, but there is nothing quite like seeing the shock on your enemy's face at the moment of their demise.

Still, the dracolich was not to be underestimated. Indrisor threw a quail's egg to the ground. It shattered—its yolk oozing forth—and an orb of iridescent energy surrounded him.

Another blast of noxious gas buffeted the arcane shield the wizard had encased himself within. Light shimmered around him. He snickered.

"You will have to do better than that, yes. Did you think I came here completely unprepared for this encounter?"

Mesorith snarled and swatted furiously about the room, each stroke of his massive claws sailing wide of their intended target. "It is only a matter of time until your game comes to an end, Aldresor. Then, my fun begins."

Time. He'd had so much of it, and now couldn't give Turin and her friends enough. Mesorith was right. It was only a matter of time until this game would betray him as long as he defined the field of play as this room.

He threw his voice toward the corner of the room. "Having

trouble seeing me?"

Mesorith spun, his tail shattering the hematite throne. He charged toward the corner where Indrisor's voice originated.

Indrisor dashed for the doorway and stood brazenly in its midst. "It seems you have missed again, yes. This shell you have possessed is surely lacking, Black Wyrm."

Mesorith snarled, his lips curled, and teeth bared. "You will die. Your little tricks cannot save you from this inevitability."

"You will have to catch me first."

Indrisor ducked out of the doorway and crossed the bridge Turin had molded in the Gilded Corridor. He waited on Mesorith in the doorway to the Chapel of Anar.

Mesorith burst into the Gilded Corridor, blowing the throne room door from its hinges, and sending a shower of rubble across the hall as the wall crumbled around him. He took a deep breath and forced his way into the hall, his wing scraping the stone overhead. "I have your scent, wizard. I shall pursue you to the end of the earth if I must."

The real chase had begun.

Indrisor scrambled through the stone chapel with Mesorith in pursuit. The enraged dracolich threw pews across the room and crushed the hallowed altar underfoot. Indrisor could not recall a time when he felt so alive.

The two raced through the Cepryn ancestral hall. The remaining revenants shambled to their feet at the disturbance. A rusty glaive whirred over Indrisor's head. A war hammer pounded the stone beside him.

Through the doorway, Indrisor coursed down the stairwell and across the great hall through which the party had entered the Zeristar stronghold. Walls exploded as Mesorith barreled after him, gaining with each stride.

The lava tubes might slow him down. The soft white glow of one of his linum seed markers caught Indrisor's eye. He darted into the tunnel.

Mesorith released a cloud of poison into the tunnel and

furiously tore at the entry, then went quiet.

Indrisor slowed his progress, his chest heaving with exertion. He doubted the dracolich had given up his pursuit. Possibly, he knew another way back to his old lair. Despite his lungs burning, he broke back into a jog and then a full sprint.

He came to the edge of the lava falls and leaped off the cliff's edge. A much more expedient way down. Gravity was helpful that way.

Just before he crashed into the dark rocks below, he slipped a small wad of goose down into his mouth and chewed. His descent slowed, and he touched down gently on the searing hot earth.

He took off running across Turin's bridge over the magma river and back to Mesorith's old lair.

Indrisor stopped outside the cavern where Mesorith once held him prisoner and listened for a moment. All was quiet but for his own heavy breathing. He entered the cavern and slipped along the wall toward the lab. The stench was horrid.

A flash in the darkness, as a giant claw shot out from the shadows and splashed into a pool of acrid sludge. A wave of acid washed over Indrisor. His eyes stung and the smell of burning flesh filled the air as the acid corroded his tissue. Indrisor screamed.

"It would seem the advantage has swung in my favor." Mesorith's voice rumbled like thunder.

Indrisor staggered backward along the wall, disoriented from the pain that tore through him.

The dracolich emerged from the gloom, his gargantuan form little more than a blur. He drew a single razor-sharp claw down the length of Indrisor's back. Hot blood streamed within the wizard's robes.

Indrisor continued toward his former lab, knowing that reaching his pocket dimension was his only chance.

"This will prove far too easy," Mesorith said, raking another talon along Indrisor's shoulders.

"Yes, yes. You have proven yourself quite superior. Come, get your precious phylactery, and assure your future resurrection and my long-awaited demise."

A mote of light across the derelict lab beckoned to Indrisor through blurred sight and radiating pain. Indrisor dragged himself across the lab, faltering at the table at its center.

Mesorith wedged himself into the recess behind Indrisor. "A fitting place for your path to end."

As the dracolich brought another claw down upon Indrisor, the Wizard spun and grasped the tip of the talon in one hand and touched the mote of light behind him with the other. He was ripped through time and space, bearing a great weight as he dragged Mesorith with him.

The blinding light abated, and Indrisor's vision cleared. His wounds healed. He felt renewed. Mesorith appeared beside him in the same disheveled condition in which they had found him.

The dracolich spun in a circle within the cramped confines of the passage. "What have you done? Where have you taken me?" He tore at the tunnel walls but could not inflict any damage.

Indrisor ran down the hallway and through the door into his laboratory. "Come, little black wyrm. You are in my lair now!"

Mesorith went into a rage and charged after his captor. The doorway expanded to accommodate his massive scale and allowed him into the lab.

Indrisor waited across the room, quite proud of himself and the panic he had instilled in his adversary. Mesorith barreled across the lab, tables covered with colorful beakers and bubbling flasks moving from his path of their own accord. As he neared, Indrisor backed up into the doorway he stood before.

Mesorith joined him in the membranous tunnel where Iolis loomed in the distance. The sun burned bright behind it, casting the planet in shadow. "It's a shame you can't see how beautiful it is," Indrisor said. "I will miss it. Alas, all this serves a higher purpose than I ever could have imagined. I spent my life running from death. Now, I embrace it. I suggest you do as well."

Indrisor produced the imitation phylactery and threw it at Mesorith's feet. The dracolich greedily clutched it in a claw. "The real one was long gone before our battle, yes. Your eagerness to destroy me blinded you to your true target. Made all too easy by your current condition, of course. You were once much more formidable."

Mesorith snarled, trying to maintain some semblance of footing in the membranous corridor. "You will pay for this, Aldresor."

"I already have." Indrisor retrieved a small vial containing a single firefly. The insect blinked in a haphazard pattern as he looked it over. He crushed the vial and blew the firefly's remains into the air between him and Mesorith. A spectral sword formed in its place, glimmering with radiant power. Indrisor flicked his head, and the blade slashed the wall, drawing a massive gash nearly the length of the temporal bridge.

Air rushed from the tunnel through the flapping tear in the membrane. Mesorith searched for purchase but found none. With one last roar, he sprayed poison throughout the chamber and was sucked out into the vacuum of space.

Indrisor exhaled and allowed space to take him. He had always wanted to reach Iolis. Now, possibly, he would. He didn't feel any pain, just tremendous satisfaction as he watched the corpse of Mesorith spiral toward Iolis's dense atmosphere below. Indrisor closed his eyes and lost consciousness.

— ▲ —

Turin was the last out of the pocket dimension. She stumbled back into Ruari, her stomach in a knot, her head pounding. She placed her hands on her knees and fought the urge to paint the floor with chyme.

The rest of the party hovered over Sena, who lay unconscious on a nearby table. Turin shook her head and rushed to her friend's side.

"Call for a cleric," she demanded.

Shadow rushed from the room.

Turin sat at the table, holding Sena's hand. It was cold. Gromley had tried time and time again on their retreat to the pocket dimension to heal her, but to no avail. While his connection with the Peacebreaker was strong, it merely amplified the powers his suffusion with Anar granted. With his god supposedly dead, there was little he could do.

Turin's heart fluttered as she awaited Shadow's return. She couldn't lose Sena, let alone Indrisor. Her entire world was unravelling.

Shadow swept back into the room; a short man dressed in tan robes behind him. The cleric hurried to Sena and placed his hand on her forehead. He closed his eyes, and the silver rose icon he wore around his neck lit with purple energy.

The same light emanated from beneath his palm and cast Sena's face in stark shadows. The light faded.

"She is stable, My Queen," the cleric said. "Unfortunately, I am not powerful enough to wake her. It may take some time."

"Try again." Turin's blood boiled.

"My Queen?" the cleric asked, his gaze darting to Gromley.

"I said, try again."

"Turin," Gromley interceded. "It is beyond his ability. It is currently beyond mine as well. Let her rest. We will keep a close eye on her."

Turin huffed and stormed from the room.

As she barreled toward the door, not quite knowing her destination, she noticed her mother and aunt approaching. Could this day get any worse?

Alessa ran to Turin and scooped her into a firm embrace.

"I'm glad you made it back safely," Alessa said through choked back tears. "We were worried sick about you. Are you alright? You look upset."

"I'm fine, mother. Sena got hurt and Indrisor didn't make it back with us. I'm unsure what's become of him."

"Terrible news," Regent Avrette agreed. "Will Sena be alright?"

"So, I'm told. She remains unconscious."

"And the phylactery? Did you succeed?"

"The phylactery is secure in Indrisor's pocket dimension as planned."

Regent Avrette nodded. "But at a cost, it seems."

"We ran into some—unexpected resistance. The Grey Queen has reanimated Mesorith as a rather disgusting green dragon. It seems Indrisor couldn't resist the opportunity for revenge and bought us the time we needed to escape with the shard."

Regent Avrette steepled her fingers and pressed them to her lips. She sighed. "Unfortunate, but I'm glad the rest of you have returned safely."

Neela sprang up from Aridon's feet, faced Turin's direction and barked with alarm.

Turin turned to the dog. "What is it?"

"Light's gone," Aridon said as he slouched in a chair behind the anxious dog.

Turin spun. The mote of energy they had used so many times to travel to and from Indrisor's pocket dimension had vanished. She scrambled to its former location and looked for any sign of its presence.

"No." She glanced over her shoulder at her mother, whose dark almond eyes welled with tears. "No. This can't be."

Turin slumped to the floor and sobbed uncontrollably. Alessa ran to her side and wrapped herself around her daughter. Their victory had come at great personal cost.

CHAPTER 20

I should like to document the customs of the six varieties of giants. To date, I have only the good fortune to have encountered two. The others, I fear, are quite reclusive.

- *A Traveler's Guide to the Odd and Obscure by Sentina Vake* Unearthed from the Homestead in Maryk's Cay, month of Riet, 1407 AT

— ▲ —

The streets of Debreth were narrow and twisted, forming an endless maze impossible to navigate. The streets, like the unstructured array of foreboding towers that were present all over the city, were also constructed of blackened iron.

Shambling masses crowded the street, their shapeless, malformed bodies deteriorated from a discernible head and arms to little more than a puddle of flesh where they met the road. They left a trail of blood littered with chunks of putrid yellow tissue in their wake.

Umhra closed his eyes and tried to steady his mind. The endless parade of the grotesque and maimed, the continuous barrage of torture and death—it was all too much. Opening his eyes in resignation, he asked, "What are these abominations?"

Trogon Podion had stopped at the gate beside Umhra and

now stared at the path, a look of what Umhra could only assume was fear on their disfigured face. "Gaulykes," they said, dismissively. "They won't bother you. They are far too consumed with their own problems. My understanding is, they are the vain and selfish who looked only at their own well-being in their mortal lives."

Umhra kneeled and inspected the street his demon guide seemed so hesitant to accompany him on. He ran his finger over its surface, felt the burn of a razor carving into him. Smearing the blood with his thumb, he returned to Trogon Podion's side.

"I don't blame you. The roads themselves are cutting these things apart, aren't they? Slowly consuming them as punishment. I wouldn't set a bare foot on them either."

Umhra unfastened his leather bracers and took a step toward Trogon Podion.

The demon jumped back, hissed.

"I was just going to offer to strap these to your feet as protection." He held out the bracers as a gift. "It might be a little awkward, but no doubt it will be better than cutting your feet to shreds or me carrying you on my back."

Trogon Podion retched and held a foot out toward Umhra.

Umhra placed the bracers on the ground and fastened them to the demon's swollen feet as best he could, careful not to touch its skin.

"That should hold. Try them out."

Trogon Podion stepped onto the streets of Debreth. They shuffled their feet back and forth, waited a moment as though they wouldn't immediately notice the pain of failure, and then waded into the morass of gaulykes.

Umhra smiled, shook his head, and followed, holding his hands high over the gaulykes as he slipped between them.

"Do you know how to find Qaresdoth?" Umhra asked, catching up to his guide.

"No," said Trogon Podion. "I only head toward the clamber of the crowd. Can you hear them?"

Umhra hadn't paid attention to the persistent din coming from deep within the city. He had admittedly been too distracted by the shambling forms surrounding him. When first among them, he found himself transfixed by their tormented faces, the squelching of their lower forms as the roadway wore them down nick by nick. Now that he had seen so many, each identical to the last, he shifted his focus and heard the cheers of a crowd reverberating off the towers and echoing through the cramped streets.

"I do. Why do they cheer?"

"Entertainment, I suppose. It occurs to me a likely place to find an arch devil."

Umhra nodded and continued to push through the gaulykes, eager to rid himself of their company. Passing a curious structure in the shape of an orb for what he was certain was the third or fourth time, a great amphitheater interrupted the path forward.

Umhra's eyes burned and teared up as a pungent sulfurous smell assaulted his senses. The sea of gaulykes parted, leaving a clear path up a narrow ramp to the enormous oval coliseum at the very center of the city. From this proximity, Umhra could discern screams of terror interspersed between the patrons' chants.

"I dislike this place," Trogon Podion said, hesitating at the foot of the ramp. "It is unlikely those within will tolerate the presence of a demon."

"Stay close to me. I won't let any harm come to you."

"You speak as though you control my fate. That you have some interest in the future awaiting me."

"You are helping me, Trogon Podion. And have been most gracious in guiding me through these hells. How could I, in good conscience, not care for your well-being?"

Trogon Podion shook his head, leaving Umhra unsure whether out of befuddlement or disgust, and trudged forward.

They ascended the ramp and entered the amphitheater

through a vast archway carved with hellish beasts, their sinewy forms locked in combat. The torchlit tunnel within arced into the darkness in both directions, a toxic orange sky setting the stairs leading to the arena aglow.

Lesser devils roamed these halls, some resembling the imps Umhra had encountered years ago in the petrified woods on the outskirts of Meriden. Others were small black creatures covered in barbs with turned-up noses, and others still had goatlike heads and scaled humanoid bodies. The crowd roared overhead, and the building shook. Dust rained from the ceiling.

The devils gave Umhra a wide berth, snickering amongst themselves from the shadows. Umhra strode up the steps to the edge of the arena. He spun in a circle—a blur of expletive jeering devils surrounded him—until he spied a balcony along the far side of the wide, oval pit where a group of large devils lounged, their every whim being catered to by lithe, red-skinned devils bound in gold chains.

Umhra hurried back to Trogon Podion, who hid himself in a darkened recess beside the stairs. "I think I found Qaresdoth. Or at least a devil important enough to point us in his direction."

"For a turn, I will follow you." Trogon Podion retched.

"Are you sure?"

"It would be unwise for me to wait here by myself." The demon pointed to a pack of the barbed devils who showed an interest in this demon among them. "I think I would rather take my chances at your side, Ascended One."

"Very well. Follow me."

Umhra put a hand to Forsetae's hilt and strode down the hall, the sea of lesser devils parting.

What have you gotten us into now?

Umhra smiled as the sword's voice resonated in his mind. *Nothing worse than usual. I hope not to call upon you.*

Coming to the apex of the arc of the hallway, Umhra found another staircase leading up to the arena. At its base stood a behemoth of a devil, the color of rusted iron. Its skin pulled tight by muscles bulging between leather straps, it snarled as the pair approached.

"I seek an audience with Qaresdoth." Umhra focused on his icon, blue ether wafting from his form.

The devil huffed, rubbed a chin covered in warts. "Deseth notar felirir."

"He says—" Trogon Podion started.

"Somehow, I know what he says. Thank you, Trogon Podion."

Umhra turned back to the devil. "Enimi satara Qaresdoth."

The devil leaned in and stared unaffected into Umhra's eyes. The elongated nostrils of his turned-up nose drew in Umhra's scent. He gnashed his fists together, his knuckles sheathed in blackened demi-gauntlets covered in barbed spikes.

"Talara iktiki semenoth," Umhra said, stepping into the devil's gaze.

"Oh," Trogon Podion said with surprise, shuffling back from the pair.

The devil roared, thick sputum covering Umhra's face.

Umhra turned from the devil and wiped the phlegm from his cheek. Turning back—the devil's pectoral muscles twitching in anticipation of the pending confrontation—Umhra focused on his icon, the blue aura around him intensifying. He growled and pointed at the fiend.

The devil's pupils dilated. The behemoth scrambled back against the wall of the stairwell and covered its eyes like a child struck affright.

Umhra took another step toward it, sending the devil sliding farther along the wall, then strode up the stairs and waved for Trogon Podion to join him. The demon tripped up the first step in a hurry to keep pace. They left the fearful devil scuttling like a crab into the hallway to the raucous jeers of the crowd, which took far too much delight in their superior's terror.

The stairway opened onto an expansive balcony of muted

red stone which cast a shadow across the crowd for an uninterrupted view of the oval arena below. A cadre of diverse devils crowded the platform, picking from platters of unidentifiable fetid meat.

Umhra put a hand on the back of a sizeable fiend nearest to him, its corpulent form mottled in shades of purple. A light enveloped the devil and smoke rose from its flesh, filling the room with the smell of sulfur. The devil howled, the room's freneticism screeching to a halt—every creature in the room turning to glare at the Mystic among them.

The crowd parted and opened a clear path across the balcony. At the center of the overhang above the arena was a plush bed with red, billowing drapes. Upon the bed, among the piles of bright pillows and luxurious red sheets, lounged a twisted pile of glossy, black devils, writhing in untoward carnal acts.

Beyond them, a lanky devil with white skin covered in purple rune tattoos stood with their back to their guests. They gripped the blackened iron railing with elongated, purple hands as they peered upon the arena below.

Raising a hand, it beckoned Umhra forward with a wave, its eyes never leaving the field below.

"Don't speak until spoken to," Trogon Podion said, their voice flecked with panic.

Umhra nodded, eyed the crowd once more, and cautiously approached Qaresdoth's side at the edge of the balcony. The devil stood unclothed, displaying its androgynous body with unabashed pride. From bony ridges along the top of their skull protruded sweeping velvety branch-like antlers adorned with gold rings and deep engravings in the same infernal language as the tattoos on their body.

Umhra peered over the edge of the railing. His head briefly spun at the unexpected height. Shaking away the vertigo, he took in the oval pit filled with black sand and dotted with iron slabs, each glowing red hot. Five figures—three Iminti and two humans—jumped from slab-to-slab. Their eyes darted wildly about the arena, and they pointed and shouted at one another as if trying to identify a common threat.

It was then, a muscular devil twice the size of the guard whom Umhra frightened at the base of the stairs, materialized above them. It had cerulean skin with deep fissures that emitted a lava-like glow from within.

The beast roared, its mouth resembling that of a mange-ridden hyena with blood-stained canine teeth. It bristled the spines on its back and swept in for an attack on tattered reptilian wings.

As one of the human men, portly with a balding head dripping with sweat, jumped from one platform to the other, the devil vanished and appeared suddenly in the space between the two platforms. It caught the man on bony claws that protruded from the back of its hands—running him through—and lifted him overhead.

The crowd unleashed a deafening cheer as the man's blood covered the devil in a shower of gore. The man screamed, the others in the arena freezing on their respective platforms as the devil cast the impaled man from its claws into the sand below.

With every tumble, blood sprayed across the sand until the man came to rest near the base of an iron platform. He tried to hoist himself up on to all fours but failed and collapsed to the arena floor.

The sand writhed beneath him. The crowd hushed. The man tried once more to push himself from the ground, but the sand clung to him with armlike strands. More pseudopods lashed out, their hooked ends piercing the man's skin along his back.

He screamed, and another pseudopod lodged itself in his agape mouth. The pseudopods embedded in his back retracted and pealed the flesh from his form. The man's skinless body shuddered and collapsed to the floor, twitching violently. Slowly, the sand devoured him. The crowd roared, and the devil and the remaining contestants continued their game.

Qaresdoth turned and cocked their head. Their eyes glowed amber, and they had no discernible mouth or nose. "A corrupt banker," they said with a scoff. Emanating from narrow slits in their face that opened only when they wished to speak, Qaresdoth's voice was deep and as smooth as silk. "Do you find the punishment unfair for such an anemic soul?"

Umhra shook his head. "Unfair, no. Distasteful, somewhat."

Qaresdoth cocked a hairless brow. "What brings an angel of Kalmindon to my place of leisure? And with a demon in tow? I dare say you are lucky to have made it this far, keeping such company."

"I seek an audience with Naur."

"And for this, you seek passage through the Flesh Gate into Syf."

"Yes. If that is required."

The devil nodded, rubbed the back of their head with an open palm. "For this, there is a cost. One does not simply open the Flesh Gate and break the seal between the realms of devils and demons. I alone am given this charge."

"Name your price. I have no currency with which to barter. But I must get to the God of Fire."

Qaresdoth rubbed their hands together. "Very well, angel of Kalmindon. You shall fight in the pit as a test of your worth. If you win, I shall grant you access to Syf. Should you lose, your soul will live within my city for eternity."

"As I said, I have no choice but to accept. Let's get on with it. I have little time to spare on your games."

"Very well."

With a wave of their hand, the iron platforms in the arena dispersed into ash and the remaining contestants fell into the sand. To their screams, the crowd cheered as the sand pulled each of them below the surface. Another wave summoned the platforms to return but rearranged them so that they were spread out farther across the arena's surface.

Qaresdoth faced the crowd and held their hands in the air.

The arena fell silent.

"Consider yourselves lucky to be welcome in the arena on this day." Qaresdoth's voice boomed with preternatural vigor. "An angel of Kalmindon walks among us and wishes to prove himself in the Sands of Debreth. Make way for him to enter the field of battle for your entertainment."

The crowd broke into a frenzied chatter. Qaresdoth held their hands in the air and the raucous crowd once more grew silent.

"Make way for our Champion of Vaila. I grant him safe passage and extend the same courtesy to his companion, the slag demon."

The crowd jeered but parted, forming a clear path from the side of the balcony to the Sands of Debreth below.

Umhra nodded to Qaresdoth and then to Trogon Podion. He hopped the guardrail into the crowd and made way to the battlefield. Devils snickered and hissed, gasped, and snarled, but kept their distance, whether out of fear of Umhra or Qaresdoth was unclear. Reaching the edge of the arena, a sickly-looking yellow devil, covered in pustules, opened an iron gate and allowed Umhra into the arena.

The yellow devil slammed the gate behind Umhra. The crowd roared in anticipation of the coming entertainment.

Umhra leaped onto the nearest iron slab and strode to its center. Upon his touch, the slab glowed red, the intense heat it generated tearing through the soles of Umhra's boots and rippling the air around him.

The devil that had impaled the banker landed on another platform across the arena floor. It roared and gnashed the claws on the back of its fists together. The light emanating from within the beast intensified, shifting from its lava-like glow to a searing white. The fissures in its skin split wide and the devil grew to a most impressive size, its bones cracking and reassembling themselves to form a larger frame. Its transformation complete, the devil roared again, and leaped into the air on enlarged wings.

Umhra focused on his icon and summoned Forsetae and his armor. Nothing happened. He thought about his wings. Nothing happened. He tried to connect to Vaila, as he had so many times since accepting his destiny on the way to Meriden those years ago. Nothing happened. His magic was of no use in this house of the damned.

He snarled and looked to the balcony where Qaresdoth stood watching, their hands splayed wide on the guardrail. The arch devil's eyes smiled fiendishly, the devil from the base of the stairs coming to Trogon Podion's side and placing a hand firmly on their shoulder.

Trogon Podion gripped the rail, but the devil pried the demon away from its perceived safety and dragged them from Umhra's sight.

Distracted, Umhra's adversary was upon him sooner than he had expected. Umhra rolled from the attack, sliding across the smooth surface of the platform to its edge. The devil crashed into the platform, two enormous fists slamming into red-hot iron.

Umhra leaped over black sand—his jump carrying him further than he had expected—and landed on the next platform. He spun to face the devil, who shook its head in disgust and took once more to the air in pursuit.

Umhra ran the length of the slab, glancing over his shoulder at the devil, who gave chase. Approaching the edge, he jumped for the next.

The devil threw a fist into the air and a wall of fire shot up from the sand before Umhra which obscured the slab on which he intended to land.

Umhra careened through the inferno, blistering heat searing his flesh. He emerged from the other side and crashed awkwardly into the awaiting slab. He beat at his hair and then his leathers to extinguish the remaining flames.

The devil's long, prehensile tail lashed out from the wall of flame and coiled around Umhra's ankle. The devil landed at the edge of the slab and casually yanked Umhra's feet out from under him.

The crowd cheered.

Umhra's back cracked against the iron slab, knocking the air from his lungs. The heat was unbearable, his leathers offering only a modicum of insulation. He coughed, fought for every breath.

The devil dragged Umhra toward him, licking his lips in anticipation of his victory. It dropped to its knees and straddled Umhra. The beast sat back, its considerable weight an anvil upon Umhra's stomach. Umhra strained to keep his core tight and not let the air escape his lungs again.

The devil punched Umhra across the face, his head snapping to the side and everything going black for a second. A warm stream of blood crossed his face and pooled in his ear. He covered his face with his arms as another blow struck him, the claws on the back of the devil's hands tearing through his forearms.

The crowd roared with delight as the devil flexed its gargantuan arms, as if to prove his strength was irrefutable.

Umhra closed his eyes and focused his mind. He searched for Vaila once more, but no connection remained. What was he without his god and the magic she granted him? What was he without Forsetae and his armor? He was just a man—even less—a half-breed Orc.

No.

It was he who jumped into the Portal of Pragarus. It was he who the Creator Gods deemed worthy. It was he who killed Mesorith and confronted the Grey Queen. He ascended to Kalmindon—the first Mystic reborn since the Age of Grace. He was no longer just a man—no longer just a half-Orc. He was Umhra the Peacebreaker.

Umhra opened his eyes, another fist hurtling at him. He met the blow with an open palm and stopped the devil's momentum with his own strength. Umhra shifted his grip to around the devil's wrist and threw the beast from atop him.

Umhra staggered to his feet and wiped the errant strands of hair from his blood and sweat soaked face. The devil arrested its slide by digging its claws into the heated iron. The two combatants squared off.

The devil charged, its eyes burning red with indignation. The two grappled at the center of the iron slab, encircled by a wall of fire. The devil lunged at Umhra, jaws snapping just shy of his neck.

Umhra used the devil's momentum to swing onto its back and bar his arm across the beast's bulging neck. With a strength even he didn't know he possessed, Umhra wrapped his other arm around the back of the devil's head and squeezed.

The devil grabbed the arm crushing its trachea, and pulled. Umhra's grip held fast. The devil punched wildly at Umhra, raining blow after blow on his shoulders and the side of his head. Umhra's grip held fast. The devil dropped to its knees. Umhra's feet met the ground, allowing him to leverage his choke hold even further.

With a forceful jerk, Umhra felt the bones in the devil's neck shatter. The beast's arms went limp and the inferno that raged around them abated. Umhra hurled the devil into the Sands of Debreth. The crowd gasped and fell silent.

With the back of his hand, Umhra wiped the blood from the corner of his mouth and looked at Qaresdoth. The arch devil offered a shallow bow of respect and waved Umhra to rejoin him on the balcony.

Umhra sprung from the iron slab. In that one bound, he cleared the guardrail of the arena and landed in the frenzied crowd. Relieved of the unfair rules of the arena, he summoned Forsetae to his hand, expecting further resistance.

Instead, the devils gave him a wide berth, offering an ample path to the balcony. Umhra strode for Qaresdoth, the crowd bowing as he passed.

"You did well, considering you did not enquire as to the rules," Qaresdoth said, running a hand over the velvet of his antler. "You really should exercise more caution. Especially when in the home of an arch devil. We aren't known to be particularly trustworthy."

"Where's the demon?"

"I gave you my word the foul beast would be safe. My word—unlike that of so many others—means something. I simply had the slag demon removed from public sight, so that should you have been torn apart in the arena, the crowd would not turn to them next. I will have them brought to you at the Flesh Gate."

"I'd prefer them returned to me presently."

Qaresdoth tilted their head with narrowed eyes. "You've grown fond of it? The Ascended are unfathomable to me. You hold us in such disdain, and yet you will fraternize with a demon? To each their own, I suppose. Very well, I'll have your friend brought to us directly."

Umhra nodded, allowed Forsetae to dissipate. Noting the still writhing mass of devils on the bed behind them, Umhra grimaced. "Can you have them stop that while I wait?"

Qaresdoth peered over Umhra's shoulder. "No. But, you can tell me what you seek from Naur. I dare say he will not take your return to Pragarus in measure."

"Why would you concern yourself with that?"

"Why wouldn't I? He led countless of my kind to their doom in his foolhardy attempt to return to Evelium. He set the balance of power between the devils and demons into disarray. I do not blame you or your god for this. I blame our naivety and his deceitful nature. If you have come to kill him, I bid you well."

Trogon Podion shuffled into the room, followed by the devil Umhra had frightened on the stairwell earlier.

Umhra snarled at the devil, who averted its eyes and nodded in a modest bow.

"Now that you have reunited with your—friend, Nolox will guide you to the Flesh Gate."

"Thank you, Qaresdoth."

Qaresdoth turned back toward the arena and threw a hand in the air. "Be on your way, Ascended One. I have souls to claim."

Umhra followed Nolox from Qaresdoth's balcony and into the bowels of the arena where they came upon an expansive room of rough-hewn stone as black as the night of the Reaping Moon. At the far side, a mass of pulsating pink flesh filled a break in the stone, purple veins running just beneath its surface. The gate writhed.

"Lovely," Umhra said, taking a step closer. "How do we get through?"

Trogon Podion shrugged. "I don't know of these things."

From the dark recesses across the perimeter of the room emerged a dozen devils, all resembling Nolox and armed with terrible looking axes and maces made of blackened steel.

"Bellera sarastrin albari, Qaresdoth," Nolox said, gnashing his armored knuckles together.

"I'm sure you've misunderstood their instructions," Umhra said, summoning Forsetae. "You don't want to do this."

"Testra uni garatharius Nolox."

Umhra rolled his eyes. "Well, I apologize for that, but I needed to see Qaresdoth, and you weren't going to let me without a fight. You should be thanking me."

Nolox took a swing at Umhra's head, but Umhra ducked before the blow connected and dropped to his knees in the ashen dirt. He searched for the surge of power he had felt within him in the arena and thought of the devils being cast across the room. He imposed his will outward with all his might. To a deafening clap of thunder, a shockwave burst forth and threw Nolox and his allies from their feet.

Nolox broke against the unforgiving stone walls of the cavern, his head splitting wide. Most of his companions also met their fate upon the walls and slumped to the ground, motionless. One of them, however, crashed into the Flesh Gate.

Countless hands reached out from the gate and grabbed the fiend. The devil screamed as the gate incorporated it into its writhing mass.

The cavern fell quiet.

Umhra sighed. "Do you have any thoughts on how we get through? We obviously can't just push our way."

Trogon Podion hadn't even had time to move during the short-lived confrontation with the devils. He waddled around in a circle, surveying the mess strewn about the room.

"I would agree that touching the gate would likely be a mistake," the demon said, unaffected. "Possibly, we need to damage the flesh?"

"As good an idea as any, I suppose."

Umhra approached the Flesh Gate, Trogon Podion a step behind him. He thrust Forsetae into the gate, the flesh giving way more easily than he expected.

The gate quivered—countless voices screaming in pain—and receded in the area around Forsetae's blade.

Umhra withdrew the sword and swiped a broad stroke across the gate's surface. Blood sprayed from the gash. The flesh again recoiled. With relentless vigor, Umhra slashed the gate repeatedly, carving a tunnel for him and his guide through the Flesh Gate.

The screams of the damned reverberated within the narrow confines of the passage. Umhra's eyes stung with sweat, the heat intensifying with every stroke of his blade. From the opaque darkness of the flesh before them emerged a muted light.

Forsetae pierced the wall, breaking free of the tissue's resistance. Umhra wrenched the blade upward and slipped a foot through the burgeoning hole. His shoulder followed, and he emerged from the Flesh Gate.

Trogon Podion followed suit and the Flesh Gate closed behind them. They surveyed the landscape. "We have arrived in Syf," the demon said, coagulated blood dappling its form. "The most elevated of the demon realms."

"Is this your homeland?" Umhra noted the twisted maze of narrow black iron bridges that spanned an endless expanse of sulfurous lakes of yellow and green, broken only by strips of brittle, burnt-orange crust.

"No. My kind are unworthy of Syf." Trogon Podion retched. "I come from Himma, the lowest of the demon rings."

Umhra nodded, the Flesh Gate healing over the wound he had created and sealing them in Syf.

Trogon Podion pointed across the maze to a tower looming against an ominous purple sky. "This, however, is where we will find Naur."

CHAPTER 21

The gods were meant to walk at mankind's side, not hide in Kalmindon while our people suffer poverty, disease, and war.

- The Elevation of Naur by Alabaster Beryl
Unearthed from the Ruins of Meriden, month of Mela, 1399
AT

— ▲ —

The bridge was no wider than Umhra's shoulders, its surface slick with oily grime. Fumes from the acrid pits below billowed into the air and burned Umhra's eyes and throat. Trogon Podion shuffled ahead, thin arms held out stiffly to the sides to maintain their balance as they navigated the labyrinth of elevated pathways.

More assured of his footing and more easily offended by the fumes, Umhra buried his face in the crook of his arm. Keeping an eye on his unsteady guide, Umhra pressed on through the maze.

They came to a fork in the path. Trogon Podion peered at each branch and shook their head. "To this point, the path has been obvious. I am uncertain which way to go."

"Give me a moment of quiet and I may be able to discern how we should proceed."

Trogon Podion turned their back and Umhra shut his eyes. He thought of Vaila—trying to connect with his god. He saw her image in his mind, but it faded. Umhra shook his head. Then, he thought of something she had said to him before he left her in Kalmindon. *It is time for you to believe in yourself, Umhra.*

Maybe none of this was about her and the power she provided through their bond. Maybe it was about *him*, the vessel. He relied upon his own inner strength within the arena and later at the Flesh Gate. It was time for him to shed his reliance on Vaila and place it in himself.

He grabbed his icon, its sharp edges digging into the palm of his hand. He focused on his inner strength and thought of all those things Vaila's power alone was not able to accomplish.

A power greater than he had ever possessed before surged through his body in a flood of warmth. He opened his eyes. Ether streamed from his form, but whereas it had always manifested as cerulean wisps, it now shown pure white. Umhra slipped his hand through the radiance.

He turned his focus back to the mission at hand. The maze revealed itself to him, and he pointed down the path to the left. "We will find what we seek this way."

Trogon Podion nodded, ignoring the change in Umhra's aura, and trudged onward.

They neared a great tower of dark stone that rose from a solitary sawtooth mountain. Upon the tower's façade swarmed untold numbers of winged creatures reminiscent of overgrown blow flies. The creatures scuttled about on stalk-like legs, regurgitating from elongated proboscises onto rotting cadavers chained to the steep walls. Two arms protruded from their bulbous green thoraxes just before the base of the wings, which they used to tear chunks of flesh from the corpses.

Trogon Podion pointed to the fiends. "Bylox. A lower form of demon employed by the lords to rid their purview of waste." Turning back to the tower, their foot caught on the edge of the pathway and Trogon Podion toppled off the side.

Umhra dove and slid further than he expected on the pathway's slick surface but grabbed hold of Trogon Podion's ankle.

The demon screeched as the flesh around their leg burned red at Umhra's touch. They craned their head to look into Umhra's eyes, as torment spread across their face.

Umhra's mind flashed back to Bat in that fateful moment within the bowels of Telsidor's Keep. He saw Bat fall from his grip and plummet into the abyss. His screams resonated as though it were yesterday.

"I know it hurts but stay as still as you can. I will save you."

Beads of sweat streamed down Umhra's face, stinging his eyes, and filling his mouth with their salty tang. He reached down with his other hand, his chest sliding over the precipice, his feet catching hold on the far edge of the narrow pathway and holding fast. He grabbed Trogon Podion's other squat leg, eliciting another scream and unleashing the unpleasant odor of burning putrescence.

"This will not be easy, but the only way I'm going to get you back up here is to swing you to the left. You will slide some when you land on the bridge, but I don't think you will go far enough to fall off the other side."

"Hurry." Trogon Podion retched. "I wish you to release me."

Umhra swung the demon back and forth, gaining momentum with each arc. As Trogon Podion's head breached the edge of the bridge, Umhra released their ankles and the demon lifted into the air and landed on the unforgiving metal with a thud. They slid across the surface to the other edge, only stopping when Umhra once again grabbed hold of their leg.

Umhra released Trogon Podion as soon as he was sure they were safe. He sat, errant hairs dangling before his eyes, and sighed.

"Why did you do that?" Trogon Podion asked, their tone flecked with anger.

"Do what? Save your life?"

"I would rather fall to my death than wear the brand of a Celestial. My kind shall forever mark me as a heretic."

Umhra looked at the demon's ankles. Where his hands had gripped them, the dirty white flesh had been seared away and replaced by glowing gold bands. "I didn't want to see any harm come to you."

Trogon Podion spat at Umhra's feet. "These markings will lead my kin to consider me lower than the bylox." There is no greater insult. I will see you to Naur and then we shall go our separate ways."

It seemed to Umhra he could do no right by his guide. He felt bad enough already for having enlisted Trogon Podion on this quest, and now he'd branded them a heretic. Exasperated, Umhra climbed to his feet. "There is a place for you in Kalmindon, should you choose a better life. I only have that to offer as an apology."

Trogon Podion turned his back and made way for Naur's tower.

Umhra followed, as he had grown accustomed to doing during his time in Pragarus. While they walked in silence, he stared at the glowing rings around the demon's ankles and thought of what he could have done differently had he known the ramifications of his actions.

Coming to the end of the maze, they climbed the twisting path lined with pikes—each boasting a robed corpse—that led to the portcullis of the tower. Dried blood stained the weathered black robes the corpses wore. Directly before the portcullis, Umhra stopped at the final pike, allowing Trogon Podion to continue without him. The corpse skewered upon it wore the remnants of a red cloak with a black inverted cross upon its chest. Its decaying face had one eyeball plucked from it, and its intestines hung to the ground like a bell rope. Beneath its chin was a terrible gash where a dagger had pierced the dead man's head.

"I suppose he took your failure personally."

The corpse's neck cracked, the head twisting awkwardly to look down upon Umhra. The remains of Evron Alabaster, former Grand Master of the Brothers of Resurrection, opened its mouth to speak, but only black oil poured forth instead of words.

Umhra nodded. "A fitting end."

Umhra strode forward to catch up with Trogon Podion as they crossed beneath iron gates and into an empty courtyard of black sand. Above, the outer walls of the tower dripped with decay as the bylox buzzed dutifully from corpse to corpse.

At the far side of the courtyard, a yawning doorway beckoned them forward to the dark interior of the tower. They complied.

The room within was lit by iron braziers along both sides that formed a wide aisle to an ornate throne carved of obsidian. In the great chair sat a demon at least twice Umhra's size. The demon's skin was a rich scarlet but for its black bat-like wings, which it held curled at its back, framing a monstrous face with beady opalescent eyes and a pair of twisted, sweeping black horns.

"Come, introduce yourselves." The demon's prehensile tail twitched enticingly at its feet. "I am eager to meet those who would trespass on Naur's sacred ground. And what an odd couple it is—a Mystic and a slag demon. I expect to be entertained."

Umhra sensed that his mission to Pragarus was nearly complete and strode forward to confront the demon. Trogon Podion dropped to their knees and bowed their head solemnly.

"I am Umhra the Peacebreaker, Champion of Vaila. I come on my god's behalf for a private audience with the esteemed God of Fire. He will remember me, no doubt. Who, may I ask, are you?"

The demon cocked an eyebrow, its lips curling into a fiendish smile of fangs. "I am Mygar, Lord of Syf and Guardian of Naur's Tower. There are but two ways to gain access to the one you seek; through that door or through me."

"We'll take the door, if it's all the same."

Mygar gestured to an iron door to his left and nodded. "As you wish."

Umhra made for the door, all the while watching Mygar. Convinced the demon had no interest in moving from his throne, he turned his attention to the banded iron before him. The door gave in to a gentle tug and swung open, exposing a corridor lined with oil lamps. At the far end, a seemingly identical door hid among the shadows.

Trogon Podion entered the hallway, and Umhra let the door close behind them. "Too easy," he whispered. "Does it strike you as odd?"

"My corruption would undoubtedly attract the attention of a demon lord and compel them to punish me." Trogon Podion retched. "Mygar made no mention of this offense."

They came to the end of the hallway, and Umhra inspected the door by the honeyed glow of the lamplight. He shrugged at Trogon Podion and pushed the door open. In the next room, Mygar sat before them on his throne, a toothy grin across his face. Umhra looked around, noting that they re-entered the room through the same door they used to leave.

"The path less fraught with confrontation is not always the correct path, Mystic." Mygar stood and retrieved an immense mace from beside his obsidian perch. Cast in a black alloy, the weapon had demonic runes carved upon the seven flanges that made up its sharpened ridged head. The weapon crackled with electricity that arced between the flanges and from its spiked finial down the engraved shaft.

The demon unfurled his wings and lifted into the air.

Umhra's heart sank. He was tired of having to prove himself over-and-over again. He was tired of sharpened steel deciding his worth relative to another's. Tired of blood drawn, of limbs severed. Of life taken. It wasn't for lack of conviction in his cause, but rather the intense conviction that there was more to his story than carving his way through heaven and hell in the name of his god. He pushed his thoughts of duty to Vaila and Kalmindon from his mind and focused on the power within himself.

Wisps of white ether surrounded him, and his armor materialized. Forsetae came to his hand and angelic wings sprouted from his back. Trogon Podion recoiled at the brilliance of his form.

Your power grows within you. Forsetae said.

Umhra leaped into the air and took flight with Mygar in his sights. The two clashed among the arching vaults of the ceiling. Their weapons locked, roots of electrical energy discharged from Mygar's mace and coursed through Umhra's body.

Mygar sneered and threw Umhra backward, sending him tumbling through the air and crashing into the wall behind him. Stone shattered under the force of the impact.

Umhra shook his head, his ears ringing. He launched himself from the wall and dashed for Mygar, with Forsetae at the ready. With gritted teeth, he swung Forsetae down upon his foe, but Mygar vanished, instantly reappearing across the room.

Umhra changed course, sweeping across the perimeter of the room. Mygar tracked his path and flourished his mace. Umhra attacked again, arresting his momentum as he approached to allow the head of Mygar's mace to hurtle past his face. He slashed Forsetae across the demon's shoulder, drawing forth a spray of molten hot ichor.

Mygar howled—his eyes burning as hot as coals—and countered with a back-handed strike from his mace. Umhra's ribs cracked, the wind forced from his lungs. Mygar lifted his mace overhead and brought it down upon Umhra with all his might, driving him to the floor far below.

Umhra coughed up blood, grabbed at his ribs with his free hand. Mygar landed beside him. "I would have expected more from a Mystic," he scoffed. "To think our realms deem us equals." He raised his mace overhead with both hands.

Trogon Podion clambered. "No." They retched. "He deserves..."

With little more than a flick of his massive arm, Mygar swatted Trogon Podion aside with his mace. The smaller demon careened across the room, crashed against the wall, and slumped to the floor.

"Tainted thrall," Mygar spat. "Now, where was I?"

Umhra rolled to his feet as Mygar turned back to him, his mace meeting the stone floor with a thunderous crash. Forsetae hummed past Mygar, narrowly missing his neck. Umhra lunged, Mygar parried with his weapon.

Umhra advanced, determined not to allow the demon any quarter. Mygar stumbled backward and then vanished.

Behind you, to your left. Forsetae resonated in Umhra's mind.

Umhra spun and released Forsetae. The blade twirled through the air toward the cloudy image of Mygar just appearing across the room. Forsetae struck Mygar at the moment he materialized and pierced his muscular chest. Run through, the demon collapsed to the ground.

"I was going to let you live," Umhra said. "But seeing as you paid my guide no such respect, I shall withhold mine." Forsetae turned to vapor and reappeared in Umhra's hand as he came to Mygar's side.

Blood streamed from the gaping wound in Mygar's chest and spread like molten lava across the surrounding floor. As the blood cooled, it hardened into black stone.

Mygar pushed himself up to a seated position and snarled, his teeth coated in blood.

"You've won your..."

Umhra took the demon's head from him with a two-handed slash of his blade. Mygar's head toppled to the floor and his corpse burst into flame.

Umhra ran to Trogon Podion who lay slumped against the wall. He kneeled in the pool of viscous blood surrounding them.

The demon was breathing, albeit shallowly. Umhra shook his head and rubbed his hands together.

Placing a palm on Trogon Podion's chest, Umhra focused on his icon and thought of sharing his life force as he had when he resurrected Gromley. White wisps of celestial energy engulfed Trogon Podion. Their flesh did not burn as it had when Umhra saved him in the maze, but instead turned a brilliant white— their lesions and rot healed along with the wounds inflicted by Mygar's mace. The light faded.

"Do not weep for me, Ascended One," Trogon Podion said, their eyes blinking open, their voice weak. "Torment has followed me for ages and the darkness that calls me seems a welcome relief. I fear not the void as long as I have no memory of this place...of this form." Trogon Podion closed their eyes, their body falling limp as they released their final breath.

An unfathomable rage welled up within Umhra. He gritted his teeth and pounded the stone floor with his fist, shattering it.

"If the little fiend means that much to you, harness their soul before it is too far gone and bring their essence with you."

Umhra looked over his shoulder to see Naur standing behind him. The demon god had three scars on his torso where Vaila's swords and Forsetae had pierced his amethyst skin and bound him to the hells of Pragarus for all eternity. His broken horn had regrown since Umhra saw him last, his wings no longer torn, but smooth and sleek and his vermillion eyes glowed bright. A fitting appearance for a god.

"Harness their soul?"

"Yes. Any Mystic is capable of such things. Just call out to their soul with your mind and beckon them to join you. If they are willing, they will come to you."

Umhra hesitated, wary to trust the God of Fire.

"Its soul won't wait forever," Naur said. "They sounded eager to depart."

Umhra closed his eyes and thought of Trogon Podion. A clear image of the demon formed in his mind. They were walking away from him into a storm of purple smoke and black ash.

Come back to me, Trogon Podion, my friend. I will carry you to Kalmindon, where you shall join the souls of the redeemed. There is no need for you to greet nothingness when you can know the meaning of tranquility after a life of undeserved suffering.

The image in Umhra's mind stopped amidst the swirling storm. It turned and looked at Umhra, tilted their head in curiosity. Umhra continued his plea.

I have seen the heavens I speak of. It will not be a straightforward path to make it safe once more, but we have already traveled a hard path together. Don't give up on me now.

Trogon Podion looked at the storm around them and shrugged. Without a word, they walked to Umhra and took his hands in theirs. Nodded.

Umhra opened his eyes to a burgeoning warmth in the palms of his clasped hands. When he unfolded them, a mote of golden energy swirled within the cup they formed. The energy coalesced into a glass bead like those he saw in the gardens of Kalmindon. He smiled and turned his attention back to Naur.

"Thank you."

Naur nodded. "I can only assume my sister has sent you to commandeer my power and become the One God."

"I am here, as it is the only course of action if we are to stop Spara's assault on the pantheon and restore order to Kalmindon. I have no aspirations to become a god. Nor do I care to intervene in your family squabbles." Umhra climbed to his feet and tucked the glass bead containing Trogon Podion's soul into the blue velvet pouch strapped to his belt.

"What made her think sending you to achieve such a feat was wise? Did she not think I would resist?"

"It was my idea. Admittedly, I expected to find you still bound to the wall where I had seen you last. I wasn't expecting to waste my time trekking through hell to track you down. To have to wade my way through devils and demons to realize my goal." Umhra gestured to Mygar's corpse with a wave of his hand.

"Hardly a waste of time. Did you not see the most deplorable of your kind? The most corrupt and twisted of mortal minds?"

"I did."

"Such a lesson is invaluable to one who seeks wisdom."

Umhra nodded. His travels had been enlightening. But now was not the time for philosophical pursuits. He could not let Spara win. He drew the diamond dagger from his belt.

"And now that you find me quite untethered and having reclaimed my strength?"

"I expect to have to kill you. Or die trying."

Naur chuckled under his breath, rubbed a clawed hand over the back of his neck. The demon god smirked and raised a hand in request for Umhra to pause.

"I assure you, Champion of Vaila, this would not end well for you. While I appreciate your zealotry and your growing power is undeniable, you are no god yet. I knew when you sealed my fate to live out eternity in these hells, among these beasts, you would one day return to release me from my imprisonment." Naur hung his head. "Alas, I tire of my existence in Pragarus, and the prospects of my future are bleak."

Naur took a few slow, calculated steps toward Umhra. His wings bristled with each step. Umhra held his ground, the diamond dagger trained on the demon god in anticipation of the coming battle.

"I agree to your ascension, Umhra the Peacebreaker. I choose to rejoin my sister and brothers as part of the One God." A few more steps and Naur was inches away from Umhra's blade. "With one caveat, of course."

Umhra drew in a deep breath. "That is?"

"We end this with civility—with a mutual respect befitting of our stations. I shall not give you the satisfaction of taking my power, but give it to you freely as my ultimate gift to Tyveriel should you answer me a simple question."

Umhra searched the demon god's face for signs of a ruse. Found none. Nodded in agreement.

"Of those untold masses who have fallen by your will, which have you not been able to forgive yourself for?"

Umhra cocked his head and stared into Naur's glowing eyes. He was silent for a long moment. "I bear the full weight of each and every one of them." He paused again. "Not because I was unjust in my actions, as I wholly believe I acted with virtue. Rather, I carry the burden as a stain that can never be washed away. It matters not that I carried my deeds out in the name of my god or for causes I deemed worthy. Each death at my hand burdens me all the same."

Naur nodded contemplatively. "You would make a terrible king. I do, however, believe you have the makings of a god. I well know how you, in your limited ability, perceive me. That I am some maniacal force of chaos, hell-bent on total dominion. But I too believe my past actions were, as you say, just. I had a vision for Tyveriel. A vision that I know would have ushered in an age of peace and equality. Because I believed so blindly in my cause, I waged war against the mortal races and my own family. I aligned myself with devils and demons. I too carry the ramifications of those actions with me." He took a step closer to Umhra and held out an open hand. "I concede to my sister's wishes and welcome our reunification."

Tentatively, Umhra turned the dagger over in his hand and offered it to Naur, pommel out. Naur gripped the diamond shard, inspected its every facet. The dagger glowed at the demon god's touch as if beckoning his very soul.

With a feigned smile, Naur plunged the dagger into his own chest. The light emanating from the dagger intensified, and Naur's eyes widened with fright. He staggered backward against the stone wall, slid sideways, and tumbled to the floor.

Umhra rushed to his side, kneeled, and took Naur's hand.

Naur laughed as the aura of the blade grew in intensity and enveloped his form. "I never thought I would fear my end, having faced it so many times before. But now, with the moment upon me, fear is all I feel. There is no pride left. No self-righteous indignation. Only the unfiltered sting of fear."

"You've done right by Tyveriel. It's what you always wanted. You will live on as a part of me and I will not shy away from it. Allow yourself the peace of knowing your legacy will not be one of obstinance, but one of altruism. I shall make that known."

Naur gripped Umhra's hand firmly and then released. A mote of scarlet light transferred from his body into the dagger and shot from its pommel into Umhra's icon. Umhra's pyramid lit and showered him in a magenta aura as Naur's power mixed with his own. Naur's body crumbled to dust. The light lifted Umhra to his feet and into the air, exalting him. It wrapped him in a celestial cocoon and then absorbed into his body.

He settled upon the floor. The heat of Naur's power coursed through his veins, flooded his mind with knowledge of the past, knowledge of alternate planes of existence, knowledge of other lands beyond Tyveriel, knowledge possessed only by the God of Fire.

Umhra opened his eyes, returned to the fluttering light of the braziers. Was he now a god? Was that all it took?

He retrieved the diamond dagger from the floor where ash now swirled about the room where Naur once lay. The shard glowed at his touch. He stared at it for a moment and considered how immortality was a ruse. Time simply moved slower for the gods. He sheathed the blade and pondered his next move.

Kemyn would be next. He thought of the majestic wild stag that greeted him in the Morion Swamp and imparted upon him the first piece of rhodium he needed to achieve his ascension to Mysticism.

Come to me, Peacebreaker. A deep, sonorous voice resonated in Umhra's mind. *I have heard my sister's plea and await our union.*

He saw the twisted roots of a dense forest floor. He focused on this tranquil place and teleported from the hells of Pragarus to the next of the creator gods.

CHAPTER 22

I plan to give my phylactery to Little One. She will know the right time to return me to the living.

- Entry from Aldresor's Journal
Undated. Discovered: The Tower of Is' Savon, month of Riet, 1444 AT

— ▲ —

Two days had passed since the events in Mesorith's lair, and Sena remained comatose. Turin had her moved into Indrisor's quarters where she had been staying as she wallowed in the wizard's loss. Life would never be the same. There would forever be an emptiness where his light once shone. She thought of his crooked smile and thick glasses—the way his hair jutted out in white tufts from the sides of his head. She cried.

Gromley and the other clerics came and went. They did what they could to heal Sena but were limited by a silver suffusion's inability to impart life. Or so Gromley said. With his own suffusion inert, they would have to wait for Sena to awaken on her own should the gods see fit.

At night, Turin slept in a chair at Sena's side. During the day, she tore Indrisor's quarters apart, looking for a way to reopen his pocket dimension. A way to get him back. She started with the bookshelves. She searched tome after tome looking for notes that would guide her in the right direction. Starting with his favorites, Turin worked her way through the library until she had scoured every page of even the most obscure book in Indrisor's collection.

Next, she rifled through his desk. Each cubby of the interior contained countless hand scribbled notes on faded parchment, none of which made much sense.

This morning, she started with the black walnut gentleman's chest, with plans to tackle Indrisor's footlocker before bed, should time allow. She paused and looked in the tarnished mirror perched atop the chest. She frowned at what looked back at her. Her disheveled raven-blue hair looked every bit like the bird's nest befitting its color. The black rings around her eyes were even darker than normal.

Turin shook off the disappointment and pulled the last drawer from the gentleman's chest. She couldn't tell if the legs were uneven or if it was the floor that caused it to wobble as she dismantled it. Either way, she didn't suppose it mattered, but it would have driven her mad if it was in her quarters.

She dumped the drawer's contents onto a nearby table, already cluttered with baubles, and tossed the drawer onto a teetering pile of its siblings.

"How long have you been going through all of this junk?" Sena asked from Indrisor's bed. Her voice was shaky, weak.

"He had to leave some clue behind. Some way to bring him back. A man doesn't simply live for thousands of years and then just disappear without a plan. If he really wanted to die, he would have done it ages ago."

Turin paused. She turned to see Sena trying to push herself up in bed. She ran to her best friend and jumped onto the bed beside her, and pulled Sena into a firm hug.

"I've missed you so much. I'm sorry about what I said on the way back from Anaris. I'm sorry I didn't listen to your advice. I'm sorry I didn't apologize sooner. I'm sorry you got hurt when we were stealing the phylactery."

"Anything else?" Sena groaned.

"I'm sure there are a million things, but those are the important ones for now."

"Well, I'm glad to be back. You were mean on the way back from Anaris, you should listen to my advice, and you most definitely should have apologized sooner. As for the dragon's lair, that's not entirely your fault."

"Anything else?" Turin asked.

"Yeah. I'd kill for some water."

"Oh. Of course." Turin jumped from the bed and hurried to a small table in the room's corner. She poured a glass of water from an earthenware pitcher and brought it to Sena.

Sena took a sip and sighed.

Turin welcomed the hot tears that streaked her face and just stared into Sena's eyes.

"Now, what's with all this?" Sena cleared her throat. "Rummaging through someone's personal belongings when they aren't around is kind of—unsettling."

Turin laughed through the tears. "Unsettling? How delicate of you."

"No, seriously. What are you doing, Turin?"

"When Mesorith attacked, Indrisor goaded him into a fight so the rest of us could escape. When we returned to Ruari, his pocket dimension collapsed. I refuse to believe he didn't have a plan before going into that lair. He had a plan for everything."

Sena nodded in agreement. "He was a necromancer trying to live forever."

"Reformed necromancer," Turin said, "but, yes."

"And it's not the necklace he gave you? That isn't the key?"

Turin grabbed Sena by the face and kissed her. "Senahrin Riora, you are a genius!"

Sena's eyes went wide with shock. "I am?"

Turin released Sena. "Yes, I didn't even think about the necklace. It's tucked away in Aunt Jenta's vault. And the inscription on the back of the stone's setting said something about love being eternal. At least, that's what Indrisor told me it said. Maybe there's more."

"It seems like a good place to start. At least, compared to destroying Indrisor's room."

"I'll have Aunt Jenta read the back for me." Turin wiped her cheeks dry.

"She'll never let you hear the end of it. She's been trying to get you to read Old Evenese since we were kids."

Turin shrugged. "It's a small price to pay if it's the key."

"Well. What are you waiting for? Go figure it out."

"It can wait a bit. At least until a cleric comes to check on you."

Sena furrowed her brow. "Just send Gromley my way when you see him and come back when you're done. I'm fine."

"Are you sure?"

Sena nodded. "I wouldn't mind a few minutes alone."

"I'll be back as soon as possible. Don't give the clerics too hard of a time. They've been working tirelessly to heal you. You were in pretty rough shape."

"I can tell. Everything hurts."

"I'm sure. Don't rush it. You'll be back to your old self in no time."

Sena brushed Turin out of the room with a wave of her hands.

Turin left the room in shambles and climbed upon the bahtreig that lazed in the rough stone corridor outside. With a gentle tap on the cheek, the bahtreig lurched into motion and coursed through the halls of Ruari toward the royal chambers.

It wasn't a long journey but, as far as Turin was concerned, it might as well have taken forever. She knew she was placing a lot of faith in little more than a hunch, but she also knew Indrisor enjoyed his little games and just may have given her everything she needed to bring him back without letting her know. He would take great satisfaction in her finding it out on her own. Well, with a little help from Sena.

The bahtreig skidded to a stop before the doors to the royal chambers. Turin dismounted, impatience fluttering in her chest. She hurried past the guards, who stood at attention, and into the compound.

She avoided the great hall and made for the vault where she had stowed Indrisor's gift.

A guard stood vigilant at the vault door. Seeing Turin approach, he bowed and unlocked the door with two distinct keys.

He hoisted the heavy door open, and Turin breezed past him.

A hint of must hung in the air, torchlight flickering off the countless treasures that cluttered the room. Turin weaved between chests filled with jewels and tables showcasing ancient artifacts and precious regalia.

She came before a small hutch and ran her fingers over the smooth lacquered surface. She opened the middle drawer. Inside were stacks of gossamer silk. A black box hid beneath one of the stacks. It glowed with a soft purple aura. She placed her thumb flush against the center of its lid, and it clicked open.

Within the box sat the necklace Indrisor gave her. The emerald in its clasp now contained a swirling vortex. Sena was right. The necklace was Indrisor's phylactery. She curled the chain around the emerald in her palm and ran to find her aunt.

When she entered the great hall, she found Regent Avrette in conference with the Barrow's Pact. "Did I miss something?" Turin asked.

Talus stood and bowed. "Not at all. We have just returned from Antiikin. What Umhra told Gromley was true. The ghost king, Eleazar, shared with us relics from as far back as the Age of Grace."

Turin eyed the vestiges arranged on the table, then the glum faces around it. "What else? I can tell something troubles you all."

"We just heard about Indrisor and of Gromley's problems in the halls of Mount Anvil. Naivara suffered a similar loss on our way back from Antiikin."

Turin smoothed her hair back with her palms. "So, we are down our three most powerful magic users and we've gained a few old, battle worn weapons."

She turned to Gromley. "Next time you talk to your friend, you might want to tell him to hurry up with his little race to kill the gods. So far, it seems like he's behind a step or two."

Gromley's eyes narrowed in contempt.

"Sena's awake. I guess I can be thankful for that, at least."

Gromley stood. "I'll go to her at once."

"I think I'll join you." Naivara said, rising alongside him.

Together, they left the room.

Laudin gathered the vestiges and motioned for Shadow and Nicholas to follow, leaving Turin alone with Talus and the regent.

Talus approached his adopted daughter. "Turin, you aren't the only one to have lost someone important to you."

"My dear," Regent Avrette said from her seat at the head of the table. "What Talus is trying to say is that you should be more careful with other people's feelings. Not solely because it is becoming of a queen, but also because it is a hallmark of a kind person."

Turin felt her cheeks flush at the admonishment. "I'll apologize to them both. Seems like I've been doing a lot of that lately. What's a few more? I also apologize to both of you. You have taught me to know better. Before I go find Gromley and Naivara, would you mind looking at something for me, Aunt Jenta?"

"Of course. What is it?"

Turin presented the necklace in an open palm. The gemstone swirled with preternatural vigor. She presented it to the regent.

"Indrisor recently gave this to me."

"I know. It's a beautiful piece."

"Yes. It is. The engraving on the setting is in the old tongue. Would you mind translating it for me? I'd like to know what it says."

Regent Avrette took the necklace. Before she looked at it, she looked up at Turin. "You should be able to do this on your own, you know."

"Another shortcoming I promise to work on. I now see the importance of knowing the old ways. I never thought it of value until now."

"We rarely realize the utility of things until it is too late."

The lessons—always the lessons. It was exhausting. Couldn't she have one conversation with her parents or her aunt, or the Barrow's Pact for that matter, that didn't end up calling attention to one of her shortcomings and advice on how to correct it? Why couldn't they let her learn her own lessons— make her own mistakes?

Regent Avrette turned her gaze back to the necklace. "I've never seen anything like it. Does the stone possess magic?"

Turin shrugged. "All he told me is that it once belonged to his mother and that it was very special to him. I'd assume it's a distinct possibility, considering the source."

Regent Avrette nodded, inspected the engraving. "This first part says, Love has many forms. All are eternal."

"First part?" Her tone was too eager, eliciting a shrewd glance from Talus.

"Yes, first part," Regent Avrette said. "The rest says Tyveriel's love gives life to us all. A beautiful inscription."

"It is. Thank you."

Regent Avrette handed the necklace to Turin. "Of course. Wear it in good health."

Turin placed it in a pocket and smiled. "I hope to. Now, if you'll excuse me, I have some more apologies to make. Will I see you both for dinner tonight?"

"You will," Talus said. "Your mother is excited to have you

home for a bit."

"I look forward to it as well. See you tonight, then."

Turin excused herself from the room.

Making her way back to her bahtreig, she wondered about Indrisor's inscription.

"What do you think it means?" A familiar voice asked from behind her. "The second part of the message."

"I'm not entirely sure. But I don't appreciate you listening in on my private conversations, Shadow."

She turned to see the Ryzarin leaning against a wall. He flipped a dagger casually by its tip and shrugged. "Sorry about that. Truly. But I figured that old curmudgeon would have a failsafe. Are you going to bring him back?"

"If I can figure out how to do it. Why?"

Shadow sheathed his dagger. "Playing God is a dangerous game."

"Spare me. Gromley decides who lives and dies all the time. How's this any different?"

"Anar entrusts—well, entrusted Gromley with a great responsibility. He is a vessel of the gods. Not to mention the most selfless and honorable man I've ever met. It's borderline disgusting, to be honest. What you're talking about is creating a lich. Nothing good ever came from such a venture."

"We're talking about Indrisor. What if it were Gromley?"

"I lost Gromley once. He died at the hands of an Orc chieftain protecting you when you were an infant. This, of course, was before we truly understood your abilities."

"Why have I never heard this story?"

Shadow ambled over to Turin. "Your aunt wanted to protect you."

"From the truth?"

"From the weight of knowing a man died for you to live. It's a burden no child should bear."

There was a certain heft to Shadow's news. She thought of how hard she'd often been on Gromley. Testing his beliefs.

Questioning his health and sometimes his sanity. And here he had sacrificed himself for her. She owed him more of an apology than she had even imagined.

"It's why he treats you with such care. Why he's so invested in your success."

"How did he come back? You said he died."

"Umhra. I don't understand it but, as a Mystic, Umhra was able to share a piece of himself with Gromley and revivify him. He was never the same, though."

"The seizures and visions?"

Shadow nodded. "I dare say Indrisor won't be the same either, if you decide to bring him back."

Turin's heart sank. Maybe Shadow was right. Maybe she should let Indrisor go. At the very least, she would have to give it the thought such a decision deserves.

A guard rode up to them on a bahtreig. The creature flashed with bioluminescence. "Queen Turin," he interrupted.

"Yes?"

"There's a man outside Prakten's Yawning. An outsider. He requests an audience with you."

"Did he announce himself? Tell you the nature of his business?"

"No. He refused entry to Ruari, although he claims to come here by your personal invitation. We thought it was wise to include you directly."

Turin looked at Shadow, who shrugged in reply. "Yes, of course. I will meet with him right away."

The guard nodded, spun his bahtreig, and rode back up the tunnel from which he came.

"What's that all about?" Shadow asked.

"The stranger that helped us in Anaris. I told him to come here and find us. That he'd be welcome."

"He certainly was useful."

"To say the least. I don't know what it is about him, but I can't wait to hear his story."

"I suppose your apologies will have to wait for later, then."

Turin nodded. There was no way she was going to risk the stranger leaving just so she could let Gromley and Naivara know she was sorry. She'd find them before dinner and set things right.

Turin climbed atop her bahtreig and patted its leathery hide. "Come on. You're coming with me. I have a feeling you're going to want to see this."

"As you wish."

Shadow climbed upon the bahtreig behind Turin, and they made for Prakten's Yawning.

The ride to the westernmost entry to the Ruari Caves was a long and boring journey through undulating tunnels and musty caverns filled with mineral columns that looked like dripping candles. By the glow of the bahtreig, pools of clear water reflected the jagged ceiling overhead.

A bead of sunlight appeared at the end of the tunnel, calling them to the surface. Turin welcomed the gentle breeze of fresh air against her face and bade her mount to a halt beside a cadre of guards that gathered before three heavy iron portcullises that were drawn shut.

"Not very welcoming, Captain," Turin noted as she climbed off her bahtreig. "Open the gates."

"Of course, my queen," the captain said, nodding to two of his subordinates who manned heavy chains on either side of the first gate. "It's just—"

"What is it?"

"There's something off-putting about the outsider. His voice sends a chill up my spine."

"I had the same reaction when I first encountered him. It's piqued my interest."

Chains rattled and the first portcullis gate groaned as it lifted into a recess in the cavern ceiling. Turin and Shadow followed the captain into the bay between the first two gates. The first gate lowered and clanked to the ground like a prison cell slamming shut.

They repeated the process two more times and then stepped out into the late afternoon sun. The last gate slammed closed behind them.

Turin squinted, giving her eyes a moment to adjust to the light of day. The stranger crouched on a rock at the base of a lone poplar as though he were a panther ready to pounce upon its prey. He wore a dark cloak despite the heat of summer and drew his cowl low, so his face was obscured by shadow.

"Wait here," Turin said. "I don't want to scare him off."

The captain took his order and stood at attention.

Shadow casually leaned against the cave entrance and grossed his arms and legs. "Let me know if you need anything. I won't take my eyes off you."

"Thanks."

Turin approached the stranger, butterflies in her stomach. "You came. I didn't think you would."

"I've wandered alone for a long time." Every word out of his mouth seemed to be accompanied by the echo of countless resonant whispers. "I thought I would test your offer. Test your word."

"Thank you for your help in Anaris. I didn't get to express my appreciation at the time."

"I was there, and you were not fairing so well with those blights."

"We were in some trouble, yes." Turin reached up and rubbed a soft, heart-shaped leaf between her fingers. A cool surge of energy flowed through her. "May I ask your name and where you hail from?"

The stranger stared at Turin from beneath his hood. His eyes lit with arcane vigor.

Turin took a step back.

The stranger stifled a laugh. "I would have thought you might not be startled so easily. I'm sure you elicit a similar response from time to time."

"I do."

"My given name is Gleriel Severe, but I have not been called this in ages. I hail from Elystine. What you would today call, Amnesty?"

"Elystine. No one has used that name since the Whispered Death.

"Yes. I died two hundred years before the plague swept through Winterashe."

"Died?"

Gleriel pushed his cowl back and revealed a skeletal head. His eyes were orbs of burning coal.

Turin gasped. "How can this be?"

"A curse. I thought the scion of Modig Forene might know of a way to undo it."

Turin sat on the stone beside Gleriel. "We had a wizard among us. He would have known about such things."

"Had a wizard?"

"Yes, but he fell in battle."

Gleriel hung his head. "For hundreds of years, I have searched for an answer to my affliction. Alas, I am no closer today than I've ever been."

"I'm sorry. You are still welcome to join us. Maybe there will be something in Indrisor's library that could help you. You can have free rein of it."

Gleriel stared into Turin's eyes. "Will your people accept me as I am? I have no interest in hiding beneath this cowl."

"I can't promise you it will be easy. It isn't for me, and I'm supposed to be their queen. They can be petty, timid, and crude. But they are good people, and I will fight for your place among us."

"I accept your terms."

"Wonderful. I know exactly where to start."

Turin called Shadow over.

"A Ryzarin." Gleriel's eyes flared. "You are a motley crew."

Shadow approached, his gait slowing as he saw Gleriel's face for the first time. "Is everything alright?"

"Yes," Turin said. "Quite. Shadow, this is Gleriel. I'm sure you remember him from Anaris."

"I do. Thank you for the help back there."

Gleriel nodded. "A pleasure to meet you, Shadow. May I ask your true name? The one given to you in the Sepyltyr."

"Barra Argith." Shadow paused for a moment and then wagged a finger at Gleriel. "I'm sorry, I need to ask. How does this all work?"

"Shadow," Turin could not believe he would ask so bold a question.

"What? You aren't curious about how we are having a conversation with a sentient, scythe wielding skeleton?"

"It is a curse," Gleriel said. "Or an enchantment, depending on your point of view."

Shadow shrugged. "See? Now, with that out of the way, I can relax. Welcome to Amari. It's terrible, but it's all we have."

"You call the caves by their Ryzarin name, yet you go by Shadow."

Shadow raised a brow. "You make a point. Welcome to Ruari."

"I have not had a place to call home in hundreds of years. Certainly, it will suffice. Until we destroy the Grey Queen and turn the blights back to the Wistful Timberlands, that is."

"I like the way you think, Gleriel," Turin said. "Come on. Let's show you your new home. There are some people for you to meet, and I have some apologies to make along the way."

CHAPTER 23

*A Guardian is bound to each Waystone. Their commitment to
the sanctity of our secrets is absolute.*

- The Tome of Mystics
Unknown Origin. Unearthed from the Ruins of Oda Norde,
month of Bracken, 1320 AT

— ▲ —

Hooves slogged through the mud which rose half-way up
Umhra's calf. All else was silent. From amidst the dense
undergrowth of the aged forest approached an enormous elk.
Umhra recognized the majestic creature as the Creator God,
Kemyn, recalling their encounter amidst the rot and decay of
the Morion Swamp. Umhra bowed.

Kemyn scratched at the muck, once again garnering
Umhra's attention. With a toss of his head, Kemyn snorted,
releasing a plume of steam into the cool evening air.

"I am honored by your presence, Kemyn. Again, you bestow
upon me a great gift."

Kemyn's eyes glowed. The glow spread across him until his
elk form transformed into a body made entirely of molten rock.
The form shifted, Kemyn rising onto two feet, his forelegs
growing into hefty stone arms, his head keeping his impressive

rack of antlers and other elk features. Assuming his true form for the first time in two millennia, he towered over Umhra.

"It is I that should bow to you, Peacebreaker. For it is only now, in your presence, the presence of a god in the mortal plane, that I may assume my true form and return to the welcoming arms of my siblings, my soul at peace. I have roamed this magical land long enough and seek passage home."

"Then you know why I'm here."

"My sister called me from Kalmindon. She is under threat from the Mystic called Spara. This time, I will heed her call, as I should have so many years ago. I long for her company but, for her safety, I would do anything. Walk with me. There is something I wish to share with you before I depart Tyveriel for the last time."

Umhra nodded. "Of course. It would be an honor."

Together, they walked through the forest for some time, Kemyn's pounding footfalls leaving no lasting effect on the gnarled ground cover. The forest grew darker, more foreboding with each step. They arrived at an area where a great fire had burned the undergrowth and canopy above. The blackened trees just now gave way to new growth, whose greens were all the more vibrant for their charred surroundings.

Blocking the path forward were the desiccated remains of a massive dragon tangled amidst the trees. A wake of vultures that had been feeding on the carcass scattered into the shadows of the canopy. What remained of the dragon's scales were a familiar rose gold, her sunken eyes a dull red which once flirted with light like flawless rubies. Umhra hung his head.

"Vendarithe. I was hoping she could best the Grey Queen. It seems I did little more than send her to her death."

"She has returned to the Fae and is at peace. You gave her freedom after two millennia of imprisonment. Her pain was tortuous for a time but fleeting. We all must walk through fire for those things we desire."

Umhra ambled the length of Vendarithe's body from tail to

head. A tree punctured each wing, a third running through her chest and protruding from her back. A gaping wound ran for several feet along the length of her throat—no doubt the Grey Queen's work. Accounting for the trees and the countless smaller puncture wounds and gashes across her body, it was obvious Silyarithe had help.

"What did this to her? Very few of these wounds are those caused by a dragon."

Kemyn pointed beyond Vendarithe's cadaver.

Umhra circled around Vendarithe's mouthful of razor-sharp teeth and saw a black monolith covered in lichens visible among the trees.

Umhra stopped, Kemyn coming up beside him. "What is this?" Umhra asked.

"This, Umhra, is the Aged One."

"May I?"

Kemyn nodded.

Umhra approached the monolith for a closer look. Below the pale green lichens, the surface of the monolith had worn smooth from ages of exposure to the elements. Umhra gently touched the monolith. The stone was warm.

Memories rushed through Umhra's mind that were not his own. He saw the dawn of time, the Creator Gods forging the material plane. He saw a youthful sun shining its first light on a planet covered in molten rock. He saw a group of great monoliths hurtling through space, approaching a new home.

"Tyveriel once belonged to them?"

"There was a great war among the gods. Those you know, those of Vaila's pantheon, took control of Kalmindon and created the material plane. Sensing burgeoning life, the primordial gods were drawn to Tyveriel from points unknown. They were allowed to stay as stewards of our creation. The Aged One is one such primordial god, older than time itself. Older than me. It rests in stasis, unaffected by our presence and yet corrupts and controls the armies of blights that lay waste to the races of men. Only through its destruction can Tyveriel be saved."

"Let's end it now, while it sleeps." Umhra summoned Forsetae, the blade feeling foreign to his hand. The hilt of the hallowed blade was now fashioned of diamond, with countless facets casting an inner light across the dense canopy overhead like a star-filled night.

"Alas, we may not. The Rescission casts a veil between the realm of gods and that of men. We may not influence it directly as we once could. The responsibility of destroying the Aged One and quelling the blights' rage falls upon the mortals."

"Then why bring me here today?"

Kemyn tilted his head, his antlers scraping the lowest hanging branches of the surrounding trees. "So, should you succeed in your quest to stop Spara, you may inform the mortals of the Aged One's role in their plight. They have but one chance of ending their war—at salvation—and that is to destroy the Aged One and free the blights from its control."

Umhra allowed Forsetae to dissipate. "Thank you. You've been most generous with your guidance. With this knowledge, they stand a chance."

Kemyn nodded. "I am ready—the blade?"

Umhra drew the diamond dagger from his belt. "This was much easier with your brother. I did not hold him in such esteem. You are another story entirely. I don't think I can do this."

"You have no choice, nor do I. The fate of everything depends on it." Kemyn's chest glowed red hot, the stone melting into magma. He plunged his hands into the pool of molten rock and pried his chest apart, exposing his heart.

Made of rock, soil and root, the organ beat only twice per minute. Umhra marveled as the secrets of the gods laid themselves bare before him.

"Now. Release me..."

Umhra stepped forward, his hands shaking, his throat

tightening. He brought the dagger to the fissure in Kemyn's chest. Hesitated. "This will only bring me sorrow."

"It will bring you untold power. And it will bring me peace."

Umhra thrust the dagger into Kemyn's heart, the heat radiating from within his chest cavity nearly unbearable.

Kemyn had no discernible reaction to his heart being pierced, simply stood, and faced his end. The dagger lit up with divine energy and quickly surrounded Kemyn's worthy body in its glow. Kemyn dropped to his knees, coming eye to eye with Umhra.

The dagger's aura shifted to green as it extracted Kemyn's soul. The radiance was concentrated in the dagger's pommel and shot forth into Umhra's icon. Wisps of pink and green ether swirled around him and combined to form a deep amber.

The energy flooded into Umhra's body, providing him with a strength he would never have thought possible. Umhra lifted off the ground among the branches of the trees as the process of his essence combining with Kemyn's reached its crescendo.

He settled to the ground. At once, he knew Tyveriel with an intimacy reserved only for oneself. Every mountain, forest, and valley became a part of him. Every creature, even those he had never before laid eyes upon, was as precious to him as if they were his own children. It was as if he too took part in their creation.

Opening his eyes, he witnessed Kemyn's body turn to ash and be carried away by a gust of wind.

Umhra found himself connected to the earth beneath him as though they were one. Tyveriel spoke in disquieted tones directed toward the monolith embedded in its surface not far away. It whispered of angry, vengeful dragons and their pact with the dark, twisted god. It wept for the needless death of the blights who were not in control of their fate and the wanton destruction of the races of men who always took more than they gave. It told of the War of Dominion and lamented how history was destined to repeat itself.

Umhra stared at the monolith and silently vowed to find a way to rid Tyveriel of the Aged One and put an end to the war between the blights and the races of men. As for tempering man's greed...he made no such promise. He knew better than to think he, even as a god, could change such things.

Alas, time was precious, and too much hung in the balance. Umhra searched his mind for Brinthor and saw in his mind a relentless ocean crashing upon towering blue marble cliffs. All too familiar with his destination, he followed a path of destruction through the woods, which he assumed Vendarithe created in her pursuit of the Grey Queen. When he came to a clearing, angelic wings sprouted from his back, and he lifted into the air. His journey called him back to Tukdari.

CHAPTER 24

His passion sparked hope in mankind. Many would heed his call.

- The Gatekeeper's Abridged History of Tyveriel
Vol. 2, Chapter 35 – Unearthed from the Ruins of Meriden, the month of Ocken, 1240 AT

— ▲ —

Silyarithe circled Mount Anvil as the sun breached the horizon over Lertmor to the east. The cloudless sky shifted color from violet to red to brilliant gold. She welcomed the warmth of the burgeoning sun on her face and the ripple of the wind beneath her weary wings.

Despite her exhaustion, she looped around a second time to be certain her keen eyes missed nothing on her first pass. Her father called it paranoia. She preferred to think of it as caution.

Convinced of her safety, she dived toward the black mountain, her eyes trained on a gaping hole in its side. As she neared, she unfurled her wings once more and arrested her descent. Her talons pierced the familiar rock of the ledge outside the entry to her lair.

The wind whistled through the crags around her, dust scraping her scales. She ruffled her wings and ducked below the claw-torn archway. The air within the tunnel was cool and carried the scent of death which Silyarithe detested but had grown accustomed to in her years with Mesorith at her side.

She slithered along the passage until it opened into a vast cavern. It had once been a banquet hall for the Zeristar—of which there were many—but she had done away with their pathetic little tables and iron chandeliers. Admittedly, she kept the silverware, as she had a fondness for the shiny things men fashioned from the earth.

Now was not the time to dwell on material possessions, however. She returned with news of a more suitable host for her father and could not wait to share her successful negotiation with the Orc shaman.

For years, Mesorith had wallowed in the decrepit remains of Felonrith the Verdant Ire. No doubt, he would want to return to his phylactery and travel to Besik Uk immediately. He desired to be useful in their conquest to ferret out the remnants of mankind, and Nezenrith the Red Fury would allow him to return to the skies.

She lumbered across her lair and through the tunnel that connected it to her father's. The adjoining chamber was a mire of stagnant pools and decaying bodies. Beauty is truly in the eye of the beholder.

"Father, I come with news from the Orcs of Besik Uk."

Her voice echoed back at her from across the broad cavern. "Father?"

There was no reply, only the drip of water into dank pools.

In his weakened state, Mesorith had spent most of his time sleeping in this room. He only left to hobble up to the Zeristar throne room to be close to his phylactery. There Silyarithe would often hear him caterwauling incessantly about his maladies.

Why he kept his phylactery upon the Zeristar's sacred chair, she did not know. Maybe it was to remind him of his rightful station. Maybe it was to force himself from his lair. Regardless of his motives, he was likely there now.

Silyarithe leaped to the tunnel entrance overhead and climbed up to the throne room. The battling scents of Ninnisrith's acrid breath and ozone hung in the air. Destruction had befallen the doorway to the Zeristar's precious gilded corridor, leaving the walls marred with burn marks. Even if Mesorith had descended into madness, he couldn't have caused this destruction on his own.

She spun for the throne, but it too lay in ruin. She threw a shattered pillar aside and searched for the crystal meant to hold her father's soul. Mesorith's phylactery was nowhere to be found.

Who would dare to infiltrate their lair and take her father's most prized possession? Hopefully, Mesorith made them pay.

Silyarithe followed the path of destruction. She crossed the Gilded Corridor, the crevasse she had created for added security overgrown by fresh stone. The adjoining chapel was reduced to little more than rubble, leading her into the banquet hall where her father kept his undead pets. Only a few revenants remained. They wandered haplessly while the others lay strewn about the room, no doubt dispatched by man's crude weaponry.

A glint caught her eye in the dreariness. Cast away into the corner of the room like the countless bones in Mesorith's lair was a simple knife. Its polished blade and clean ivory handle spoke of someone who invested in its care. This was not the weapon of a revenant, but that of an intruder.

Silyarithe retrieved the tiny blade and tucked it under one of her scales. It could be of some value to her when this was all done.

She continued through a hole blown through the far wall. Stones crumbled to the floor around her as she descended the remnants of a flight of stairs and beyond the limits of the Zeristar stronghold to areas of the mountain she was yet to explore.

The residue of battle led her to the mouth of the lava tubes where Mesorith had seemingly abandoned his pursuit. The stone was too hard for him to breach in his weakened state. No, he would not have given up so easily and allowed the intruders to escape with the key to his immortality. He must have found a more amiable path.

Silyarithe closed her eyes and thought of her father in his younger years, when he was a vibrant and powerful black dragon. Before he became a lich. Before he decayed at the bottom of the Sea of Widows for a millennium. Through his young eyes, she saw a lair deep within the base of the mountain. Her father barreled through a vast tunnel that connected it with the outside world.

She spun and followed another lava tube, more becoming of her size into the depths of Mount Anvil.

The stone turned darker as she ran until the tunnel opened into a cavern rife with the scent of death and decay. Cutting through the foul odor, however, was something Silyarithe found less offensive—the smell of fresh blood. Fresh Farestere blood. Mesorith had caught up with them.

She picked up the trail across the room and followed it into a derelict laboratory filled with dust-covered tables and vessels of clouded glass. The streak of coagulated blood led her to the corner of the room and stopped in a modest puddle. There was no body, no evidence of further struggle. There was no sign of her father. The trail simply stopped. A dead end.

Silyarithe roared, but it did not quell her frustration. Her heart rate quickened, and her jaw tensed as anger welled up within her. Whomever was responsible for this would pay a heavy price for their brazen crimes. She would see to that where her father had failed.

She thrashed the table behind her with her tail, grimy glass vials exploding against the wall. She trampled the rest of the equipment underfoot and released a torrent of plasma into the room, setting it aglow in purple flame.

Her chest heaved; her eyes burned with fury. If she was

going to locate the perpetrators, she would need to calm her mind first. That was unlikely to happen in this cesspool. How could anyone focus in such a deplorable place?

Silyarithe trod back to her lair, all the while ruminating on this travesty of events. How could her father have just vanished? He would not dare leave the mountain in his frail state. Who could have orchestrated such an affront? She would find out soon enough. They had made one fatal mistake.

Having flown from Orrat Skaag without rest only to stumble upon the infiltration was too much. She needed rest. Silyarithe collapsed to the floor and exhaled. She closed her eyes.

It was a short, fitful sleep plagued by nightmares. She saw her father in Ninnisrith's frail body being tormented by devilish forms—human, Iminti, and Zeristar among them. They jabbed him with spear and sword, hacked at him with axes, and burned him with magic. He fought bravely, but his blind, feeble host failed him.

When she awoke, she felt no better than she had before. Her head pounded behind her eyes.

She climbed to her feet, yawned, and scratched her flank against the wall. Once she satisfied her itch, she brandished a talon and plucked the knife she had found from within her scales. The knife clattered to the floor. What a delightful addition it would make to her ever-growing collection of glimmering metal. Today, however, it served a higher purpose.

She covered the blade with a fore claw and took a measured breath to help calm her mind.

"Lothryk darmot vrenom."

The draconic spell she had seen her ancestors use in the memories they shared with her took hold. Her head spun and her vision went black. In her mind's eye, all she saw was the knife. It was a beautifully crafted instrument with a fine edge and a vine of roses carved into its handle.

The knife led her from her lair and over the Bay of Tailings. They flew over Lertmor and the ruins of Ember's Watch.

Farther still, they continued past the Seorsian Mountains and crossed the River Torrent.

The blade descended upon a set of rolling hills covered in lavender grasses. It entered a cave and delved far below Evelium's surface. Here, it passed countless people—those she sought to snuff out. They bustled about like ants. Repulsive.

Silyarithe continued after the knife until she came upon a young woman like none she had ever seen. The woman had grey skin much like her own and pupilless amber eyes surrounded by dark rings. She was different than the rest. Special. She was also the thief that carelessly left her blade behind and somehow was responsible for Mesorith's apparent demise.

For nearly two decades, Silyarithe had searched far and wide for the remnants of humanity—those that escaped her assault on Vanyareign and the days after. She had found little in the north where word of her conquest no doubt reached before she had the opportunity. South of the capital, however, had been a thriving garden of death and destruction.

The knife hovered before its owner, who stood in conversation with a Zeristar man with a short, dark beard. An icon in the shape of the sun dangled from around his neck as he inspected a gold helm with a single horn jutting from its side.

Silyarithe's vision flashed to a great hero who donned the helm along with matching heavy armor. He leaped over a chasm and brought a gilded axe inlaid with green glass down upon his adversary. The axe cleft the intended's head in two and it fell into the canyon below, a blur of blue wings and reptilian scales.

"It's exquisite," the Zeristar said. "If not a little ostentatious."

"The others agreed you were best suited to wear it," the grey-skinned intruder said. "It could be of great value to our cause."

Silyarithe's vision faded, and she returned to the present. She shook her head and removed her claw from the blade and admired it. How useful such an insignificant thing can be when knowledge is applied.

She laughed. "Value to your cause, indeed. Now I know where you hide, little bug. And I intend to squash you and your cause."

With a swipe of her claw, she sent the knife sliding across the floor. It came to rest at the base of a towering pile of favored trinkets, causing a few to slide down from on high and cover it.

Tomorrow she would return to the Wistful Timberlands and inform the Aged One of her discovery. Together, they would mount an attack that would crush the resistance and avenge her father's destruction.

CHAPTER 25

*Our time on the Tukdari plains brought us in direct contact
with not only the land's barbarians but also the terrifying Tuk
Lion.*

- A Traveler's Guide to the Odd and Obscure by Sentina Vake
Chapter 29 – Unearthed from the Homestead in Maryk's Cay,
month of Riet, 1407 AT

Umhra soared overhead, searching for the exact place along
the cliff side he had seen when he tried to locate Brinthor.
He considered the last time he had flown over the open sage
grass fields and barbarian settlements of Tukdari. How blind he
was to Spara's plans—how effortlessly she used him to get the
Eketar egg and dispatch the Guardians. He shook his head. At
some point, you need to clear your mind of the past. There was
no value in dwelling on these things. Learn from your mistakes
and look forward.

Spotting the thin crescent beach he had seen in his vision,
Umhra swept down over the sheer marble cliffs that surrounded
it and set down upon its soft blue sands. Beyond the edges of the
cliff that jutted from the shoreline, the Dari Sea raged, dutiful in
its endless pursuit to grind the sapphire blue cliffs that

dominated the landscape to dust. Within their protective walls, however, the waters gently lapped the sands, no more threatening than a bucolic pond.

Crabs scuttled among the scattered stones as Umhra walked to the water's edge and looked for some sign of the last of Vaila's brothers. A gull cried over-head and the back of a massive beast breached the surface just within the last set of breakers. Umhra froze.

The creature approached at incredible speed, only its immense silhouette and the wake it cast in its path were visible. Reaching the shallows, an enormous blue dragon burst from the water and roared. Umhra held his ground.

Brinthor thundered ashore. Water cascaded from his body, and steam rose from his nostrils into the sky. Pulling himself onto the beach, he touched his forehead to the sand before Umhra as a sign of reverence.

"Please, you owe me no such honor," Umhra said.

Brinthor kept his head low to the ground, his eyes averted. Umhra bit his bottom lip. Not sensing that Brinthor was going to give in, he took a step closer to the dragon and placed a friendly palm upon the crest of his head.

Under Umhra's touch, Brinthor's wings and legs receded, and his body elongated into his natural serpentine form. He looked his body over and flicked his tongue into the salty air.

"Years ago, you came to me," Umhra said, "and, along with your siblings, imparted upon me the rhodium I needed to ascend to Kalmindon. Today I come to you asking for something much more precious than a bit of rare metal."

"I have sensed the passing of my brothers—and my sister's desperation," Brinthor hissed. "Our powers wane. Ages ago, it was decided that this day was inevitable. I shall reunite with my siblings and see you fulfill your destiny. I am ready. End me now."

The request took Umhra aback. "Is there nothing else you request before we proceed?"

Brinthor did not answer. He simply prostrated himself along the beach at Umhra's feet, awaiting the inevitable.

"As you wish, mighty Brinthor." Umhra drew the diamond dagger from his belt and drove it into Brinthor's neck, not wanting to have him wait a moment longer than he wanted. Blue blood poured forth from the wound, disappearing into the sand.

"I leave you with a gift," Brinthor said. "Take the time you need. A few of Tyveriel's fleeting moments will not decide Kalmindon's fate."

A vibrant white light coalesced around Brinthor, concentrated around the gash in his neck. The dagger gathered the light in its pommel, the mote of energy nearly blinding. The dagger released a beam of energy into Umhra's icon, shifting its color from amber to pure white. Umhra's icon pulsed with Brinthor's essence, and wisps of ether enveloped him. Umhra's feet remained grounded in the blue sands, as he was now more able to resist the surge of power. As the radiance faded, Brinthor's body turned to ash and fell into the lazy waters of the lagoon. Umhra watched as the cloud that was his remains dissipated and became one with the sea.

Umhra sat, the powdery sand coating his fingers. He grasped a handful and let it cascade back to the beach like an hourglass biding its time. He closed his eyes and considered what to do next. Having claimed the power of each of Vaila's siblings, he was unsure of which god to pursue. Surely, the rest wouldn't be as willing as Naur, Kemyn, and Brinthor.

Something sharp jabbed at his back and broke his concentration. He looked over his shoulder and a burly man with tan skin covered in red tribal tattoos greeted him. The Tukdari barbarian was at least seven feet tall and wore leather pants and boots but flaunted a bare, muscular chest. The spear he held to Umhra's back was sturdy and tipped with a flaked flint head.

"What are you doing here, outsider?" The man asked in Tuk.

"I mean no offense," Umhra said, having never known but a few words in the language before this moment. "I was called to this beach by my god and will leave you in peace."

"Your god is a fool for calling you to trespass on Tukdari land." The man thrust the spear forward. The flint spearhead shattered against Umhra's form. Its pieces remained suspended in the air for a moment and then settled to the ground like a lazy snow.

The barbarian staggered backward in awe. "What curse do you bring to our land?" He asked.

Umhra rolled to his knees and held his hands in the air. "I mean you no harm."

Another fifty Tukdari, all armed with crude weaponry, filled in behind the spearman from a weathered path amongst the cliffs. The hunting party gathered close and investigated the intruder on their shores.

"Umhra?" A familiar but distant voice called from behind the wall of spears and clubs and axes. "Is it truly you?"

From amongst the anxious crowd emerged a woman with greying hair pulled back in a tight braid adorned with shells. She wasn't particularly tall or beautiful, but she held herself with strength and dignity, and bore the tattoos of both Tukdari and Orc royalty. While age lines now creased the corners of her eyes and mouth, Umhra instantly recognized her gentle features, her grey eyes reminding him of his own.

"Mother?" Tears streaked down his face.

Joslin pushed between two burly men clothed in furs and ran to her son. She dropped to her knees in the sand and held his face between her hands. She cried.

"My sweet boy. My Na'ranna."

Na'ranna. Umhra had not heard that word since he was four. His mind flashed back to the night before the Tukdari raided his village in Goshur Uk. The invaders were likely members of this very tribe. He was curled up in his mother's arms, his eyes tired. She called him her Na'ranna only when they were alone, as it was a Tukdari word his father forbade her to use. The next morning, his world would shatter.

"What are you doing here? I did not know you still lived. I mourned your death ages ago."

"I..." Umhra was at a loss for words. He hadn't thought twice about the gift Brinthor promised and here it was the greatest gift he had ever received. He just stared into his mother's eyes— stared into his past.

"Come. Come back with us to the settlement. We have much catching up to do." Joslin climbed to her feet and beat the sand from her leather skirt with open palms. She turned to her tribe. "This is no stranger. This is my lost son, Umhra. He is one of our own."

The hunting party erupted in whispers.

Joslin offered Umhra her hands and a kind smile, the grime on her face smeared by tears. He gladly accepted.

"My, you filled out nicely. Look at you...you have the physique of a god."

If she only knew. Umhra smiled. "Thank you."

"Come. Tonight, we will celebrate your life and our reunion."

The Tukdari hunting party led the way up a narrow passage along the cliff and into the sage grass plains. Umhra and Joslin followed close behind. It had been a long time since Umhra felt this kind of peace, this depth of belonging. It was a shame it would only last the better part of an evening.

"Do you mind?" Joslin asked as she took Umhra's hand.

Umhra fought the lump in his throat. "Of. Of course not."

Joslin clamped onto Umhra's hand as though, if she let go, he would slip away, never to return.

Surrounded by leather huts, Umhra and Joslin admired the sky set afire as the sun flirted with the horizon. The fire crackled, sending an army of sparks into the air, only to flicker out and join the pillar of smoke that trailed to the east. They sat beside each other, an empty bowl between each of their feet and an earthenware goblet in hand.

"So, tell me. What have you been doing with your life?" Joslin took a sip of wine. "I want to hear about all your exploits. I've missed so much."

"I'm not sure you'd believe me if I told you."

"Try me. I knew you were destined for greatness. And now, after all this time, you inexplicably arrive in Tukdari, no boat to be seen, after our scouts reported seeing a man with eagle wings soaring over the cliffs."

"I must know something first."

Joslin nodded, permitting Umhra his question.

"It's plain to see that you hold a position of influence among these people. They are your own, no?"

"By birth, yes."

"And, when the horde raided our home in Goshur Uk and slaughtered our family and left my father's head on a pike. Did they kidnap you as I always thought, or did you leave of your own free will?"

Joslin frowned for the first time since Umhra's arrival. "That morning, I was gathering bitter roots out in the Wastes. Upon my return, the siege was already underway." She gestured to the bustling Tukdari encampment with a sweep of her hand. "They, my people, had come for me after five years in captivity."

She placed a hand on Umhra's cheek. He swallowed the lump in his throat.

"Umhra, you must understand. It was Yargol who had taken me as his prize. You were the only reason I continued for all those years. Without my Na'ranna, I would have ended my life rather than stay with that beast."

Joslin's words stung. Umhra had never considered how his mother and father had come to be together. All he had of those times were the idealized memories of youth and the terror of losing everything he knew on that fateful day.

"When I saw what was happening, I frantically searched for you. My plan had always been to bring you with me and raise you among the Tukdari. I screamed your name, tore the village apart, asked anyone I could if they had seen you. There were many children among the dead—most of them unrecognizable, whether from weapon or fire. I searched until my people had their fill of spoils and then left with them."

Umhra nodded slowly. "A dead tree. Father hid me in the hollow of a dead tree outside the village before running to meet his end. I hid there for days, and nobody came for me."

"I can't tell you how sorry I am to have abandoned you like that. You must have thought the worst of me."

"No. I never considered that you left of your own free will. I thought they had taken you. I thought the Tukdari had stolen you from me and killed my father for no reason other than he was an Orc."

"Finding out the truth cannot be easy for you. All I can say is that I assumed you were dead with the others. If I had the slightest hope that you were alive, I would have done anything to find you."

Umhra took a sip from his tankard. The ale was warm and bitter, but better than the stale taste he had in his mouth.

"Please, tell me, what became of you after that terrible day?" Joslin asked.

"Eventually, I made my way through Wicked Pass and into the arms of an Evenese monk who raised me as his own and trained me as a Paladin. I grew up in Travesty and, when the monk died, I set out on my own, roaming Evelium as a sell sword. Over time, I found another family—a group of half-Orcs much like me. We fit in nowhere but with each other. They too were taken from me, and I have been on a personal journey since." He flashed the rhodium icon that hung around his neck on a simple but unbreakable chain. "I ascended to mysticism and have walked among the gods in Kalmindon and the devils and demons in Pragarus."

Joslin furrowed her brow in disbelief. "What are you saying?
"I speak plainly, mother. In the years we have been apart, I have attained immortality by the will of Vaila." He summoned his wings and holy armor. Instead of the small rhodium plates he had grown accustomed to since becoming a Mystic, his armor materialized as a suit of flawless diamonds.

Joslin gasped.

The flash of brilliance from Umhra's form attracted the other Tukdari who came running to Joslin's aid.

Joslin remained seated. She waved her would be heroes off dismissively. "It's alright. It seems my son is even more special than I could have imagined. Tonight, we feast in the presence of a god."

The Tukdari dropped to their knees, touching their foreheads to the ground. They chanted in unison. "Ulaoula, Ulaoula, Ulaoula."

Umhra inspected his new armor, flexing his arms within its confines and peering into the depths of its many facets. It reminded him of the gown he'd seen Vaila wearing, first in Pragarus and later in Kalmindon.

"Please, have them stop." Umhra allowed his armor and wings to dissipate. "I don't want to be worshipped. I want to spend what little time I can with my mother."

Joslin hushed her tribe. "Go about your preparations. I wish to have time alone with my son."

The crowd dispersed, some bowing to Umhra as they departed.

"There's someone I'd like to introduce you to," Joslin said, rising from the log upon which they sat. "Come, walk with me."

Umhra followed his mother from the fire hearth, the cool evening breeze carrying a sweet scent. Chella blossom. He had never heard of such a thing before today and yet was familiar with them all the same.

They came to an expansive hide tent, its skins painted with the same markings Joslin bore. "You are their queen?" Umhra asked as he ducked under the flap Joslin held for him.

"The term is, Falla. All women of child birthing age compete in physical competition and combat to earn the tribal vote. Once nominated, you are Falla for life. But it is not like a queen. I do not sit on a throne and ring my bell for servants. I am an equal part of the community. I hunt, gather, and fight with the others."

"But you lead them?"

"Yes. I guide the tribe on its journey. But come, I have a kindred spirit for you to meet."

Umhra's eyes adjusted quickly to the dark interior of the tent. A pot simmered on the hearth at its center, filling the air with the scent of herbs. There were woven grass mats on the ground around the hearth and an intricately carved ebony wood chair that looked distinctly out of place among its surroundings. A linen sheet hung across the far side of the room to create what Umhra assumed were sleeping quarters.

Joslin cleared her throat. "Mother, please come. I bring you a present from our hunt today."

Mother? Umhra's throat tightened. He brushed his leathers and smoothed an errant strand of hair from his face. His heart pounded in his chest.

Joslin smiled.

From behind the linen curtain emerged a frail, ancient woman with hair the color of dry straw. She had a slight hunch to her back, and her paper-thin skin showed every vein in her body. She shuffled ever so slowly into the room. "What's this? A gift you say?" Her voice was little more than a dry croak.

She took no notice of Umhra as she approached the hearth at a snail's pace. "It better not be another Na'ranna. You know I no longer have the energy for such things. And you say the companionship is good for me. I say those things are nothing but a bother."

"But it is a Na'ranna, mother. But not just any. Mine."

The old woman came within a few feet of Umhra, craned her

neck and squinted into his face. "By Vaila's grace. You're Joslin's Umhra? I've dreamed of this day ever since your mother returned to us and told me about you. She thought you were gone, but I always told her there was hope. Just like the hope I kept in my heart all those years she was gone."

"It's wonderful to meet you ..." Umhra trailed off awkwardly, not knowing how to address his newfound grandmother.

"You are welcome to call me Bita. I've always longed for someone to call me that. Now, come down here, boy. Sit with your grandmother by the fire. I need to get a better look at you and the light with help."

Umhra nodded. "Yes, Bita."

Bita flashed a wide smile at hearing the name and sank into the ebony chair. Umhra joined her by the fireside, kneeling on a grass mat and coming to her eye level. She looked him over for a few moments as a child would a new doll.

"My, you are just about perfect, aren't you?"

Umhra replied only with a smile as he knew his words would only ruin the moment by being disagreeable.

"How long will we have you with us?" Joslin asked, taking a seat beside her son.

"I'm afraid only tonight. I have pressing matters to see to. I hope to return when I have completed my mission. I should like to spend more time here with you both."

"To think I have not seen you in forty-seven years and now that you are here, I only have you for a few hours."

Umhra's mind raced. He had forgotten about the disparity in time caused by his ascension. It had been ages since he saw his mother but, for her, it had been nearly twenty years longer. For the first time, he considered the possibility that her losing a child and thinking him dead was greater than the pain he still held onto from his childhood. There were times, when he was with Ivory, that he'd nearly forgotten about his mother. He had fleeting moments of peace where the thought of his parents didn't plague his mind. She, likely, carried the burden of her loss around like those wretched souls on the Slopes of Phit carried their laden yokes.

He turned to his mother. "Forty-seven years is such a very long time in the life of an Orc or a Tukdari. I'm sorry it has taken me this long to find you."

"Yes. Forty-seven years ago, this Prien. But you don't owe me any apologies. Despite the wait, I will always cherish that you found your way back to me."

"For me, it has been twenty-eight years since you were taken—left."

Joslin tilted her head, the age lines in her face deepening as she frowned. "How is that possible, Umhra?"

"I don't know. Possibly, it has something to do with my ascension to Kalmindon. I can't think of any other reason for it. I'm sorry you've had to wait so long for this. For me, it seems like a lifetime, but I'm grateful we've had the opportunity, nonetheless."

Joslin wept and threw her arms around Umhra's neck. "One evening hardly seems fair."

"It is more than you ever thought you'd have, Joslin," Bita said, laboring to rise from the chair. "Wipe those tears and celebrate your reunion. You are the luckiest woman alive."

Joslin wiped the tears from her eyes. "Yes. Let's join the others and rejoice." She climbed to her feet and Umhra followed. Together, the three of them left the tent and made for a great bonfire that raged at the center of the encampment. Music blared from beyond the fire, young women and men dancing feverishly in its glow.

The dancers cast long shadows across the rest of the tribe, who gathered around an array of exquisite Evenese banquet tables worn from years of use out in the elements. Piles of roast boar, flat bread, and root vegetables smothered the tables.

Umhra paused at the edge of the feast, that familiar sense of dread washing over him. Joslin took his hand. "You are among family, Umhra. There is nothing for you to fear here."

Umhra nodded, offered an unconvincing smile, and continued into the fray alongside his mother.

A shrill call rattled Umhra awake. He rubbed his eyes and rolled onto his side. It was the first time he had slept since his ascension to Kalmindon. He wasn't even certain he had needed the rest, as mortal afflictions such as fatigue and hunger now eluded him. It did, however, allow his mother and Bita an excuse to retire for the night.

The bonfire was now little more than a smoldering pit, the smoke choking the air between him and a large black bird with a needle-thin orange beak and long, ruddy legs. The bird squawked again and then drove its beak into an insect mound at the edge of the firepit.

The insect mound burst with activity, angry little creatures pouring forth in defense of their queendom. The bird used a foot to scrape the bugs from its beak and then plucked as many as it could from the surrounding earth. Apparently sated, it ran a few steps and lifted into the air.

Umhra climbed to his feet, dusted his leathers with open palms. Tukdari lay strewn around the firepit, some tangled together in post-coital knots. Stale food and ox horn tankards littered the ground around them. Umhra nudged a tankard aside with his boot and made for Joslin and Bita's tent.

He quietly pushed the flap of the tent and entered. Bita was at the hearth, stoking the fire and fiddling with her pot of aromatics. She smiled as he sat down next to her. "You wear the expression of a man ready to move on."

"I'm not so much ready as I am resigned. The matter that brought me to the shores of Tukdari remains unresolved. While my heart beckons me to stay, I know my fate lies elsewhere."

"Go see your mother, boy. Spare as many moments for her as you can."

"It was a wonderful surprise getting to meet you, Bita. I never thought I would know the sweet smell of family. I leave with a full heart that I shall carry always."

Umhra hugged Bita and left her at the hearth tending to her morning rituals. Joslin stepped out from behind the linen sheet, tears coming to her eyes as soon as she saw Umhra's face. "It is time for you to leave." She bit her bottom lip. "May I walk with you back to the beach?"

"It would be as good a place as any for me to depart. I would welcome your company."

They took their time on the way back to the blue marble cliffs. Umhra knew greater things hung in the balance, but he found it difficult to leave Joslin and Bita after only yesterday, knowing they lived. Certainly, he had felt a sense of family with Ivory, and the Bloodbound, and the Barrow's Pact, but this was different. It went beyond love, beyond admiration, beyond respect. The bond of a child to his mother and the generations before her. These were his very roots to Tyveriel. And here, he could only offer her a few fleeting moments. She deserved more.

The path leading to the beach somehow seemed narrower and more foreboding on their descent than Umhra had recalled. Maybe it was the euphoria he had experienced upon reuniting with Joslin, maybe it was his dread toward leaving her, but it felt as though the winding strip of sand and rock now begged him to reconsider leaving. After all, he did not know where he was headed next, having commandeered the power of three creator gods. He assumed Vaila would offer some direction on how to proceed. He would return to her and the sanctity of Kalmindon.

"I can't imagine the burden you bear," Joslin said, greeting the sun and welcoming its warmth on her face with a smile. "If there was anything I could do to help—"

Umhra cradled his mother's cheeks in his palms. She was warm, welcoming, loving. "It wasn't always clear to me. In fact, I neglected my duty for some time and now wonder, if I had embraced it earlier, would the peril I now face have been avoided? I spent so many years running from the day you were ripped away from me. I lost sight of what I was running toward. Maybe, had things been different, I would find peace at your side in Tukdari. How I love the thought of that future. The gods have other plans, however. My path is one that must be walked alone. I look forward to a day when we shall be together again. Until then, I shall keep you in my heart."

Joslin smiled, again wiped the tears from her eyes. "I will always treasure this day. I never thought I would feel this way again. Please, take care of yourself. I love you, my Na'ranna."

Umhra embraced Joslin. She felt small, vulnerable in his arms. He released her, nodded, and walked to the edge of the water. He thought of Vaila and of Kalmindon. A high-pitched screech pierced his mind, forcing him to his knees. He gripped his head.

Joslin ran for him, but he waved her off. She skidded in the powdery blue sand, eyes wide with fear.

Instead of the image of Kalmindon which Umhra expected to see, there materialized a desolate, windswept wasteland of purple-grey stone spires reaching into a sky blanketed with ominous clouds. He saw Spara fighting her way through a terrible dust storm, a fiendish grin on her face. Umhra allowed himself to be ripped through time and space, leaving Tukdari and his mother behind and with Wethryn in his sights.

CHAPTER 26

It was not long until the blights turned their attention to Winterashe. We fled to the Bite, where even they dare not venture.

- Entry from the Diary of Vred Ulest
Dated 14th of Riet, 908 AF. Unearthed from the Ruins of Ohteira, month of Lusta, 1399 AT

— ▲ —

Silyarithe landed in a familiar clearing, the outcrop at its center baking in the afternoon sun. The anger that consumed her after the intrusion into her lair and the disappearance of her father had given way to the spark of opportunity.

Without hesitation, she ducked below the canopy and weaved her way into the dark tangle of the Wistful Timberlands.

The smaller of the blights scrambled from her path, while their larger siblings ambled forth from the darkness to assess the disturbance.

At the center of a circle void of undergrowth, the Aged One paced. Lit by will o' wisps that hovered overhead, the primordial god muttered to itself. Silyarithe had never seen it so incensed.

"What troubles you?" she asked, eyeing Vendarithe's

desiccated remains with satisfaction.

The Aged One pointed at two sets of footprints in the mud.

"The gods of Kalmindon have found the Aged One's sanctuary. They stood here as the Aged One rested. Kemyn, himself, trod this very soil."

The gods of men and other common beasts held no significance to Silyarithe. She did not concern herself with their affairs, and they seemed all too happy to sequester themselves in their precious heaven and allow their disciples to fend for themselves. It had been so since the end of the Age of Grace, and there was no reason for it to change now.

Yet, she could tell that the presence of this Kemyn and whomever the smaller set of tracks belonged to disturbed the Aged One greatly. Her ally would be of little use to her if thoughts of self-preservation distracted them. She needed them focused on an assault on Ruari.

She sniffed at the air. "If they sought to harm you, would they not have taken advantage of your slumber and shattered you?"

The Aged One glared at her from eyes set well below its broad granite shoulders. "The Aged One assures you they are quite resilient in their resting state. The intruders would have gotten nowhere."

"Then where does your concern lie?"

"The Aged One must return to their sleep. Until this threat is eliminated, the Aged One will not awaken again."

Of course. The Aged One had lasted so long by hiding in stasis. In its living form, it was somehow vulnerable. The primordial god's anguish now made sense.

The Aged One returned to the center of the barren forest floor.

Silyarithe took a step forward. "I know where they hide. The remnants of mankind."

The Aged One turned and faced her. "How did the Grey Queen learn of such a well-hidden secret?"

"I too had intruders enter my lair. They stole Mesorith's phylactery. My father has gone missing."

"A disturbing development. Unfortunate you had not secured a more suitable host for him."

"There's more. One intruder left behind a blade. With it, I was able to locate the owner. The owner and the final holdout of mankind in Evelium. They live like ants beneath the surface in a series of caves in the southeast."

The Aged One approached Silyarithe. "What are you suggesting?"

Silyarithe paused for a moment and admired her own reflection in the ancient god's glossy black eyes. "I suggest we mount an offensive. We flush them out of their hole and destroy them in the open fields. We put an end to their resistance."

"The blights do not travel below the surface willingly. It is not in their nature, nor is it in the Aged One's nature to force it upon them."

A memory flashed in Silyarithe's mind. For a moment, she saw through Mesorith's eyes when he was a youthful dragon waging war against the armies of men as she did now. He stood on a rocky outcrop at the edge of the Wistful Timberlands, a vast force of the enemy marching toward him with siege engines and other terrible war machines in tow.

Beside him stood the Aged One. The primordial god stepped forward into the open field and pointed a finger at the throng of armored men. From the wilderness behind it came countless blights. Some towered over Silyarithe as would an ancient redwood, and others were no larger than a common garden weed.

The Aged One held its other hand to the air, the appendage barely reaching the top of its barrel-shaped shoulders. The blights stopped.

A stillness held in the air as both armies appraised the other.

The catapults at the rear of the opposing army unleashed flaming boulders into the air. The stones rained down on them like meteors. The blights screamed as the catapult fire set them aflame, their cries echoing through the field.

A boulder crashed into the earth at the Aged One's feet. They stepped through the flames and thrust their hand forward.

The blights bellowed a war cry and raced across the fields with clubs and spears held high.

Silyarithe returned to the present.

"Then I ask the Aged One to lead the blights into battle, as you once did alongside my father. Together, we can put an end to the army of Evelium and expand our cause beyond its borders. There will be little to stand in our way and all Tyveriel shall be ours."

"The gods of Kalmindon will meet their end. A just cause worthy of sacrifice."

The Aged One held its arms out wide and the blights that lurked in the shadows beyond the glow of the will o' wisps crept into the eerie light. Their cores brightened in a menagerie of vibrant colors.

"Children of the Aged One, you have fought a war as my proxy for nearly two decades. The time has come for the Aged One to join you on the battlefield and return the blood of mankind to Evelium's soil."

Blights pounded on tree trunks, stomped on the ground, and thrust their crude weapons into the air. The largest among them released a guttural chitter. The smaller blights joined in. Their chorus grew until the canopy shook overhead.

The Aged One again held out its hands. The blights fell quiet.

"Call together your brethren," the Aged One said. "Every last blight shall witness our glorious victory. We follow the Grey Queen south at once."

Silyarithe roared. Blights scattered, opening a path back to the clearing.

"I shall see you at the outcrop where you once stood in battle with my father. From there, I will lead you to the caves in the south."

The Aged One nodded.

Silyarithe hurried from beneath the dense canopy, her heart racing in anticipation of their siege. As the clearing broke overhead, she welcomed the warmth of the late afternoon sun on her scales and took flight.

CHAPTER 27

In the depths of Wethryn he found the alloy necessary to forge the Circlet of Everlife.

- The Gatekeeper's Abridged History of Tyveriel
Vol. 3, Chapter 1
– Discovered: Private Library of Solana Marwyn, the month of Vasa, 889 AT

—▲—

Umhra guarded his eyes against the relentless dust storm that lashed the austere wasteland of Wethryn. His hands and knees sunk deep into the powdery, barren soil. He sat back on his heels and took in what landscape he could discern. Towering pillars of purple-grey rock shot into the heavens, their peaks obscured by the raging tempest.

Peering fruitlessly into the storm, he climbed to his feet and labored into the buffeting wind, a familiar thrum in his right ear drawing him toward Spara. He forged onward through blasting dust and debris. Lesser abominations scrabbled from his path into small caves and hollows within the rock pillars to seek refuge from the storm.

Umhra waded through drifts of dust and ash, coming to a small village of domed, windowless hovels. He skirted the edge of the village, thinking better of disturbing its inhabitants despite the horrific conditions. The rhythm in his ear grew with every step.

Climbing over a ridge of jagged stone, he spotted a glimmer of light amongst the desolation. Umhra skidded down a narrow ashen path and came to a circle of crudely hewn stones, each three times his height. The glimmer that had caught Umhra's eye from above emanated from the circle's center and drew him within its perimeter.

There, in brilliant diamond armor, stood Spara. In one hand, she grasped a diamond axe reminiscent of the sun, like the one she forged by combining Shatter and Quake to break the Waystone in Shent. In the other, she lifted the lifeless body of a bird-like creature partially off the ground by its head. The entity was deep crimson and had long, sinuous legs and two sets of arms beneath sweeping feathered wings. It wore gold robes adorned in black embroidery—now rent and stained with blood—and gold rings on its clawed fingers and toes.

Umhra forged ahead to thwart Spara's conquest, but the winds of Wethryn hampered his advance.

Unconcerned, Spara hung the axe on her belt and drew a diamond shard in its place. She drove the shard into the creature's head at its temple. The creature's body shuddered and fell limp. Light coalesced around the wound and escaped from a beak of razor-sharp teeth from which a long tongue lolled. The light grew in intensity, spreading over the entity's form, and then flooded into Spara's icon.

The light abating, Spara turned to face Umhra, her icon pulsing red with freshly absorbed power. "Cylin, God of Chaos," she shouted over the raging wind. She tossed the god at Umhra's feet, its formerly gold eyes already dull, vacant.

As Umhra stepped over the corpse, Cylin's form turned to ash and became one with the dust storm.

"You're too late, Umhra, Champion of Vaila." Spara held her hands out wide, showing off her diamond armor in a grandiose gesture. "I am a God Ascended. All is mine."

Umhra summoned Forsetae and his own diamond armor, eliciting a look of dismay from Spara. Her top lip quivered with anger at the unexpected contest. "At first, I must admit, I considered you useful, if not a bit dim. You were even fun to be around for a time. Now, you're just irritating. A boil on otherwise unblemished skin."

Umhra took a step forward, Spara pointing her axe at him as a warning not to come any closer. "What would you expect?" Umhra asked. "You played your part in creating me. Every deceit and manipulation. Every lie that led to your ultimate betrayal. Did you honestly believe I would just sit back and watch you destroy my god and all she built?"

Spara shook her head and charged Umhra.

Umhra reciprocated in kind. Their weapons clashed, casting the interior of the stone monument aglow in a shower of celestial light. Spara spun, her axe blade whirring inches from Umhra's face. Umhra leaped back, assessed his enemy's newfound speed and agility. Spara slowly circled Umhra, eyeing him up and down, as though she were doing the same.

"Just because you wear the armor of a god doesn't make you my equal. Desperate to see their vision fulfilled, willing fools have given you their power. You've done nothing of consequence. I've taken what I deserve from the others, and I will take the rest from you."

Spara lunged forward, bringing her axe down upon Umhra. He dodged the attack and countered, slashing Forsetae across Spara's back. The blow struck true, but the blade careened off the shimmering armor instead of finding flesh.

Spara scowled and came for him again, sweeping her axe in an uppercut. The weapon screeched across Umhra's armor, catching Forsetae with the brunt of its impact and throwing the sword from Umhra's hand. She continued her pursuit, furiously swinging her axe as Umhra stumbled backward.

Umhra dodged another axe blow and stepped into Spara, his

forehead butting her in the nose and sending her staggering into an immense stone that jutted from the landscape at a steep angle. Wiping the blood from her nose, Spara growled. She feigned another onslaught and ran with the wind at her back. White, angelic wings sprouted from between her shoulder blades, and she took to the air.

Umhra gave chase, his own wings catching a gale. Dust and debris lashed his face as he climbed—Spara a shadow through the roaring storm.

The wind shifted, and Spara reeled wildly. Umhra closed in. A chunk of stone hurtled past them, clipping the leading edge of Spara's left wing, sending her into a spin. Umhra grabbed her ankle and held fast with all his strength. He dove back toward the earth, pulling Spara behind him. As they neared the desolate Wethryn landscape, he pulled up and slammed Spara into the ground.

Spara tumbled through the arid soils, a plume of dust trailing her. Umhra landed before her, summoned Forsetae back to his hand. He flourished the blade on his cautious approach.

You must end her now. Do not hesitate with this one. She will be the ruin of everything.

Umhra nodded, looming over Spara as she labored to push herself from the earth. "This game of ours ends now."

The earth trembled. *Her beast comes to her aid.*

"Yes, it does." Spara smiled through blood-stained teeth.

The Eketar burst forth from the earth, threw Umhra from his feet, and unleashed a deafening roar. Umhra crashed through a rock pillar and slid to a halt at the base of another. He regained his footing and shook his head, his ears ringing.

Spara came before the immense worm and waved goodbye coquettishly. She closed her eyes and vanished, leaving Umhra alone with her pet.

The Eketar coiled its rust-colored body, its rear-most segment pulsing and the eye at its center glowing chartreuse. The second segment quivered and lit up, then the third.

Umhra charged, leaping into the air amidst a deluge of dust and rock. The eyes on the Eketar's back dimmed. Spinning faster than any beast of its size should be allowed, the creature thrust the barbed stinger at the base of its tail. The spike screeched across Umhra's armor, sending him spinning into the dirt.

The Eketar attacked, its mouth agape with razor-sharp fangs running in concentric circles down its throat. Rows of fangs gyrated in alternating directions, black venom dripping from each.

Umhra stood his ground and focused on the surrounding space, drawing it inward and taking control of the storm. Obscured by the dust devil around him, he released a concussive blast. The explosion leveled rock pillars and sent a shower of debris into the Eketar, but it surged forward despite the chunks of stone impacting its pulpy flesh.

Umhra dove to avoid the monstrosity's path, but the Eketar slammed him in the back with a swipe of its enormous head and sent him crashing into another rock pillar. The pillar shattered and its pieces were swept up by the storm.

The Eketar spun and charged after Umhra, who scrambled to his feet, laboring to get air into his lungs under cracked ribs. He rolled clumsily from the Eketar's attack, not knowing what else to do. As the Eketar thundered past him, it lashed out with its stinger and drove it between the diamond plates of Umhra's armor at his shoulder.

The stinger's barb caught and yanked Umhra forward, tearing at his flesh. The wound burned. With a pulse of Umhra's heart, the pain spread throughout his chest. With a second beat, it flooded his body.

The Eketar lifted Umhra from his feet and thrashed him back and forth. The stinger ripped free—a spray of blood swept up by the wind—and sent Umhra plummeting to the ground.

Umhra landed on his hands and knees, his arms giving out as the Eketar's poison surged through his form. He vomited and clutched his pyramid.

The Eketar reared up high overhead, the eye on its hind-most segment once again coming to light.

I am no god. Forsetae resonated in Umhra's mind. *This monstrosity holds no power over me.*

Umhra focused his mind and regained control of his labored breath—his heart rate slowing to a discernible rhythm as the eyes along the Eketar's body came to life one at a time. When the illumination reached the eyes within the bony plate on the creature's head, the effects of the poison faded, and Umhra jumped to his feet and threw Forsetae into the storm.

The sword windmilled through the tempest in a wide arc, the gales guiding it to its target. The three eyes on the Eketar's head burst aglow and the monstrosity roared, sending forth a wave of energy that tore at Umhra's form. He guarded his face with his arm, diamonds tearing away from his armor.

The Eketar's roar stripped Umhra bare. Forsetae streaked into the giant worm's open maw. Flesh peeled away from Umhra's face and chest. As his footing gave way, Forsetae burst through the back of the Eketar's head and spiraled out into the storm until falling out of sight.

The Eketar's eyes faded, their vibrant chartreuse glow growing murky and dull. The creature swayed as black ichor spewed from its mouth and the exit wound Forsetae had left. Umhra saw his opportunity and ran for the Eketar. His wings sprouted from his bare back, and he drew the diamond dagger from his belt and leaped into the air. The storm lifting him quickly above the worm, he collapsed his wings and fell toward the Eketar.

He buried the dagger deep in the worm's throat, just below its agape mouth. Gripping the dagger in both hands, he wrenched it downward. The flesh gave way and Umhra slid down the worm's body, leaving a laceration the length of its form in his path.

Coming to his feet, Umhra stared up at his handy work as the Eketar thrashed about, its lifeblood pouring forth in a deluge. It finally toppled over and crashed into the earth, sending a plume of dust into the restless air. The behemoth quivered and then came to rest.

Umhra's dagger sparkled as though it were new. He sheathed it and placed his hands on the Eketar's rubbery hide. He shook his head and said, "You shouldn't have to pay such a price for acting upon your nature—for doing all you know. I hold no ill will and welcome you to Kalmindon's gardens." Umhra drew the Eketar's fleeting soul into his hands and forged another glass bead and another promise.

He peered into the storm and summoned Forsetae to his hand. The vaunted sword did not heed his call. He could no longer feel the connection he had grown accustomed to since bonding himself to the weapon in Manteis's crypt. He felt hollow. Broken. But there was no time to search Wethryn for his steadfast companion. He had to find Spara. Possibly now, without the help of her precious monstrosity, she would be vulnerable, and he could put an end to her misguided quest. She had already brought the pantheon to its knees...who could say what untold danger she posed to Tyveriel and beyond if she were to destroy Vaila and acquire her power.

He closed his eyes and focused on Spara. A vision of her standing before a tower of glass came to him. No. Diamond. Umhra growled. Was it possible he was already too late? That his prolonged battle with the Eketar had given Spara the window she needed to return to Kalmindon and challenge Vaila? Umhra willed his mind to take him to the image it had shared, but a vision of a great hall made of black stone interrupted him. Spirits swirled before a throne carved of blood red obsidian that showed a wolf holding a serpent in its mouth as the serpent's body coiled around its own in a grim embrace. His heart told him to return to Kalmindon and defend his god, but something in the pit of his stomach told him otherwise.

He focused on the red throne and celestial light enveloped him.

CHAPTER 28

Barra Argith was cast out from his colony for looking upon the sun. Since, he preferred to be known by the Evenese translation of his name, Shadow.

- *The Legend of the Barrow's Pact by Nicholas Barnswallow* Chapter 3 – Unearthed from the depths of Peacebreaker Keep, month of Jai, 1422 AT

— ▲ —

Turin crossed her ankles on the seat next to her and smiled. She scanned the faces that stared back at her with consternation in their eyes. Her aunt always said that a good leader knew when they needed to shake things up. From the look of things, she'd done just that. And it felt right.

"With all due respect," Gromley said, nodding at Gleriel, "he is undead."

"You died once, did you not?" Turin asked.

Gromley's brow furrowed. He glared at Shadow, who shrugged in reply.

"What you refer to is revivification. It is well-documented that the Mystics had the ability to perform such miracles. This. This is fundamentally different. Whatever necromantic curse gives life to your new friend here is poorly understood and has created some of the worst abominations in history. One need to go no further than the dracolich, Mesorith, to grasp my point."

"Well, Gleriel is different. Not only did he come to our rescue in Anaris, but he has a storied past. Maybe you should all get to know him before you cast your all too predictable dispersions. Open your minds to the possibility the world isn't black and white. That there is room for exception in everything."

Naivara placed a hand on Turin's. "My dear, if you've taught us anything, it's that grey is beautiful. That there is more to a person than the color of their skin or their lack thereof. Gromley, you assert that Gleriel is cursed. How many said the same about Turin?"

"Innumerable fools."

"And what has been your response every time?"

"To defend her from their ignorance."

"Maybe. Just maybe, we now must defend Gleriel from our own. Certainly, we have never come across anything like him in our vast experience, but that does not mean he is not what he so plainly seems to be. A thoughtful and courageous man."

Gromley bit his bottom lip as if to stifle the terrible words about to escape. He sighed.

"You are, as always, a voice of reason, Naivara."

"Well, I can't turn myself into a dragon anymore, so I have to find new ways to be useful." She smiled, but the pain showed through the cracks in her veneer.

Laudin took her hand and kissed it.

"Gleriel, we are not the only ones at war. The gods themselves are under siege. As they die, those connected to them through suffusion lose their abilities. Naivara and Gromley have both suffered such a fate. Our friend, Umhra, fights to save the pantheon. Unless he succeeds, I'm afraid we are not at our full strength."

Gleriel tapped a bony finger on the table. "You speak of the Peacebreaker. I've heard his tale. Alas, I have no remedies for his strife—only our own. I will fight to the death with you against the Grey Queen. Together, we can bring her to her knees."

"We've been trying to do that for nearly twenty years," Shadow said. "What do you see that we don't?"

Gleriel's eyes shifted to Turin. "Our own grey queen. She is the key to the dragon's destruction."

Regent Avrette's brow furrowed. "While it is obvious that Turin's powers grow, I will not allow the last of the Forene bloodline to risk her life in combat with the Grey Queen."

"If you aren't willing to take risks, I see little chance of you reaping rewards," Gleriel said.

Regent Avrette blushed but bit her tongue.

"I appreciate your concern, Aunt Jenta, but I will decide what risks I will take on behalf of our people. No one will forbid me from bringing them a better future in the name of my own safety. There is, however, another issue we cannot afford to overlook," Turin said. "The blights. Naivara and I have both had visions of an evil force that corrupts the Wistful Timberlands and turns them against us. If we are to turn the tide, we must free them from this control."

"Not to mention our promise to King Eleazar," Nicholas said.

Gleriel made a guttural clicking sound that wreaked with disgust. "I'm not sure this is going to work. You put too many restrictions on yourselves."

"Gleriel," Laudin said, "we are of the belief that if we do not hold ourselves to a higher standard than our enemy, then we are no better than those we fight."

Gleriel nodded. "I respect the sentiment. It is noble. Sometimes, however, good people need to do deplorable things to put evil in its grave. If the enemy seeks to burn down your home, you must be willing to burn down their village."

"I like you, Bones," Shadow said. "We need a little attitude in this gang of do-gooders."

Gleriel snarled like a feral dog.

"What? You don't like the nickname?"

"I do not. I'm sure you can imagine why."

Shadow raised his hands in the air. "Okay. Okay. I've struck a nerve. I apologize."

Gleriel huffed and turned his attention back to Turin. "When we were in Anaris, you used powers I have not seen since the days wizards walked among us. But you didn't learn magic from a book, and you haven't Suffused with a god, have you?"

"No. I was born with certain abilities and have learned more since."

"What is the source of your strength?"

"Tyveriel, itself. There is a connection between us. Nothing born of Tyveriel can hurt me. Other than blights, for some reason."

"This corruption you speak of may have something to do with that. You would presumably be vulnerable to dragons then, as their kind originated in the Fae and only claimed Tyveriel as their home toward the end of the Age of Grace."

"I haven't cared to find out."

"Have you asked Tyveriel her feelings on the Grey Queen? Does she want the dragons here?"

Turin wondered why she never thought of asking Tyveriel her wishes? Their connection had grown stronger along with Turin's abilities, but Tyveriel had only recently shared glimpses of her desires.

"I have not. She has shown me her disdain for the being that corrupts the blights, but she has shown me nothing of the dragons."

Talus sat quietly, his fingers steepled as he listened to the conversation. "Can you do that? Ask Tyveriel what she needs?"

"She gives more of herself each time we connect. I suppose it wouldn't hurt to try."

"Talking to Tyveriel now, are we?" Gromley asked. "At least I only speak with actual people."

Turin deserved that, and she knew it. She smiled. "If you think I'm apologizing again, you are sadly mistaken."

Gromley laughed. "My dear, one sincere apology is always enough. A second only cheapens the sentiment."

Right again. Turin hated that there was always a lesson in Gromley's words. Or did she hate she had so many lessons to learn? If she was honest with herself, it was more—but not entirely—the latter.

"Well, I'm glad I won't disappoint you. I'm going to get Sena and take her to the surface with me. She hasn't been outside in days and would enjoy the trip. I'll be able to focus better up there. Hopefully, that will improve my connection with Tyveriel."

"Then, we will await your return and Tyveriel's answer," Jenta said. "Good luck, Turin."

"Thank you. Would you like to come with me, Gleriel?"

Gleriel surveyed the table. "If it wouldn't interfere with your process."

"Not at all. And it would give Sena someone to speak with while I'm meditating. Aridon isn't the best conversationalist, and she's spent all day with him. She'll be looking for a conversation and that would interfere."

Gleriel sighed, hundreds of voices meeting his in a grim chorus. "I am not the right choice for such a job."

"Nonsense," Turin said, rising from her seat. "She'll do most of the talking."

She waved for Gleriel to follow and coursed from the room.

The animated skeleton came to her side, his footfalls even and light on the stone floor. Together, they walked in silence to Sena's quarters, three rings above the royal hall. Here, the path narrowed and the distance between doors shrank. Time and time again, she had offered Sena accommodations closer to her own and time and time again, Sena declined despite their close friendship—even when she was asked to stay in Indrisor's spacious home. She was born and raised near the surface of

Ruari and saw no need to pretend otherwise. Turin loved her for it. For her honesty. For her authenticity. You could trust a person who knew themselves and embraced it proudly. If only Turin found it so easy to embrace being queen.

Turin stopped before a wooden door worn smooth with age. Rust flecked its black metal hinges and handle. They rattled as she knocked.

Neela barked within and the door groaned open, revealing Aridon's smiling face.

"She's having moods," he said. "Been a long day."

Turin hugged Aridon. He wrapped an arm around her and pulled her tight to his chest. Warmth radiated off him...drew her in further.

She looked into his gentle eyes and pursed her lips. "Why don't you go get some rest?"

"Yes. I would feel better."

"Then, off you go. Gleriel and I will take it from here."

Aridon grimaced at Gleriel. "Don't scare her. Her head is fuzzy."

Gleriel offered Aridon a sincere nod but said nothing.

Aridon patted his leg and Neela came to heel. She panted, her docked tail wagging furiously. "Come on. Nap time."

The two set off, leaving Turin and Gleriel alone.

"He's a pleasant man," Gleriel noted. "I wish he didn't find me so off-putting."

"He'll come around once he gets to know you," Turin said. "You have to approach him as you would a child."

"That normally doesn't go well."

Turin laughed. "I know the feeling all too well."

She entered Sena's room and Gleriel followed, but came no further than necessary to close the door behind him. The cramped room barely had enough space for a small table with two chairs. Turin always imagined it as being like what Talus had told her of his childhood home in Tayrelis when he would recount his and her mother's daring escape from the clutches of her biological father.

"Sena?" Turin called.

Sena poked her head out from the adjoining room. "Oh, great. You're here. I think Ari's had enough for one day. Did you two figure anything out?"

"Maybe. Gleriel believes my connection with Tyveriel could be the key to defeating the Grey Queen. We are heading up to the surface so I can ask Tyveriel for guidance. Do you want to come and keep Gleriel company while I do?"

"Do I ever! I need some fresh air and I have plenty of questions for our new friend here."

Gleriel's eyes flared with arcane fury.

Turin flashed him an uneven smirk. "I told you so."

"Very well," Gleriel said. "We go to the surface together. I am an open book."

— ▲ —

A gentle breeze lifted Turin's hair from her shoulder and sent it snaking across her face. She took a deep breath and tucked the errant wisps securely behind her ears.

Sena and Gleriel sat a short distance off. Sena chattered feverishly, eliciting the occasional nod of acknowledgement from her hooded counterpart. They made an odd pair—one so full of life and the other devoid—and yet, Turin had brought them together. Maybe, if she could forge such a bizarre friendship, there was yet hope she could find a way toward peace for her people. Maybe Tyveriel could help with that.

She closed her eyes and welcomed the warmth of the afternoon sun on her face. Her mind raced. She squirmed on the cool earth upon which she sat and tried to let the stress melt away. Steadying her mind, she focused on the tension in her jaw and allowed it to unclench. She let her neck hang and rolled her head from side-to side, the accompanying pain in her shoulders lessening with each stretch.

Soon, the worries that plagued her faded, and she placed her open palms upon the soil. She dragged her fingers through the dirt and reached out to Tyveriel in her mind. Her hands went cold as though she held them beneath the frigid waters of the River Torrent in the months before the Sowing Moon, when ice still clung to its banks.

The cold crept up her arms and rushed through her body with every beat of her heart. Her mind went blank.

You showed me your hatred for the being that corrupts the Wistful Timberlands, but what of the Grey Queen? She no more belongs to you than the other.

From the shadows in her mind emerged the image of a grey dragon coursing through a cloudless sky. The beast folded its wings and dove toward scrambling masses of entangled people and blights. It snarled on approach, the sound of the wind rushing over its reptilian wings drowning out the screams below.

The Grey Queen opened wide its mouth of dagger-like teeth and unleashed a torrent of purple plasma into the frenzy. She landed in the chaos and grinned triumphantly.

Turin's stomach twisted with rage. Despite sharing the sentiment, this anger was not her own. It was not the anger of a queen helplessly witnessing the massacre of her people, but the anguish of a world losing itself to the unrelenting aspirations of an invader.

The dragon's visage faded, and Turin's own face took its place. She felt Tyveriel grow calm—hopeful.

She stood before a wall of sheer stone. People ran past, putting her between them and the Grey Queen. She ran at the dragon.

A surge of heat tore through Turin's body. It burned in her chest like a hot coal until the pain was unbearable. Then everything went black.

Her jaw stung.

Turin's eyes flitted open. As the haze cleared, she saw Sena and Gleriel kneeling over her with a dusky sky behind them.

"You really have to stop doing that," Sena said with tears in her eyes. "This time, it was harder to wake you."

Gleriel placed a bony hand beneath Turin's shoulder and helped her sit up.

"Sorry. I wasn't expecting her response to be so intense."

"So, Tyveriel spoke to you?" Gleriel asked.

Turin nodded. "Just as you suspected. She doesn't want the Grey Queen here anymore than we do."

"What did she show you?"

"She showed me the Grey Queen laying waste to our people amidst a great battle with the blights. Then she showed me myself amidst the fray. She believes I may be able to help."

Gleriel nodded contemplatively. "And then?"

"There was a searing pain in my chest, and I blacked out."

"Do you feel different?" Sena asked.

Turin stared at her friend.

"You know, like, more powerful or something?"

"Not unless you include this splitting headache."

Sena frowned.

"No. It was worth it. She showed me what we need to do."

"What's that?" Sena asked as Gleriel hoisted Turin to her feet.

"To bring the fight to the Grey Queen before it's too late."

CHAPTER 29

Many have left for Ruari. Still more have perished. I will stay behind with those who remain.

- Entry from Xavier Pell's Journal
Undated. Unearthed from the ruins of Anaris, month of Vasa, 1152 AT

— ▲ —

Silyarithe soared over the Wistful Timberlands, intent on arriving early at her rendezvous point with the Aged One so she would have time to prepare before their offensive. She thought of her father and what he would do if he were at her side. She huffed. No doubt, he would throw caution to the wind and wreak havoc as only he could.

A memory of Mesorith's forced her own thoughts aside. Through his eyes, she saw him emerging from the mouth of a cave. The cavern behind him cast an eerie indigo light that pulsed rhythmically. He inspected the dense stand of white-barked aspen trees with yellow leaves and relished his success at crossing over from the Fae to this new land.

Here, the metallic dragons could not hide behind their self-righteous laws and persecute his kind. The only wars waged in Tyveriel would be those he, himself, sanctioned. Here, he would be king.

Mesorith turned back to the cavern and roared. A beautiful white dragon that Silyarithe immediately recognized as her mother stepped forth from the cave. Golden aspen leaves rustled overhead.

"You've done it," she marveled. "We have a new home. A chance at a better life. You are miraculous."

Mesorith bowed to his bride. "I would not have seen it through without your encouragement. What once was only a dream, today becomes reality."

"Shall I call the others forth?" Zalinrithe asked.

"No. We will find a suitable home before opening the gate to the others. I have no interest in leading our kin from one fire blindly into another."

Mesorith leaped from the ground and burst through the canopy of aspens. He spiraled up into the sky and waited for his bride to join him. As Zalinrithe neared, he set off to the west in search of refuge.

Silyarithe shook her head as if she could throw the foreign memory from her mind. Clarity returned. She wondered why this memory presented itself now. The memory of her parents' arrival in Evelium. Then, ahead of her, a stand of golden aspens appeared amidst the sea of green that encircled it.

She swept over the anomaly and decided it was worth disrupting her own plans to see where her father's memory would lead.

The grey dragon rolled into a dive and plummeted toward the aspens. She unfurled her wings at the edge of the stand and arrested her descent. White trunks splintered like twigs as she broke through the dense canopy and came to rest at the center of the grove.

She shook the debris from her back and circled like a feral cat. She saw no signs of danger, only golden leaves and an ample cave built into an outcrop of dark granite.

The mouth of the cave pulsed the same blue-purple glow she

had seen in Mesorith's memory. A portal to the Fae.

She craned her neck in curiosity, but the cavern gave her nothing in the way of detail of what awaited her inside.

Silyarithe knew little of the home of her ancestors. All she had to go by were vague flashes of recollections of those who came before her. Without context, they were useless. What she knew for certain was that Mesorith came to Tyveriel to escape persecution. Undoubtedly, it would be an inhospitable venture should she decide to go.

She took a tentative step forward, an aspen tree creaking as it bent against her shoulder.

Now, she could see the pulsing light came not from within the cave but that the mouth of the cave itself contained a thin membrane as though an ethereal spider had spun a web in its span, hoping to catch its next meal.

A streak of light in her peripheral vision caught her attention.

The trail darted toward her through the trees in a haphazard path. It looped around her entirety three times before hovering before her face, undeterred by her size or demeanor.

The creature was no bigger than a sparrow, with long, pointed ears and oversized eyes. Its skin was porcelain white, and its limbs were long and thin.

"A Fae Hobb, perhaps?" Silyarithe wondered aloud.

The Fae Hobb dashed to the gate on pearlescent dragonfly wings and flitted about the portal's surface.

Silyarithe snarled and approached the cave entrance. She pressed a claw against the portal. It resisted her effort to pass through.

"Dormant," she said, the curious little Fae Hobb racing about her head. "Useless."

She backed away and unleashed a torrent of violet plasma over the gate out of frustration.

As the cloud of noxious fumes dissipated, the gate shone brighter than before. The glow unwavering.

Without hesitation, the Fae Hobb plunged into the gate and vanished from sight.

Silyarithe huffed. *Sometimes rash behavior is your best option.*

She stood before the gate, weighing her options. Surely, if such an insignificant creature did not so much as hesitate to cross over, the Grey Queen was brave enough to follow suit.

She shook her head and bound toward the gate.

As she passed through its surface, a blur of indigo surrounded her. Her stomach reeled as space twisted around her.

Instead of the dark interior of the cave she entered, she emerged in a foreign realm of yellow skies and vibrant orange grasses; a vibrant sun perched low on the horizon. The earth beneath her feet was spongy and cool, reminding her of the fen on the northern shores of Lertmor.

Silyarithe looked over her shoulder at the cavern through which she had arrived. A sheer cliff face of glossy grey stone rose into the sky. It stretched out for what seemed like miles in either direction. The gate remained intact.

Around her, thousands of Fae Hobbs fluttered about, doing whatever it is that Fae Hobbs do. High overhead dragons soared, a spectacle of gold, platinum, bronze, and silver. She shuddered. A sneer spread across her face as she thought of Vendarithe, the ancient rose gold dragon that would have killed her in the Wistful Timberlands if not for the Aged One intervening. How she despised their kind.

She scanned the horizon, hoping to locate some refuge from the open skies. Nothing but open plains except for the escarpment behind her. For now, she would stay close to the cliff face until she found better cover.

A memory of this very place flashed through her mind. For a moment, she saw the Fae through the eyes of her mother. She trailed behind a group of dragons that followed Mesorith along the escarpment, heading away from the glowing gate behind them.

Silyarithe followed their path and slinked along the smooth stone wall, one eye on her way forward, the other on the beasts gliding overhead. Common sense told her to return to Tyveriel but something deeper, something ancient and irresistible drew her farther into the Fae. So far, it seemed the odds of finding death far outweighed those of finding an ally. And yet she pressed on.

For hours on end, she crept—Fae Hobbs, her only company—until the path she followed descended, and she found herself in a narrow canyon. The skies cleared of any sign of threat, and she shook off the cramps from her prolonged crouch. Standing tall, she continued.

Rounding a turn in the canyon, she came upon an enormous red dragon that blocked the path ahead. He was a handsome beast with a pale orange chest and matching curved horns, which he held low to the ground as he snarled.

"You should know better than to enter our territory, platinum scum," the behemoth hissed. "Name yourself and your business or you will not see the rising of the second sun."

"My name is Silyarithe the Grey Queen, and I am not a platinum." Silyarithe puffed out her chest for the red dragon to get a better look. "I am the daughter of Mesorith and Zalinrithe if those names have meaning to you."

The red dragon laughed. "Of course you are. And I am Kryarith the Garnet Rage, son of the Alldragon."

"Tell me, son of the Alldragon. Have you seen another grey dragon such as me? Can you explain how I come before you if I am not the progeny of the Liege of Darkness and the White Death?"

Kryarith raised his head high and narrowed his eyes.

"Do I smell like a metallic dragon?" Silyarithe asked.

"No. And your business?"

"I come from Tyveriel, the land my father left the Fae realm for. I am in search of an alliance with my brothers and sisters."

Kryarith huffed, smoke billowing from his nostrils and dancing up the canyon walls. "Mesorith left us here to die. He never returned as promised. Why would we ally ourselves with his kin?"

"I assure you his desertion was not by design but out of ill fortune. It would seem the gate he opened to leave this realm closed behind him. He was unable to return without the key. That being me."

"And where are the great Mesorith and Zalinrithe now? Why do they not return with you?"

Silyarithe hung her head despite not mourning her parents' deaths. She had never known love for another—only their utility. "My mother sacrificed herself to assure my survival as a hatchling. My father recently perished at the hands of my enemy."

"What of the others that went with him?"

"Also, dead. I am the last of our kind in Tyveriel."

Kryarith turned, exposing a gaping cavern in the canyon wall. "Then be on your way. You offer nothing we need."

He ducked his immense head into the entrance of the cave.

"I offer you passage to Tyveriel where not a metallic dragon is to be found and where the remnants of mankind hide in fear of me, as you do here. I offer you a land devoid of true threat."

Kryarith stopped in his tracks. From within the dark interior of the cave, his eyes glowed like stars on the night of the Reaping Moon. "Follow me. You may bring your case before the others."

He disappeared into the cave.

Her heart pounding in her chest, Silyarithe followed.

"You are lucky you weren't killed, coming here," Kryarith's voice echoed from the across an expansive cavern encrusted in ice. It reminded Silyarithe of her mother's lair deep below the Sea of Widows. While the cold never bothered her, the red dragon wore his discomfort plainly, shuddering as he spoke.

Silyarithe crossed the slick floor. "It was not without risk.

The metallics seem to be everywhere."

"Everywhere but here, I assure you. This is our last refuge, and we tire of it." Kryarith continued into the adjoining cavern.

This room dripped with green sputum that bubbled in vast pools on the floor. The dragons navigated the narrow path that snaked between the acrid pools.

"I never learned to tolerate the greens and their poison," Kryarith said with a sneer. "Fortunately, the metallics hate it even more than me. If they breach the ice—which they haven't in a century—they quickly turn back here. For that, I'm grateful to the greens."

Silyarithe nodded. She hadn't had the opportunity to know many other dragons. For the last several years, Mesorith had lived as a green, but she assumed his reviling ways were more because of the decrepit state of his host than the broader species' proclivities.

"And what is the nature of your breath?" Kryarith ducked into another tunnel. "You are unlike the rest of us."

Silyarithe spat a globule of violet plasma over his shoulder onto the wall of the passage. It dripped down the wall, leaving a trail of flame in its wake.

Kryarith studied the flame as it licked the dark stone. "Impressive. Your breath has permanence unto itself. Mine requires kindling to burn. It cannot last on stone."

Silyarithe huffed, eliciting a glare from Kryarith. She didn't flinch, despite his enormity. She knew she was superior, and now he did as well. There was nothing wrong with that. It is the way of things. Life is full of inequity. The earlier you understand that then the wiser you will be.

Kryarith turned from the globule of flame and continued down the corridor.

The passage gradually widened until opening into a massive cavern with a high ceiling covered in stalactites. Unlike the other caverns they had crossed, this one was devoid of ice or poison, or other traps laid for the metallics. It was a vast expanse of dark stone, the circumference of which was marked by seven darker holes.

Kryarith roared. "This is where the Convocation meets. We have hidden our lairs deep below the surface. We leave only when we must and never alone."

"You were alone when we met in the canyon."

"Was he?" a voice hissed from behind.

Silyarithe looked over her shoulder to see a green dragon slink into the cavern from the tunnel behind her.

"This is Nisorithe the Jade Deceiver."

"Yes," Nisorithe said, coming alongside Silyarithe with the grace of an adder. "My apologies for the deception. One must be cautious in these times, and you can easily be mistaken for platinum under the first sun."

Silyarithe considered grabbing the smaller dragon and tearing her throat out. She did not like being played the fool. Alas, she came here for help and murder often interferes with such ventures. Instead, she simply bared her teeth for a moment to make the smaller dragon aware of her prowess.

Nisorithe bowed her head in reverence. "Again, my apologies."

A white dragon of considerable age soon met them, its ice-blue eyes framed by a mane of elongated scales with nearly translucent tips. He paused at the sight of the Grey Queen, a smile crossing a mouth of blunted teeth.

"Long have we awaited your arrival, youngling." His thundering voice commanded caution and respect. "Many have tested the gate through which Mesorith and the others left and have failed. And here you are before us, with the gate reopened."

Other dragons filtered into the room from the passages along the far wall. Soon, dragons great and small filled the room—although not as many as Silyarithe had envisioned. Some were old and lame, others young and still fragile. Only a few would prove useful in the assault on mankind's caves. Most were unlikely to survive.

"Mesorith and Zalinrithe succeeded," a young black dragon exclaimed from the crowd. "The Grey Queen lives. She returns to deliver us from oppression."

A frenzy of chatter overcame the group until the white dragon bellowed, calling for order. "Of course, my daughter succeeded. Tell me, youngling, what news do you bring from Zalinrithe?"

"You are Zalinrithe's father? My grandfather?"

"Indeed, youngling. I gave the one you call mother her name."

Silyarithe bowed her head to the floor in a rare sign of reverence. After a long moment, she looked her grandfather in the eye. "Zalinrithe gave her life so that I could come into the world at a time of weakness for mankind."

Her grandfather roared with such force stalactites rained down from the shadowed roof and broke upon the cavern floor.

"Yes, grandfather, it hurts me as well that her sacrifice was necessary."

"And what of Mesorith and the others he brought with him to the new world?"

"All dead, I'm afraid. I am the last of our kind in Tyveriel."

Some dragons from the Convocation hung their heads in defeat. Others turned their backs.

"Not all is so bleak," Silyarithe said. "In my brief life, I've nearly rid Tyveriel's greatest continent of mankind. I come to seek your aid in destroying them once and for all and securing our kind a new homeland. A homeland free of the metallics. Free of threat."

The Convocation once again broke into uproarious chatter. The ancient white dragon bared his teeth, plumes of icy breath billowing into the air, and they again grew quiet.

"We have been waiting for untold ages for Mesorith's prophecy to come to fruition. Long ago, he promised us safe passage to a peaceful world. He spoke of a daughter that would free us from our bondage at the hands of the metallics. We had all but given up on any hope of salvation until this very day. Now, the Grey Queen stands before us, offering the freedom we have desired for many second suns. Are we to stay here and cower or follow her and spread our wings in a new world?"

At first, silence reigned. Then, a burly yellow dragon with deep garnet eyes and ridged horns that swept forward from the sides of its head along its jawline stepped forward. "I tire of these caves. I yearn to soar among the clouds. Is that not what we are meant to do? There is no future for our kind in the Fae. I head to Tyveriel with the Grey Queen."

Kryarith and Nisorithe came to the yellow dragon's side. "Us as well," they said in unison.

Silyarithe's grandfather nodded his head. "I too will follow the Grey Queen and help create a new world where we shall thrive once more."

More dragons stepped forth in support. When all had joined, Silyarithe roared. The rest joined in the chorus.

"Then it is settled," the ancient white dragon said. "This very day, under the fading light of the second sun, we shall follow the Grey Queen through the gate to Tyveriel. Make ready."

The Convocation broke and Silyarithe approached her grandfather. He looked down upon her with eyes that reminded her of her mother's.

"It brings me comfort that Zalinrithe lives on in your form. I see her fearless wit within you."

"Thank you, grandfather. Tell me your name."

"Alolith. First named of the Alldragon."

Silyarithe again bowed her head. "Tell me, grandfather. Is this the extent of your numbers?"

"Those who gathered for the Convocation and swore themselves to follow you to Tyveriel are all that remain of our kind, yes. In the millennia since Mesorith left, our ranks have succumbed to age and predation."

Silyarithe stood tall and met Alolith's gaze with as much

conviction as she could muster. "Some of us will not survive the final war with man. Others are not fit to join us. The few of us that fly into battle will be risking everything for the young and weak we leave behind so that our kind may thrive once we claim our victory."

Alolith nodded. "An acceptable sacrifice. Their names shall be bound to the Alldragon for eternity."

"Yes, I am certain that is a great honor. When do we leave?"

"The second sun has risen. It will not be long until the sky dims at the setting of the first and we will have cover from the metallic scouts. We will follow the path by which you arrived and cross through the gate unnoticed."

"I should like to witness the rise and fall of the suns you speak of. I have seen so little of my homeland."

"Very well," Alolith agreed. "But it is forbidden to go to the surface alone. Kryarith will accompany you. This, I must insist on."

Silyarithe huffed. "That will not be necessary. I can take care of myself."

"You openly admit to not having knowledge of the Fae. You have no reference for the threat that looms on the surface. As long as you are here, you will abide by my laws. You can act the queen when we reach Tyveriel."

"Very well," Silyarithe agreed. She admittedly knew little of the Fae and the plight of the chromatic dragons in this realm. Someday she would return and liberate her ancestral homeland from the metallics, but she had to secure Tyveriel first. She had to create a refuge where her ranks could grow.

She turned to Kryarith. "I should like to see the setting of your first sun. Will you accompany me to the surface?"

Kryarith nodded. "It would be my honor to keep time with the Grey Queen. Follow me."

Silyarithe followed her guide back through the antechambers and out of the cavern system. The scent of honeysuckle filled the air as the sun that greeted her when she arrived in the Fae sunk below the horizon at one end of the canyon and another rose rapidly at the other.

In contrast to the warm amber glow of its predecessor, the second sun brought a cold blue light that cast the sky in shades of sage green. The beauty of the unexpected change struck Silyarithe.

A dragon screeched overhead, its shadow coursing over the canyon.

"The metallics struggle to see in the light of the second sun," Kryarith said. "It is the only time of day we are safe to hunt as they flee to their lairs. Rarely do they patrol late in the day."

Silyarithe had many questions about the land of her ancestors and their subjugation to the metallic dragons, but there would be time for questions. For now, she was content to admire the foreign landscape's beauty and that of the company she kept.

Soon, the others emerged from the cavern, with Alolith the last to reach the surface.

"We are ready," the ancient white dragon said. "Let us not waste another moment on our journey to Tyveriel."

"As you wish, grandfather."

Silyarithe set off down the canyon with Kryarith at her side. The others followed in close proximity. Silyarithe glanced over her shoulder at her dragon army. Some kept their heads down like frightened dogs as they traveled, while others looked to the sky, their eyes darting back and forth in search of a threat.

Pathetic. Only Kryarith and her grandfather held themselves with any sense of dignity, their heads held high, and chests puffed out as they strode. They were true dragons. These other things were little more than rodents scurrying from danger.

They trudged for hours until the landscape opened, and orange grass replaced the pale moss of the canyon floor. They were not far from the gate and the morale of the procession improved.

Staying close to the cliff face, Silyarithe continued until the indigo glow of the gate welcomed her. As the gate came into view, however, a massive figure sat before it and blocked their escape.

Identical platinum dragons of nearly equal size flanked the rose gold dragon on either side. As the chromatics filed into the field, three bronze dragons landed behind them.

"I could smell you the moment you entered the Fae," Vendarithe said, her form gleaming with radiance cast from the gate. She bore no injuries from her death at the hands of the Aged One, and her ruby eyes glinted with vigor. "Did you think you would pass unnoticed?"

Silyarithe snarled. "We intend to leave the Fae to your kind. Do with it what you will. We only want passage to Tyveriel."

"Why should I allow that? So, you can breed undeterred and return in numbers when you tire of the mortal plane? I think not. The scourge of the chromatics ends here."

Alolith thrashed his mighty tail at one of the bronze dragons behind him. With a resounding crack, the bronze dragon's head whipped back, a spray of green blood painting the grass.

The other two bronze dragons snarled and leaped at Alolith with outstretched talons.

Kryarith and the burly yellow dragon each charged at the platinum twins that flanked Vendarithe. The smaller and older chromatics darted about, some seeking cover from the battle, others scrambling to do what they could to help Alolith.

Vendarithe gave a casual glance at one of her talons as chaos erupted around her. "I guess that leaves you and me."

The rose gold dragon charged Silyarithe with a speed unnatural for a creature so large.

Silyarithe swatted a small black dragon into Vendarithe's path, causing her adversary to stumble. She lunged for Vendarithe and sank her teeth into her flank.

With one fore claw, Vendarithe batted Silyarithe away and with the other, she pinned the helpless black dragon to the ground. She bit into the flailing dragon's neck and tore its head free from its body and cast it aside.

Silyarithe spewed her noxious plasma across the field between them, setting the grass ablaze. In the moment of reprieve, she came to Kryarith's side as he recoiled from his adversary, a fresh laceration running the length of his shoulder.

"I will lure them from the gate," Kryarith said. "You lead the others to freedom."

"But." The notion had not entered Silyarithe's mind. "You are more worthy than the rest combined."

"What is my worth if I leave my kin here to die? Now go."

Vendarithe strode through Silyarithe's wall of purple flame, her mouth agape and filled with a burgeoning flame.

Kryarith barreled into the rose gold dragon and sent her reeling. The platinum dragon he was engaged with prior leaped through the fire and landed on Kryarith. It bit into his back. Kryarith roared and rolled, taking the platinum with him, and casting it into its twin.

"To the gate," Silyarithe bellowed.

She dashed for the glowing portal, the footfalls of the other chromatics behind her. As she came upon the gate, she spun and allowed the others to disappear through the membranous surface before her. Once Alolith was through, she looked back at Kryarith, who was locked in a hopeless battle with five metallic dragons.

He fought fiercely, but she well knew his fate. What could have been. With melancholy filling her heart, she dove into the portal and returned to Tyveriel.

CHAPTER 30

The locals informed us of a portal along the cliff face. After a treacherous climb, we found ourselves in a desolate and inhospitable wasteland, teeming with abominations. Our retreat from Wethryn was swift.

- *A Traveler's Guide to the Odd and Obscure by Sentina Vake*
Unearthed from the Homestead in Maryk's Cay, month of Riet, 1407 AT

— ▲ —

Smoke. Umhra choked as the light faded, leaving him in near darkness. The scent of burning wood filled the air, but no fires were visible in any direction as he turned. A stiff breeze blew, clouds of smoke rushing by as though in a great hurry. Maybe it was smoke that he saw in his vision before the garnet throne, not spirits. Always hope for the best and plan for the worst. At least, that's what Ivory was fond of telling him.

He searched for a clue as to which way he should travel, but he could not see through the thick grey clouds that blanketed the landscape. His eyes watering, he kneeled and inspected the earth at his feet. Charred black like the remains of a dry summer forest after a great fire swept through, everything he touched crumbled to ash between his fingers.

Umhra wondered where he was and why his vision called him to this desolate place. Surely, Spara had killed all the lesser gods if she had returned to Kalmindon to confront Vaila. What could be more important than following her and putting an end to this once and for all?

From his knee, a dim white light flickered through the smoke for a fleeting moment and then was gone. It was as good a sign as any.

Umhra climbed to his feet and waded into the miasma. The smoke stung his eyes and burned his throat, but he pressed on, every so often getting a glimpse of the light that guided him.

He approached a temple made of black stone. On one side of the arched doorway stood a statue of a wolf, its lips curled, exposing a mouthful of sharp teeth. On the other side was a similar statue of a coiled snake, ready to strike. The façade surrounding the doorway was carved to resemble a magnificent tree, its branches obscured by the haze above.

He willed Forsetae to his hand, but there was no reply. He summoned his armor—again, nothing. All he had was the icon around his neck and the diamond shard Vaila had given him to use in dispatching the gods. So far, they had all been willing participants. Umhra swallowed a lump in his throat at the notion that this time, he wouldn't be so lucky.

The dim light emanated from within the temple, which tapered up at a steep angle until disappearing into the unrelenting smoke. It was a foreboding place; one he had no desire to enter.

Umhra paused and muttered a quick prayer to Vaila. His icon fluttered but did not sustain itself.

"You can do this," he said. "You must do this."

He bit down on his bottom lip, welcoming the prick of his tusks.

His icon lit in amber ether that swirled around him. His heart slowed. He took a deep breath and entered the temple.

Tiered racks of recently lit blue votives flickered as he

passed. He approached one rack that had a single unlit candle at its center awaiting a vow.

Umhra plucked an incense stick from the edge of the rack and lit it upon a candle. A stream of black smoke danced into the air, bringing with it the earthy aroma of saffron. When the coal at the stick's end was strong, Umhra used it to light his own candle and then returned it to the incense holder.

"May I have the strength to see this through."

A hot tear streaked Umhra's cheek. He wiped it away and turned toward the room beyond.

Crossing a threshold carved with ancient glyphs, he entered an expansive room unadorned but for the red obsidian throne he had seen in his vision. A myriad of spirits swirled about the room, their ghostly forms sending a chill up Umhra's spine.

On the throne at the center of the frenzy sat a young woman with fair Evenese features. She sat askew with her knees pulled tight to her chest. A flowing white gown covered all but her bare toes, which dangled over the edge of the seat. Her flawless skin was as pale as fresh snow and her platinum blond hair cascaded over her exposed shoulder. She rocked back and forth gently and hummed to herself.

"So, my time has come." Her voice flowed like sheer curtains in a soft breeze. "Each of the others passed through here as they departed. I could only assume you would eventually come for me."

Umhra approached cautiously. "I'm afraid it was her or me. I never intended for any of this."

"Does intention justify your extinguishment of the Creator Gods? For their great light no longer burns."

"There is justification for my actions. I act to stop evil from ruling Kalmindon and imposing its will on the mortal plane. I mean to see it through to the end."

The goddess released her knees and turned to face Umhra. The other half of her body was a desiccated husk. For as delicate as her initial features were, the rest of her was reviling. The skin was stretched thin and the musty green of an aged corpse. Whereas one eye was the pale blue of a shallow lagoon, the other was sunken and milky white. The red of her lips abruptly ended in a jagged, toothy sneer.

Umhra took a step back.

The goddess rose to her feet, the left side of her body languid. "You come to a temple of death, and you are surprised by the sight of it?" She scoffed. "I am Gurtha. Goddess of Death. The moment of passing. You must be Vaila's Champion."

"Umhra. The name is Umhra."

Gurtha cocked an eyebrow. "That name has died to all but a few. The mortals now refer to you as—the Peacebreaker. Dramatic, is it not? They put their faith in you. Of that, I've heard much from those that pass through this temple. In fact, Kemyn and Brinthor themselves advised I grant myself to you."

"But you're not going to do that, are you?"

Gurtha put a finger to her lips in contemplation. "I think not."

The spirits that swept about the room vanished, leaving Umhra in darkness but for the distant flutter of the votive candles behind him.

Umhra's heart jumped as Gurtha appeared just inches away from him, her entire form having taken on the visage of her dead half. Her hair flowed around her preternaturally, framing her desiccated face like a star's corona.

Umhra jabbed the diamond shard into her abdomen, but it passed through her form, his hand burning from the intense cold of their contact.

"You will have to do better than that." Gurtha thrust her hands through Umhra's tattered leathers and into his chest.

Umhra felt as though his heart was in a vise. It strained with each beat under Gurtha's grasp.

Through gritted teeth, Gurtha's intimate embrace promised Umhra's end. She bore down, her clouded eyes narrowing with grim satisfaction.

Umhra closed his eyes, the pain excruciating. He pushed the pain from his mind and drew upon the energy around him. A surge of warmth fought the chill that grew within his core. He would not succumb so easily.

Power welled within him. He opened his eyes to see the flames of the votives from the antechamber encircling him and Gurtha.

Umhra unleashed the force outward, releasing a concussive blast through the temple. Stone walls cracked and the red obsidian throne scraped across the floor. The votives' flames fought the onslaught but were snuffed out. Gurtha vanished in a plume of sickly green dust.

Umhra put his hand to his chest where a purple scar now marked where Gurtha had penetrated his body. He snarled, knowing his fight with her was not yet over.

Skittering in the darkness.

Umhra spun just in time to see a spike career out of the gloom. He rolled from its path, and it retracted as quickly as it appeared. An enormous pincer snapped closed around his ankle and dragged him toward the worrying mouth of a scorpion.

The creature spat on Umhra's legs. The sputum bubbled and acrid smoke rose into the air as the acid ate away at Umhra's leathers.

Umhra attacked the scorpion's claw with his diamond shard. Repeatedly, the dagger screeched off its chitinous armor.

The stinger once again whirred out from behind the scorpion, this time striking Umhra in the right shoulder. Pain pulsed through his body. He screamed, but grabbed hold of the bulb at the base of the stinger.

The scorpion tore the stinger free, poison dripping from its tip. Umhra strained against the monstrosity's brute strength, his foot stuck in a pincer and his arm wrapped around the end of its tail. The scorpion writhed with anger, but Umhra held fast.

With all his might, Umhra pulled the tip of the tail down toward the scorpion's head. As the scorpion released his foot, he spun and drove the stinger through the scorpion's armor and into its head.

The scorpion screeched, its legs stamping like a poorly controlled marionette.

It threw Umhra from its back. He tumbled across the unforgiving stone floor and cracked into the base of the red obsidian throne.

The scorpion reeled, tore its stinger free from its head, and then fell limp on the floor.

Umhra's head rang. His stomach cramped with every labored heartbeat as poison coursed through his body. He vomited white foam onto the floor.

The scorpion transformed into Gurtha's bifacial form. She wheezed, tried to push herself up, but collapsed back to the ground.

Umhra dragged himself over to the goddess of death. He laid his hand upon her and focused on his icon, willing his life force into her as he did for Gromley on the altar of the Kormaic temple in Vanyareign.

The withered half of Gurtha's body gradually regained its appearance to match her living side. Her skin grew supple and fair, her clouded eye glimmered like a cerulean pool, her lips became as red as a garden rose.

She lay flat on her back and marveled at her hand as life imbued it once more.

"Thank you," she said. "I never thought this possible."

"Sorry," Umhra replied. "I am running out of time. You shall live on through me should I succeed."

He thrust the diamond shard into Gurtha's chest. Her eyes went wide as she stared into Umhra's. She tilted her head and exhaled for the last time.

Umhra wept.

A deep violet light gathered within the diamond shard. It

shot forth into Umhra's icon and Gurtha's essence flooded his body. He came to know death as a beautiful moment at which life transitioned from one form to another. A moment when the struggles of mortality give way to eternal bliss. When a life well led is rewarded for its efforts.

He rolled onto his backside and pushed himself up onto his hands. The wounds he sustained healed, but the discolored scars remained. But scars were meant to linger, less one forgets their shortcomings—their mistakes. Nobody bears the same scars as another. Individuals earn them through their own trial and tribulation. They are to be worn with pride.

Gurtha's body crumbled to ash, and a spirit lifted into the air and circled around the red obsidian throne. Umhra watched as it glided about the room. He felt it ask him permission to pass on to Kalmindon.

He nodded, and the apparition vanished.

There was only one place left for Umhra to go. He looked himself over. The wastes of Wethryn had claimed Forsetae, and the God Slayer had destroyed his armor. Even his leathers were now little more than tattered rags. He looked at the scars that covered his body and hoped he, alone, would be enough.

294 | JEFFREY SPEIGHT

CHAPTER 31

I have forged a crown of unmatched power. It shall not belong to me, but anyone the people of Evelium see fit to wear it.

- The Collected Letters of Modig Forene
Letter to Turin Archedyne dated 20th of Lusta, 999 AC. –
Unearthed from the Ruins of Vanyareign, month of Ocken, 1301 AT

— ▲ —

Turin was startled awake. Her heart racing, she sat up and fought to catch her breath. She was used to having the occasional nightmare. It came with the territory of leading a people under existential threat by a numberless, unyielding enemy. This time, however, the screams seemed so real. So close.

She tossed her cover aside and lit a candle she kept on her bedside table. She rolled her head back and forth, rubbed a kink at the peak of her shoulder, and climbed out of bed. Her footsteps were unsteady as sleep's cobwebs still dulled her mind, but she found her way into the adjoining room and poured herself a cup of water from an earthenware pitcher. She took a sip and yawned.

Another scream rang out—Turin jumped. *What in the hells of Pragarus was going on?*

She poked her head out the door despite only wearing a thin linen chemise.

Guards ran past, weapons drawn. A bell rang. From the level of chaos, not for the first time. Ruari was under attack.

She grabbed a guard by the arm as he rushed by. He spun to look at her—eyes wide.

"What's going on?" she asked.

"My lady," the guard panted. "It's the blights. They've overrun the hills and are now pouring in through the surface tunnels unabated. Our orders are to push them back to the surface and mount a counterattack from there."

"Go. I'll secure the regent and rally the Barrow's Pact."

The guard nodded and ran down the hallway, the cold of his steel bracer lingering on Turin's fingertips.

Turin returned to her quarters and hurried out of her chemise and into her leathers. Hopping across the room, she pulled on her boots and threw open the door.

She took off in the opposite direction the guard had run, navigating the crowd that flooded the tunnel with the determination of a salmon swimming upstream to its spawning site. A flash of auburn hair caught her attention. She recognized it as Naivara's and made to intercept her.

Hand in hand with Laudin, Naivara's emerald-green eyes flashed with worry.

"I'm glad I found the two of you. Where are the rest of the Barrow's Pact?"

"Roused awake, by now, I'd guess," said Laudin, Sem'Tora slung over his shoulder. "We heard the bell toll and now we head toward the surface to assist the common guard. The others know to meet us there in such an instance as this."

"Naivara, come with me," Turin insisted. "I need someone I trust to oversee the security of Aunt Jenta and my mother."

Naivara nodded and kissed Laudin. "Don't do anything more reckless than usual up there. I'll send the others if we cross paths."

Laudin held Naivara's gaze for a moment and then disappeared into the throng of guards, his fingers clinging to hers for as long as he could.

"Come on," Turin said. "Once we get to the royal chambers, I'm going to find Sena, Aridon, and Gleriel. I can't for the life of me figure out how the blights found us. We took every precaution."

"It's here," Naivara said, keeping stride with Turin.

"What is?"

"The primordial god. Before the first toll of the bell awakened me, I had a dream of the primordial god stepping forth from the Wistful Timberlands for the first time in ages. It welcomed the sun on its face and set Ruari in its sights. Its powers conceal the blights' numbers."

Turin stopped and stared into Naivara's eyes.

"It would seem remnants of my connection with Tayre remain," Naivara said.

"So, this is it. The great battle of our time. And we find ourselves unprepared.

"It would seem so. I will do what I can to help, but I fear Gromley, and I will be of limited value."

"You could never be of limited value—powers or not."

The crowd thinned, and they hurried past the guards standing watch at the entrance of the royal chambers.

"You two, with me," Naivara commanded as she passed.

The guards fell in line behind them as they strode for Jenta and Alessa's private quarters.

None to Turin's surprise, Talus was standing guard outside the doors in full regale.

"Your mother's been worried sick," he said. "There is a reason she and Jenta want you within these walls."

"And there's a reason I don't live within them. But now is

not the time for this conversation. Are they alright?"

"Yes. Nervous but safe."

"Good. Naivara will take over security for my mother and Aunt Jenta. I'm going to find Sena, Aridon, and Gleriel. Are you coming to kill some blights or staying here?"

Talus drew Aquila from its sheath. "You know I'm with you."

Turin hugged Naivara. "If the bell rings again, head to the depths. I'm certain many are already on their way. Join them and be safe."

"They are in good hands," Naivara assured.

"I know. Thank you."

Turin and Talus ran from the royal chambers toward the Iris. Turin hoped there would be a stray bahtreig available to make the journey to the surface less onerous, but each stable they passed was empty. They would have to proceed on foot.

When they reached the end of the tunnel, chaos erupted as commoners headed into the depths and soldiers and others who were willing and able to fight made their way to the surface.

Turin dragged her fingers across the rough stone of the tunnel wall and called upon Tyveriel. She took no time to welcome the rush of cold that flooded her body but willed the stone to draw across the mouth of the tunnel, sealing those beyond within and, more importantly, the blights out.

She frowned. It wasn't her best work, but she was in a rush. It would have to do.

Talus led the way into the Iris. The pair wove through the frenzied crowd and up the spiraling ramp. There was a resounding crack overhead and blights rained down upon them. Most shattered on unforgiving stone, while others scrambled to their feet, their inner lights raging with fury.

Talus ran the nearest of them through and kicked it off the edge of the ramp. It fell into the depths, its life force flickering into the darkness.

Another was upon them, and Turin thrust a hand in the air. The rock beneath them jutted from floor and impaled the blight on its honed point.

She surveyed the area. "These are only scouts and shrubs."

"The larger of their ranks can't fit into the tunnels," Talus said, cleaving another blight in two. "They must be waiting for the vanguard to drive us to the surface."

A blight jabbed at a nearby guard with a spear. Another jumped on a man's back and thrashed him with its claws. The man fell to the floor.

Shadow came out of nowhere and drove his Savonian glass dagger into the blight's back. The green glass flashed as it penetrated its barky skin.

The blight released the man and clawed at the blade to dislodge it. A black necrosis spread over the blight's body. It wailed in agony. Shadow wrenched its neck until the brittle wood splintered and the blight fell quiet and limp to the floor.

Gromley donned Barofyn upon his head and met the other blight with a swing of his war hammer. The impact shattered the blight, sending what little splinters that were left of it off the edge of the path into the abyss below.

He tapped the golden helm. "I may not be able to heal, but I can still deliver a mighty wallop. Nice to see you two. What's our plan?"

Turin put a hand on Gromley's shoulder. "I aim to find Sena, Ari, and Gleriel, and then get a better sense of what we're dealing with on the surface. Naivara will head to the depths with my mother and the regent. She told me she believes the primordial god is here leading the blights."

"It's always a damn god," Shadow said. "Worthless meddlers."

Gromley gave Shadow a shove. "Heresy. Watch your mouth."

Shadow shrugged. "I'm not wrong."

"Hopefully, we'll have time for this argument later," Turin said. "We have more pressing matters at hand."

"Aye," Gromley agreed. "Another time."

Emboldened by their union, they proceeded up the winding ramp of the Iris. Without hesitation, they met each blight they crossed in combat. As they proceeded, the path became littered with the corpses of blight and man alike, and the numbers of blights grew with each step.

A balding man who wielded a hatchet screamed as a blight repeatedly stabbed him with a wooden spear. Another took a blow to the head from a gnarled club and toppled from the edge of the path. Yet another fell, a small blight no bigger than a cat jabbing sharpened sticks into the base of his neck on either side.

Turin stone shaped an offshoot that led to the surface to close it off from the assault. It held for a fleeting moment, but the blights crashed against it from the other side and broke through. There were just too many of them.

Turin led Talus, Gromley, and Shadow through the morass and ducked into a side tunnel that led to Sena's quarters.

Talus hesitated.

"My Queen," he called, drawing Turin to a halt.

She turned and looked her adoptive father in the eyes. She'd seen that look before. It said both, 'I'm sorry' and 'I'm the bravest man you'll ever know' all at once. He normally reserved it for her mother when duty called him into harm's way.

"I can't let my men walk into an ambush. I'll lead them in pushing the blights from our halls and hold them from pursuing them into the fields until we get your signal."

Turin fought a lump in her throat. "Go. They need you."

Talus nodded to Shadow and Gromley. "Take care of her or I'll have your heads."

"Yes, General," Shadow said, his tone unusually sincere.

Turin watched Talus run back toward the Iris. The truth was, she needed him too. But she knew all too well that duty came above all else. It was Talus himself that taught her the virtue of sacrifice in the name of the greater good.

As Talus fell from sight, Turin led Gromley and Shadow down the corridor toward Sena's quarters.

"I don't know why she insists on living up here," Turin said as the blight she froze in her grasp shattered and fell to the ground in jagged pieces.

"Stubborn like her best friend," Shadow said, flashing a smile.

"No weeds in my home." Aridon's voice boomed through the tunnel.

Not far down the hallway, a blight lifted into the air on the shaft of a halberd. It was thrashed about like a flag rallying an army into battle until it was shorn in two and crashed against the stone wall in a spray of splinters.

Shadow dashed into the crowd, his Savonian dagger in one hand and a blackened steel blade in the other. He made light work of the blights standing between Turin and her friends. With each glint of glass and steel came a flash of light as the orb at the center of each blight's torso burst.

The others followed Shadow's lead and soon cleared the passage of intruders.

Before Aridon stood Gleriel. His eyes glowed like raging infernos as he swung his scythes with wild abandon. Blights fell at his feet with every angry swipe, the sound of shattering wood reverberating through the passage.

Aridon flashed a broad smile at Turin's approach. Sena heaved behind him.

"I'm not ready for this. Are they everywhere?"

"Yes," Turin said. "I'm afraid so. We are going to the surface to see exactly what we are dealing with. We came to get you three first."

Neela barked.

"You four. Sorry."

"How do you plan on getting to the surface?" Gromley asked. "The tunnels have been overrun."

"The tunnels *you* know of are overrun. I've kept one for myself. It's narrow and steep, but it will hopefully put us away from the fray so we can assess the situation."

Gromley bit his bottom lip. "It may be our only chance. Lead on."

Turin continued down the corridor, past Sena's quarters. The door was left open, offering a glimpse of her tousled bed. Coming to the ring, she followed the passage around the outer edge of Ruari until coming to what was little more than a crack in the dark stone wall. She slipped through the fissure into a tunnel barely more than the width of her shoulders.

Inside, she found a satchel stowed behind a rock and retrieved a drift globe from within. Setting the globe into the air, she scrambled up the first few lengths under its soft glow. She lost her footing, nearly kicking Shadow in the face and abrading her knee. The others followed with a procession of grunts and curses.

Soon, the slope lessened, and she could stand upright. Her knees stung as she helped the others up the last few difficult steps.

"Another twenty minutes and we should be at the surface. The worst is behind us."

"That depends on what we find on the surface," Shadow replied.

Gromley nodded. "Needless to say, it isn't likely to be any better than what we saw within the Iris."

Grim reality set in, and the party proceeded in silence to the end of the tunnel. Turin stopped before the mouth of the corridor, moonlight streaming in from a cloudless violet sky. She took a deep breath of cool early morning air and steeled her nerves.

"Stay low. I don't want to give away this position."

She squeezed through the opening, running her hands against the rough stone.

"Stay with me," she whispered. "I fear that, tonight, we will need you more than ever. And you will need us."

Tyveriel answered by sending an intense chill up Turin's arms. Her grey fingers burned and turned black with frostbite.

Turin threw herself against a stone that jutted from the earth in a circle and stared at the digits. Finger by finger, she made a fist with her hand. They looked bad, but she was no worse for the wear.

She smiled. "I guess that's my answer."

The others huddled behind the rocks next to her, careful to remain hidden from whatever awaited them in the open fields below.

Turin peered between two canted stones and gasped. Unlike the chaotic throngs she had grown accustomed to encountering on her rescue missions, an army of countless blights stood in regimented formation.

While those wreaking havoc within the tunnels of Ruari were little more than shrubs, those that spanned the fields counted among them some of the largest sentinels Turin had ever seen, towering the full height of an old growth hemlock and as sturdy.

Dispersed between the sentinels were smaller blights, including the Soul Carriers who carried their wicker cages slung over their shoulders. Each cage glowed with the light of a Will-O'-Wisp that would periodically crackle with lightning in anticipation of their coming meal.

At the very back of the massive formation stood a lone figure. Backlit by the waning moon, Turin could not make out the detail of its form—only that it was unlike the myriad of others that stood before it. It was short and stocky and had no internal glow that hallmarked the blights.

Turin withdrew from her vantage point and returned to the others.

"There are *so* many of them. They must outnumber us a thousand to one."

Grim faces looked back at her, speechless.

"To make matters worse, it would seem Naivara's fears were warranted. There is a figure at the rear of their formation that is unlike the rest. I can only imagine it to be the primordial god in her dreams and that Tyveriel has shown me."

Shadow frowned and peaked between the rocks. "I told you. It's always a god."

"I can't believe it would expose itself like this."

Nicholas took his own look. "It's just like Umhra always says—hubris. This is our chance."

"So, what's the plan?" Sena asked. "We can't just run out there and take them on."

Turin smeared her palm across her lips. She didn't have a plan. Anything she considered seemed pointless against a force that massive.

"No. We can't just run out there and take them on. For now, we will wait until Talus, Laudin and the others drive the blights from within the tunnels. Assuring the safety of our people is my primary concern."

"Well, you can't seal us all in the caves." Sena poked her head out from behind the stone and quickly squatted back down. "And I don't think *they* are going anywhere, anytime soon."

Gromley crept past Aridon and kneeled beside Turin.

"When we were in the depths of Antiikin, King Eleazar told us the blights were not to blame for this—that they were once a peaceful species that lived in harmony with humanity. What we need to do is kill the primordial god who controls them."

"Kill the primordial god?" Sena scoffed. "How do you suggest we do that? Your suffusion is inert. So is Naivara's."

Gromley tapped Barofyn, the tinny ring making his point before the words escaped his mouth. "Maybe these will help. Otherwise, why would Umhra have sent us to Antiikin? Barofyn grants me strength of body and mind..."

Turin rolled her eyes. Gromley grimaced in return and cleared his throat.

"Shadow's dagger is stronger and sharper than any material forged by man or god."

Shadow flipped the dagger. "It's true."

"Nicholas's bracers make him one with the wind," Gromley continued. "He can now move faster than any creature I've ever seen. And Laudin has Sem'Tora...Tie Breaker. That sure sounds like it wouldn't hurt our cause."

"Good name," Aridon said. "I agree."

Gromley patted Aridon on the shoulder. "Send the Barrow's Pact to kill the god."

Turin let it all sink in. It could work. Maybe. What other choice did they have? Surely, the paltry army she had at her disposal would not last long against all those blights.

"We draw the blights into battle while the Barrow's Pact goes after the primordial god."

Sena scrunched her nose and nodded. "Now, we're talking."

"Let's do it," Turin said. "What do we have to lose?"

CHAPTER 32

Turin Archedyne took to the battlefield alone. A sea of blights before him, he charged.

- The Gatekeeper's Abridged History of Tyveriel
Vol. 2, Chapter 36 – Unearthed from the Ruins of Meriden, the month of Ocken, 1240 AT

— ▲ —

Everything smelled of damp moss and blood. Clumps of green vegetation lay trampled throughout the corridor, rivulets of red running between them. The blights had been driven from Ruari, but at great cost.

Soldiers dragged the corpses of their fallen brothers in arms down the tunnel so that the grave clerics could give them a proper send off at a more suitable time. They carried the gravely wounded on stretchers or over their shoulders into the depths to be seen by healers or to await infection to set in and claim what the blights could not with immediacy.

For each body brought deeper within the caves, they returned with countless blight husks and threw them upon great pyres set at the mouth of each entrance as both a deterrent to further incursions and a warning to the enemy.

In the distance, the blight army screeched and wailed as the flames licked higher, fueled by their kin. It would seem the cost was great for both sides.

Talus stood at the entrance, ignoring the fresh gash on his face that reached from ear to chin and was caked with dirt and dried blood.

"They won't come back as long as we keep these fires burning," he said as Turin approached with Sena, Aridon, and Neela in tow. "And it would seem we have plenty of fuel to see that it happens."

Turin gave him a hug, eliciting a wince. When she released him, he rubbed his ribs. "I hadn't even noticed that until just now."

Turin smiled. "You and your soldiers did fine work here this morning. Without your efforts, we would have surely been overrun. At least now we have a chance."

Talus frowned. "A chance at what? We have no way out. It's only a matter of time before we run out of food. What we produce within the caves isn't nearly enough to sustain us."

"That's why we are going out there."

"Going out there?" Talus seemed to notice his wound for the first time. He dabbed at the gash and hissed. "Turin, that's insane. Look what we've gone through just driving them from the caves. They will decimate us out there in the open fields."

"We need to march out there as though we plan on fighting to provide a distraction for the Barrow's Pact," Gleriel said, crouched against the wall.

Talus raised an eyebrow. "I'm not sure there still is a Barrow's Pact. Naivara and Gromley are no longer what they once were. Umhra is gone. Laudin, Shadow, and Nicholas can only do so much. Even if they were at full strength, what would they be able to do against so many blights?"

Turin shook her head. "Nothing. They would barely put a dent in their ranks. They, however, think they stand a chance against the primordial god who leads them."

Talus's head dropped, and he took a deep breath. "Who put

that idea in their heads? They can't fight a god."

"Primordial god," Sena quipped as she leaned against the stone wall beside Gleriel, the inferno outside lighting half her face in a warm glow. "Barely a god, really."

"Gromley proposed the idea," Turin said. "I was against it at first as well. He thinks the vestiges they took from Antiikin will give them the edge. It makes sense when you think about it. Why else would the Peacebreaker have sent them there?"

"And you want me to march your army out into the open and draw the blights toward us to buy them time and space."

"No. I want you at my side when I march my army out into the open and draw the blights toward us."

"That, I can't agree to."

Turin recognized the resolve in Talus's expression. He had sworn to protect her at all costs and had never broken a promise as far as she could remember. She had to play the only card left in her hand. "General Jochen, I'm not asking for permission. I'm giving you an order. As your queen."

Talus smiled. "Now, you're ready to lead us as queen?"

"I am."

"Then—when will you need us?" Talus's tone reeked of resignation.

"The Barrow's Pact is making preparations. Gromley will let me know as soon as they are ready."

"I will rally our troops and await your word."

"Thank you, General."

Talus bowed. "My Queen."

— ▲ —

"You're not going." Laudin said. "We can't take that risk."

"Excuse me?" Naivara paced the torch-lit room. "How about the rest of you? Do you feel the same way? Nicholas? Shadow?"

Nicholas shifted uneasily in his seat. "It's just that your suffusion is inert. Without it, you..."

"I what?"

Laudin swore he saw a flicker of flame in Naivara's green eyes. Impossible. It was probably just the reflection of the torch behind him. He took her hand as she strode past him, halting her in her tracks.

"What Nicholas is trying to say is that, without your suffusion, it would be too dangerous for you to confront a god."

Naivara rolled her eyes. "What about Gromley? He's inert too."

"That's different." Laudin stared at the empty copper bowl on the table in preference to Naivara's narrowed eyes. "He has his war hammer and Barofyn."

"Yes, and why is it he has Barofyn, you have Sem'Tora, Shadow has his Savonian glass dagger, and Nicholas his fancy bracers, while I am to be removed from the party when it matters most?"

"Removed from the party?" Laudin could not believe what he was hearing. "We aren't doing any such thing. We just want to keep you safe until we figure out how to get you your powers back?"

"And what if I don't get them back?" asked Naivara, swinging her arms wide. "What if I am like this forever?"

"Then you would still be the most amazing and unique person I know."

Naivara scowled.

"Naivara," Shadow said, drawing her ire from Laudin. "What Laudin is struggling to convey is that your suffusion does not define you. Nor does it define our view of you. We know little of this primordial god other than it somehow controls the blights and brings them to our doorstep. We will not sentence you to death by having you join this hairbrained scheme. If the roles were reversed, you would do the same to protect one of us."

Naivara slumped into a chair and rubbed her eyes. "Fine. I will stay behind. May I remind you, though, Tayre told me I would destroy the primordial god. Not the Barrow's Pact."

Nicholas nodded. "Naivara, we are doing our best with the cards the gods have dealt us. I wish more than anything that you could be there with us."

Laudin rose from his seat. "We best be going. Wish us luck?"

Naivara feigned a smile. "Of course. Know your limits. Run if it is too powerful."

Laudin nodded, but he knew there would be no running. By the tears welling in Naivara's eyes and the redness of her nose, he assumed she knew as well. Humanity's salvation relied on destroying the primordial god, and the Barrow's Pact—hobbled as they may be—would throw everything they had at what might be their only opportunity to do just that.

He kissed Naivara's forehead and led Gromley, Shadow, and Nicholas from the room.

The corridors were quiet—deserted. Those able to fight had rallied to the surface and those too weak had descended into the depths, leaving little in the party's way other than smoldering blight husks and fallen soldiers.

"Shadow, remember the passage we took when we came here from Vanyareign?" Laudin asked in full stride.

"Of course. I led the way."

"Are there any exits that would bring us to the surface behind the blights' ranks?"

"One. It will be a bit of a hike back to the battlefield, but only a couple of miles at most."

"Then I ask you to lead us again. We will send a smoke signal from north of the primordial god when it is time for Turin and Talus to engage the blights. Then we will launch an attack from the rear when our quarry is distracted. Hopefully, it will give us the edge we need."

"And, if it doesn't? Nicholas asked, not in the least bit struggling as he normally would to keep up with his friends.

"If it doesn't, then we die along with everyone else we know and love. There will be no stopping the blights if they destroy what we send at them as a distraction."

Shadow led the party into the Iris and down the spiral ramp into darkness. He took a passage that descended at a sharp angle until the stone shifted from grey to purple, noting their arrival in Sepyltyr. They came before a banded iron door secured by three formidable locks.

He retrieved his pick set and went to work. With one satisfying click after another, the locks sprung open, Shadow casting them to the floor in succession. He strained against the heavy door but met with little success in opening it.

Gromley stepped forward and swept Shadow aside with a wave of his hand. The door groaned in protest, but its heft was no match for Gromley's enhanced strength. With little effort, it swung wide, and a plume of dust filled the air.

The stench of mold was repugnant.

Laudin buried his nose in his sleeve. "I hate this place."

Shadow drew in a deep breath. "Smells like home to me."

Without hesitation, he strode into Sepyltyr. The others glanced at each other in trepidation.

"Fine," Nicholas said. "I'll go next."

The tiny Farestere bounded through the doorway.

Laudin put his arm around Gromley. "Come on. Let's go give this god hell."

— ▲ —

Golden pine straw covered the ground, making for a slippery exit from the small cave. Evening was setting in, and the sky was painted in a tapestry of colors that faded to deep purple in the east.

Shadow stood at the edge of the copse and stared out over rolling hills blanketed in phlox, the mirror image of the sky above. "From here, a two-mile trek due south will put us directly behind the blights and their primordial god. The trek down to the hills will be the hardest of it."

Laudin put a hand on the Ryzarin's shoulder and looked at Gromley, then Nicholas. "Then we travel with haste. When we are in position, we will notify the others that we are ready."

There was a time, many years ago, when Laudin would have asked for Taivaron's help in such a situation. How he wished to have those days back. He was better with the harrier at his side. More content. At peace. But Taivaron had left when the races of man sequestered themselves in the depths of Ruari and Laudin had not seen the raptor since.

Alas, a fire would have to do the job. Crude, but effective.

Laudin's strides were effortless as he led the party south along a craggy ridge, the scent of vanilla and clove filling the evening air. Shadow followed with little struggle, as did Nicholas, thanks to the bracers that hastened his every move.

It was Gromley who clambered over exposed rock and tripped over the uneven footing. His heavy armor clanked with each step, eliciting the occasional glare from his companions.

Eventually, they came to a steep wall of jagged stone that seemed to be the only way down to the fields below. Shadow was the first over the edge, his head dipping below the ledge before Laudin could even say a word.

"You said we travel with haste." His voice echoed from below.

Nicholas leaped off the precipice and floated through the air toward the ground like an autumn leaf dropped by a weary tree.

Laudin looked at Gromley, who heaved with exhaustion, his hands on his knees. His brow glistened with sweat. For the first time, Laudin realized he had not trimmed his beard in some time. Likely, since his suffusion with Anar left him. He was no longer a Strongforge Cleric, and the ranger supposed that meant he no longer needed to adhere to the norms of one.

"Do you need a minute?"

Gromley waved Laudin off. "I'm fine. This helm might give me strength of body and mind, but it doesn't give me longer legs. Get going. I'll be right behind you."

"Alright. See you at the bottom."

"Looking forward to it."

Gromley's cynicism brought a smile to Laudin's face. How lucky he was to have found such friends. So fearless and irresponsible. So trustworthy and capable.

He peered over the edge and saw Shadow nearly to the ground below and Nicholas standing in a patch of phlox against the side of a knoll, staring up at him with a hand guarding his eyes from the glare cast by the remnants of daylight.

Laudin rolled onto his stomach and found sturdy footing on the rock face. He glanced at Gromley one last time and began his descent.

The rock was sharp but offered ample handholds for a reasonable down climb. It wasn't long before Laudin greeted Shadow and Nicholas at the base. He looked up to see Gromley about halfway down the escarpment, making light work of his descent.

In the distance to the south, Laudin could barely discern the distinctive shape of the rocky outcrop that marked the north-most entrances to Ruari. It was there Turin and Talus awaited his signal. That meant that somewhere beyond the hill they huddled behind was the primordial god and his blight army.

He looked at the sky. Despite the sun still hanging low on the horizon, it was already specked with stars. A cloudless night augured well for sending his message, and the waning moon would only help as it lifted into the sky.

"We'll need visual confirmation of our target before sending word to Turin," he said as Gromley joined them at the base of the hill. "I don't want to risk our people being exposed without good cause. We will weave between the hills until we can see the primordial god, then we will retreat and send our signal."

In agreement, they coursed along the gaps in the landscape. As they neared a final ridge, Laudin called the party to a halt with fist thrust in the air. Evening dew glistened under the light of the gleaming moon. He climbed to the top of the hill before him and lay down in a clump of tall grass.

There, in the open field with its army of blights stretched out before it was a stout figure the likes of which Laudin had never seen. Its head was set below its burly shoulders and its form, made of dark stone, was covered in pale green lichens and rich moss. He could only assume this was the primordial god he sought.

He slid back down the embankment, bringing a small avalanche of loose rock and stone with him. "It's there," he whispered. "Or, at least, something that fits the description Turin gave us is there."

"Did it see you?" Gromley asked.

"No." Laudin retrieved a tinderbox from his satchel. "Not that I can tell. Let's head back behind that next hill and set our signal fire there."

Laudin rose to a crouch and followed Shadow and the others along the path they took on their journey south.

Shadow froze. A high-pitched wail echoed through the night sky and a massive blight sentinel emerged from the darkness, an equally immense club in each hand.

CHAPTER 33

Atalan has fallen for her. I must admit, she possesses a
certain allure, but nothing good will come of it.

- *The Tome of Mystics*
Unknown Origin. Unearthed from the Ruins of Oda Norde,
month of Bracken, 1320 AT

— ▲ —

The blinding celestial light faded and Umhra found himself on the expansive staircase leading to Vaila's Grace. The crystalline façade of the tower seemed to have healed since he was here last, the damage Spara and her worm had done giving way to new growth of pristine diamond that knitted the building's gaping wounds.

His battle with the Eketar left him standing in tattered olive-green leathers. When he tried to summon his armor or Forsetae since Wethryn, he encountered a silence he had never experienced before.

He drew the diamond dagger from his belt. It was the only thing he had left. Spara was now a god—that he knew. With a little luck, the shard might be all he needed.

Resigned to the inevitability of confronting Spara one more time, he bounded up the stairs. Hopefully, Vaila still lived, and he could meet his enemy on equal footing. If he were too late, his chance of survival would be small—never mind victory.

Crossing beneath the reconstructed archway, he raced for Vaila's throne room. The great hall within was also rebuilt. Its sleek pillars and flawless walls climbed to untold heights. Light painted the hall in a spectrum of color, Umhra's reflection appearing in each facet he passed. He stopped and spun in a slow circle.

He did not need the constant reminders of the sorry condition he was in—the burning cuts and muscle aches were enough to instill humility in the most brazen of egos. Alas, with every passing visage, his spirit spiraled further toward despair. How could he possibly best Spara in such state?

Metal crashed into something resilient and brittle, a resounding crunch echoing through the hall. Countless shards of diamond clattered across the floor. Umhra snapped out of his stupor and took off in a sprint. Abandoning any sense of caution, he burst into Vaila's throne room.

Vaila's swords lay strewn on the floor in the center of the room. One of the rhodium blades had shattered at its midpoint. Its surface was dull, lifeless. The other still glowed with celestial light, seemingly unscathed. Before Vaila's angelic throne stood Spara in flawless diamond armor that hugged her form, a bloodied great axe held high.

She gleamed with unfettered radiance as though she emitted her own internal light. Umhra looked at himself—little more than tattered leather rags and bloodied lacerations.

Spara loomed over Vaila's motionless body, a trail of pearlescent blood running down the steps from a glistening pool surrounding the fallen god. Vaila's diamond gown was riven across her chest where the axe had cleaved deep.

"My, you look terrible," Spara scoffed, letting her axe drop to her shoulder. "You should really take better care of yourself. Although, I suppose that no longer matters, as you so eagerly rush to your death."

With preternatural speed, Umhra dashed for Vaila's swords and swept the blades from the floor as he coursed through the room. The intact blade gleamed in his hand, warmth spreading up his arm and flooding his body. The other was missing the top third of its length but was still better than no blade at all.

Spara frowned. "Straight to the swordplay, as usual." She held out her hand, and the air rippled between them. "Why don't we slow things down and chat for a moment?"

Umhra expected the spell and slashed Vaila's sword through the aura. The air swirled like eddies in a well-trafficked harbor, sparks coruscating from hundreds of little vortices. The spell dissipated.

Umhra charged up the dais stairs with nothing but rage in his heart. One way or another, this would end here and now.

Spara spun to meet Umhra's attack, barely deflecting the first wild swipe of Vaila's unbroken sword. He lunged at her with the sundered blade he held in his off-hand and came between her and Vaila. He growled like a rabid dog.

Spara leaped back, just out of reach. Had the blade been whole, Umhra would have run her through. "Always one step behind, Umhra. It's almost charming if it weren't so costly a flaw. Your god lay dead. I've absorbed her essence. Our game is over."

Umhra peered over his shoulder. His gaze darted between the pool of blood, the mortal wound across Vaila's chest, the pale hue of her skin, and the blank stare in her dark eyes. He grimaced and shot Spara a glare of unfettered hatred, his icon fluttering erratically.

"Our *game* isn't over as long as my heart beats. As long as *her* body remains."

Spara smiled, licked her lips, and backed down the stairs onto level footing. "The Eketar might have failed to kill you, but it did its job well enough. How brazen you are to come before me with neither your armor nor your precious sword. You are so little without them, not to mention without her." She nodded toward Vaila's lifeless body.

"I'll almost feel bad cutting you down. Almost. What Vaila saw to elevate you to be her Champion I shall never know. Without the bells and whistles you are nothing more than a half-witted mongrel orphan whose been fed stories of his own greatness."

A sword in each hand, Umhra bounded down the stairs, Spara effortlessly dodging the whirring blades and countering with a swing of her axe, the trailing edge slicing through the remnants of Umhra's leathers at his shoulder. She winked. "You'll have to do better than that."

The wound burned. Blood ran down Umhra's arm in a hot stream. He spun, Vaila's broken sword leading the way. The blade collided with the broad side of Spara's axe, knocking it aside, the blade shattering further, leaving only a jagged shard above the hilt. The second sword followed, humming through the air.

Spara released the axe with one hand and threw her free hand into the air. Despite Umhra putting all the strength he could yet muster behind the stroke, Vaila's sword affixed in space inches from Spara's neck. Umhra gritted his teeth and screamed as he forced his weight behind the blade. It wouldn't budge. He released the sword and dove at Spara, his broad leather-clad shoulder connecting with her chin.

The axe came free of her grip, clattered across the floor, and reverted to her hand axes, Shatter and Quake. Spara reeled from the force of the blow and came to a knee. Umhra pounced on her and pinned her to the ground with a knee on each shoulder. She struggled beneath him, his weight and will holding her in place. He stabbed at her, the sundered blade screeching across her faceted breastplate. He raised the weapon again, and she closed her eyes.

Space collapsed around them as Spara drew in Kalmindon's energy. The force of the heavens crashing down upon Umhra's back was too much to bear. Knowing he could not withstand the pressure for long, he directed the sundered blade toward Spara's chest and allowed the force to drive him to the floor atop her.

Spara's diamond armor crunched beneath Umhra, his face drawn to within inches of hers. Her breath was labored and hot in his face. She screamed as the blade broke through breastplate and pierced flesh.

"Shall we see if you still bleed red?" Umhra grunted.

Spara released a concussive blast, throwing Umhra from atop her. He hurtled through the air as the walls of the throne room shattered around him. The blast cast him into the next room, where he crashed into a massive hearth. His head sang, bones cracked. He slumped to the floor.

He shook his head, the double vision clearing as Spara stepped through the gaping hole in the wall with Shatter and Quake in hand. Chunks of diamond rained down around her like countless teardrops. As though Kalmindon wept for her pending victory.

The wound in her stomach caused by Vaila's shattered blade healed, the rent breastplate reforming as she strode forward. She wore a wicked smile on her face.

"This has gone on long enough." She leaped across the room, so she straddled Umhra.

He thrust the broken sword at her, but she caught the blade and twisted it from his grip. She carelessly tossed it over her shoulder and kneed Umhra in the face.

The tusks in his lower jaw pierced his upper lip and his teeth crashed together. A spark of pain ran up his jaw into his head. Fresh blood filled his mouth. He spit it to the floor.

Spara grabbed him by the collar and lifted him to his feet with one hand. Umhra raised a hand to strike her back, but his muscles gave out and it fell limp to his side.

She propped him up against the hearth. He stood on his own despite not being able to feel his legs.

Spara buried Shatter in his chest just below the clavicle. She followed with Quake between his ribs.

Umhra's blood flowed over the rhodium axes and streamed to the crystalline floor.

Spara came in close for a whisper, like she held words only intended for her lover's ear. "I really should thank you, Umhra." She torqued Shatter and a shock of pain surged through Umhra's chest. "You did most of the hard work and now deliver to me the souls of the most vaunted gods. I must say, I wouldn't have been able to do this without you."

He head-butted Spara in the face. Her head snapped back with a spray of red blood from her nose.

"I see you do still bleed red. You're no different from me. You only hide behind your diamond armor. Beneath it, you are still trapped in that cage in Oda Norde with nothing but fury in your heart."

Spara licked the blood that now dripped from her nose. She sneered—her teeth bloodied—and tore Quake free from Umhra's stomach. The axe cast gore across the floor but, itself, gleamed anew.

Umhra screamed.

To the sound of cracking ribs, Spara buried the axe back in his side once more.

With little more than a flick of her wrists, she tossed Umhra across the room, his body tearing free of her axes.

He crashed into the wall close to the hole created by Spara's concussive blast. The wall cracked on impact and Umhra again slumped to the floor. The room went black.

Emerging from the darkness, he saw the faces of each of the Bloodbound. Drog was first, dutiful as ever. Gori and Thurg followed, as they had departed the mortal world together and remained tethered in death. Behind them was Bat, whose terrified face still haunted Umhra when the memory of Telsidor's Keep crept into his dreams. Last, there was Xig. He stood tall and proud—a welcome change from the desiccated shell Umhra peeled from Manteis's wall.

"We've been waiting for you, mate," Drog said. "What's taken you so long?"

A sense of warmth overwhelmed Umhra. Belonging. Home. He looked down upon his wounds and found none, his leathers in perfect condition. "I am yet to finish my work. I'm sorry I led you into that horrid place, not knowing the evil we would face— that I was too weak to show my true self and keep you safe."

Thurg dismissed Umhra's apology with a wave of his hand. "Water under the bridge, boss. We all did our best under the circumstances. Gori and I burned that pit of undead as you ordered. Didn't we, Gori?"

Gori smiled, though his disfigured jaw made the expression a grim spectacle. "We sure did. They didn't stand a chance."

Umhra smiled.

Bat took a step forward. "Umhra, are you ready to join us? We've missed you."

How easy it would be for him to let go and join his brothers in the afterlife. After all, he never asked to be a god. All he'd ever wanted was a place to belong. He'd had it for a time—with these great men before him. Like all else in life, the peace he once felt died along with them. He yearned to have it back.

No. It could not end this way.

"Not yet, boys. I am compelled to finish what I started before I rest."

"Well then, have at it," Xig cheered.

"Bound by blood," Umhra said.

"And, bound to spill it," the Bloodbound replied in unison.

Umhra's eyes flitted open. The room came into focus, and he rolled to his knees. He crawled to the jagged opening that led back to Vaila's throne room, grabbed her broken sword. Every inch of progress brought with it the agony of a life's worth of torture. His own personal Slopes of Phit. Maybe he deserved this as much as those who aimlessly trudged up its slopes. After all, his hands were as red as any man's.

Spara sauntered up beside him and put a boot on his back.

"You just don't know when to give up, do you?"

Umhra grunted.

Spara laughed. "Is that all you have left? The mighty Umhra the Peacebreaker, Champion of Vaila and Savior of Tyveriel crawls on his hands and knees and grunts like the common swine he is. Alas, you find a posture worthy of your station."

She kicked Umhra in the ribs, but he held fast to her leg. He drew what power he could from Kalmindon before she could strike again and forced his will outward. The blast took everything he had left, but it was enough—just enough—to send both Spara and him flying in opposite directions.

Umhra crashed into the base of the dais in Vaila's throne room and collapsed to the floor.

CHAPTER 34

I returned to Ohteira empty handed—a failure. And yet, in Avanla's arms, it is as though I am a king among kings.

- Entry from the Diary of Vred Ulest
Dated 3rd of Ocken, 907 AF. Unearthed from the Ruins of Ohteira, month of Lusta, 1399 AT

— ▲ —

The branch-like appendages that protruded from the blight's back and head bristled and juddered. In all his interactions with the blights, Laudin had never seen such a display. If it were not so threatening, it would almost be beautiful.

The blight arched its back and bellowed an unmistakable warning call into the night sky.

Shadow let a dagger fly. The ebony blade whirred end over end, flashing in the moonlight. It struck true in the blight's agape mouth, cutting short its resonant plea.

The blight heaved, but the dagger remained lodged deep in the back of its throat. It dug into its maw with twiggy fingers, tearing away bits of bark as it tried to rid itself of the obstruction.

"Well?" Shadow said. "What are you waiting for?"

Gromley charged the creature, his war hammer held

overhead.

Laudin drew Sem'Tora—the bow's runes glowing red—and loosed two arrows over Gromley's shoulder.

Nicholas dashed wide of the stomping behemoth and released a fireball from his ruby ring.

Mid-flight, Laudin's arrows burst into flame and struck the blight in the chest. Nicholas's fireball hit just after.

The blight lit ablaze like dry tinder. It shifted its attention away from the dagger in its throat and batted at the fire that raged across its torso.

Wood shattered as Gromley's war hammer crashed into the blight's leg, taking it clean from the rest of its body just above the knee.

The blight hopped awkwardly and toppled against the side of a hill. It rolled along the slope, unable to arrest its momentum with flailing arms. With a heavy thud, it hit the ground, its face buried in the soil.

Flames danced across its back as it tried to push itself upright, but Gromley struck down with his hammer and crushed its brittle head.

"I think we found the fuel for our fire," he said.

Laudin searched the surroundings for any sign of another threat. "Break it up. There's enough greenery to create the smoke we need."

Without hesitation, Gromley went to work with his hammer.

While Gromley broke the blight down into manageable pieces, Laudin and Nicholas dug a shallow pit and encircled it with stones. Shadow gathered pieces of the blight's husk and arranged it in the center.

With a controlled burst from his ring, Nicholas set the bonfire ablaze. They heaped more fuel on the fire until it was burning hot and then added fresh bows from their victim's back.

White smoke billowed into the night. They stepped back

from the fire, craned their necks, and watched their signal drift up to the heavens.

Laudin slung Sem'Tora over his shoulder. "Let's go kill a god."

— ▲ —

Turin dug at the cavern floor with a splinter of wood. They had been waiting since morning for Laudin's signal and she grew impatient.

Sena sat at the mouth of the cave, her form a silhouette against the light of the moon while Aridon slept beside her, an arm draped over Neela.

Gleriel worked tirelessly along with the soldiers of lower rank to keep the pyre outside burning with a seemingly endless supply of blight husks from within Ruari. He seemed to relish the work and the men he helped treated him as one of their own. Turin swore she heard him laughing as he and a young, sandy-haired soldier dragged a gnarled old blight from the caves.

The rest huddled along the walls of the tunnel as they awaited their orders, their faces covered in grime and their eyes bleary.

"There it is," Sena shouted. "They're ready."

Turin jumped to her feet and rushed to Sena. Talus and Gleriel joined her.

Butterflies set flight in Turin's stomach the moment she saw the streak across the sky.

The blights had noticed it too and had turned to face the moon that was now bisected by the plume. They howled and jeered at the man-made fire somewhere off to the north but did not stray from the battlefield.

"We go now," Turin said. "General, please ready your men and send word to the other tunnels that we are to march into the fields at once."

"Yes, my queen."

Talus called a soldier to him. The Iminti man was tall and

slim, and one of his pointed ears had been shorn from his head some time ago. He wore studded leather armor and a gold sash that draped between two ceramic epaulettes on each shoulder. The adornment marked him as a bell guard.

"We head out to meet our enemy in battle," Talus said. "Notify the others, so we may show a united front."

"Yes, general." The guard saluted and ran down the passage toward the bell station.

A moment later, the bell tolled four times in rapid succession. The soldiers that littered the corridor in various states of despondency snapped to attention and formed a column five abreast and at least one hundred men deep behind their general. They halted.

Another bell thundered. Then another.

Turin stepped to the front of the formation at Talus's side. Gleriel, Sena, and Aridon filed in behind them.

More bells rang out and then silence hung in the air.

Turin looked at Talus. She did not know what she was looking for in his face, but she searched for it, anyway.

He looked back at her, narrowed his eyes, and nodded.

She drew in a deep breath and strode forward.

A thousand footsteps followed.

The bonfire just beyond the mouth of the cave raged as it turned the dead blights that fueled it to ash. Smoke choked the air, and the intense heat of the blaze bit at Turin's face as she passed.

She led the column around the inferno and the cool evening air that followed the blaze's heat sent a chill up her spine.

Six other trails of soldiers spilled out from their respective caves like ants pouring from their colony in search of food. Maybe they would number three thousand when they met in the fields. Whatever their number, it would pale compared to the vast army of blights that awaited them with their backs turned.

It was not long before the blights realized their approach. They shifted their attention from the trail of smoke that billowed from the hills behind them to the streams of men that brazenly converged to form an army in their midst.

They bellowed an alien war cry and shook the earth as they stomped and pounded the earth with their crude weapons.

Turin stopped, careful to leave enough space between her and the enemy, so a retreat was possible when needed. She surveyed the ranks that fell in behind her. She saw human, Evenese, and Iminti faces staring back at her expectantly. Scattered among them were some Zeristar and diminutive Farestere.

She considered saying something profound and motivational—to rally these weary soldiers to greatness. Something like Aunt Jenta would say. The words did not come easily. What could she say to three thousand tired soldiers who stood before an army a thousand times their size?

She cleared her throat. "There is nothing more that I want than to give you all the lives you deserve. Tonight, we find ourselves on the brink. If we are to survive as a people, we must give the Barrow's Pact the time they need. I thank each of you for being here with me. I love you all as brothers and sisters. Know that if we don't stand our ground against this massive force, there will be no tomorrow. If, however, we succeed, we can rebuild what we once had. I will not falter. All I ask is that you stand with me."

Silence reigned, the breath of a thousand men and women rising into the air in plumes of steam.

Turin looked at Sena, who shrugged.

Talus drew Aquila from its scabbard and hoisted the fabled blade overhead. "For Evelium!"

The soldiers drew their weapons in response. "For Evelium!"

The blights roared. Turin's army roared back.

Laudin loosed the opening salvo. His arrow whistled through

the air, a trail of ice vapor in its wake.

The Aged One turned as the arrow approached and caught it in its hand. Before it could cast the arrow aside, ice grew up its arms and across its torso.

The Barrow's Pact charged from multiple angles.

Nicholas ran past the primordial god—a blur to the naked eye. A bolt of lightning detonated on the Aged One's back.

The Aged One stumbled as it tried to follow Nicholas's path, ice growing over its legs.

Shadow threw his Savonian dagger. The green glass buried itself in the Aged One's side. Shadow recalled the dagger which reappeared in his hand.

Gromley charged forward with his war hammer held overhead. As he neared the Aged One, the ice shell Laudin's arrow had cast across its body shattered, frozen shards exploding against Gromley's armor.

The Aged One emerged from the mist, its eye flashing with verdant preternatural energy.

Gromley swung his war hammer, but they had lost the element of surprise and the Aged One caught him in its glare. The hammer careened off an invisible shield that now surrounded the primordial god, a wave of energy coursing around its rotund form with the point of impact its epicenter.

The Aged One pushed its hands outward and Gromley flew through the air and crashed into the slope of the hill behind him.

"Who dares confront the Aged One?" The primordial god's voice rumbled like a landslide. "Name yourself so the Aged One knows whose doom is wrought this night."

Laudin loosed another arrow, the bowstring humming in his ear.

The arrow split apart in the air to form six smaller missiles that swirled about each other and left a trail of smoke behind them. The first of them sent the Aged One's shield flickering erratically, while the others collided with the Aged One and exploded across his form in a deafening display of flashes.

The Aged One staggered backward.

Shadow threw two daggers. Green glass pierced the Aged One's shoulder. The second dagger, the primordial god caught in its hand. It crushed the black iron blade and cast its mangled remnants to the ground.

"I liked that one," Shadow shouted. The Savonian blade disappeared from the Aged One's shoulder and returned to Shadow's hand.

He leaped upon the Aged One's back and plunged the blade into its neck. The Aged One reeled. It grappled Shadow's leg and pulled him free from his perch.

Shadow dangled upside down in the primordial god's grasp.

Nicholas struck from behind, a fireball erupting in the darkness.

Laudin aimed for the Aged One's eye and released his bowstring.

The Aged One swiped its free hand to the side, and the arrow veered wide, falling away into darkness. With an open palm, it pushed forward, and Shadow flew from its grip and tumbled to the earth.

Laudin knew this was going to be next to impossible, but he needed to find a weakness—a weakness that, at the moment, eluded him. Ice did not seem to slow this entity down, nor did lightning or fire. Savonian glass pierced its stone-like body but was little more than a nuisance. He thought of acid and Sem'Tora's color shifted to yellow. He let another arrow fly.

As the Aged One attempted to once more swipe Laudin's arrow aside, the arrow liquified and covered its intended target in acrid fluid. Fumes rose into the air and the Aged One scraped at its eyes to wipe the acid clear.

Gromley leaped from the shadows and slammed his war hammer into the Aged One's head. The resounding blow sent the blinded primordial god staggering.

The Aged One threw its hands in the air. Trees erupted from

the earth.

Gromley shattered one with his war hammer and dove from another's path as it grew forth.

Nicholas dashed past the Aged One and touched its legs with his fingertips. Ice grew from the point of contact and froze its leg to the earth.

Despite his great speed, the Aged One grabbed Nicholas by the neck as he passed and hoisted the Farestere into the air. It tore its legs free, slammed Nicholas into the ground, and stomped on him with its full weight.

Nicholas screamed. Bones snapped. Silence.

"No!" Shadow threw two daggers that deflected off the Aged One's torso.

Laudin drew his scimitar and charged the primordial god.

Gromley leaped out from the trees, swinging his war hammer in wild arcs.

Together, the three pushed the Aged One back and Gromley dragged Nicholas's mangled body from the fray. Gromley held a hand on his icon and another over Nicholas's bloodied head.

"Answer me," he yelled. There was no reply. There was nothing he could do.

"Gromley, we need you here," Laudin said, his scimitar ringing off the Aged One's hardened form. No matter how much he wanted Nicholas healed, he knew Gromley's efforts would prove pointless, and that the priority was to kill this wretched god.

Gromley grimaced and returned to the fight.

The Aged One pushed its hands outward and Laudin felt the hair on his arms stand up on end as the air electrified. The blast of energy that followed threw Laudin and Shadow from its proximity.

Laudin tumbled, the air and earth replacing each other in his vision over and over until he hit the ground and slid through the dirt. The air driven from his lungs, he forced himself to his feet.

He looked at Shadow, whose landing was more graceful. The Savonian glass dagger coursed past Gromley and embedded itself in the Aged One's chest before reappearing in Shadow's hand.

Gromley charged the god alone. The Aged One's eyes flashed, and it again forced its hands outward and generated another blast. Gromley withstood the detonation and forged a path to the Aged One, so they stood toe-to-toe.

He screamed and brought his hammer down upon the primordial god with reckless abandon. Each furious blow chipping flakes of stone from the Aged One's body.

The Aged One stomped the earth, its heavy brow furrowing. The earth quaked.

As Gromley stumbled, the Aged One struck Gromley with the back of its fist, sending him down on a knee. It then turned back toward its blight army and pointed toward Ruari. "Leave none alive," it said.

— ▲ —

The blights suddenly charged.

"Hold your ground," Turin yelled, sensing the nervousness of those around her.

The ground shuddered with each step as the horde's attack neared.

Turin dropped to her knees and brushed her blackened fingers through the loose soil and trampled grass. "It is time."

As the blights bore down upon her people, she swept her hands into the air and spikes of stone broke through the earth and jutted toward the onslaught, creating a spear wall before her.

The front line of blights crashed into the stone spikes and impaled themselves. Their inner lights fluttered out. More followed.

Some of the spikes shattered under the force of the charge, blights pouring through the gaps in the defense.

Gleriel rushed forward, his scythes a blur of glinting steel. He cleaved blight after blight as they came through the wall. Aridon and Talus joined him and hacked and slashed at anything within reach.

Turin raised her hands again and a second row of spikes thrust forth, running more blights through.

Sena put a hand on Turin's shoulder. "We need to back up."

Turin climbed to her feet and turned to order the army to push back when she heard a thunderous flapping sound, like the sails of a ship being lashed by a great storm. She looked up to see a massive form diving from the night sky.

"Run!" she yelled. "Back to the caves."

The Grey Queen strafed the center of the panicked formation with a torrent of violet plasma. Everyone scattered as more dragons followed, the night sky alighting in an eruption of color. Turin watched as her army succumbed to the dragon's breath.

The dragons landed behind the army and cut them off from their planned retreat. Turin's army was surrounded with little hope of salvation.

Turin screamed, her voice drowning out the dragons' roars. She ran at the Grey Queen.

CHAPTER 35

*Those who follow their path and reach beyond shall be
rewarded with the bond of suffusion.*

- The Book of Korma
Unknown Origin. Unearthed from the Ruins of Travesty,
month of Riet, 1287 AT

— ▲ —

Umhra tried to push himself onto his knees but fell back to
the floor. His head throbbed. His wounds burned. He was
unsure of what to do or how much more he could take. Maybe
Spara was right—he was always a step behind. He wasn't
enough.

He placed a hand on the first stair. It was cold, unyielding.
He wiped his bloodied chin on the remnants of his sleeve and
placed his other hand beside it. His arms shook, but he
managed to lift his chest from the floor. One hand after the next,
he dragged himself up upon the dais and collapsed. If he was
destined to die, he would die at his god's side. It was where he
belonged.

He closed his eyes and gave in.

"Umhra. My Champion." A cool, weak hand grabbed his.

He opened his eyes and saw Vaila looking back at him. Her

eyes were dull, and yet she forced a shallow smile.

"I need your help," Umhra rasped. "I can't beat her on my own."

"There is one last gift I can give you." Her voice was fragile—a distant memory of its former presence. "There is no saving me now. My time has come, and I wish to rejoin my brothers. Take my life. What remains of my power will be enough to overcome her. I give it to you freely."

Umhra sat up. Spara did the same in the adjoining room, shards of diamond raining from the ceiling between them. He rolled to his knees and stared into Vaila's fading eyes. "How do you expect me to do this? It goes against everything I've ever wanted. Everything you taught me to be."

"You do it because you have no choice—because your god commands it of you. I have had my time and I cherish it. Now, I grant you yours."

He knew that if he hesitated, he would not be able to go through with it. Umhra slipped the diamond dagger from his belt and plunged it into Vaila's heart.

"No!" Spara screamed, running into the room as Vaila shuddered and wisps of gold ether escaped her body through the pommel of the dagger and enveloped Umhra.

Time slowed and Umhra's senses sharpened. He could hear each individual diamond clink on the floor, and each of Spara's footfalls as she neared. He could smell the ozone-like remnants of Vaila's essence mixed with the ferrous tang of the blood coursing from the gashes he bore. He could feel Vaila's innate power flooding his body—joining that of her brothers—and fortifying him. He could see the totality of her experiences from the dawn of time.

Vaila's body turned to ash, her delicate hand crumbling in her hero's.

As he became one with his god, Umhra was lifted to his feet in exaltation, and the aura of his rhodium icon shifted from amber back to blue. Where he once found power in the tether between him and Vaila, the void her death left was now filled with a connection to Kalmindon itself. He felt rooted for the first time in his life, as if he belonged to Kalmindon and it belonged to him.

As the rush of newfound power faded, a sense of rage overcame him. He was accustomed to sacrifice—to loss. He'd lost his family, he'd lost Ivory. He hid within himself as the vampire Manteis destroyed the Bloodbound. He witnessed Balris fall to the devils in Meriden. Each of them an anvil upon his heart.

But he had given all of himself to his god. Every scar on his marred body bore her name, every life he took was for her glory. And now she was gone—his hand forced to take her life because of Spara's greed and aspiration. He snarled, Spara bearing down on him with Shatter and Quake at the ready.

Umhra met Spara's eyes. The storms within them were raging tempests. She lunged wildly and swung her axes at Umhra's chest.

He stepped from the path of the first strike, Shatter hissing past him. Quake followed, but he caught Spara's wrist and swatted her away with the back of his fist.

She staggard backward and stalked around him in a wide arc.

Again, she attacked. She spun, her axes a blur of glimmering metal. Her speed was unparalleled.

Umhra ducked beneath Shatter. He deflected Quake with the remnants of Vaila's sword.

Spara continued her pursuit, crouching low and swinging her axes at Umhra's stomach.

Again, he deflected the first attack, the second hitting him in the torso with a blaring clang.

He looked down at where the axe should have been buried, but a band of diamonds had rebuffed the blade. The diamonds grew around him, forming a suit of armor. Gone were his tattered leathers. Healed were his wounds. He felt the pain abate.

Spara attacked again.

Umhra caught her arm and threw her the length of the room.

She tumbled to the floor and slid into the wall with a grunt.

She climbed to her knees and glared at Umhra; the hatred worn plainly on her face. She dabbed the corner of her mouth and stared at her bloodied fingers.

"It's now *me* that finds *you* a nuisance." Umhra strode toward Spara deliberately. "Concede defeat and I will show you mercy."

Spara spat blood on the floor at Umhra's feet. "You are not my god. I bend a knee to no one."

Umhra shook his head and sighed. How many times had he bested one who thought they were his superior? Humility was, indeed, an element more precious than the rhodium he wore about his neck or the diamond that now encased his body. Yet he had no desire to destroy Spara. He only knew that he could not allow her to become the One God. He could not allow Vaila's legacy to be besmirched. With a flick of his fingers, he beckoned her forward. "Have it your way. Let's finish this."

Spara climbed to her feet, her diamond gown glimmering. "Whether I win or lose, it is me who has changed the course of history. The Creator Gods are dead, Vaila's pantheon destroyed. I am the Catalyst. You are but the unworthy beneficiary of my vision."

They met once more in combat. Spara slashed at him with her axes, but Umhra grabbed her wrists and twisted. The strength of his grasp forced Spara to drop Shatter and Quake to the floor. Umhra crushed them underfoot.

Spara screamed in abject rage.

Umhra felt the initial pull as Spara drew upon Kalmindon's energy around her. Unlike the last time she called for Kalmindon's aid, however, Umhra did not succumb to the immense force. Space closed in upon them, but he felt no strain.

Spara released another concussive blast and tore another wall apart, but it did not so much as flutter the strands of grimy hair that hung in Umhra's face.

Umhra grasped the rhodium orb that dangled from Spara's neck on a simple but unbreakable chain. He pulled and envisioned its chain rent in his hand. The chain shattered, links of rhodium scattering across the floor.

Spara's face twisted, her eyes wide with shock.

Umhra held the remnants of the chain in his hand, Spara's icon swaying in the space between them. He released Spara's hand and gathered her icon in his palm.

Spara scratched and clawed at him to retrieve her icon, but Umhra paid her no notice. He bore down on the orb of rhodium in his palm and felt it burst like soft fruit.

Wisps of prismatic ether bled between Umhra's fingers and drifted into the air. The essence of the gods Spara had killed in her great conquest swirled around her more-worthy adversary. In a flood of light, the ether entered Umhra's icon. The power of the entire pantheon coursed through his body. He was unstoppable. He was the One God.

Spara's diamond gown dematerialized. Once again clad in celadon chiffon, Spara dropped to her knees. "It is done, then." She held her open hands out wide in resignation. "I must admit, I didn't think you had it in you."

"None of this was by choice." Umhra's chest heaved as he loomed over Spara. "I didn't ask for this."

"You still don't get it, do you? Your entire life has been guiding you to this moment—this is your destiny. It's *because* you didn't want it, you are so worthy. You were not driven by self-gain, but by virtue. You will have no one to squabble with, like the Creator Gods. Tyveriel's course, and that of countless other realms, lay at your discretion. And you will be a just steward. I will take pride in having your first act, as the God I created, be that of claiming my life. It is your right."

Spara closed her eyes and tilted her head back regally,

awaiting her sentence.

Umhra dropped her crushed rhodium icon on the floor and placed a hand on each of Spara's eyes. Her skin was warm and soft beneath his calloused palms. Spara's life flashed through his mind, thousands of years whirring by in a moment. He felt her pain as Vaila's magic seared her eyes from her face as she banished Naur to Pragarus. He sensed her sorrow at being left behind by the other Mystics and her despair at her millennia of imprisonment by King Hallgeirr and the frost giants.

A vibrant light glowed beneath his hands, and Umhra allowed a portion of his life force to flow into Spara. He removed his hands from Spara's face, and her eyes blinked open. In place of the violent storms Umhra was accustomed to were glinting, almond-shaped eyes that matched her celadon gown.

Spara dabbed at her healed eyes. "Thank you. You are a just god."

Umhra put a hand on each of Spara's shoulders and smiled.

She let a diamond shard slip down into her hand from her sleeve and jabbed at Umhra.

He caught the attack and bent her arm, redirecting the shard into her chest. With no armor to protect her, the dagger delved deep within her. Her eyes went wide, and she staggered back from Umhra's grasp.

Umhra let her go. He watched as she stumbled off the edge of a table and stabilized herself with a bloody palm on the wall behind her.

"Finally," she coughed. "You did something worthy of respect. And here I thought you were uncorruptible."

"You forced my hand, as usual."

"If that makes you feel better." She smiled and collapsed to the floor.

Umhra kneeled at her side. "I hope you find peace. I'm sorry this is the only way I could bring it to you."

Spara grabbed his wrist. Her nails bit into his skin as she seized in pain. Her breathing grew quick and shallow. "I wouldn't have been an angry god," she said, barely able to form the words. "I was just angry at them." She coughed and blood ran from the corner of her mouth. "I needed to make them pay for what they did."

Umhra nodded and smoothed Spara's hair from her face. "You were wronged by everyone you loved and who were supposed to love you. It's not how life should be. It's not fair. But you allowed revenge to consume you. That's not how life should be, either."

He held his arms wide and gestured to the destruction around them. "Look what you did. Now, let it go."

Spara looked into his eyes and smiled, the color fading from her face. She shuddered and then was still. Everything was still. Spara's body turned to ash and scattered on the gentle breeze that blew through the gaping hole in the façade of Vaila's Grace.

Umhra was alone.

The building shuddered. Diamonds rained from the ceiling.

Umhra stood and looked up as the roof of Vaila's Grace caved in. Walls crumbled and pillars toppled. The entirety of Vaila's Grace collapsed around him.

The floor beneath Umhra fractured. With each new crack, innumerable glass beads surfaced. They slowly covered the ruins until they were all that was left.

His diamond armor fell in flawless gems to the ground. They too sunk below the surface.

Umhra stood alone in an open field. A gentle breeze blew. Kalmindon awaited his vision for its future. He looked at himself and envisioned his leathers anew. And they were. Otherwise, he left himself as he was. He did not wish away the scars that covered his body as they were each a reminder of the hardships he had faced. He did not ask for diamond towers to hide within or gilded banquet tables. All he desired was peace.

Finally, there was peace.

CHAPTER 36

Naivara Marabyth was the only member of the Barrow's Pact to hail from outside Evelium. Viewed as a witch by her Reshinta tribe, she stowed away on a trade vessel to escape persecution.

- The Legend of the Barrow's Pact by Nicholas Barnswallow
Chapter 4 – Unearthed from the depths of Peacebreaker Keep, month of Jai, 1422 AT

— ▲ —

Naivara paced the room. She had not felt this useless since the day she was exiled by her own people. Even then, at least she held a sense of hope for her future. She knew she would be better off without them. Now, her stomach twisted with dread.

"My dear," Regent Avrette said from her seat at the table, having just been debriefed on the battle raging above. "We all share your anguish. Have faith in the rest of the Barrow's Pact. I have never known them to fail our people."

"It's not a question of faith, Jenta. We couldn't be in better hands, given the circumstances. It's a question of my worth. I should be up there with them, not down here..." Naivara bit her tongue.

"Babysitting me and Alessa?"

"That's not what I meant. Well, it was but..."

"It's alright. I know you would rather be amidst the action. I take no offense. There was a time where I longed for the same."

"I belong at their side. Thank you for understanding."

The rooms spun, reminding Naivara of the last time she drank too much honey wine. She steadied herself on the corner of the table.

"Are you alright, my dear?" Regent Avrette asked.

"Yes, I'm just feeling a bit dizzy."

"Here, take a seat." The regent pulled a chair back from the table.

Everything went black.

Naivara found herself in a foreign land. She stood in a lush garden with plants with which she was unfamiliar. The sky overhead was a delicate pink—the color of cherry blossoms.

Two men sat on a stone wall in the shade of a common pear tree—quite out of place among the exotic foliage. The setting was somehow familiar despite her confidence she had never been here before.

"I'm sorry it took me so long. I realize it seemed like ages for you, although I assure you it was only a matter of weeks for me."

Naivara peered into the shadows. "Umhra?"

She stepped beneath the canopy of the pear tree and her eyes adjusted, though the second man remained obscured by shadow.

"Nice to see you, Naivara," he said. "I'm glad you are well."

Umhra looked different than she remembered. Scars riddled his face, and his body emanated a soft amber aura. Naivara rushed in and hugged him.

Umhra reciprocated, his strength comforting.

As they embraced, she watched the shadowed figure who remained seated on the wall with his back to them. He was small, his hair a wild tangle atop his head.

"Where are we?" Naivara asked, her gaze returning to

Umhra's grey-green eyes. "Who is that?"

Umhra spread his arms wide. "Welcome to Kalmindon in all its glory. *He* is not ready for visitors."

"Am I dead?"

Umhra laughed. "No. You are most certainly not dead. I am communing with you. I killed Spara. My journey is over. I have become the One God."

"I don't understand. What are you saying?"

"In order to defeat Spara, I had to assume the souls of the other gods. Spara was attempting to do the same."

"That's why I lost my suffusion. She killed Tayre."

"Yes."

Naivara felt herself get pulled away from Umhra. She grabbed his hand.

"You can't stay long," he said. "Tayre lives within me now. Go. Go put an end to your war."

"Will we see you again?"

Umhra frowned. "I'm not sure. This is all new to me. I will do my best. Tell everyone I fight for you still."

Naivara's hand slipped from Umhra's grip, and she was torn through time and space.

"Naivara?"

Her eyes fluttered open. Jenta crouched above her. The regent's eyes welled with tears, her lips quivering. She helped Naivara up and gave her a firm hug.

"Are you alright?" she asked.

Naivara's head ached. "I think so. What happened?"

"You blacked out. Convulsed for a bit. I was terrified."

"I dreamed of Umhra."

Jenta's jaw dropped. Her eyes went wide with shock.

"I know. I couldn't believe it."

"I don't think it was a dream," Jenta said. "Your circlet is glowing."

Naivara looked up to see tendrils of green ether dancing around her head. Her stomach jumped. The warmth of her suffusion with Tayre flooded her body.

Hope. It was always there—lurking in the shadows. Not always obvious when you need it most, in time it presents itself.

Jenta smiled. "Go. You have a god to kill."

Naivara climbed to her feet and opened the door to Jenta's cavern. A guard stood on either side of the entry to the modest room and snapped to attention as the door swung wide. Naivara polymorphed into a harrier and flew from the room. The guards jumped back, startled by the shape shifter, but Jenta came to the door and assuaged their fears.

"Fly, Naivara. Wake us from this nightmare."

Naivara flew along a winding corridor, coursing over grimy-faced children and disheveled elderly—those the Barrow's Pact sought to protect. They ducked and pointed as she flew past.

Reaching the base of the Iris, she swept upward and climbed through the levels or Ruari. She felt a cool breeze ruffle her feathers and leveled off. Flying into the draft, she wove along another passage. Unlike the worried and expectant faces she saw below, here the vacant eyes of corpses of people and blights alike stared back at her.

Finally, she burst from the cave and lifted into the air. It was then the horror of what Turin and the others were up against struck her. The battlefield was lit in purple flame, a massive grey dragon—its wings held out wide—breathing it upon the confused army. Other stretches were frozen solid and yet more of the field was covered in a green noxious cloud, countless dead lay writhing in its confines.

Her first instinct was to change shape and attack the dragons, but she thought better of it when she saw Turin charging them with Gleriel, Aridon, and Sena flanking her. The dragons would have to wait. The primordial god was her primary concern. This might be the only chance they would get to destroy it and end their war of attrition with the blights. Turin would have to do what she could on her own.

Further away, blights poured over a wall of spiked stone that had erupted from the earth. She only knew of one person other than herself capable of shaping stone, but she had never seen it done on such a massive scale. Could Turin have wielded such magic? Could her connection with Tyveriel have grown so strong that she could will it to her aid in such a manner? These were the things of Mystics and gods.

Her keen vision spotted Talus as he led the front line against the blight assault, Aquila in constant motion as the enemy swarmed his position. Again, there was nothing she could do. He would have to hold out for as long as he could. It was difficult to choose between the terrors that beckoned her, but she remained focused on her objective.

She followed the streak of smoke that cut across the low-hanging moon like ink across a sheet of parchment. She only hoped that she wasn't too late.

A flash of blue lit up the land below, followed by a crack of thunder. Sem'Tora. At least there was hope that Laudin still lived.

Within the burst of light, she saw the silhouette of a humanoid form. It was stout, with its head set below broad shoulders. The primordial god.

As the light faded, a burst of energy emanated from the form. The blast leveled the few trees that stood in the area and threw two smaller bodies through the air.

Naivara collapsed her wings and dove for the Aged One.

The wind whistled past her as she fell from the sky, her quarry square in her sight. As she neared, she called upon Umhra—a green aura surrounding her—and shape shifted into a storm elemental.

An enormous ball of angry wind, rain, and lightning, she collided with her target and sent it tumbling through the grass. A clap of thunder rang out as she skidded to a halt, never touching the ground. In her wake, a blazing inferno of blue flames ignited.

She looked to Laudin and Shadow, who charged out of the

darkness toward her.

"How?" Laudin asked in astonishment.

"It doesn't matter," Shadow replied. "All that matters is that she's here."

Naivara barreled forward along the gouge in the earth the Aged One's body had created with Laudin and Shadow in tow.

— ▲ —

Turin ran for the Grey Queen. She seethed with a hatred she did not know she possessed. Everything else was a blur but for the massive grey dragon that laid waste to her people so dispassionately. As she bounded forward, hurdling the dead, Gleriel shouted behind her.

"You two, hold off the white one. I'll handle the green."

Aridon and Sena split off to one side to confront an ancient white dragon with ice mist leaking from its open maw. Gleriel leaped and in one bound had his scythes buried in the neck of a reeling green dragon who sprayed poison into the air.

Despite being showered in the noxious slime, Gleriel remained unaffected.

Silyarithe spun and her large purple eyes caught Turin in stride. She sneered.

"You. The slayer of my father." Her voice resonated in Turin's mind. "I will kill you and everyone you love, and still I won't be sated."

Turin threw her hands in the air as she ran, and Tyveriel answered. Stone spikes shot up from the earth. One scraped off the Grey Queen's side. Another tore a hole in the membranous tissue of her wing, eliciting a roar of pure fury.

The Grey Queen tore her wing free and lashed the protrusions with her tail. Rock exploded—a shower of boulders cast across the field between them.

Turin dove from their path and ducked behind another as Silyarithe released a flood of purple plasma over her.

A burst of ice doused the flames and Turin placed her hands

in the earth. She grabbed a handful of soil in each palm and watched as the black necrosis on her fingers spread over her hands.

Huddled behind the boulder, she felt the wind pick up as the Grey Queen flapped her wings to lift into the air. Turin stepped out from behind the rock and focused on the exposed stone jutting from the Ruari caverns. She drew it forth in two barbed spikes.

The cold that coursed through her body was nearly unbearable. Turin screamed as she willed the stone toward her.

Silyarithe leaped into the air and narrowly avoided the jagged stone. She roared and released another deluge of purple plasma that set the world aflame between her and Turin. She took flight.

The green dragon bellowed, garnering Turin's attention for but a moment. Gleriel tore a scythe free of the beast's skull and jumped from its back as it thrashed wildly. A horrid gash now ran through its eye. The dragon snapped at Gleriel. He rolled from its path and again buried his scythes in its skull. The dragon spit blood and green poison. With one more blow, the dragon was still. Gleriel stepped on the side of its immense face and wrenched his blades free with a spray of gore. One down.

The Grey Queen circled once overhead and dove at Turin.

Turin held her ground and waited for the dragon to draw near.

Silyarithe opened her mouth wide, and a violet glow grew in her throat. *Her tell.* Turin thought, thankful for all the time Shadow spent teaching her to play cards. She rolled as flame raked the ground where she had stood just seconds ago. The Grey Queen lifted back into the night sky.

Turin knew that, if she were to have a chance against the Grey Queen, she had to get her back on the ground.

Sena and Aridon poked and prodded the white dragon with their weapons as a volley of arrows rained down upon it. The dragon swatted at Sena, but she proved too lithe for the monstrosity and dodged the attack. Aridon hacked at its flank.

The Grey Queen reared about and dove once more. As she approached, Turin thrust her hands in the air and stone erupted from the earth in a series of spines that followed the Grey Queen's path. One struck Silyarithe in the side, exposing a streak of flesh. She spun awkwardly and crashed to the earth.

She shook rock and clumps of grass from her back. Snarling like a rabid timber wolf, she spun to face Turin.

Her strong hind legs rippling with muscle, she bounded forward.

Turin clambered backward, trying to put some distance between her and her foe.

Silyarithe's jaws snapped shut just shy of a death blow. The dragon seethed, her breath acrid and hot in Turin's face.

Turin threw more stone into the air.

Silyarithe's tail crashed through the defenses and struck Turin in the chest.

The force of the blow sent Turin hurtling through the air. She smashed into a wall of rock beside a cavern entrance. A searing pain shot through her ribs. She gasped for breath that refused to come.

She climbed to her knees and saw the ancient white dragon rear up on its hind legs as Neela nipped at its ankles. Sena dodged a blast of ice and Aridon wedged his halberd into the soil and supported it with his foot. He kneeled beside it, the tarnished steel pointing at the dragon's chest.

She tried to call out to him, but the words would not come.

The dragon came down upon him and he disappeared from sight.

The white dragon reared up again. This time it dragged Aridon with it as he held fast to his weapon lodged in the beast's chest.

With a swat of its fore claw, the dragon ripped the halberd clear and sent Aridon toppling to the ground.

Dark green blood poured from the wound. Aridon's halberd

had run deeper than Turin thought.

The dragon breathed ice over the wound and lashed out with an angry maw.

Aridon wedged his halberd in the dragon's mouth, giving him enough time to crawl out from under the behemoth and escape being trampled.

The white dragon took two steps forward and then staggered sideways. It snapped the halberd in two and spit its pieces to the ground at Aridon's feet.

Gleriel leaped for the beast and slashed into its side, but the damage had already been done.

It made to bite down on Aridon, who stood defenseless before it but wobbled awkwardly. From the gaping hole Aridon's halberd had left, blood came forth in waves with each beat of its heart. The ancient white dragon collapsed to the ground with a thunderous crash, one of its horns shattering upon the rocks.

Unphased by the calamity around her, the Grey Queen attacked.

— ▲ —

Naivara came upon the Aged One as it climbed to its feet. The primordial god's eyes glowed bright with anger.

It threw its hands toward her, a wave of preternatural energy washing past her, throwing Laudin and Shadow backward. In her storm elemental form, however, Naivara was unaffected and swept forward.

She landed a vicious blow on the Aged One's chin. She struck it again in the chest. With each successive punch, lightning crackled about them.

The Aged One raised trees from the earth, but they passed through his enemy, causing little discernable damage as the raging winds that made up Naivara's form regathered in a swirling vortex.

The Aged One floundered as blow after blow rained down

upon it, none of its godly powers slowing the assault.

An arrow passed through Naivara's form and struck the Aged One. Ice froze it in place. The Savonian glass dagger flew out of the darkness and sunk deep into the center of the primordial god's chest. This was the chance they'd been waiting for.

Naivara punched the Savonian dagger deeper into the Aged One's torso. The ice shell of Laudin's arrow shattered and the Aged One gripped at the dagger, its eyes wide with astonishment.

With one stride, Naivara was upon the ancient being that had caused so much trouble for her people over the ages. That had corrupted the blights to do its bidding and wage war against the gods and their beloved creations.

A crack propagated in the Aged One's body from where the Savonian dagger lay buried. A garnet glow leaked from deep within the primordial god.

Naivara struck the dagger again and drove it deeper still. Bolts of lightning danced over the Aged One's form and the crack spread from shoulder to hip.

The Aged One cried out. It was not a cry of rage or hatred, but one of sorrow. The sorrow of unfulfilled dreams. The sorrow of time cut short.

The fracture spread over its entire body, light seeping from each fissure with ever-increasing intensity.

"You are a cancer," the Aged One said. "A malignancy that will destroy this planet. You cannot help but spoil everything you touch."

Naivara's hands were restless tempests. "You may be right." Her voice rolled like thunder. "But it is not for you to decide our fate, for you are no better."

She struck the Aged One in the center of its chest, and it exploded into countless motes of energy that hung in the air. The embers whirled around one another like fireflies in mid-Jai and then faded to nothing.

Shadow's Savonian glass dagger fell to the ground and Naivara dropped her elemental form.

"I've never been so glad to see you," Shadow said, his chest heaving. "That wasn't looking good."

Laudin embraced her. "You were amazing. What happened?"

"Umhra. He communed with me from Kalmindon. He has defeated Spara and has become the One God. He gave me my suffusion back."

"Maybe that's why Gromley fell."

"Gromley." Shadow's voice quavered. He ran into the night.

Laudin and Naivara followed and came upon Gromley sitting with Nicholas's head in his lap amid a patch of phlox.

Gromley's icon glowed amber, but tears streaked Gromley's face as he stroked Nicholas's hair.

"I was too late," the cleric said. "He is lost."

Shadow dropped to his knees. Naivara burst into tears and buried her face in the crook of Laudin's neck.

CHAPTER 37

Their first adventure proved fruitful. They returned from the barrows with untold wealth in tow.

- The Legend of the Barrow's Pact by Nicholas Barnswallow
Chapter 5 – Unearthed from the depths of Peacebreaker Keep, month of Jai, 1422 AT

— ▲ —

Talus thrust Aquila into the scarlet orb at the center of the blight's chest. It grabbed Talus's arms with white claws scarred with dark lenticles. The blight's eyes widened as Talus drove his blade deeper. The blight screeched.

The mindless rage with which it had attacked washed away from its face and was replaced by something gentle and loving. Talus stared into its eyes as its life force flickered and then faded. He pulled Aquila free and searched the battlefield for his next adversary.

There were none to be had. All he saw were the backs of tens of thousands of blights trudging away to the north. Had they won?

Arrows loosed—blotting out the moon—and struck the blights at the back of their formation. Some dropped to the ground, others staggered. None turned back to the battlefield.

"Hold!" Talus cried. "Hold! We've won the night!"

Soldiers dropped their swords to the earth. Others fell to their knees. All of them yelled in celebration.

Turin.

Talus spun.

A sea of soldiers cheered. Grimy faces and the stench of sweat and blood surrounded him. There was no sign of his adopted daughter.

He felt the urge to vomit but pushed it down.

Where was she?

Talus pushed his way into the crowd. He searched the fallen, expecting that any one of them could be her.

But none were. Despite the death around him, hope grew in his heart that Turin was safe. That was until he saw the Grey Queen spit a stream of plasma across the landscape.

The hillside burst into flame as the enraged dragon unleashed hell.

He sprinted toward the Grey Queen. His legs felt like lead balloons and his lungs burned, but there would be time for pain later. He hurdled mangled corpses and wove between the throng of soldiers.

Amidst the revelry, a barrel-chested yellow dragon crashed down up the crowd. Soldiers were crushed underfoot, while others ran for cover as the behemoth thrashed its forward swept horns through their ranks.

The dragon gored soldiers on its horns and shook them into its gluttonous mouth. It then turned to those willing to stand and fight and unleashed a wave of super-heated air into their midst.

The air rippled like the desert in the high sun.

Skin blistered and sloughed from soldiers' bodies as they screamed. Metal armor glowed red.

Talus flourished Aquila. The glint from its jeweled hilt garnered the dragon's attention.

The beast laughed.

"I applaud your bravery, child of Tyveriel. Nonetheless, this will end poorly for you."

The dragon exhaled another wave of searing breath.

Talus dove from its path. The skin on his hands and face burned.

He rolled to his feet and dashed for the dragon. Running between the beast's legs, he slashed Aquila against soft flesh.

The dragon lumbered as it tried to locate its adversary beneath him.

Talus drew Aquila along the dragon's stomach.

The dragon collapsed upon him, but Talus tumbled out from beneath it before it crashed to the ground in a plume of dust. The dragon whipped its tail about as it searched for Talus.

"Where are you, runt?"

Talus drove his blade between the scales at the dragon's knee.

With more speed than Talus thought it possessed, the massive dragon spun and caught him in his jaws.

He lodged between two of the dragon's teeth beside a piece of rotten meat. He tried to slip between them, but his armor caught on a tooth's serrations. He sheathed Aquila and worked furiously to free himself.

The dragon's tongue ran over its teeth in search of the nuisance. It shook its head and Talus broke free and fell deeper into its mouth. With one gulp, he was consumed.

— ▲ —

Naivara soared over the battlefield. Blights marched north in their retreat toward the Wistful Timberlands, and men and women cheered their victory. Beyond, a yellow dragon loomed, locked in combat with a soldier whose sword gleamed above all else around it. Talus. Who else would be so rash to confront such a beast?

Laudin, Gromley, and Shadow gripped onto her scales as she dove to Talus's defense. As they neared, the dragon plucked

Talus from the ground and swallowed him whole.

Naivara roared, and the others jumped from her back as she crashed into the other dragon. She bit the beast's neck, her razor-sharp teeth slicing through scale and flesh.

An arrow whistled over her head and struck the yellow dragon in the face. Lightning crackled over the dragon's eye.

The dragon batted Naivara with its tail. Her smaller dragon form tumbled through the grass in a flash of platinum scales.

"Talus is inside the dragon," Shadow said. "We must keep it on the ground."

The yellow dragon unfurled its wings and lifted into the air.

Laudin loosed another arrow and pierced its wing. Ice covered the appendage, and the dragon crashed back to earth.

Naivara locked jaws with the beast to keep it from attempting another escape.

Laudin continued to pepper the dragon with arrows.

Shadow looked at Gromley. "Be ready to heal him."

Shadow rushed toward the dragons as they thrashed in battle. He ran up Naivara's back and along her neck.

"Now," he yelled.

Naivara released the dragon's jaw, and the beast opened its mouth wide. Shadow leaped from Naivara's head and dove head-first into the dragon's maw.

The dragon choked. Naivara locked jaws with it once more.

Moments later, a green dagger pierced the dragon's stomach from the inside. The blade drew a long gash, and Shadow and Talus spilled from the wound covered in digestive juices.

Naivara turned her full attention back to the yellow dragon. She released its jaw and bit again at its bulky neck. She tasted blood.

The larger dragon bore down upon her and took a chunk of flesh from her shoulder. It raked both of her sides with its fore claws. It was too big—too strong. She would not last much longer.

As the beast lunged at her again, she bit into its neck and pulled it atop her. The monstrosity lurched forward further than its strike should have carried it, and Naivara jabbed her barbed tail into its abdomen where Shadow's dagger had left a gaping wound. She tore the barb free from its stomach and green blood sprayed across her.

The dragon roared in pain and reared up on its hind legs. Naivara scrambled out from under it as it unleashed a wave of blistering air upon her.

Even in her platinum dragon form, the heat was unbearable. It tore at her scales and bore into the exposed flesh of her wounds.

The pain was so great, she could no longer maintain focus on her spell and reverted to her Reshinta form.

The dragon's breath stopped with a gurgle. Naivara saw Laudin rushing toward her with his scimitar dripping with green blood. Everything went black.

She saw endless beaches and pink skies. Standing at the shore with his back to her was Umhra. She walked to his side, gentle azure waters lapping at their feet.

"That was rough," Umhra said as he peered over the water at the sunless horizon.

Naivara chuckled at his unexpected candor.

"Yes. That was rough. There wasn't much else I could do, though."

Umhra nodded. "You were the only one who stood a chance."

"So, what do we do now that I'm actually dead?"

Umhra looked at her for the first time and smiled. He plucked a glass bead from the beach and placed it in her palm.

It was warm to the touch and swirled with an energy of its own, as though it contained a galaxy within. Naivara had never seen anything like it.

"That's what you'd look like if you were dead," Umhra said.

Naivara stared deeper into the bead. "So, I'm not?"

"Laudin got to him just in time. You're lucky to have each other."

"I suppose we are."

"Go back to him. You two have a long life ahead of you."

"Nicholas fell."

"I know," Umhra said. "It was his time. He is healing."

Naivara smiled at the notion and then frowned. "And you? Can't you come back with me now that you've put Spara's ambitions to rest? Shouldn't the One God be able to go wherever he wants? Do what suits him?"

"Alas, I cannot come back to you. The Rescission cast a veil between us, and I know of no way through. Rest assured, there is a place with me for each of you when your days are done, and we shall be together again. But be in no rush, for I have seen eternity, and it is not as precious as the fleeting moment that is our mortal lives. How insignificant a thing—a single life. To so many, it goes unnoticed. To so few, it is cherished. I tell you, having seen this in a new light, there is nothing more valuable. Even the beggar who lives unseen in the streets, even the slave that toils without care—their lives are worth more individually than all the glory we saw together. More than all the wealth of this decadent age in which we—you live. Treat them each as such in my name. Let them know my grace, as so many carelessly knew my blade when I walked among you. Tell my story—the story of the Peacebreaker."

Naivara cried freely. How unfair that Umhra would have to give so much of himself and get so little in return. What did it mean to have the power of a god if you could not be with the ones you loved? What glory was there in isolation?

Umhra put a hand on her cheek and wiped a tear away. "Don't cry for me. I can now rest knowing I did all I could for Tyveriel and our people. I will, of course, miss you and the rest of the Barrow's Pact terribly. But this is my home now. This is where I belong. Go."

Naivara felt the undeniable pull of Tyveriel and snapped

awake. She sobbed uncontrollably.

Laudin embraced her. "Oh, thank the gods, you're alright."

"God," Gromley said. "Thank the One God."

CHAPTER 38

One day, they will follow her to the brink of their own reckoning.

- Entry from Aldresor's Journal
Undated. Discovered: The Tower of Is' Savon, month of Riet, 1444 AT

— ▲ —

Turin threw up a wall of stone before her. It absorbed the initial blast of Silyarithe's plasma, but the heat from the ensuing fire overcame the persistent chill she'd felt within since calling for Tyveriel's help. Still, she endured, knowing her only chance was to draw the Grey Queen closer.

Turin retreated further toward the mouth of the cave. The air reeked of charred flesh and wood, but she dared not choke unless she gave up her position.

Silyarithe shattered the wall with a swipe of her tail, sending a shower of rock over Turin.

"There is no sense in hiding," Silyarithe said, her tone flecked with annoyance. "Win or lose, I will have my way with you tonight."

The Grey Queen thundered forward through the black smoke and purple embers that hung in the air.

Turin passed beyond the bonfire of blights that now smoldered with charred limbs. Part of her wanted to run for the cavern entrance and hide in the depths of Ruari with the rest of those too frightened or frail. She looked at the black void that offered her refuge. No. The other part of her—the part that made her a queen of men—knew she must stand and fight. It was time to draw this chapter of Evelium's harrowed history to a close.

She stood her ground and awaited the Grey Queen. Alone.

The earth shook with each step and a vibrant violet glow shone through the dense smoke. Turin anticipated the blast and dove from its path. But there was no blast. Silyarithe held her breath until Turin popped to her feet and then unleashed fury upon her.

Turin drew forth a wall of stone but was too late. The plasma splattered on her and set her leather cuirass aflame. She dropped to the ground and tried to smother the fire, but it would not die. Flame spread over her. She unfastened the buckles at her chest—her hands burning in the purple flame—and cast the cuirass aside.

The Grey Queen charged forward and destroyed the stone wall, leaving Turin exposed in little more than her black linen shirt.

A grim smile spread over Silyarithe's face.

Then she howled.

As if she had forgotten about her desire to kill Turin, she spun and snapped at something at her rear.

Between the Grey Queen's legs, Turin spotted Sena and Aridon. They hacked at the dragon's tail like they were chopping a tree, while Neela nipped at her ankles. It was when the dragon turned, however, that Turin saw the real nuisance.

With his cowl tattered and singed, exposing his skeletal head, Gleriel stood on Silyarithe's back. His eyes were balls of arcane fury as he cleaved the Grey Queen's flesh above her spine.

The dragon snapped again but met the full force of Gleriel's scythes. Her chin split wide. Blood sprayed over Gleriel.

Silyarithe reared back and opened her mouth. The inferno within raged as she fixed Gleriel in her aim.

Turin once again felt the cold surge through her. The discoloration on her hands spread up her forearms as the sensation grew into a searing pain. She thrust her hands toward Silyarithe and willed the stone from the wall behind her forward.

Turin screamed as serrated shards broke free from the wall and flew toward the Grey Queen.

The dragon swatted Gleriel from her back like a fly and turned back to her primary concern. Her eyes went wide as the shards bore down upon her. She beat her wings in a panicked effort to escape but was too late.

The first shard punctured her shoulder. Two more tore through her wings. More followed and impaled her chest and neck. Silyarithe staggered backward with each blow, sending Sena and Aridon diving from her erratic path.

There was no last burst of flame—no enraged roar. The Grey Queen simply slumped to the ground—her lifeblood soaking the soil. She closed her violet eyes. Her massive chest stilled.

Turin stopped screaming. The rest of her shards fell. Each struck the earth with a deafening thud.

All she heard was her own labored breath. All she felt was the pounding of her heart. All she saw was the Grey Queen lying dead before her. She dropped to her knees and placed her hands on the cold earth. *Thank you. We are free.*

Tyveriel was silent. At peace.

Smoke wafted from Sena's leathers as she sprinted for her friend. She slid to a stop and wrapped Turin in a firm embrace.

"That was so amazing. Did you even know you could do that?"

The truth was that Turin did not know what her connection with Tyveriel would allow her to do. She had no idea if she would be strong enough to defeat the Grey Queen and deliver her people a new life—one worthy of her serving as their queen. She only knew that failing to rise to the challenge would result in the loss of Evelium and, likely, all Tyveriel.

"I had a pretty good idea." She showed Sena her stained arms.

Sena inspected around her collar. "It's spread all the way up to your neck."

Turin shrugged. "A small price to pay."

Aridon came up behind Sena. "We each killed a dragon except for Sena." He laughed, eliciting a high-pitched bark from Neela. The dog jumped into his arms and licked his face.

Sena grimaced and then joined in the laughter.

"Where is Gleriel? What happened with the blights?" Turin asked.

Sena pointed over his shoulder. "Bones is with the Grey Queen. I'm not sure what happened with the weeds. The cheering is a good sign, I'd think."

Turin had not heard it before. She was too consumed with her own war. "They did it. The Barrow's Pact killed the primordial god."

Sena shrugged. "It seems like it's turned out to be a pretty good day."

Turin climbed to her feet. Only now did she realize how much her body ached. Every breath sent a shot of pain through her. Every muscle begged for rest. Her head pounded.

"Give me a moment with him," she said.

Sena nodded, flashed Turin a crooked smile.

"Time for a nap, anyway," Aridon said.

Turin walked through the haze and found Gleriel standing before the dragon with his head hung.

As she approached, he threw his shredded cowl up to cover what it could of his exposed skull.

"You don't need to do that," Turin said. "You will always be welcomed and respected here. Your appearance is not something that influences the way I feel about you, and the way I feel about you is the way our people will feel about you."

Gleriel nodded, left his torn cowl up.

"You were a true hero here today," Turin continued. She hoped Gleriel would stay but, in the pit of her stomach, she knew he was no more meant to be tied down to a queen and her castle than was a phoenix to a cage. "I can never thank you enough."

"Such a beautiful creature. The only of its kind, I suppose." A myriad of raspy whispers followed Gleriel's words. He looked at Turin with fiery eyes. "It's a shame her heart was so poisoned. I would like to think there is enough room on Tyveriel for us all."

Turin felt a flutter of unexpected guilt in her chest. "I. I had no choice."

"I am well aware and took part willingly, myself. It had to be done. But if you are to return Evelium to glory, you must do better than your forefathers or you will fail as they did. You should know better than any the harsh judgement of your people. Even when reduced to living in these caves, they hold to their norms as though they are at court in Castle Forene. Do not rebuild Evelium—envision it anew."

Turin had never considered what the future of Evelium would look like. She grew up hearing stories of its former greatness. She had, of course, seen the ruins of its cities and bucolic towns. But maybe, those are not the things that make a kingdom great. Maybe she could do better than her forefathers.

"I promise you, I will."

Gleriel nodded. "Then, I wish you luck, my Queen. I wish you a thousand years of rule. May Evelium be all the better for it."

"So, you are leaving, then?"

Gleriel looked up at the night sky and sighed. "I am. While I appreciate your offer, my own quest is not yet complete. I learned much from your wizard's library and will travel Tyveriel until I find a cure to my affliction. Only then can I be at peace."

"Well, then it is I who wish you luck. You deserve nothing less than the peace you seek. If you should ever need anything, I hope you will find me."

Gleriel bowed, his hands folded over his chest where his heart should be. Without another word, he walked away.

As Turin watched him disappear into clouds of smoke, she called after him.

"Where do I start?"

Gleriel kept walking but called over his shoulder in reply. "With their hearts and minds. That is where change always begins."

With that, he was gone. Turin's heart sank.

As though he materialized from Gleriel's shadow, Talus emerged from the haze with the Barrow's Pact at his back. She had never seen such worry on his face. Putrid slime covered him as he rubbed the back of his neck, his eyes darting over the bodies strewn in his path. A stream of blood ran down his chin from where he chewed his lip.

Their eyes met, and he dropped to his knees and buried his face in his hands. His shoulders shook as he wept. Turin ran to him.

She wrapped herself around him and squeezed. Usually, it was his firm grasp that brought her comfort, but now she did everything she could to let him know how important he was—how much she loved him for everything he had done for her.

Talus put his cold hands on her cheeks and smeared the grime away as best he could. "I thought I lost you."

"It was admittedly a little closer than I would have liked, but we won." Her gaze darted to each of the Barrow's Pact. "It would seem we all won."

"We certainly did," Talus said. "Your plan worked. Well, minus the dragons."

Turin laughed and her ribs screamed. She put a hand to them, and Talus noticed the discoloration on her arms.

"Your mother will not like that," he said. "She always thought you were perfect just the way you were. We both did."

Turin inspected her arms through torn linen sleeves. "It's actually growing on me. A reminder of the great things we all did here today."

"I'm proud of you," Talus said. "You've proven yourself an outstanding leader. Evelium is lucky to have such a queen."

"Thank you. I couldn't have done it without each of you at my side."

It then dawned upon Turin that Naivara was with the Barrow's Pact and not in the depths with her mother and aunt as she had left her. "Your powers?" she asked.

Naivara smiled. "They're back with a vengeance."

"And yours Gromley?"

"Umhra came through for us once more. He defeated Spara and has become the One God."

Turin never had much use for the gods. She had never put faith in them. After all, what were they but absentee parents who neglected their responsibilities? Maybe the Peacebreaker was different. Maybe he was worthy of the faith the Barrow's Pact and the others put in him. Maybe he was a god worthy of his people, as she was finally a queen worthy of hers.

"The One God," she pondered aloud. "A new faith for a new age. Come, we must let the others know of our victory. I shall not have them hide in worry a moment longer."

Gromley clasped his icon and helped Turin to her feet with his free hand. She felt his power flow into her. The stabbing pain in her side abated. Her headache faded. She hugged him.

Together, they returned to the cavern from which Turin and Talus had led their army into the fields before the blights. Turin brought them before a chain that disappeared into a hole in the ceiling and motioned for Gromley to step forward.

"Would you please, Cleric Strongforge?"

Gromley smiled, rubbed his scruffy beard. He stepped forward and pulled on the chain. A bell rang out overhead. He

364 | JEFFREY SPEIGHT

pulled again and again, and the bell tolled in response.

From deep within Ruari's belly, a raucous cheer resounded throughout the caverns.

With the rising sun, a new age dawned. Evelium would rise from the ashes.

CHAPTER 39

It was not until my later years that I found my true faith.
After my friends passed and my love reserved for Evelium
and the Peacebreaker alone.

- The Collected Letters of Turin Forene
Letter to Bella Ketch dated 7th of Prien, 137 AT. Unearthed
from the Ruins of Farathyr, month of Mela, 1411 AT

— ▲ —

The early morning sun cast long shadows across the field. The Grey Queen and her companions were put to the flame where they lay on pyres fueled by blight husks. Fires raged for days, a constant reminder of the terror the dragons had inflicted.

Turin toiled alongside the others. They buried their own dead as soon as the grave clerics saw to their last rites and painted their shrouded bodies in ochre paint. It was not a pleasant job, but it was the least Turin could do to thank them for the sacrifice they made to save their loved ones. Someone once told her there was no victory in war, only degrees of defeat. She had never understood the meaning until now.

Death's stench gave way to the spicy scent of phlox that

bloomed with ubiquity around the caves. Ash took to the wind, but it would take some time for the dark scars across the landscape to heal.

"You better get cleaned up," Sena said as she leaned on her shovel. "You have a big day ahead of you."

Turin had felt nauseas since she woke up. She was not looking forward to her coronation, not because she did not want to be named queen of her people, but because she hated being on display like the porcelain doll she would never be.

"Don't remind me. I've been dreading it for days. I can't tell if this ceremony is for me or my mother and aunt."

Sena wiped her brow. "They're making me wear a dress."

Turin laughed. "How horrible of them. Seeing that might make this all worthwhile."

"Your aunt was going on about the duties of a woman of my station. I honestly had no idea what she was talking about. I've never had a station that I know of."

"It's because I told her I was disbanding the Elders Syndicate and that you were going to be the first person named to my new advisory council."

"I what? Disband the Elders Syndicate?"

"We don't need their bickering. I need people that aren't afraid to speak their minds. That aren't afraid to act in others' best interests. I'd like to have you help me rebuild Evelium."

Sena shrugged. "I don't have much experience with nation building. Are you sure that's a good idea?"

"There's no one I trust more."

"While I question your judgement, you're probably going to make me do all the hard work, anyway. I might as well get something out of it. I accept."

"Then, the dress it is."

Sena rolled her eyes and took Turin's shovel. She passed it and her own to a wiry Evenese man with a tangle of dirty blond hair.

"Do you mind, my dear? The queen and her most trusted

advisor must be on our way."

"Of course, my Lady. Anything for the queen."

"And her most trusted advisor?" Sena drew out the words.

Turin gave her a shove.

"What? I'm just trying it on."

"Thank you, kind sir," Turin said.

"A pleasure, Queen Turin."

Turin threw her arm over Sena's shoulder and Sena wrapped hers around Turin's waist. Together, they sauntered back to the caves.

Despite the afternoon's coronation, Turin struggled to recall a time when she felt so at peace. She was still adjusting to life without the specter of the Grey Queen or the threat of the blights and their primordial god. She did not know how to live this way. She was not sure anyone did.

Turin grasped the emerald Indrisor had given her. He would have known how to move forward. He had an insatiable love for life, even at its worst moments. She peered into the depths of the uncut stone and thought of him. She remembered running on the bluffs of Maryk's Cay as her mother and Talus gave chase. Every time she looked over her shoulder, she saw Indrisor watching from afar with a smile on his face. That feeling of love and belonging was what she sought for every child in Evelium.

She thought of bringing him back. She missed him more than she thought possible, but now was not the right time to meddle with death's grasp. How could she bring Indrisor back and then look into the eyes of a child who lost a father, or a wife that lost a husband, or a mother who lost her son or daughter? For now, she had to focus on her promise to the living. To deliver to them the life they deserved. Until then, her memories of Indrisor would have to suffice.

At the Iris, she said her goodbyes to Sena and gathered a bahtreig from a nearby stable. She barreled down the spiral pathway, her mind running through the events that led to this day. She thought about the Barrow's Pact and everything they taught her. She regretted how often she took them for granted. She thought about her Aunt Jenta and her undying patience with a stubborn girl that wanted nothing to do with the great honor her bloodline bestowed upon her. Most of all, she thought of Talus and her mother and their unconditional love for an oddity of a daughter.

Her bahtreig flashed with bioluminescence, a burst of teal in an otherwise mundane world. Turin steered her mount into the royal chambers where her aunt awaited her arrival flanked by guards.

Jenta stood with her hands on her hips and a stern expression on her fair face. She wore her hair up in an intricate weave decorated with teardrop diamonds. Her gown was a rich forest green—the color of the Forene bloodline. How proudly she wore it. How proudly she clung to the past.

A guard grabbed the horn of her saddle, and Turin dismounted.

"Even your mother is almost ready," Jenta said. "And here you are, with your coronation in a matter of hours, looking like a farm girl."

"And, when we rebuild Hylara, I will lay the first stone, Aunt Jenta. If there is anything you have taught me, it's that a ruler does not hide in ivory towers. They fight for what they believe in, just like you were willing to do when Uncle Vred's army marched on Vanyareign."

"My dear, you take it to an extreme." Jenta chuckled. "But I cannot argue with the results. Your people adore you. Now, let's get you tidied up for the coronation. You can go back to looking like a pauper as soon as the celebration is over."

Turin sighed. "Let's get on with it."

Jenta ushered Turin into the quarters they maintained for her, but she never used. Clusters of white candles flickered across the ruddy walls of the sitting room. In the adjoining room, maids waited with hands crossed over their honeycomb stitched aprons.

"Ladies," Jenta said. "Please see to the queen's care with expediency. Send for me when she is ready. Her mother and I shall like to inspect her before the ceremony."

"Yes, Regent. We will do our best."

Inspect? Do our best? Turin felt more like the family silver in need of polishing than a person. Never mind a queen.

Jenta left, and the room went into a frenzy. The maids buzzed about like bees as they stripped Turin of her leathers and led her to a tub of steaming water. They scrubbed every inch of her body, paying special attention to the blackened skin on her arms and neck as if it would rub free. They combed the tangles from her raven blue hair. They dug the grime out from beneath her nails and filed their rough edges. Turin loathed the invasiveness of it all.

Helping her from the tub, they dried her with soft linen towels. They dabbed her bare skin with rose oil and dressed her.

She had to admit the gown was perfect. Muted blue silk and fine pewter embroidered trim that complemented the grey of her skin. Tight sleeves that barely clung to her shoulders and a square neckline showed more than she thought her mother would approve. She felt powerful and beautiful, like how she always saw Jenta. Maybe a single day like this wouldn't be so terrible after all.

The maids left her hair long and straight, draping it over her shoulder. Otherwise, her head was unadorned to leave room for the Circlet of Everlife.

Finally, they clasped Indrisor's emerald around her neck.

She looked at herself in the mirror. Sure, her pupilless eyes were still yellow and ringed with black, and her skin still the color of cold steel, but she liked what she saw. Instead of the dread that dwelled within her for the last several days, butterflies flitted excitedly in her stomach.

Her mother appeared in the mirror over her shoulder. Her bronze skin and ebony hair were perfect, as always.

"You are the very image of radiance," Alessa said. She

turned her daughter around and held her hands. She looked her up and down and shook her head. "Perfection."

"You always say that."

"I always mean it. It's you that never believed me. Never believed in yourself. I hope you can now see what I've aways seen."

Turin hugged her mother.

"It's time," Jenta said from the doorway. "Let's not make the people of Evelium wait for their rightful queen any longer."

"Yes," Turin agreed. "They have waited long enough already."

EPIL◊GUE

There are times I wake up in the middle of the night and feel as though he is close. There are others when I feel like I will never see him again.

- *The Legend of the Barrow's Pact by Nicholas Barnswallow*
Chapter 22 – Unearthed from the depths of Peacebreaker
Keep, month of Jai, 1422 AT

— ▲ —

Indrisor's ward lapsed upon his death. Ivy and weeds overran the grounds at Peacebreaker Keep. Laudin surveyed the gardens where vines climbed the olive marble statues of the Bloodbound. There was much to be done.

"Is there any point in even starting?" Shadow asked. "It's not like Anaris will return to its old form anytime soon."

Laudin put a hand on Shadow's shoulder. "We're not here for Anaris. We're here for ourselves. For Umhra."

Shadow cocked an eyebrow, his lavender eyes twinkling in the sunlight. "I don't think he needs us here. He'll find us wherever we are when he can."

"I was hoping I'd feel closer to him once we got here," Gromley admitted. "So far—"

"What is it?" Laudin asked.

Gromley waded into the tangle of weeds between the towering statues. He tore a bunch of the overgrowth from the ground and tossed it over his shoulder.

Blue light streamed from the cleared space.

Gromley looked up—his eyes wild with excitement. "Don't just stand there. Help me."

The others joined Gromley in the morass. With each unwanted clump they cast aside, the light from beneath strengthened.

Laudin scraped away the dirt. His fingers slid across a smooth stone hidden beneath the surface.

He had only seen something like this once before at the mouth of the Stoneheart Pass. "A Waystone."

"I'm certain this was not here before," Gromley said.

Naivara stood upon the center of the glowing stone and spun in a slow circle.

"The sigil. It's a pyramid."

The realization sent Laudin's heart racing. He dusted the remnants of earth from the stone's surface and climbed to his feet.

The Barrow's Pact stood at the perimeter of the stone. The carving of Umhra's icon glowed between them.

Shadow ran a hand through his white hair. "Now what?"

Naivara shrugged.

"How does it work when you commune with him?" Laudin asked.

"I focus on him, or he focuses on me, and we meet," Gromley said.

Laudin wondered why whenever he thought of Umhra, it didn't end in such an outcome. "Maybe if we all focus on him while standing on the Waystone it will activate."

Gromley stepped onto the stone. Its glow intensified. "It's certainly worth a try."

The others took a step forward.

"Should we hold hands?" Naivara asked. "You know, just in

case something goes awry?"

They clasped their hands and shut their eyes.

Laudin thought of Umhra. He smiled as his friend's image grew clear in his mind. How far they had come since he found the mysterious half-Orc nearly dead and about to be devoured by dire wolves outside of Telsidor's Keep all those years ago.

He saw Umhra's kind, but vigilant eyes. The tusks that jutted from his bottom jaw. His long black hair and pointed ears. How he missed him.

Umhra's visage gave way to a blinding light and Laudin hurtled backward. For a moment, he felt like he was weightless, a great force pulling him at breakneck speed. Then, the light faded, and he saw the rest of the Barrow's Pact.

They held hands in a circle but were no longer in the garden at Peacebreaker Keep. Rather, they found themselves in a barren wasteland of purple-grey stone. Laudin squinted into the lashing wind that threw dirt and debris with relentless vigor.

Shadow dropped Naivara's hand and dashed into the deluge. Laudin gave chase, towing Naivara behind him.

Through the windstorm, Laudin could make out the silhouette of a hulking figure standing bedside what looked like a young child.

Shadow lifted the smaller of the two into the air and drew the figure in close to his chest.

Gromley crashed into Umhra and threw his arms around him. Umhra hugged him back.

"I've missed you, Gromley. How have you been?"

"Well enough, Umhra." Gromley sniffled. "Am I still allowed to call you that now that you are a god?"

Umhra chuckled. "Of course. You are a dear friend. I wouldn't have you treat me any differently than you always have."

He looked at Laudin and Naivara.

"Naivara." He nodded. "It hasn't been nearly as long since we last met. Laudin, it's wonderful to see you."

The two embraced. The strength behind Umhra's grasp was stronger than Laudin recalled.

Shadow returned Nicholas to the ground, a warm amber aura surrounding him that did not in life. The group took turns greeting one another.

"Is this Kalmindon?" Laudin asked.

"No. We are far from Kalmindon, and we are not communing. We are in Wethryn. I called you here for a very specific purpose."

"And what is that?" Shadow asked. "What could we possibly do to help a god?"

"In my quest to defeat Spara, I lost something here and I wish to find it. I have figured out how to create Waystones that will allow you to come to me. I have yet to learn how to return to Tyveriel, myself. The days are long and quiet in Kalmindon. You can help by keeping me company. Follow me. I apologize for bringing you to such a deplorable place."

Umhra waded into the gale, Nicholas glued to his side.

They fought through windborne rock and debris until they came upon the carcass of a monstrous worm. Its rust-colored body obscured the landscape, and its three massive eyes were clouded over. The wind thrashed its form, so its thick skin flapped like the shell of a tent during a summer storm.

Behind its mouthful of wicked teeth, it had a hole torn through the base of its head. Dried ichor clung to its side and formed a pool of thick gore on the ground. The Barrow's Pact huddled around Umhra beside the Eketar. The stench was overwhelming, but they welcomed the brief respite from the storm.

Laudin marveled at the size of the creature. "Did you do that?"

Umhra nodded. "It's an Eketar. A god killer. Spara used it to further her cause."

"By yourself?" Laudin asked in amazement.

"It's not *that* big," Shadow said.

"Its sole purpose was to kill gods. It did so indiscriminately. I barely survived the fight and sacrificed Forsetae in the process."

"And we're here to help you find it?" Gromley asked.

"If you wouldn't mind."

"How'd you lose it?" Naivara asked.

"I threw it at the worm."

Shadow smirked.

"It was Forsetae's idea and worked quite nicely, actually."

Naivara nodded contemplatively. "Where were you standing?"

Umhra took a few strides away from the party and looked around. His hair whipped around in the tempest. He took another few strides and stood his ground. "I was here. The Eketar was roughly where it fell but reared upright by roughly half its length."

Laudin came to his side. The wind buffeted his face. He drew Sem'Tora from his shoulder and aimed an arrow at the approximate height of the Eketar's mouth, as Umhra described it. As his bow creaked under his draw, he imagined a streak of lightning across the night sky. Sem'Tora lit with blue radiance and Laudin loosed his arrow.

The fletching whirred past his cheek and the arrow flew into the storm at a steep angle. It burst to light with a clap of thunder. Branches of electrical energy arced from its shaft.

The wind caught it and swept it from its intended course. Laudin followed the streak of blue until the haze obscured it.

"That's new," Umhra said.

"All thanks to you and King Eleazar."

"Another debt I owe the dead."

"I'm sure, in your new position, you'll be able to make amends. Come on, let's find your sword."

Umhra put a hand on Laudin's shoulder, and they followed the path of his arrow beyond the Eketar corpse. The others joined them, fighting Wethryn's rage with each step.

They trudged onward until a pulsing glow broke through the haze. There lay Laudin's arrow stuck in the powdery earth.

"Spread out," Laudin shouted over the storm. "Forsetae must be buried in the silt somewhere in this area."

Umhra and the Barrow's Pact fanned out—the arrow their epicenter. They shuffled between one another with their gazes affixed to the ground.

Gromley dropped to his knees and dug into the earth. He produced a rusted sword with a sweeping blade that had two chinks along its edge. He tossed it away.

Nicholas yelled something unintelligible through the gales.

Laudin ran to him as the others also converged upon his location. Nicholas kneeled beside a stone. As Laudin drew near, Nicholas stood, his hair a tousled mess. Flawless metal glinted over his shoulder. The Farestere struggled with the weight of the fabled blade but dragged it in a semicircle to face his approaching friends.

Umhra was the last to reach him. He slipped between Gromley and Shadow and crouched before Nicholas.

Nicholas presented Forsetae's hilt.

"I owe you a great debt, Nicholas." He looked at the others. "All of you."

"I assure you, Umhra, you owe us nothing," Naivara said. "This is what family is all about—selfless acts for one another without expectation of return."

Umhra smiled. "Regardless, I thank each of you for heeding my call."

He grasped Forsetae and studied the flawless blade. The hilt transformed from rhodium to diamond within his grip and glowed with celestial light.

Umhra closed his eyes and drew in a deep breath, like a mother reunited with a lost child.

"Of course, I came back for you," he whispered. "We are one, are we not?"

Laudin felt the earth tremble beneath his feet. A moment

later, he felt another quake, this one stronger than the first. He shielded his eyes and peered into the storm.

A shadowy form appeared within the tempest. Easily twice the size of the Eketar, Wethryn trembled with each successive footfall.

"We might have a problem on our hands," Laudin said.

The others turned to bear witness to Laudin's concern. Naivara gasped.

The monstrosity was as black as the night of the Reaping Moon, but for two angry orange eyes with narrow slits for pupils. It stood on towering front legs that ended in razor-sharp claws that pierced the ground with each step. Its hind legs were short but strong, muscles rippling in its hindquarters.

The creature had a solid and sinewy body from foot to shoulder, but its hunched back and porcine head consisted of black smoke that swirled discontentedly in the storm.

Slowly, the Barrow's Pact fanned out with Umhra at their center.

"A Chasm Wraith," Umhra said.

The Chasm Wraith opened its mouth and roared, exposing rows of massive tusks backed by a vortex of white fire.

Laudin looked at Umhra. "Shall we have one more go before we part ways?"

Umhra summoned diamond armor that grew around him one faceted stone at a time. "I think so."

Laudin lifted Sem'Tora from his shoulder and nocked an arrow. He nodded to Naivara who transformed into a platinum dragon in a cloud of green ether. He then looked to Shadow, who held his Savonian glass dagger in one hand and a newly fashioned blade of blackened steel in the other. Gromley stood beside him, his war hammer in both hands.

Nicholas came to Umhra's side and looked up at the half-Orc with a smile on his face. "One more time," he said. "The Barrow's Pact and the Peacebreaker."

ACKNOWLEDGMENTS

When I began writing what became Paladin Unbound, I had no idea what the future had in store for me. It wasn't until my dear friend, Kevin Fanning, did me the favor of reading the book and suggesting that I pursue publication that the wheels were set in motion. Today, I can't imagine my life without writing...without the Archives of Evelium. Kevin, thank you for giving me the nudge I needed to share Umhra's story with the world and for all the support you've given me since.

I wanted to make sure that God Ascended delivered on all the promises I made in Paladin Unbound and Mystic Reborn, so I could give the trilogy a proper conclusion. As such, I enlisted three beta readers that I respect greatly for their love of books, breadth of knowledge, and unwavering sincerity. Their advice helped hone God Ascended to a razor-sharp finish. Thank you, Charlie Cavendish, Jodie Crump, and Tom Bookbeard for giving God Ascended an early read and offering such fantastic feedback.

I'd like to think I've grown a lot as a writer since I set off on this journey. What's the point of a journey, after all, if you don't learn something along the way? Nobody has had a greater impact on refining my storytelling than my friends in the Forge. Thank you, Blake, David, Jason, Stephen, and Zack for challenging me to be a better writer. I hope I've returned the favor a bit since joining the group.

Susan Brooks and I have been on our own epic adventure over the last several years. As my editor and publisher at Literary Wanderlust, Susan has been invaluable to the process of getting AoE out into the world. With the trilogy now complete, I am thankful for all the hard work she put into each of my books, and that we became good friends in the process.

Of course, I'd like to offer a special thanks to my family and friends, without whose support, I wouldn't have gotten very far. I'm grateful to you all for believing in me.

Umhra's trilogy is over, which is a bittersweet moment form me. I have more planned for Tyveriel, though. The Archives of Evelium offers an expansive world in which to play, and there is a lot I have yet to share. Thank you to my readers for being the fuel to my creative fire and the bloggers, booktubers, and bookstagrammers that have helped spread the word.

ABOUT THE AUTHOR

Jeffrey Speight's love of fantasy goes back to an early childhood viewing of the cartoon version of *The Hobbit*, when he first met an unsuspecting hafling that would change Middle Earth forever. Finding his own adventuring party in middle school, Jeff became an avid Dungeons & Dragons player and found a passion for worldbuilding and character creation. While he went on to a successful career as an investor, stories grew in his mind until he could no longer keep them inside. So began his passion for writing. Today, he lives in Connecticut with his wife, three boys (his current adventuring party), two dogs, and a bearded dragon. He has a firmly held belief that elves are cool, but half-orcs are cooler. While he once preferred rangers, he nearly always plays a paladin at the gaming table.

Printed in the USA
CPSIA information can be obtained
at www.ICGtesting.com
CBHW020026231124
17750CB00003B/11